Praise for *Fire, Burn!*

"As history, as romance, as mystery, as detection, the story is splendid, with an exact and detailed picture of the Yard's early days, an alluring love story, copious action and a solution wholly surprising."
—Anthony Boucher, *The New York Times*

"Just the sort of rare fooling that Mr. Carr, the Grand Wizard, brings off so well."
—*New York Herald Tribune*

Other John Dickson Carr mysteries
available from Carroll & Graf:

John Dickson Carr
Fire, Burn!

Carroll & Graf Publishers, Inc.
New York

For Sir Allen Lane

Copyright © 1957 by John Dickson Carr
Copyright © renewed 1985 by Clarice M. Carr, Julia McNi-
ven, Bonita Marie
Cron and Mary B. Howes.

Reprinted by arrangement with Clarice M. Carr

First Carroll & Graf edition 1987
Third Carroll & Graf edition 1995

Carroll & Graf Publishers, Inc.
260 Fifth Avenue
New York, NY 10001

ISBN 0-7867-0175-7

Manufactured in the United States of America

Contents

1

"Then Who Will You Send to Fetch Him Away?"

The woman couldn't have been killed, in the broad corridor with the fringed lamps. She couldn't have died before the eyes of three witnesses. And yet she had.

In short, as Cheviot will tell you, the most baffling murder case in his experience occurred in the year 1829.

Now that was fully eight years before Queen Victoria came to the throne. It flared up during the last sunburst of the dandies, and of the prettiest courtesans with white skins and enigmatic mouths and rooms full of rich *bijouterie,* in the dance of scandal before old, obese King George the Fourth gasped out his life against a table at Windsor.

Therefore, since Detective-Superintendent John Cheviot is very much alive in these years of the nineteen-fifties, being not yet middle-aged, some explanation of such statements ought to be made.

At about ten o'clock on an October night, present-day, Cheviot hailed a taxi in Euston Road. To the driver he said, "Scotland Yard." Then he slammed the door and sat back.

Cheviot was Superintendent of C-One. Under the Commander of the C.I.D. there are nine C-departments; and C-One is the Murder Squad. Cheviot owed his position to the fact that the present Assistant Commissioner believes in promotion by ability rather than seniority.

Nowadays it is no disgrace to have entered the Force by way of Winchester and Trinity College, Cambridge. And, provided a man does his work well, nobody will object if he rummages much in the ancient police-records preserved at Scotland Yard Central.

Then, too, Cheviot had learned to control his over-imaginativeness; to appear as stolid as everybody else. Public-school austerity is no bad training for the semi-military discipline of the police. If he was saved from what swooped down on him, he was saved by a woman and by his own sense of humour.

Cheviot, let it be repeated, got into a taxi in Euston Road and told the driver to take him to Scotland Yard.

It was a muggy night, though not warm, and with a slight mist. He did not notice where they were going. His thoughts were absorbed in a case which does not concern this narrative. To this day he swears that he had no cold premonition, no warning that a bit of the dark world had pierced through and pinioned him, when the cab drew up and stopped almost at the place where it should have stopped.

"Now if that charwoman," he thought, "is telling the truth . . ."

Stooping down towards the left, he twisted the handle of the cab's door. He opened it to step down. And the top of the door-frame knocked off his hat, which fell off backwards on the floor of the cab.

Startled out of his thoughts, he stood humped in the doorway. He was wearing a soft felt hat. It should not have hit the floor with such a heavy bump and bounce, or rolled when it did.

Instead of glancing over his shoulder, he looked ahead. Through the mist he saw a dim gas-lamp, in a sort of glass coffin, where an ordinary lamp-standard should have been.

Well, that should cause no shock at the heart or even any surprise. Many parts of London were still lighted by gas.

Carefully he bent down and picked up the hat by its hard, curled brim. He climbed out: not to a running-board, but to a high step. The cab in which he had travelled bore two brass-bound carriage-lamps, burning oil. Beyond the light of the offside lamp he could not see either the driver or the horse. But he could smell the interior of the cab now, and smell the horse too.

Cheviot did not say anything. The expression of his face remained unchanged. He jumped down into an inch of mud, which spattered and was more unsavoury still, over a cobblestone road. But his voice was too loud when he spoke.

"What's the fare?"

"Shilling," said the driver.

That was all. But, more than any of these discrepancies, of the night or of a disaffected brain, Cheviot was startled by the hatred and vindictiveness in the cabman's low voice.

"A shilling. Oh," Cheviot said mechanically. "Where did I hire you?"

An invisible whip cracked, pouring more hatred.

"Euston Road. Yer said 'Scotland Yard.' But yer meant 'Great Scotland Yard'; w'ere else? And yer meant number bloody four White'all Place." The whip cracked again. "Well! There 'tis!"

Cheviot looked at the hat in his hands. It was something like a modern top-hat, but much higher and heavier, its nap of beaverskin with a furry gloss. There seemed to be something damnably wrong with his hair, which was far too thick, when he carefully jammed the weight down on it.

His right hand slid down to his right-hand trousers pocket. His coat, of fine broadcloth, was too long; he had to push it completely aside before dipping into the pocket of rather tightly fitting trousers, and fishing out a handful of change.

Silver coins glimmered between mist and cab-lamp light. When he saw whose head was on every one of those coins, Superintendent Cheviot stood very still.

And, all the time, that eerie invisible voice still poured hatred at him.

"Quite the nob, ain't yer?" it jeered. "Fr'all I knows, yer may be one o' the two new Commissioners of Bobby Peel's brand-new ber-luddy p'leece. . . ."

"What's that?"

"You 'eard!" The voice grew softly frantic. "Got coloured

clothes on, ain'tcher? And, for all that, you'd try to gammon me out of me fare. Wouldn't yer? Say I didn't pick yer up in—"

Cheviot looked up.

"Be quiet," he said.

Once upon a time a female reporter had written that Superintendent Cheviot, of the Murder Squad, was "quite distinguished-looking, with rather sinister light-grey eyes, though to me he seemed good-natured enough."

No doubt this was gush. And yet, as those same light-grey eyes were raised now, they held a look so sinister that the cabman's voice stuck in his throat. The eyes were set in a lean face, above the two white points of the collar and the casually tied black-satin stock.

"Walk-er!" thought the driver. He didn't want no row. He didn't want no real trouble with a nob who looked as dangerous as this 'un.

"Here; take this," Cheviot said mildly. He handed up two shillings to a cabman who should already have jumped down and held open the door.

If the fare all the way from Euston Road happened to be only a shilling, then that extra bob was an enormous tip. The cabman seized at the money. Almost soundlessly, muffled in mud, the cab backed and shuffled and clopped away down Whitehall into an eerie night. But the invisible voice still cried two words of hate.

"Peeler!" it said. *"Spy!"*

John Cheviot turned and strode left into the little turning where, beyond the gas-lamp bracket, was the only brick house showing a few furtive lights on the ground floor. The chill mud clogged his trousers and oozed unpleasantly across his shoes.

That was reality, surely?

But it wasn't. Cheviot knew better.

"This is Old Scotland Yard," he thought, "exactly as it ought to be. Only a few hundred yards up from where I want to go. It hasn't changed, of course. It's *my* eyes, *my* senses, *my* brain."

And then, in sheer terror and despair:

"Oh, God, it's happened. I never really thought it would, even when I was over-worked. But it's happened."

That was when he first saw the woman.

A closed box of a carriage, painted in dark lacquer, with gilt wheels and glossy bay horses, had been drawn up close to the windows of number four Whitehall Place. Cheviot hardly saw it, because the carriage-lamps had been turned down to mere blue sparks, until a top-hatted coachman in red livery sprang down from the box.

As the coachman twisted a tiny wheel under the lamp, its flame blossomed up bright and yellow. The carriage-door was opened. A woman put one foot down on the step and hesitated, waving away the coachman. She looked steadily at Cheviot from a distance of only ten feet away.

"Mr. Cheviot!" she called gently. Her voice was very soft and sweet, with a hint of demure formality. She lowered her long eyelashes in confusion, and sat back into the carriage.

Again Cheviot stood still.

This was worse than ever. He had caught only a brief glimpse of her. And yet, though he had never seen her before in his life, he thought he knew who she was.

She was no girl. She may have been thirty, or perhaps more. The hint of maturity in that slender figure only added allure. She wore a gown of white brocade, with faint yellow stripes, well off the shoulders and cut low at the breast, with bare arms.

Her hair, clear golden, was parted in the middle and drawn across the forehead so as to expose the ears, ending in flat round plaits well behind her head. It exposed the soft beauty of face and neck, faintly coloured despite a dusting of rice-powder. Her mouth, unpainted, was small but full-lipped, like her rounded chin. Most of all, beyond her gracefulness, you noted the eyes: large, long, heavy-lidded, of a clear dark blue, outwardly as innocent-looking as those of a girl of fourteen.

But she was not in the least innocent.

One of the hardest tasks in Cheviot's life was to walk straight across to that carriage. Out of the corner of his eye he noticed that the top-hatted coachman in red livery again sat straight-backed on the box, staring ahead.

"I am blind," the coachman's back seemed to say. "I hear nothing; I see nothing."

Cheviot removed his hat. He mounted the step of the carriage, and bent his head inside.

This was no hackney cab. It smelled of jasmine perfume, even its claret-coloured cushions. The woman was leaning back, her innocent-looking blue eyes half closed; but she sat up as he entered.

"Dearest!" she said, in a voice so low it was barely audible.

Then she lifted her mouth to be kissed.

"Madam," said Cheviot, "what is your name?"

The blue eyes flashed wide open.

"Isn't your first name Flora? *Isn't* it?"

"As if you didn't know!"

"You are Lady Drayton. You're a widow. You live at—"

Even at her most intent or her most passionate, as he was to discover, she would colour with that air of timidity or even shyness.

"I live," she whispered, "where I am waiting to take you home. As always."

Cheviot, the outwardly stolid, never quite understood his behaviour then. Dropping on one knee, he locked his arms tightly round her waist and put his cheek against her breast.

"Don't laugh at me," he said. "For God's sake don't laugh at me."

Flora did not answer that she would not laugh at him. She did not say he was hurting her, though his grip did hurt. Instead her arms went round his neck, and her own cheek was pressed against his hair.

"My dear! What is it? What is the matter?"

"I'm out of my senses. I'm mad. I'm a cursed Bedlamite! You see . . ."

For perhaps thirty seconds he whispered or shouted wild words. It is doubtful that Flora, who could remember everything he said and repeat it to him afterwards, understood one tenth of what he spoke.

But the black fear-sting was being drawn out of his brain,

slowly, as he talked. He could feel the soft, perfumed flesh rise and fall under his cheek. He felt the pressure of her arms round his neck.

"This is one fine position," he thought, "for a police-officer on duty."

Cheviot stumbled to his feet, inadvertently treading on the hem of a white-and-yellow gown tight at the waist but wide in the skirt according to the prevailing mode. He could not stand upright in the carriage. Bending over, he put his hands lightly on her shoulders as her head went back.

Flora's neck seemed too slender to support the weight of the heavy golden hair. Her long, large, innocent-seeming eyes were blurred with tears, and she trembled. Her presence was so sensually disturbing that—

"You are not mad," she told him gently. Then she made a wry mouth, turning her head away. "Except, to be sure, that you wish to become Superintendent of their Central Company, or Central Division, or whatever name they give it." Back turned the disturbing eyes. "And, if you be mad, what am I?"

"Oh, you're out of a picture-book!"

"Dearest?"

"To be exact, from a folio of coloured drawings at . . ."

About to say "the Victoria and Albert Museum," he checked himself.

"Nobody knows," he said, "how long I have loved you. Nobody will ever know."

"Well. I should hope not." Yet she took fire at his mood. "Oh, how I wish we were at home now! But—but are you not late for your appointment?"

"Appointment? With whom?"

"With Mr. Mayne and Colonel Rowan, surely?"

Beside Flora, on the cushions, lay a large Leghorn hat and a red cashmere shawl. Cheviot studied them in the dimness. As one who had delved much in ancient records, he knew that the names of the first two Police Commissioners, acting with joint authority, had been Mr. Richard Mayne and Colonel Charles Rowan.

He knew their portraits, their histories. He knew—

"You refer," he said, and cleared his throat, "to Sir Robert Peel's . . .?"

"*Sir* Robert?" Flora looked perplexed. "I had heard old Sir Robert was very ill, and not expected to live. But has he died? And has Mr. Peel inherited his father's baronetcy?"

"He hasn't, he hasn't! Not yet!" Cheviot cried out. "Forgive me," he added more mildly. "It was only a mistake."

"We-el," murmured Flora. "I suppose you must go. But don't, please *don't*, remain away too long."

And once more she lifted her mouth.

What happened in the next few minutes need not be told here. And yet, as Cheviot left the carriage and strode confidently towards the door of number four Whitehall Place, the fit of horrors had departed.

"Come, now!" crackled a satiric voice in his own brain. "Isn't this only the other part of your dream, the secret dreams all men hide and cherish? Didn't you want to see, in action, the first Scotland Yard in history? When the mob was a tiger, when gangs were more murderous, when the police were hated and attacked as interferers with personal liberty? When puzzling crimes, of house-breaking or murder, could be solved only by a blunder of luck or the whisper of the informer?

"Murder, let's admit," whispered that same satiric voice, "is always sordid; usually dull; not at all the stuff of novels. Still! Didn't you want to amaze them by solving some such mystery, with fingerprints or ballistics or modern deduction? In your heart, now, don't you still want to astonish them with what can be done?"

"Yes!" Superintendent Cheviot muttered aloud.

Number four Whitehall Place was a handsome brick house, showing glimmers of light through drawn curtains of windows on either side of its door. Cheviot lifted the knocker and rapped sharply.

Was it only in his imagination that someone, close at hand, uttered a laugh?

Cheviot whirled round. Yes; it was illusion. There was nobody there.

The door was opened by—yes, by the sort of person Cheviot expected to see.

The man was of middle height, red-faced, and by his stiff military bearing clearly an ex-Army ranker. His coat, stretching halfway to his knees, was of dark blue and had a line of metal buttons to the waist. His trousers were dark blue. Few would have guessed that his tall hat was reinforced inside by a leather crown and supports of heavy cane, against the lash of clubs and bottles.

As he eyed Cheviot's bearing and clothes, he became more stiff and respectful.

"Yes, sir?"

"My name is Cheviot," the latter said carelessly. "I believe I have an appointment with Colonel Rowan and Mr. Mayne."

"Yes, sir. Will you follow me, sir?"

The Peeler's hardwood truncheon and rattle were hidden by the skirts of his coat. In fact (as was Mr. Peel's strongest wish) you could see little to distinguish him from an ordinary civilian, except for the blue-and-white band round his left arm, which indicated merely that he was on duty.

Cheviot sauntered after him, into a wide and spacious hall with doors on either side. But the passage was going to ruin from its smell of damp, from the spreading patches on its scarlet wall-paper.

The policeman, stiff-backed, marched across to a door on the right. He threw it open.

"Mr. Cheviot," he announced in a hoarse brandy-voice.

Cheviot felt a second's blind panic, worse than any he had known. He was committed. For good or ill, for ease or death, he must walk the path to God-knows-where. Well! All the more reason why he should walk it with good grace, as Flora would have him do.

He caught only a glimpse of a good-sized room, its oak-panelled walls cluttered to confusion with military trophies.

Colonel Rowan, he vaguely remembered, was a bachelor and kept living-quarters here. Then, throwing back his shoulders and with a lazy smile, Cheviot strolled in.

"Good evening, gentlemen," he said.

2

A Problem in Bird-Seed

Actually there were three men in the room. But, since one was sitting at a writing-desk in a far corner, Cheviot at first saw only two.

On the floor lay a red-patterned Turkey carpet, so spattered and trampled with tobacco-ash that its original colours remained dubious. A polished mahogany table, much burned at the edges, stood in the middle. On it, amid scattered documents and a paper of cigars, was a lamp with a fluted red-glass shade and a red-glass bowl burning a broad flame of petroleum oil.

Cheviot wondered, not for the first time, why petroleum-burning lamps didn't blow up; and was soon to learn that they often did.

Sideways to the table, in an easy-chair of padded purplish silk, sat a tall, slender, rather handsome man in his late forties. His thinning and greying fair hair was brushed up and curled back from a high forehead. What you first noticed were the large eyes and wide nostrils; they added an air of sensitiveness and intelligence to the thin face.

This was Colonel Charles Rowan, of course. Except for the absence of sword or sword-belt, he wore dress uniform: his scarlet coat, with heavy gold epaulettes, bore the buff facings and silver lace of the 52nd, a Light Infantry regiment. His white-trousered legs were crossed. His left hand held a lighted

cigar; with his right hand he slapped at the chair-arm with a
pair of white gloves.

Cheviot glanced across the table at the other man.

Mr. Richard Mayne, a bouncing barrister in his early thirties,
was also smoking a cigar. At first glance his face appeared to be
perfectly round. This was because of his shiny black hair and
shiny side-whiskers. Though the side-whiskers did not completely encircle his face and meet at the chin, they came within
an inch or more of doing so. Out of this frame peered dark
eyes, also shiny and shrewd, above a long nose and a wide mouth.

Mr. Mayne's clothes were much like Cheviot's own, though
of less fine quality. Mr. Mayne wore a sombre-hued coat,
pinched-in at the waist but long and loose almost to the knees.
The high sides of his collar showed above a white neckerchief.
His trousers were of brown velvet, strapped under the shoes
like Cheviot's.

"Now steady!" thought the latter. "I'm perfectly cool."

And yet he kept on clearing his throat as he bowed formally.

"I—I must apologise for my lateness, gentlemen."

Both his companions rose to their feet and returned the bow.
Both of them threw away their cigars into a china spittoon
under the table.

"I beg you won't mention it," smiled Colonel Rowan. "Speaking for myself, I was rather gratified at your application. This,
I take it, is your first visit to Scotland Yard?"

Slight pause.

"Well!—" said Cheviot, and made a noncommittal gesture
with his hat.

"Ah, yes. Kindly be seated, in that chair there, and we'll
consider your qualifications."

Mr. Richard Mayne, who had sat down, bounced to his feet
again. His face, circled with the dark hair and whiskers, was
not at all unfriendly; but it was dogged.

"Rowan," he said in a deep voice with a faint trace of Irish
accent, "I have no liking for this. Forgive me, Mr. Cheviot,"
and his dark eyebrows twitched back towards the Colonel, "but
this gentleman is too plainly a gentleman. Rowan, it won't do!"

"And yet," mused the other, "I am not sure."

"Sure? Damme, it's against the express orders of Peel himself! The Force, in general, is to be composed of ex-Army privates, commanded by non-commissioned officers. *Non*-commissioned. Peel don't want gentlemen, and says so." Here Mr. Mayne squeezed up his eyes in memory. " 'A sergeant of the Guards at two hundred pounds a year,' " he quoted, " 'is a better man for my purpose than a captain of high military reputation who would serve for nothing, or if I could give him a thousand a year.' What do you say to that?"

Colonel Rowan's thin, fair-grey head, atop the high black-leather stock which gave his courtesy so stiff-backed a look, turned slowly towards Mr. Mayne.

"At our very first parade," he said, "we were obliged to dismiss five officers for being drunk on duty. Not to mention the nine men we dismissed for complaints at what they called the long hours."

"Drunkenness?" scoffed the young barrister. "Come, now! What else can we expect?"

"Better than that, I think. One moment."

With another polite bow, Colonel Rowan walked to the desk in the far corner of the room. There he exchanged a few words in a low voice with a man sitting behind the desk. This man, whom Cheviot could not see very well, handed him a long sheet of foolscap. Colonel Rowan returned to the table.

"Now, sir," he added, looking at Cheviot. "Your record."

He sat down. So did Mr. Mayne and Cheviot, the latter turning round and round the brim of his hat in unsteady hands.

Under the eye of Colonel Rowan, light-blue and mild as it appeared, he felt very small. He remembered, ghost-like, the painting of Colonel Rowan with the five medals across his coat. This man had fought in every major battle of the Peninsular War, and had commanded a wing at Waterloo.

"I believe," continued the Colonel, glancing at the foolscap-sheet, "you served in the late wars?"

He meant the Napoleonic Wars, of course. But Cheviot could speak truthfully about the only war he knew.

"I did, sir."

"Your rank?"

"Captain."

Mr. Richard Mayne grunted. But Colonel Rowan was not ill-pleased.

"Yes. In the 43rd Light Infantry, I think." Then he spoke of Cheviot in the third person, as though the latter were not there at all. "Served with distinction at . . . hum! I will not embarrass him."

Cheviot said nothing.

"Lives," pursued Colonel Mayne, "in chambers at the Albany. Is of independent means: intelligence kindly supplied us by his bankers, Messrs. Groller of Lombard Street. Moves in the—the *beau monde*. Noted as pistol-shot, wrestler, and singlestick-player." He glanced with approval at Cheviot's shoulders, and looked at Mr. Mayne. "His private affairs . . . hum! These are no concern of ours."

Cheviot's voice rang out loudly in the smoky, dirty room.

"If you don't mind, sir, I should be interested to hear what you have gleaned about my private life."

"You insist?"

"I request."

"Is at times a heavy gambler," read Colonel Rowan, without looking up, "but goes for months without touching cards or dice. No friend to temperance societies, but is never observable as being drunk. His friendship with Lady Drayton is well known—"

"H'm," grunted Mr. Mayne.

"But is, I repeat, no concern of ours."

And he dropped the sheet of foolscap on the table.

Too many shocks were having on Cheviot just the opposite effect. They induced in him a mood of exhilaration, a don't-give-a-damn high-heartedness; he was ready to seize at one dream amid dreams.

This was just as well, because Mr. Mayne's deep voice came driving in.

"Now, Mr. Cheviot!" said the barrister, thrusting an arm so

suddenly across the table that Cheviot feared the lamp would singe his whiskers. "By your leave, I'll ask the question Rowan was about to ask."

Mr. Mayne rose to his feet, putting his hands under his coat and waggling the coat-tails. This disclosed a velvet waistcoat, in which arabesques of black dominated arabesques of green, and which was crossed by a gold watch-chain with a bunch of seals.

"Sir," he continued, "you have applied for the post of Superintendent at our Central or Home Division. You are, we hear, of independent means. But your emolument would be only two hundred a year. You would be on duty twelve hours a day. Your work would be hard, dangerous, even bloody. Mr. Cheviot, why do you want this post?"

Cheviot also sprang to his feet.

"Because," he retorted, "the duties of the police comprise more than suppressing brawls, or hauling away drunkards and prostitutes. You agree?"

"And if I did?"

"Well, what of crimes committed by a person or persons unknown? Thievery? House-breaking? Even," and Cheviot rounded the syllables, "murder?"

Mr. Mayne frowned at the table and flapped his coat-tails. Colonel Rowan did not speak.

"Such crimes, I believe," said Cheviot, "are now dealt with by the Runners. But the Runners are corrupt. They can be hired by a private individual, or rewarded by the Government with prices according to the scale of the crime. Oh, yes! Bow Street can always produce a victim to be hanged. And how often do you hang the right man?"

Colonel Mayne interposed with unusual sharpness.

"Seldom," he said. "Damned seldom!—In good time, a dozen years or so," he added, "we shall abolish the Runners altogether. We shall then create a new force of our own, to be called the 'detective police.'"

"Good!" said Cheviot in a ringing voice. "But why shouldn't *I*, in addition to my ordinary duties, become the first member of your detective police? And begin those services *now?*"

There was a silence.

Colonel Rowan looked startled and even displeased. But in Mr. Richard Mayne could be sensed a new and different mood.

"Eh, and why not?" exclaimed the barrister, firing up. "We live in a new age, Rowan. Of steam, of railways, of power-looms for the mills!"

"And therefore," the Colonel retorted, "of worse and worse poverty. This cry for Reform will cause riots; remember that. If we can assemble seventeen divisions by this time next year, we need every man. You go too fast, Mayne."

"Do I? I wonder! Always provided, that is, Mr. Cheviot could manage this work. What makes you think, sir, you could manage the work?"

Cheviot bowed.

"Because I can prove it," he said.

"Prove it? How?"

Cheviot had been looking quickly round the room.

The blood-red glass of the lamp cast a dim, rather ghastly light. Patterns of swords, pistols, muskets, and metal cap-badges glimmered with dull polish round the walls. In the back wall, beside a white marble mantelpiece, loomed up a stuffed and moth-eaten brown bear; the bear stood on its hind legs, fore-paws out, seeming to leer and listen with one glass eye gone.

Cheviot addressed Colonel Rowan.

"Sir," he said, gesturing round, "is there a loaded pistol among all these trophies?"

"At least," the other answered gravely, "I have one here."

Colonel Rowan drew open a drawer of the table. From it he produced a medium-weight, medium-bore pistol; the whole of its handle, Cheviot rejoiced to see, was plated with pure silver bearing Colonel Rowan's initials.

Just as gravely its owner drew back the hammer to half-cock, above the percussion-cap on the firing-nipple. Then he handed the pistol to Cheviot.

"Will that do?"

"Admirably. With your permission, sir, I will try an experiment. You gentlemen will be the two witnesses. Stop!" Cheviot looked at the figure behind the desk. "I see there is a third. Three witnesses would make my task more difficult."

Colonel Rowan craned his neck round. "Mr. Henley!" he called.

There was a bumping noise, and the rattle of an unlit lamp, as someone pushed his way clumsily from behind the desk. Out of the shadows emerged a shortish, stocky man in his middle fifties.

He was partly lame in the right foot, from a wound at Waterloo, and supported himself on a thin ebony walking-stick. But he had a merry brown eye, a flattish nose, and an amiable fleshy mouth. Even his thick side-hair and short-cut side-whiskers, reddish in colour, could not hide the broad runnel of baldness in the middle.

You would have thought him something of a ladies' man, a dasher, a lover of good food and wine. You would have thought so even despite his very dark clothes and the air of portentousness he assumed under Colonel Rowan's eye.

"May I present Mr. Alan Henley, our chief clerk?"

"Your servant, sir," intoned Mr. Henley, portentously and in a cultured voice which had not always been quite so cultured.

He directed at Cheviot a private grin which Colonel Rowan did not see. Then he propped up his stick at the narrow end of the table, assumed an air of deep wisdom, and leaned on the table with both hands.

"But, I say!" burst out Mr. Mayne. "What's this demm'd experiment? What does the fellow mean to *do?*"

"Observe!" said Cheviot.

With an immense and vari-hued silk handkerchief, whipped from the tail-pocket of his coat, he had been polishing the pistol as though only to give it a higher gloss. Next, left forefinger on the muzzle and right forefinger under the handle, he put it down under the lamp.

"Out in the passage," he continued, restoring the handkerchief to his pocket, "you have a constable on duty. I propose to go out there. Tell the constable to engage my attention; at any event, be sure I cannot possibly see what occurs in here."

"Well? Well? Well?"

"Then close the door; lock it. One of you gentlemen, I suggest, shall take up the pistol. Let him fire a shot, from any distance he likes; say at that stuffed bear beside the fireplace."

All swung round to look at the brown bear, which leered back with one glass eye.

"Finally," said Cheviot, "give me a sign to return. I will then tell you which of you three fired the shot, from what distance it was fired, and what the man in question did before and afterwards. That's all."

"All?" echoed Mr. Richard Mayne, after a stupefied pause.

"Yes, Mr. Mayne."

Mr. Mayne smote the table a blow with his fist.

"Man, you're mad!" he almost yelled. "It can't be done!"

"May I try?"

"Poor old Tom," Colonel Rowan said rather sadly, and looked at the brown bear. "I got him in Spain many years ago. One more bullet won't hurt him.—At the same time," the Colonel added with some sharpness, "our guest may well be able to tell us at what distance a shot is fired. By reason of the powder-burns."

Cheviot's heart seemed to turn over. These people couldn't possibly . . .?

His momentary consternation was shared by the chief clerk as well as the barrister. Mr. Alan Henley rolled up his heavy, half-bald head, opening his eyes wide. A drop of sweat trickled down beside one reddish side-whisker.

"S-sir?" he demanded.

"Come, Henley, you have been to the wars! Have you never observed the nature of wounds?"

"No, sir. Can't say as," here Mr. Henley coughed and instantly corrected his grammar, "can't say I have."

"If a firearm is discharged close against the body, there will be black burns on the uniform. Even at ten or a dozen feet, granting a heavy charge of powder, there will be faint marks. Otherwise, if Mr. Cheviot will forgive me, I find his offer incredible."

"Incredible?" cried Mr. Mayne. "I tell you it's impossible!" He looked at Cheviot. "A small wager, perhaps," he suggested, "that you can't do it?"

"Mr. Mayne, I—"

Cheviot paused.

A wave of revulsion, almost like nausea, rose up in his throat. What he intended was a trick, and a very cheap trick at that. It is all very well to imagine yourself dazzling the ignorant with your superior knowledge, and playing the great omniscient. But, when you are face to face with this, you shy back and find you can't do it.

"Five pounds?" inquired the barrister, diving into his pocket and waggling a banknote. "Shall we say five pounds?"

"Mr. Mayne, I can't take your money. This is a certainty. You see—"

Rat-tat-tat. Rat-tat-tat. Rat-tat-tat.

It was only a sharp knocking at the door to the passage. Yet none of them realized how great had grown the tension. Mr. Mayne jumped. Even Colonel Rowan, the imperturbable, jerked up his chin.

"Yes, yes, what is it?" he called out.

The door opened and closed behind the constable. The constable's tall hat seemed even taller in this light. Standing stiffly at attention, he saluted. Then he marched towards Colonel Rowan, holding at arm's length a four-folded sheet of paper sealed with a conspicuous crest in yellow wax.

"Letter for you, sir. Personal, and by 'and."

"Thank you."

The red-faced constable marched backwards stiffly and stood at attention by the door. Colonel Rowan, after glancing at the letter, swung round again.

"Billings!"

"Sir."

"This letter has been opened. The seal has been pried up from underneath."

"Yessir," instantly and hoarsely replied Billings. "I reckon it was the lady, sir."

"Lady? What lady?"

"The lady, sir, has got her kerridge pulled up smack to the front winders. Fair-haired lady, sir, as pretty as any pictur you ever see."

"Oh," murmured Colonel Rowan. But his eye strayed towards Cheviot.

"By your leave, sir!" said Billings, saluting again. "I hear some horse a-coming up outside. I thinks it's one of the Patrol. I opens the street-door. But 't'an't that at all. It's a footman in livery, on an 'orse. An 'orse!" he added, with much disgust. "In my time, sir, they made us run. And run like blazes too."

"Billings!"

"Very good, sir. Oh, ah; well. The lady puts her head out of the kerridge-winder. The footman stops and looks smarmy. She says something to him; can't hear what. He gives her the letter into the kerridge. Presently she gives it out again. He wallops up to me, gives *me* the letter, and wallops off without waiting for a reply. Can't say no more or that, sir."

("Now what, in God's name," Cheviot was thinking furiously, "has Flora to do with this affair? Or, in fact, any affair that concerns the police?")

But he did not speak. The door closed after Billings. In silence Colonel Rowan opened and read the letter. His expression changed and grew more grave. He handed over the letter to Mr. Mayne.

"I greatly fear, Mr. Cheviot," he said, "we must postpone our experiment with the pistol. This is a matter of serious import. Someone has again been stealing bird-seed from Lady Cork."

Pause.

The words were so grotesque, so unexpected, that for the moment Cheviot could not even laugh. He was not sure he had heard aright.

"Bird-seed?" he repeated.

"Bird-seed!" declared Mr. Mayne, who was quivering with excitement. Suddenly an inspiration gleamed in his dark eyes, and he struck the letter. "By Jove, Rowan! Since our good friend Cheviot fancies his abilities as a detective policeman, here's his opportunity. Mind you, I mean to see he makes good his boast about the pistol. Meanwhile, here's a test to decide whether he gets what he wants!"

"To be honest," the Colonel admitted, "I had much the same idea too."

Both pairs of eyes were fixed on Cheviot, who slowly bent down and fished up his hat from the floor.

"I see," he remarked with much politeness. "Then you wish *me* to investigate this abominable crime?"

"Mr. Cheviot, do you find the matter so very amusing?"

"Frankly, Colonel Rowan, I do. But I have been given far more nonsensical assignments in my time."

"Indeed," said the Colonel, breathing hard. "Indeed!" He waited for a moment. "Are you acquainted with Lady Cork? Or, to give the lady her proper title, with the Countess of Cork and Orrery?"

"No, sir."

"Lady Cork is one of our leading society hostesses. She keeps many birds in cages, as pets. There is also the famous macaw which draws out, clips, and smokes a cigar. For the second time in a week, someone has stolen the bird-seed from the containers at the side of a number of bird-cages. Nothing was stolen except bird-seed. But Lady Cork is very angry."

Colonel Mayne, an undemonstrative man, hesitated.

"We—we are a new institution, we Metropolitan Police. I need not tell you how the mob hate and fear us. If we are to succeed at all, we must have the good-will of the gentry. The Duke himself, as Prime Minister, is not too proud to assist us in this. Are you too proud, Mr. Cheviot?"

"No," Cheviot answered, and lowered his eyes. "I understand. And I beg your pardon."

"Not at all. But we must act at once. Tonight Lady Cork gives a ball for the younger people. As a gentleman, your presence will pass unnoticed. You see the virtue of my method, Mayne?"

"Deuce take it, Rowan, never say *I* objected!" cried Mr. Mayne.

"Mr. Henley had better write you a few lines, signed by both Mayne and myself, to serve as your authority. Henley!"

But the chief clerk had already limped back to his writing-desk, and sat down. Flint-and-steel crunched up a brief yellow-blue flame; a lamp-wick, this time in a green shade, burst up with a loud *pop*. Mr. Henley was mending the nib of a pen.

"Henley, I think, had better accompany you should you wish to take notes. We must ring for horses. Stay, though!" Colonel Rowan's face grew blank and detached. "Am I correct in assuming that the carriage outside is Lady Drayton's?"

There was no sound in the room except the scratching of the chief clerk's pen.

"You are correct," Cheviot said. "May I ask where Lady Cork lives?"

"At number six New Burlington Street.—You accompanied Lady Drayton here?"

"I did."

"Ah! Doubtless she has a card of invitation to the ball; and you would wish to ride there with her in the carriage?"

"With your permission, yes."

"By all means." Colonel Rowan looked away. "You must consult your own conscience as to what questions you ask her about an opened letter. Now, Henley!"

The chief clerk lumbered up with four lines written in a neat round-hand on half a sheet of foolscap. This he put on the table, together with pen and inkstand. Mr. Mayne and Colonel Rowan hastily scratched their signatures. Mr. Henley sanded the document, folded it up, and gave it to Cheviot.

"Now make haste," advised Colonel Rowan, "yet not too quickly! Henley must be there before you, on horseback, to explain matters. One moment!"

John Cheviot felt an inexplicable chill at his heart. Colonel Rowan's large eyes and thin face swam at him with calm but inflexible authority.

"The affair may seem trifling. But I say again that it is of grave import. You won't fail us, Mr. Cheviot? You will do your best?"

"I will do my best," said Cheviot, "to solve the mystery of the missing bird-seed."

And he bowed satirically, his hat over his heart. His last glimpse was of the polished pistol, shining and evil-seeming on the table under the lamp, as he strode out into a worse nightmare than any of which he had ever dreamed.

3

Carnival by Gaslight

Fully a dozen fiddles, animated by the twang of a harp, sang and dipped and raced in the fast tempo of the dance. Open gas-jets, in their flattish glass bowls, jumped and swayed to the music.

As Flora Drayton's carriage turned into New Burlington Street, a very short and rather narrow lane to the left of Regent Steet, they heard the music even at a distance.

Number six New Burlington Street was a large double-fronted house of dark red brick, with a dingy whitish pillar on either side of the street-door, and window-frames picked out in white. The door was uncompromisingly closed. Yet tremulous gaslight, yellow-blue, shone out on the white mist. It shone out through curtains, tasselled and looped, which were only half closed on every window in the house.

Thump, thump went the feet of the dancers, advancing and retreating. Shadows appeared at the windows on the floor above the street: appeared, grew bloated, then faded and dwindled away. The window-frames rattled to the noise.

"Who-o-a!" softly called the coachman, to restive horses creaking in heavy harness. The horses' hooves clopped, swerved badly, and drew up.

"Flora!"

"Y-yes?"

"That music. That dance. What is it?"

"But, J-Jack, it's only a quadrille. What on earth do you think it is?"

To Cheviot it sounded like an old-fashioned square-dance, which in effect it was. But they carried it at a pace which he, for one, would not have cared to try.

Flora, cowering back in a corner after what she had endured even during that short drive, pressed one hand hard against her breast.

She loved him. Seeing him now, the light-grey eyes, the high forehead with the heavy dark-brown hair, the sardonic-humorous lines from nostril to mouth, it came to her with a stab how deeply and passionately she loved him.

Flora was not possessive; or, at least, not very. Being wise, she did not seek to pry into every mood. Soon, she felt, his conscience would be troubling him as usual; then he would turn to that fierce tenderness which had carried her away from the first. But he mustn't quiz or tease her; he mustn't pretend! That frightened her too much.

And Cheviot himself?

Ever since he had left number four Whitehall Place, stepping out again through the mist and dim gas-gleam towards the carriage with the gilt wheels, he had been wondering what he should say to her. As they turned into New Burlington Street, his mind went back to that scene at Great Scotland Yard.

The coachman in red livery had jumped down and held open the carriage-door. Cheviot had hesitated, hat in hand, on the step.

Flora sat back against claret-coloured cushions, breathing emotion though not looking at him. She was still hatless. Her golden hair, exposing the ears and drawn to such a long sweep at the back, did not seem suited to a hat. But she had drawn the red cashmere shawl round her shoulders. Her hands, now white-gloved to the elbows, were thrust into a large muff of fur dyed in yellow-and-white stripes to match her gown.

"Well!" she breathed, still without looking at him. "Did you obtain this odious and inferior position for which you so horribly longed?"

"Inferior!" exclaimed Cheviot, still hesitating on the step.

Flora tossed her head.

"Is it not?"

"If I obtain the position, I shall command a force of four inspectors and sixteen sergeants, each sergeant in charge of nine constables."

"*If* you obtain it?" At last she turned to look at him. "Then you have not?"

"Not yet. First I am being given a test. Flora, would it trouble you too much if we drove to Lady Cork's? I—I suppose you have a card of invitation?"

Had she opened that letter, or hadn't she?

As a rule Cheviot counted himself a reasonably good judge of human character.

But Flora's whole being, the mock-innocent mouth and mock-innocent blue eyes now wide open, disturbed his senses and upset his reason. Besides, what the devil did it matter whether she had opened the letter or not? Her blush, as she lowered her eyes, was vividly real.

"My reputation is not yet so tarnished," she retorted in a very low voice, "that all doors are closed to me. Yes! I have my invitation, and yours too."

From her muff she drew out two engraved cards, square and very large, much too ornate for his conservative taste; and then put them back again.

"But you swore you wouldn't go," she whispered reproachfully, "because you detest bluestockings. I'm not fond of them myself, I allow. And Lady Cork, goodness knows, was the original bluestocking of all. Jack! Please get in!"

"Mr. Cheviot!" called a heavy voice behind him.

Flora shrank back. Cheviot swung round.

On a skittish, eye-rolling black horse sat Mr. Henley, the chief clerk. But his short, stocky figure bestrode the saddle like a centaur, reins gripped in two fingers of his left hand. His glossy beaverskin hat was stuck on rakishly.

The horse clattered and danced. Mr. Henry restrained it. As more suited to an outdoor excursion, his right hand held a thick cane of knobby wood, as well as the flattish shagreen-covered case for his writing-materials.

He bent down towards Cheviot.

"I'm off," he said. "But a word in your ear, sir."

His brown eyes, ordinarily merry in the broad fleshy face, grew very sombre as he glanced left and right in the mist.

"Look very sharp when you talk to Lady Cork. Ay! And to Miss Margaret Renfrew too. That is, if you do talk to her."

"And all this," Cheviot thought rather wildly, "about stolen bird-seed?"

But the chief clerk, he knew, was no fool. Instinctively subservient, Mr. Henley touched two fingers to his hat. Then the black horse clattered away, spurting mud; past the Admiralty, looming dim and unfamiliar at the other side of the street, at a canter and then at a gallop up Whitehall.

"Jack!" Flora pleaded softly. "Do get in!" She addressed the motionless coachman in red livery. "Robert. To Lady Cork's, if you please."

Cheviot got in. The door closed. The carriage lumbered out to the crack of a whip.

Then she even knew his Christian name. Everybody, at least at the Scotland Yard of his own time, had called him Jack. It was all so fantastic that—

" 'Reputation,' " Flora said, almost to herself. "As though it mattered! Oh, as though I cared one farthing for that! My dear . . ."

And again she was in his arms, in an intoxication which blotted out thought.

Yet other thoughts and emotions, always as palpable as the perfume she wore, stirred in Flora. She moved her head back.

"Jack. Who was that man? The man with the despatch-box?"

"His name is Henley. He's the chief clerk to the Commissioners of Police."

"Margaret Renfrew—" Flora began.

"Yes?"

"You are not acquainted with Lady Cork," said Flora. "I'm *quite* sure you are not acquainted with Lady Cork. But you may have met Margaret Renfrew. Yes; I daresay you know Margaret Renfrew?"

"Flora, I . . ."

"You do know her, don't you?"

Suddenly, to his amazement, Cheviot felt he held a tigress in his arms. A soft tigress, but a tigress all the same. Her small fists beat frantically at his chest. She wrenched and writhed, with surprising strength, to draw away from him.

"Flora!" He was more astounded than angry. *"Flora!"* he shouted.

Instantly she was submissive again. He knew, with this power of sympathy which was like a physical touch, that she was near to tears.

"Listen to me, my dear," he said gently. "I had never even heard this woman's name, whoever she is, until Henley mentioned it. One day, soon, I may tell you who I am and what I am. I may tell you where, in a sense, I first saw you; and why your image has been with me for so long."

He felt, rather than saw, the long-lashed eyes stare at him in bewilderment.

"But I won't tell you now, Flora. I won't frighten you; I could not frighten you for worlds. There is only this. In a place I don't know, amid people I don't know, I have been given an idiot's mystery to solve. And I need your help."

"Dearest, of course I'll help you! What is it?"

Cheviot told her his mission.

"Oh, yes, it's comic enough!" he said, though Flora did not regard it as at all comic because it concerned him. "But I see why they think it important. Even a character called 'the Duke,' whoever *he* is, thinks—"

Look out!

Cheviot stopped, just in time, as memory opened and showed him the gulf.

"The Duke," of course, was Prime Minister the Duke of Wellington. Though sixty years old, he was still spry enough to fight a pistol-duel with Lord Winchilsea in March of this year.

("Now, then, Hardinge," he had said to his second, "look

sharp and step out the ground. I have no time to waste. Damn it! don't stick him up so near the ditch. If I hit him, he'll tumble in.")

Those gruff words seemed to echo in the night. The Duke, frosty-headed and beakier than ever, was very much alive and growling at Apsley House. He loomed into reality, dragging his whole century with him, as the carriage rattled and bumped. Sir George Murray held the Colonial Office; Lord Aberdeen was Secretary for Foreign Affairs. Mr. Robert Peel, above all, was Home Secretary.

John Cheviot's slip had gone unnoticed. Flora was fascinated, deeply fascinated, as is any woman whose aid has been sought in a puzzling question.

"But why . . .?" she was persisting.

"Why bird-seed? I can't tell. Nothing else was stolen. Are you well acquainted with Lady Cork?"

"Very well. *Awfully* well!"

"H'm. Is she in any way (how shall I say it?)—is she in any way eccentric?"

"No worse than many others. She's very old, to be sure; she must be well past eighty. And she has crotchets. She'll tell you for the hundredth time what Dr. Johnson said to her when she was a girl, and what she said to him. She'll tell you how poor Boswell got fearfully lushy with Lord Graham, and staggered to one of her mother's parties, and made the most indecent remarks about ladies; and afterwards was so ashamed of himself he wrote her a set of verses in apology, and she still keeps them in a sandalwood box."

"True, true!" exclaimed Cheviot, who was remembering his Boswell's *Life*. "Wasn't Lady Cork originally a Miss Maria Monckton?"

"Yes!—Jack!"

"My dear?"

"Why must you pretend you never even heard of her, when you have? And become as tensed and nervous as though—as though you were going to an execution?"

"Your pardon, Flora. Does Lady Cork ever keep large sums of money in the house?"

Flora drew still farther back from him.

"Mercy on us, no! Why should she? Why should anyone, for that matter?"

"Has she jewels?"

"Some few, I think. But they are always kept in a big iron box in her boudoir, the pink boudoir; and she alone has a key to the box. What has this to do with . . .?"

"Stop, stop! Let me think! Do you know her maid?"

"Really, Jack! One does not know one's friends' maids!"

But Cheviot's gaze remained steadily on her, while he drummed his fingers on his knee; and Flora relented.

"It is true," she answered, with a lift of her rounded chin, "I have some acquaintance with Solange. Yes, her maid! Solange, which is often embarrassing, positively adores me."

"Good, good! That will be useful. Finally, has Lady Cork relations? Children? Nieces or nephews? Close friends?"

"Her husband," said Flora, "has been dead more than thirty years. Her children have grown up and gone." Impulsively the warm-hearted Flora seized his arm. "Don't laugh at her," Flora pleaded gently. "Most hostesses, I know, make sport of her loud voice and old-fashioned ways. But who else would have the good-nature to give a ball for the younger people, when she prefers tea and conversation about books? They'll only smash her china and stain her carpets and break her furniture. Don't laugh at her, Jack; pray don't."

"I promise you I won't, Flora. I—"

More than once, on that drive, he had glanced searchingly out of the window. Now, for some time, they had been driving uphill on what seemed a broader road much better paved.

Cheviot bent away from her side. Letting down the offside window with a bang and bump, he thrust out his head. Then he was back again, putting his arm round Flora's shoulder.

"Come!" he said, as though carelessly. "I knew there wouldn't yet be a Trafalgar Square, or a Nelson Monument, or a National Gallery. But, my God, where are we now? What's this?"

"Darling! It's only Regent Street!"

"Regent Street." Cheviot pressed his hands to his forehead, and became casual. "Ah, yes. They've—they've finished it?"

That was the point at which the carriage swung sharply to the left, into New Burlington Street off Upper Regent Street. That was the point at which he saw gaslight streaming out through windows only half curtained up four floors to the dormers.

He heard fiddle-music sawing and jigging in a rapid whirl. He asked what the dance was. At long last Flora cowered back into the corner, terrified and uncertain. And, as the carriage stopped, Cheviot soundlessly cursed himself.

Before anyone else, he was certain, he could control his speech. But Flora's presence seemed so intimate, so familiar, in some way so right (why?), that he spoke to her and did not stop to think. Without her he was lost.

"Flora," he said, swallowing hard, "hear me again. I promised not to frighten you. I seem to have done little else." Then all the sincerity, all the earnestness of which his dogged nature was capable, rang in his voice. "But that, so help me, is because you don't yet understand. When I explain, as I've got to, you'll understand and I think you'll sympathize. Until then, my dear, can you possibly forgive me? Can you?"

Flora's expression altered as she looked at him. Hesitantly her hand stole out. Then he seized her, kissing her mouth hard, while the shadows of dancers grew and dwindled on the mist above them.

"Can you?" he demanded presently. "Forgive me, I mean?"

"Forgive?" she stammered in astonishment. "Oh, Jack, what is there to forgive? But don't be a quiz. Please! I can't endure it."

Then he became aware of the patient coachman, waiting outside to open the door, and he released her.

Flora, too, played her part. She gave little touches to her hair, little touches to her gown, as though she were alone in the carriage. But her cheeks were pink, her eyelids lowered, as

Cheviot jumped down and handed her out. Flora slipped the two cards of invitation into his hand.

"You're not in evening-dress," she murmured, rather reproachfully. "But—there! Many gentlemen drink so much, before they go to a ball, that they forget to change."

"Then it won't signify if *I* act a little drunk?"

"Jack!" There was a curious new note in her voice.

"Well, I only wondered."

Actually, he had been wondering how any intoxicated gentleman could carry a square-dance at that pace without taking a header and landing on his ear. The front door of number six remained uncompromisingly closed, despite the runner of red carpet across the pavement.

But their arrival had not gone unobserved. As he and Flora went up one step, between the dingy pillars and the line of area-railings, the door was opened by a footman in orange-and-green livery. And, stupefying, another blast of noise smote out at them.

They entered a rather narrow foyer, though with eighteenth-century panels painted by some imitator of Watteau or Boucher; a waxed and polished floor; and a rather fine staircase, under ugly carpeting, against the right-hand wall.

Out of the foyer, left and right, doors opened on big empty rooms tonight laid out for a lavish buffet-supper. The noise came not alone from the music and the stamp of dancing, which made the ceiling shake and the gas-jet chandelier rattle. From somewhere invisible, probably a back parlour with a punch-bowl, more than a dozen male voices roared out in song.

> A frog he would a-wo-o-o-ing go,
>   "Heigh-ho!" says Rooow-ley!
> Whether his lady would have him or no,
> Whether his lady would have him or no,
>   With a roly-poly, gammon, and spinach—!
>   "Heigh-ho!" says Anthony Rowley!

"Ho!" shouted the owners of all the voices at once, and wildly began applauding themselves. A cork popped. Somebody smashed a glass.

Flora handed her cashmere shawl to the impassive footman; though, rather to Cheviot's surprise, she retained the large fur muff. She attempted to say, "We're awfully late," but stopped in the uproar. In any case, Cheviot might not have heard her.

He had again, as usual, become the police-officer. He had a job to do. It didn't matter in what strange age this occurred. He had a job to do; he would see it through, though he must make his speech sound like theirs or be betrayed in ten minutes.

To the footman he handed his hat and the invitation-cards.

"I—" he began.

Abruptly the uproar ceased. With a flourish the fiddles and harp made an end, despite cries of protest. Overhead, footfalls merely shuffled. The singers in the back-parlour were silent. Only a few voices, beginning at a yell and then sinking to normal, set up a vague murmur. You were conscious of the odour of coal-gas; of a damp, stuffy smell even in this rich foyer.

"I am not here," Cheviot said to the footman, "altogether for the ball. Be good enough to take me to Lady Cork."

The footman, in orange-and-green livery, eyed him with very faint insolence.

"I am afraid, sir, that her ladyship . . ."

Cheviot, who had been looking for bird-cages and seeing none, wheeled round.

"Take me to Lady Cork," he said.

To do him justice, he had no notion of the air of power and authority he carried as he stared the footman in the eyes. The footman moistened his lips.

"Very good, sir. I will tell—"

Then, simultaneously, two things happened.

Out from under the staircase, where he had been put away to sit on a chair away from notice, emerged Alan Henley, with his knobbed cane in one hand and his case of writing-materials in the other.

And, at the same time, a slender woman in a white gown came slowly down the stairs.

"The matter has been arranged," said the woman in a husky contralto voice. "Good evening, Mr. Cheviot."

Flora, who had been pulling and adjusting her elbow-length gloves so as to take only one hand at a time out of her muff, did not turn round. An expression of utter indifference went over her face. She spoke without moving her lips, in a whisper which Cheviot only just heard.

Yet Flora, who in his estimation could conceal so little, did not try to conceal her bitter, intense scorn and dislike.

"There's your precious Miss Renfrew," she said.

4

The Woman on the Stairs

Yes, Margaret Renfrew was beautiful. Or almost so.

She was a dark brunette, in contrast to a very fair complexion. There were half a dozen hair-styles fashionable in this year, as Cheviot was to learn. Miss Renfrew wore her hair in thick, glossy ringlets, just below ear-length, and parted in the middle. The fair complexion was perfect, with a tinge of red colour in the cheeks. Her eyebrows were straight and dark, above eyes almost too vivid a dark grey; the nose a trifle long, with wide nostrils, but redeemed by the chin and mouth, whose lips gleamed dark and glossy red.

She smiled, a very little. Straight-backed she moved down the stairs, one white-gloved hand on the banister-rail. Her white, low-cut gown, tight at the waist but wide of skirt like Flora's, carried across its bodice a design of vivid red roses edged out with black.

That almost-beauty shone with its own power in the hot foyer, under fluttery gas-jets. And yet—Cheviot couldn't for the life of him understand or analyze why—there was about it something wrong, something inharmonious or savage, almost repulsive.

Margaret Renfrew reached the foot of the stairs. Her husky voice rang out again.

"Ah. Lady Drayton." And she dropped Flora a deep curtsey. Even Cheviot could see it was too deep a curtsey. It was sarcastic, defiant. Flora, who had turned round, inclined her head coldly.

Observed close at hand, Miss Renfrew's gown was an old one, though carefully cleaned and mended. But she flaunted it, seemed proud of the fact, taunted you with it.

"Forgive my boldness," she said to Cheviot, with an edge of satire on the final word, "in presenting myself to you. But I have seen you ride in the park; I am not unaware of your accomplishments, sir. Permit me: I am Margaret Renfrew."

This time she made a real curtsey. Under the straight dark brows her vivid eyes studied Cheviot and found him favourable. In the next second the eyes hardened and grew opaque.

Cheviot bowed in reply.

That word "accomplishments" brushed his mind with dread. Back flashed Colonel Rowan's words, "Noted as a pistol-shot, wrestler, and singlestick-player."

He had a silver cup to prove he had been the best revolver-shot in the Metropolitan Police. How he might fare with an unrifled muzzle-loader, whose bullets were seldom perfectly moulded, might be another matter. He knew nothing of wrestling, except insofar as they had taught him judo. He was not even sure what a singlestick might be. No matter, no matter!

"Your servant, Miss Renfrew. I have had the pleasure of seeing you too," he lied with the best possible grace. "You are related to Lady Cork, I take it?"

Margaret Renfrew's voice went high.

"Related? Alas! I am only the daughter of one of her old friends. I am merely a courtesy poor-relation, sir. I exist by Lady Cork's bounty."

"As a companion, no doubt."

"What is a companion?" asked the woman, with extraordinary intensity. "I have never learned. You must define it for me, one day."

The rose-painted bodice of her gown rose and fell. Confound the woman! What *was* the meaning in that air of lurking mystery, of fierce repression, of mingled shame and pride? Miss

Renfrew dragged away her eyes from him, and glanced at Mr. Henley.

"This—this gentleman," she added with a flick of the glossy dark curls, "has told us to expect you as Colonel Rowan's representative. Very well; so be it! Follow me, if you will."

Her skirts swirled as she turned towards the stairs. Whereupon, with a combined whoop, the foyer was invaded.

Half a dozen young men in evening dress, together with a scarlet-coated young Guards officer moustached as well as sidewhiskered, raced and reeled out from the back-parlour in a fuming aroma of brandy-punch. Their tight-fitting black tailcoats, and very tight-fitting black trousers, against the white of frilled shirt or waistcoat, made them all appear horribly thin, spindly, unreal, like caricatures.

But they were not caricatures at all.

"Jack, old fellow!" cried a hearty voice Cheviot had never before heard.

His hand was wrung, in an equally hearty grip, by a flushed young man who could not have been more than twenty-one or twenty-two. The newcomer's snub nose, wide mouth, and blurred eyes were encircled in bright-brown hair and whiskers, rather like those of Mr. Richard Mayne.

"Freddie!" exclaimed Flora with real pleasure, and extended her left hand.

"Flora! D'lighted!" cried the young man called Freddie. He bent over her hand, making passionate gobbling noises like "M-mm-m!" as he kissed her glove, and straightened up with a graceful stagger.

"By Jove!" he added with enthusiasm. "Must be—what? Fortnight? Yes! Fortnight at least, b'Jove, since I saw either of you." He waggled a white-gloved finger at Cheviot, and laughed uproariously. "Sly dog, sly dog! Nem'mind. Envy you. I say," he pointed upwards. "Dance?"

"Not at the moment, Freddie." Cheviot forced out the name. "The fact is—"

"The fact is," he was thinking, "that a man who begins ask-

ing himself 'Who am I? What am I?' is already on his way to a
strait-jacket."

Fortunately or unfortunately, such morbidities were swept
away. The young Guards officer, with the single epaulette of
a captain, and a red stripe down his thin black trousers, lifted
his chin to intervene.

"Weally!" he said in a languid, bored, high-pitched voice,
with a definite lisp. "I twust one *can* weach the ballwoom to
dance?"

The languid one was thin, but tall and powerful. Suddenly
seizing one of his companions by the frilled shirt-front, he flung
him aside and sauntered forward.

Cheviot saw him coming, and all his hackles rose. He set his
shoulders and braced himself. The Guards officer, who could
not be troubled to alter his course for anyone, cannoned straight
into him—and bounced off as though he had struck a rock.

Freddie yelled with delight. The Guards officer did not.

"Weally?" he said again, in a loud but even more bored voice.
"Why don't you look where you're going, fellow? Who are you,
fellow?"

Cheviot ignored him.

Margaret Renfrew had now gone four steps up the stairs,
and was studying Cheviot sideways past her curls. He addressed
her.

"If you will lead the way, Miss Renfrew?"

"I spoke to you, fellow!" snapped the Guards officer, and
seized Cheviot's left arm.

"I didn't speak to you," said Cheviot, whirling round and
flinging off the other's hand. "I hope it won't be necessary."

Captain Hogben's long face, behind the black feathery moustache and whiskers, went as scarlet as his coat. Then it grew
mottled-pale.

"By God!" he whispered, beginning to swing back a white-
gloved right hand. "By God!"

Immediately, with a shout of laughter, four of his friends
fastened on him and dragged him, writhing and struggling, up
the stairs.

"Keep your temper, Hogben!"

"Wouldn't call out the best shot in town. Now would you, Hogben?"

"Isabelle's waiting for you, Hogben! She's pinin' and dyin' for you, Hell-fire!"

The scrimmage bumped the wall past Miss Renfrew, who shrank back in fury; it staggered again, and pushed on up the stairs. Cheviot caught one glimpse of the Guards officer's face, long and malevolent, with the feathery black hair waving above, as the face was thrust out.

"I'll wemember this," it said.

The young man called Freddie, after a broad beaming wink at Flora and Cheviot, scrambled after them. The tails of their tight-waisted coats flew out as they whooped after their quarry. In an instant they were gone.

Margaret Renfrew lifted one shoulder.

"What puppies they are," she said without inflection. Then, with great intensity: "How little amusement they provide! Give me an older man, with experience."

Now she would not look at Cheviot. Her gaze, curious and cryptic, appeared to be fixed at a point past his shoulder. Afterwards she turned round, and delicately marched up the stairs.

Flora, if she felt any anger at all, did not show it. Flora was only disturbed, nervous, even frightened, as she went up with Cheviot at her side.

"You'll never be warned," she said in a low voice. "But I beg you to be warned of one thing!"

"Oh?"

"Don't quarrel with Captain Hogben; pray don't!"

"Indeed."

"Don't vex him or trifle with him. He's notorious for not playing fair; I abhor to say it, but you'll be hurt!"

"How you terrify me."

"Jack!"

"I said nothing except, 'how you terrify me.'"

Flora wrung her hands inside the fur muff. "And—and you weren't very cordial to poor Freddie Debbitt, either."

Cheviot stopped nearly at the top of the stairs. Once more he pressed his hands hard to his forehead. But his voice was little louder than hers.

"Flora, how many times must I ask your pardon? I am not myself this night."

"And do you imagine I don't know that? I am trying but to help you!" She was silent again, timid after that soft outburst. Her thoughts seemed to dart away.

"Freddie hasn't a penny, poor fellow, even if he is Lord Lowestoft's son. But he admires you tremendously; that's why I like him. He may upset Lady Cork with his mimicking and his tales. . . ."

"Tales? What tales?"

"Oh, only vapourings! About thieves, since you're so concerned with this wretched bird-seed."

"What about thieves, Flora? Tell me!"

"Oh, that someone might steal Lady Cork's adored macaw, the macaw that smokes cigars, and carry it away perch and all. Or that he wouldn't trouble to break the lock of her strong-box; he'd fetch away the whole strong-box."

"So!" muttered Cheviot, and snapped his fingers. "So!"

They had come to the top of the stairs; they were in a broad passage, well illuminated. He broke off to study it with interest.

It was decorated after the Chinese fashion, much admired forty years before, now a trifle musty. The wall panels, of black lacquer thinly patterned in gold dragons, glistened under the light of oil-lamps with fringed silk shades and painted but hollow porcelain bases. These lamps stood on small, low, black teakwood tables, with a carved teakwood chair between each, down both sides of the walls.

Midway down the wall on his left, as Cheviot faced the rear of the passage, he saw closed double-doors painted a brilliant orange with gold arabesques. These led to the ballroom; beyond he could hear a murmur of voices, the *plunk* of tuning fiddles.

All the doors, in fact, were painted orange with gold twinings. They stood out against the black-lacquer walls. A second set of double-doors, also closed, was at the end of the passage. In the right-hand wall were two more single doors set wide apart. The modern, dull-flowered carpet was stained with footmarks in mud and dust.

"Mr. Cheviot!"

But Cheviot was examining the bird-cages.

"Mr. Cheviot!" repeated Miss Renfrew, who had reached the double-doors at the end of the passage facing him.

There were eight bird-cages, four hanging from the ceiling on each side above the teakwood chairs against the walls. Each cage contained a canary, all restless, sometimes trilling song. Each case, gilded, was very large. He had hoped for that.

He reached up and detached the white china seed-container from one cage. It was correspondingly large. The cage swung; the canary squawked and fluttered up; and Cheviot, as he gently replaced the seed-container, saw out of the corner of his eye that Margaret Renfrew was gripping her hands together hard.

"Is it quite kind," she called, "to keep Lady Cork waiting?"

Then, unexpectedly, Flora spoke out.

"I'm sure, Miss Renfrew," she said in a clear voice, "Lady Cork won't mind if *I* detain Mr. Cheviot for one moment more?"

"You usually detain him, don't you? Still! On this occasion?"

"Oh, most particularly on this occasion!"

"Lady Cork's affairs, you know, are *rather* important."

"I'm sure they are," Flora agreed sweetly. "So are mine. Exactly one minute, then?"

Cheviot, about to protest, swung round and for the first time saw Flora in a bright light.

She was taller than he had imagined; taller, more fully developed of figure. Perhaps he had imagined her as very small, in the carriage, because of her soft voice and small hands. The light shone on the smooth, glowing skin of her face and shoulders. There was a provocative smile on her mouth. Her appearance took his breath away.

At the same moment the double-doors behind Miss Renfrew,

doors plainly leading to Lady Cork's boudoir, opened and closed softly.

Out slipped an olive-skinned girl of eighteen or nineteen. Her lace cap covered her ears; her long apron was of lace. She was pretty, with those shining brown eyes which often seem black, and are at all times expressive.

To Margaret Renfrew the girl murmured, "Beg-pardon-miss." Then she hastened towards the stairs at the front of the passage. On the way she dipped a curtsey to Flora, with a furtive and sidelong glance of sheer adoration.

"Mr. Cheviot!" said Miss Renfrew. "Don't you think, after all—?"

"Madam!" interrupted a portentous voice.

Cheviot had completely forgotten Mr. Henley, who had followed them upstairs. But he was glad of that stocky, sturdy presence.

"By your leave, madam," the chief clerk went on, addressing Miss Renfrew and hobbling towards her, *"I'll* take the liberty of going in first. Mr. Cheviot won't be long, I promise."

"As you please, then."

She opened one side of the door and marched in. Mr. Henley, after a brief, appealing glare from between his red side-whiskers, followed her and closed the door. Cheviot was alone with Flora in the gaudy, painted passage.

"What is it?" he asked. "Have you something to tell me?"

Flora tossed her head, shrugged her shoulders, and would not meet his eyes.

"We-el!" she murmured. "If it isn't asking too much, and you could spare me *one* dance . . .?"

"Dance? Is that all?"

"All?" echoed Flora, opening her eyes wide. "All?"

"I can't, Flora! I'm on duty!"

He said this. But he couldn't resist her, and very well she knew it. And, because of this very reason, it seemed that her heart melted and she would not press him too far.

"No," she said, yielding with a wry-mouthed smile, "I suppose this dreadful police business must come first. Anyway the next dance will be a waltz, and some people still think the waltz is improper. Very well! In that event I shall sit down here," and she did so, gracefully and languorously, in one of the black chairs, "to wait until you've had done."

"But you can't wait here!"

"Why ever not? I daren't go into the ballroom; they'd think me unescorted! Why mustn't I wait here?"

"Because . . . well, I don't know! But you mustn't!" With a violent effort Cheviot regained his emotional balance. "However! If you still wish to help me—?"

Instantly Flora straightened up eagerly. "Yes, yes! Anything!"

"That dark-eyed girl in the lace cap. The one who passed through here a moment ago. Am I right in thinking she's Lady Cork's maid? What did you call her? Solange?"

"Yes. What of her?"

"This is what I want you to do."

He gave brief, concise instructions. Flora leaped to her feet.

"Oh, I'll do it," she agreed, after biting at her lip. "Though it's so—so embarrassing!"

"Why on earth should it be embarrassing?"

"No matter." Her eyes, dark-blue and with a luminous quality under the lamp-glow, searched his face. "You seek something, don't you? You find it suspect, don't you?"

"Yes."

"What is it? Who is it?"

"I can't tell. Not yet. I'm not even sure I've grasped the right thread. I must get round this dragon of a hostess; and there's little time." His memory brought back the image of the cold supper set out downstairs. "Flora! Does Lady Cork customarily join her guests at supper?"

"Yes, of course. Always!"

"At what time will they take supper?"

"At midnight, to be sure." She was regarding him curiously. "Then (as surely you know?) they'll dance until one or two in the morning. We're—awfully late, as I said. They did not even offer me a dance-programme, which I thought most ill-mannered. What's the time now?"

Automatically, without thinking, Cheviot thrust out his left arm, pulling back the sleeve to consult his wrist-watch. No wrist-watch was there. Flora stared at him still more strangely.

He dived down for the heavy weight in his left-hand waist-coat pocket. The watch was a thick gold repeater, double-cased. However his finger-tips pried and probed, the case wouldn't open to show the dial.

"Jack!" She spoke in a low voice, but with sudden terror. "Can't you even open your own watch?"

If it had not been for her disturbing presence, he would never have made that blunder at all. He pressed down the watch-stem; the lid flew open.

"It's twenty-five minutes to midnight," he said, and cleared his throat.

"Oh, God," Flora whispered, as though praying.

She had shrunk away from him, both in body and spirit. Mentally he touched mist.

"At first," said Flora, breathing hard, "I thought you joked. You haven't been—it can't be—after all you promised—!"

Then she fled from him. She ran lightly down the passage, over the dull-flowered carpet, between the black-lacquer walls and gold dragons, towards the staircase Solange had descended.

"Flora! What have I done?"

There was no reply. She had gone.

Cheviot shut up the watch with a snap, conscious of the weight of watch-chain and seals as he put it into his pocket. He was sweating badly.

He wished, even prayed, he could understand the emotional undercurrents which accompanied every word spoken tonight in this house. They were there; he could feel if not interpret them. They might be an undertow to sweep him away. And yet—

"This won't do!" he said aloud, and straightened up.

He knocked sharply at the double-doors. He could not foresee that, partly because of his own words and actions that night, within twenty minutes there would be murder.

5

The Waltz Played Murder

"Come in!" called a gruff voice.

Cheviot turned the knob and pushed open one side of the door.

He was greeted by so appalling and inhuman a screech, a screech like "Ha-ha-ha," that for a second he thought it must have been uttered by the very old woman who sat by a fireplace at the opposite side of the room, her hand on a crutch-headed stick.

She was short, thick-bodied rather than fat, with almost no neck. Her white cap, whose frills stuck straight up above a big head, crowned straggling grey-white hair. Her gown was white too. And yet, despite age, her skin was fair and retained some outline of a face which had once been pretty. Her little eyes were fixed on Cheviot with cunning and expectancy.

"Well, well, shut the door," she said in a loud voice.

Cheviot closed it behind him.

Just across the fireplace from her, like the beloved companion it was, a large red-and-green macaw stood on a wooden perch. The macaw was not caged; it was held to the perch by a thin chain round one leg. In its head, a colour between mauve and white, rolled a wicked eye. It fluttered its feathers, scraped its claws on the perch like a man cleaning his shoes on a doormat, and threw back its beak to utter the same inhuman screech Cheviot had already heard.

The latter felt his flesh crawl.

"Lady Cork, I imagine?"

"Imagine? God's body! Don't ye *know*?"

"I am a police-officer, Lady Cork—"

"Hey? What's a p'leece-officer?"

"—and I am here to ask a few—"

"What's this?" demanded Lady Cork. "And from George Cheviot's son too? No pretty compliments? Not a word of how well or handsome I am for my years? Where's manners these days?"

Cheviot pulled himself together, controlling his temper.

Lady Cork might sit in a room crammed with tables and consoles of tortoise-shell or ormolu, with spindly chairs and china vases. The pink walls might be covered with the paintings, the miniatures in gold or silver frames, of the year 1829. But she herself was as much of the eighteenth century as though her thick white gown smelled of it.

He must find not only the proper attack, but precisely the right words too.

"And yet, madam," he smiled, "I had never heard that the late Dr. Sam Johnson paid you pretty compliments at your first meeting."

Lady Cork, who had opened her mouth, kept it open without speaking.

"Indeed, as I have read, he named you a dunce. But he also called you 'dearest'; and, some time afterwards, made handsome apology for calling you dunce. May I, madam, offer both compliment and apology at our first meeting rather than our second?"

There was a pause. Lady Cork was startled, but not at all displeased. She stared at him, mouth open. Then, instantly, her whole speech and manner changed.

"It gives me much pleasure, sir," she intoned, rearing up with real dignity, "to entertain a gentleman who at times beguiles his leisure with books rather than at cards or dice. You speak a compliment the better for speaking it backwards, like a wizard."

"No wizard, madam, I beg! To the contrary, I would quote

Mr. Boswell's lines to you, 'While I invoke the powers above, that I may better live.' "

"Ecod!" cried Lady Cork. "Ecod!"

("Oh, lord," Cheviot thought desperately, "what a ruddy fool of myself I'm making!")

He thought so the more because Margaret Renfrew, who was standing at the left of the marble mantelpiece, her elbow leaning on the edge of it, watched him with ironic eyes.

Some distance back, as befitted a clerk, Mr. Henley sat unhappily at his writing-case, pen poised above a sheet on which he had written no word. But Cheviot's tactics had been admirable.

"My dear young man," Lady Cork said cordially, "sit down! Pray sit down! Do sit down, there's a dear!"

She was beaming all over her face, as lively and animated as a girl.

With her crutch-headed stick she pointed to a broad-backed, padded chair not far from the macaw's perch. The macaw, alive with evil, scraped its claws on the perch and made bubbling noises. Cheviot eyed it with as little favour as the macaw eyed him.

"Tush, have no fear!" scoffed Lady Cork. "*He* won't fly at you, poor fellow, since I've had him chained. He has committed but one crime in his whole life."

"I rejoice to hear it."

"It is true he made a bit of an assault on the King's stocking. But that was an *offence* merely," Lady Cork pointed out with severity. "The crime was running away with a piece of Lady Darlington's leg."

Nobody smiled, though she seemed to expect it. Evidently her words reminded her of Cheviot's errand. Though the short, squat figure reared up with immense dignity in the chair, Lady Cork looked uncertain and even uneasy.

"H'm. You've been told, I apprehend, of our—trifling problem here?"

Cheviot sat down.

"It may not be so trifling as you think," he said.

A queer, cold little stir went through the room. Lady Cork poked with her stick at the very small fire in the grate.

"I have heard everything," Cheviot went on, "except of the place from which the bird-seed was taken. From the kitchen, perhaps? The pantry? The scullery?"

"No, no, no!" said Lady Cork. Beginning to point, she found no bird-cage in the boudoir. "From the thingumbobs. You know. The things that hold the seed on the side of the cages."

"Yes. I had supposed so. But we must make certain and not guess. Madam, how many bird-cages are there in the house?"

"Well, there's four parrots in me bedroom there."

Lady Cork pointed towards another door in the boudoir, well apart from the double-doors. If Cheviot had been just entering by the double-doors, this second door would have been on his right. Therefore her bedroom was one of the rooms opening on the passage outside.

"Four parrots!" she said with emphasis. "There's six more cages, birds all different but almighty exotic and wonderful, in the dining room beyond me bedroom. And eight canaries, as you must ha' seen, in the passage. That's all."

Twice more the stick jabbed. That, then, accounted for every room on this floor; the ballroom contained none.

"Sir!" hissed Mr. Henley's sibilant whisper from behind. "Do you want me to put this down in shorthand?"

Cheviot nodded with decision, seeming only to nod at Lady Cork.

"The seed-containers, I understand, were—were attacked twice?"

"Ay! Once on Tuesday, that's three nights ago; again on Thursday, that's last night. Emptied out as clean as a hound's tooth, not a bit o' seed dropped on the floor, and in the middle of the night too."

"Thank you, madam. Then all eighteen bird-cages were robbed?"

"No, no, no, no!" Lady Cork eyed him with a slight change of manner. "Only five in all. Four on Tuesday night, in me very bedroom where I was sleeping. One canary cage last night, in the

passage out there. That's not much, you say? But it made me
mad. God's body, it made me mad!"

"Aunt Maria—!" began Miss Renfrew as though in protest.

"You be silent, m'gel!"

Cheviot remained unruffled.

"May I ask, madam, whether any person in particular attends
on the cages? Cleans them, and so on?"

Lady Cork looked pleased and proud, her white frilled cap
waggling.

"You may, and there is. Ay! Jubilo!"

"I beg your pardon?"

"Jubilo! Black boy," explained Lady Cork, holding her hand
about four feet up from the floor. "Me personal servant, special
green livery, and cap with black plumes. Lady Holland, or Lady
Charleville either," she added, with a majestic sneer as she mentioned London's other two leading society hostesses, "can't match
him, I'll be bound!"

"No doubt, madam. I believe you never keep money in the
house?"

"Money? Money? Down with the Rich!" shouted the wealthy
Lady Cork, who was a radical Whig. She hammered her stick on
the floor. "If they put up a Reform Bill, I'll hang flags out of the
windows to cheer 'em. Ecod I will!"

"But you do keep jewels—Madam, may I see the strong-box?"

Lady Cork, eighty-four years old, did not hesitate.

She rose up from the chair, and bustled across the room with
great animation. From inside the neck of her gown she drew out
a string on which hung two keys.

With one key she unlocked a Boule cabinet, and opened it.
From a shelf inside she took out the strong-box. Though it was
not large, and seemed to be made of ivory, it was lined with
iron. She lifted it out and plumped it down on the top of the
cabinet, pushing a blue vase to one side.

Cheviot hurried after her.

She unlocked the box and opened the lid.

"There!" she announced, and bustled back to her chair as
though dusting her hands of an unpleasant duty.

"My most humble thanks, madam."

Hitherto there had been hardly a sound except the scratching of Mr. Henley's pen, or an occasional click as he dipped the pen too deeply into the ink-pot. Lady Cork was oblivious to this. But Margaret Renfrew glanced at him several times, shaking back her glossy ringlets. Now the pen stopped.

Cheviot could hear his watch ticking in his pocket. Time, time, time!

The box was not filled or even heavily lined. Except for a tiara and a number of bracelets, most of the pieces were small despite their large value in rubies, emeralds, and especially diamonds. There were rings, pendants, a tiny diamond-crusted watch. He counted them, setting out each on the cabinet as he did so.

Then, in the midst of a silence stretching out unendurably, out smote the music of a waltz from the ballroom.

He would never have believed that fiddles and a harp could make so much noise, or that the one-two-three beat of a waltz could go so fast. With joyous cries the dancers flung themselves into it. He could picture them dipping, swaying, whirling like lunatics across a waxed floor.

But Cheviot, as well as his three companions, heard the soft insistent knocking at the double-doors to the passage.

"Forgive me," he said politely.

He hastened across to the doors, over the thick carpet, and opened one door only a dozen inches.

Outside stood Flora. She would not or at least did not look at him. But her hand (the left hand in a glove, he noted vaguely) thrust out a folded piece of paper.

He took the paper, closed the door, and went back to the cabinet. Jewel colours burnt in a shifting glitter under the low light, reflected back from pink walls crowded with pictures. Opening the paper, he ran his eye slowly down what was written there.

"Well?" demanded Lady Cork from her chair. "What's to do now?"

Since Mr. Henley was craning round against one high point

of his collar, Cheviot made a sign for him to continue the short-hand.

Smiling, he sauntered back towards his chair.

"Lady Cork," he said, "I count thirty-five pieces of jewellery there. And yet, according to my information, there should be forty. Where are the other five?"

"Why, as to that—" She stopped.

"Come, madam!" He spoke in that persuasive manner he had used so often. "Wouldn't it be better to tell me the truth?"

The loud waltz-music rose and fell.

"Where'd you get that bit o' paper?"

"Information received, madam. The other five jewels have been stolen, have they not?"

"Ha, ha, ha," screeched the macaw, and danced and rattled and flapped its wings all over the perch. From the corner of his eye Cheviot saw that Margaret Renfrew had drawn herself up straight. Her shining red mouth (lip-salve?) was open as though in amazement.

"Are you accusing me," asked Lady Cork, loudly but without inflection, "of stealing me own gewgaws?"

"Not of stealing them, madam. Merely of hiding them."

"Freddie Debbitt said—!"

"Yes. Freddie Debbitt seems to have said many things. Among them, doubtless with mimicry and gesture to alarm you, that a thief would spirit away your whole strong-box. In our experience, Lady Cork—"

"Whose experience?"

"—a woman's natural instinct is to hide things of value, and hide them close at hand, if she thinks them in danger. This is especially so if the things have a great sentimental value too."

Cheviot still spoke gently, softly, persuasively.

"I can hardly think of a better place to hide rings, brooches, any small pieces of jewellery," he went on, "than in the seed containers of bird cages. It does credit to your wit. Who will suspect it? Or, if suspected, the detaching of a container from the side of a covered cage at night may set up a flutter and cry to betray the thief. And so you hid your most valued trinkets. Do I speak the truth?"

"Yes!" said Lady Cork.

It was those words "sentimental value" which had stabbed her. She twisted round her very short neck and stared at the fire. Grotesquely, from under her wrinkled eyelids, two tears squeezed out and ran down her cheeks.

"From me husband," she said to the fire, choking a little. "Ay! And from another man, dead these sixty years."

The swell of the waltz-music seemed to beat against Cheviot's brain.

"I must remind you," he said softly, "that these jewels were stolen. The thief has not yet been found."

Lady Cork nodded without looking round.

"Aunt Maria," interposed Miss Renfrew, in a voice of deep compassion, "they will be found. Don't fear. In the meantime, it is near midnight. Your guests must be advised of supper. Have I your leave to go?"

Again Lady Cork nodded, violently, without turning round. The old, squat shoulders were trembling.

Miss Renfrew, in her white gown with the black-edged roses round the bodice, slipped away by the door to the bedroom rather than the double-doors. Cheviot watched her, began to speak, and changed his mind.

"Lady Cork, I can't and I won't distress you too much. But why didn't you say the jewels had been stolen? Why did you conceal it?"

"And have 'em all laugh at me again? As they always do?"

"Yes. I see."

"The man who can laugh at you, your ladyship," suddenly interrupted Mr. Henley, with suppressed violence, "shall answer to me. By God, he shall!"

This roused her. She turned her head, giving Mr. Henley a singularly gracious smile. But, to conceal the fact that she was openly crying, she glared at Cheviot.

"Now, who'd ha' thought," she almost sneered, with more

tears streaming down, "that George Cheviot's son would have had the wit to fathom *this?*"

"It's my job, madam."

"Your what?"

"My work, I should have said. May I venture a further question?"

"Ye may."

"On Tuesday night, as an experiment, you hid four treasures in the seed-containers of the parrots' cages in your own bedroom? Yes. You were struck with horror, amaze, wrath, when you found them gone next morning. On Thursday night you concealed another trinket in a canary's cage in the passage: something of little or no sentimental value, and perhaps to lay a trap for the thief?"

Lady Cork cowered back.

"Yes! True! But man, man, how did you know all that? Aforetime we spoke of wizards. Odd's life. Are you one?"

Cheviot, taken aback at her reception of his commonplace reasoning, made a fussed gesture.

"It's the most likely supposition, madam. No more."

"Ah! Then tell me this, Signor Cagliostro!" Shrewdness peered out through the blur of tears. "Why did this curs't knave empty out the containers, into a bowl or whatnot, and leave 'em empty? Why not fish with his fingers? Draw out the pretties? And leave the seed as though untouched?"

"Madam, there are several explanations. Again I can but give you the most likely."

"Well!"

"Wasn't it certain, Lady Cork, that next morning you would immediately hasten to the cages, and make sure your treasures were safe?"

"God's body!" said Lady Cork. "So I did!"

"And the thief, he or she, must act very quickly in the night. It's no easy matter to disturb parrots' cages without a great commotion, which might have aroused you. No doubt the thief cared little whether or not the containers were left empty. But you understand what this means?"

"Hey?"

"For instance. Is your house, on the outside, locked up safely at night?"

"Like Newgate! Like the Fleet! Or more so, from what I've heard."

"Do you lock your bedroom doors at night?"

"No! Where's the need?"

"Then the thief, he or she, must be someone close at hand. On your honour, madam: you have no notion at all who the thief may be?"

"No." She rounded the syllable carefully, after a pause.

"Did you confide to any person your intent of hiding the jewels?"

"To nobody!" snapped Lady Cork, with more assurance.

"Then but one more question, madam. You are *sure* you heard no noise or movement, saw no glimmer of light, in the long watches of the night?"

"No. It's—it's the laudanum."

"The laudanum?"

"Old women, boy, sleep very little." Then she raged at him. "I drink it every night, to give peace. I can't help it! Even when I laid a snare on Thursday, with a worthless ring in a canary's cage, I yielded and drank. And where's the harm? Don't the King drink laudanum to ease the pain in his bladder? And, when his Ministers go down to talk o' state affairs, an't he so hocussed he can't speak to 'em?"

She brooded, fiercely, clasping and unclasping her hand on the head of the stick. Yet her tone changed.

"The King," she said. "They hate him, don't they? Ay! They hate him. But I knew him when he was young, as handsome as a god, and a-paying court to poor Perdita Robinson."

Again the muscles of her face were writhing past control. Despite herself the tears overflowed and trickled down.

"Be off!" she shouted, clearing her throat. "I've had enough this night. Be off with ye!"

Cheviot made a sign to Mr. Henley.

The chief clerk sealed his ink-well, put away his pens, closed the writing-case, and limped over softly on his own thick cane to yank the tapestry bell-pull beside the fireplace. Then he and Cheviot moved towards the double-doors.

"Stop!" Lady Cork said suddenly.

She rose to her feet with strange dignity, for all her tear-draggled look.

"A last word to you! I hear everything. I have heard, no matter how or from whom, about my diamond-and-ruby brooch, formed like a ship. It was the first gift I had from my husband after we were wed. And I hear it's been pledged at Vulcan's."

Even the surge of waltz-music seemed to infuriate her. She hammered her stick on the floor, so hard that the macaw screeched once more.

"My brooch!" she said, swallowing. "At Vulcan's!"

"Vulcan?" Cheviot thought. "A pawnbroker? A money-lender?"

He couldn't ask her who Vulcan was. Clearly she expected him to know. But there were others he could ask, and so he merely bowed.

"Good night, Lady Cork."

He motioned the clerk to precede him, and they both went out.

There, in the long and broad passage with its two lines of Chinese lamps, they stood huddled in muttered conference as Cheviot closed the door with a loud snap.

"Now, what," asked Mr. Henley, "did you make of that?"

"The fact is," Cheviot answered truthfully, "she's so much of the eighteenth century I could hardly understand her pronunciation, much less try to imitate her speech. It's a relief to speak naturally."

(To speak naturally. Over ninety years before he had been born!)

"Ah!" muttered Mr. Henley, assuming a wise look. "I had a bit of trouble myself, once or twice, though I'm a good deal older than you. But what I meant—!"

"She's not telling us the whole truth. She knows, or guesses, who stole those jewels. If it weren't for their sentimental value to her, she might not have spoken at all. It's fairly clear that—"

Cheviot paused, because his companion had swung round from the door. Mr. Henley was staring ahead; his reddish eyebrows drew together; he half-lifted his cane to point. Cheviot swung round too.

About a dozen feet ahead of them, with her back to them, stood Flora Drayton.

There was nothing unusual in her presence there. She stood somewhat to the right, on the dull-flowered carpet, in the direction of the closed double-doors to the ballroom.

It was her rigid, unnatural posture, head held a little back and hands thrust deeply into the fur muff. Though they could not see her face, yet her whole body was instinct with agony and despair.

Cheviot's heart seemed to contract as though squeezed in fingers.

Two seconds later, a door opened. It was one of the single doors, painted brilliant orange, in the wall now on their left as they faced forwards towards the stairs. It was, in fact, the passage-door to Lady Cork's bedroom.

Out walked Margaret Renfrew, closing the door sharply after her. She was turned sideways, showing little more than the line of her cheek. Miss Renfrew passed well ahead of Flora, hurrying diagonally as though towards the doors to the ballroom.

Then she hesitated, seeming to change her mind. Making a gesture of impatience, she turned slightly and walked straight down the middle of the carpet towards the stairs. She was then about ten feet ahead of the agonized Flora.

And at that moment—let it be the chronicler who states it— somebody fired the shot.

They scarcely heard the shot, for reasons to be explained. A dozen fast-sawing fiddles and a harp, the swish and swirl of shoes as dancers whirled and dipped, the giggles of women and the shouts of men, filled the passage with incredible noise.

But the bullet struck Margaret Renfrew just under the left shoulder-blade.

Cheviot's long eyesight saw its black speck leap up against the back of the white gown. It was as though someone, with hands more than human, had flung her forwards. She pitched two steps, staggered, and fell flat on her face.

For what seemed minutes, and must actually have been two or three seconds, she lay motionless. Then her fingers, frenziedly, clawed and scrabbled at the carpet. She tried to push herself up on both arms, and succeeded in straightening out to the elbows. But a violent spasm shook her body. Margaret Renfrew's shoulders collapsed. Her forehead bumped against the carpet, the glossy black ringlets tumbling forwards. She lay still.

Up and down whirled the waltz-music.

While we glide on summer's tide, to what dream's end?
As we ride, our thoughts abide with . . .

Cheviot raced forwards, past a blur of black-lacquer walls and gold dragons. He knelt down by that motionless figure.

The bullet-hole was small; only a little sluggish blood had trickled down. A small pistol, with a light powder-charge, would have made comparatively little noise. It should not have done much damage, even, unless the bullet pierced the heart.

But it had.

Snatching out his watch, he pressed open the lid. Sliding one hand under the woman's forehead, he lifted her head up and held the face of the watch close against painted lips, automatically noting the time as he did so. Not a breath clouded the glass. She had died within twenty seconds.

Cheviot lowered her head. He shut up the watch and put it in his pocket.

Mr. Henley, as pale as paper and with a sagging fleshy mouth, loomed up over him. The chief clerk all but sprawled on his face as he knelt down too.

"What—?" he began.

Fortunately he was looking at Miss Renfrew's body. Cheviot glanced behind him, and went cold.

Flora's rigidity had changed. She was now facing him, from ten feet away. Her eyes looked at him without seeing him. She began to tremble all over, beyond control of all nerves. As her arms shook, the big fur muff slipped sideways.

Though she still held the muff with her left hand, her right hand—in an elbow-length glove with one seam split wide open along the back of the hand—fell nervelessly out of the muff.

And a smallish pistol, with a golden lozenge-shaped plate let into the wooden handle, fell with it. The pistol dropped on the carpet and gleamed there.

Flora dropped the muff, too, gasped, and pressed both hands over her eyes.

⑥

Nightmare in the Passage

Cheviot, who had stood up, clamped his hand firmly on the shoulder of the still-kneeling Mr. Henley.

"Turn her over!" he said.

"Eh?"

"Turn her on her back, and make sure she's dead. You've been to the wars; you won't lose your head. Don't let anything distract your attention!"

"Whatever you say, sir."

If the chief clerk looked round . . .

But he did not look round. His lame foot gave him difficulty when he wrenched at the limp but dead-weight body.

Then Detective-Superintendent John Cheviot did what he would never have believed he could have done.

Silently he ran to Flora. Her eyes, changing, were now fixed on him in mute, irresistible appeal. He picked up the pistol, gripping it hard with forefinger and thumb round the edge of the muzzle.

Only a few feet from her side stood one of the very low black teakwood tables. Though the lamp with fringed and silk-brocade shade appeared to have a heavy base of dark-painted porcelain, he knew the base was hollow.

He lifted the lamp with his left hand. With his right he put the pistol underneath. The base of the lamp easily fitted over it and concealed it.

But not before he had noted several things. The pistol was still warm. His middle finger, against the muzzle, came away with traces of burnt black powder. The little golden lozenze-shaped plate, inlaid in the wooden handle, was carved with the entwined initials A D.

To hide the pistol under the lamp, it had been necessary to turn away briefly. He whirled back again, Mr. Henley had not glanced round. But . . .

God Almighty!

He thought that one of the double-doors to the ballroom had opened only two inches or so, and then closed again. He had a wild impression he had seen something black, a coat or perhaps hair, between the brilliant orange oblongs with their arabesques of gold.

But he couldn't be sure. It was only a flash at the edge of the edge of the eye; uncertain, possibly a complete deception. There was no reason for his nerves to jump.

Margaret Renfrew lay on her back, with her eyes wide open and her jaw fallen. She could not hear the music, or would ever hear it again.

Mr. Henley, still pale but beginning to regain his wits, staggered to his feet.

"Mr. Cheviot," he said, "who done this?"

Cheviot risked a look at Flora. His eyes pleaded with her as silently they asked the question, "Flora, Flora, why did you . . .?"

Just as desperately her own eyes replied, "I didn't! I didn't! I didn't!"

"Mr. Cheviot," the chief clerk repeated in his hoarse, heavy voice, "who done this?"

Mr. Henley had not even observed his slip in grammar.

"*You* didn't do it," he said. "*I* didn't do it. With all due respects to the lady, and suggesting nothing," he jerked his head towards Flora, "she didn't do it either. I was watching her, and she didn't take her hands out of that muff for one instant."

It was true.

It was so true, striking like a blow, that Cheviot spoke without thinking.

"You saw the wound. It was a small pistol, what they call a pocket pistol. If you or I fired through a pocket, muffling the flash too . . ."

Mr. Henley, startled out of his wits, uttered an expletive.

"Look at my clothes!" he said, staring down over himself. "You're as good as Superintendent of the Home Division. Go on: look at 'em! I'll do the same for you!"

"But . . ."

"By your leave, sir! I insist!"

Cheviot did so. He even opened the writing-case and examined the cane. He found nothing. But he knew he wouldn't, as Mr. Henley examined him. His thoughts were on Flora's muff. There wasn't any—

"Merely as a matter of form?" he suggested, with what must have been a stiff and grotesque smile. And he picked up Flora's muff.

She could not even have fired through the muff, without leaving a black burned rent from the exploded powder. As he turned the muff over in his hands, he found no such rent; and he gave it back to her.

Flora was no longer trembling. Her fear of him, her shrinking back from him, whatever had been its inexplicable cause, was gone. Her lips scarcely moved when she spoke.

"Darling!" she whispered, in so low a voice that he hardly heard. "Darling, darling, darling! You *know* I never did."

Whereupon Flora spoke aloud.

"But who did?" she cried. "There was nobody else in the passage."

True again; there had been nobody else in the passage.

Eerily the oil-lamps shone on black-lacquered wood. The canaries hopped, defying the surge of music and competing with it. Cheviot looked back at Mr. Henley.

The latter, instinctively subservient, touched two fingers to his forehead.

"It's no business of mine, Mr. Cheviot. *But*," and he gestured around, "there's only one way. One of these doors must have opened, and somebody stuck out a barker."

"I could take my oath," Cheviot answered quietly, "that not one of the doors opened when the shot was fired."

"Certain of that, sir?"

"Dead certain."

"But—!"

"Stop, stop! Let me think!"

He stared at the carpet. A woman can't be dead of a bullet wound when there is no human hand to fire the bullet; yet it happened. Mainly Cheviot was conscious of the watch ticking in his waistcoat pocket.

This roused him. Snatching at the watch again, he found it was three minutes past midnight. That waltz must stop soon; it had been going on long enough. Miss Renfrew had been on her way, or so she said, to announce supper. In a short time the whole crowd must come pouring out. If they found a dead body in the passage . . .

"Just a moment!" Cheviot said to his two companions.

He went to the ballroom doors, opened the right-hand one, and looked inside.

Nobody noticed him, or seemed to notice him.

A hot gush of air, stuffy yet scented, swirled out at him with the dipping and whirling of the dancers. The dozen fiddlers sawed and sweated like mad on their little platform. Women's gowns, wide-skirted and some with puffed sleeves like day-dresses, wove a flying pattern of pink, blue, green, white, and primrose-yellow.

He saw the half-dozen hair-styles; many girls had flowers threaded in their hair, some wore feathers. From each slender wrist, a dance programme hung on a thin thread. All the ladies were gloved to the elbow, as the black-coated men wore white kid gloves.

Some people, Flora had said, still considered the waltz improper. Cheviot couldn't understand this. Each man held his partner almost at arm's length. And yet . . .

And yet, in that dream scene under dim fluttery gaslight, there pulsed underneath a queer, repressed excitement. Cheviot himself could feel it. The women's faces were flushed with exercise; the men's with exertion or drink. On a floor waxed to glassiness, past windows with very heavy green curtains looped back, emotions were unloosed and uncovered.

"What accompanies all this?" he wondered. "Yes, the first thought is easy. But the second is something just as primitive; it could lead to murder."

On the inside of the door, he saw, there was a large brass key in the lock. Cheviot stepped a pace inside the ballroom. Unobtrusively he put his hand over the key, worked it out of the lock, and slipped it into his pocket.

"On the surface," ran his racing thoughts, "it's as proper and decorous as a nursery school. But underneath the surface?"

Look out!

A circling couple, unseeing in the colour-whirl and uncertain light, bore down on him. He had no time to dodge.

There was a soft, flesh-thudding shock. The dancers lurched, but did not lose their footing. Instantly Cheviot was all apologies to the young lady.

"Madam, I entreat you to forgive me. The fault was entirely mine. I had ventured out too far."

The young lady, a pretty and breathless girl with light-brown hair and wide-set hazel eyes, in a blue silk gown and with forget-me-nots in her hair, breathed fast from the tempo of the dance.

But she did not forget to curtsey prettily, raise her large eyes, smile, and lower her eyes.

And at last Cheviot understood the quality common to all these women, especially Flora herself. It was their intense femininity, the strongest weapon a woman can possess and the one which makes most trouble among men.

"I beg you won't mention it, sir," smiled the girl, gasping at him as though the matter were of earth-shaking importance. "Pray don't mention it! Such accidents are quite usual. I am sure my partner agrees?"

She turned. Cheviot found himself looking straight into the eyes of the Guards officer, Captain Hogben, with whom he had already exchanged words on the stairs.

For a few seconds Captain Hogben, exuding wrath and brandy-punch, spoke no word. Yet he did not seem angry; only tall and languid. He stroked his moustache and side-whiskers.

"You again, fellow?" he drawled. "Well! I must chastise you pwopewly, fellow; at the pwopew time and place. Meanwhile, fellow, be off with you!"

His long right arm darted out to give Cheviot a contemptuous shove in the chest.

It was still more strange a thing. Wrath, which Cheviot seldom felt and never showed, none the less boiled up inside him. By inches and half a second he beat the companion to the shove. His open left hand, with weight behind it, struck like a battering-ram against the Guards officer's padded chest.

Captain Hogben's heels twitched and twitched on the waxed floor. He sat down with a crash which shook the gas-jets. Immediately he was up again, sure-footed in his pointed military boots under the thin black trousers, but with furious eyes.

It would not be true to say that the brown-haired girl fastened on him. Yet she seized his hands in a position for the dance, pouring out low-murmured, soothing, indistinguishable words.

Cheviot waited, looking Captain Hogben in the eyes.

But decorum prevailed. Captain Hogben bore his partner away. Nobody else, deeply absorbed, had so much as glanced at the incident. A girl in lilac giggled loudly. Round-faced Freddie Debbitt, entranced, sailed past holding at less than arm's length a queenly brunette in a pink gown.

Cheviot backed out of the ballroom. Closing the door, he took the key out of his pocket and locked both doors on the outside. The key he left in the lock.

But a bead of sweat ran down his forehead.

What the devil was wrong with him? Had he too been affected by the atmosphere of the ballroom? Or was it, more deeply buried in his mind, some scratching and nagging doubt about Flora—and Flora's innocence, after all?

Flora herself, moving farther and farther away from that dead body, cried out at him in the quieter passage.

"Jack! What in mercy's name were you doing in the ball-room? At a time like this?"

Cheviot was himself again.

"Locking them in." He spoke lightly. All the time he studied the limpid sincerity of Flora's eyes and mouth. "We can't have the place overrun, can we? Gently, now! There's no need for haste."

"But this is horrible." She nodded her golden-haired head towards Margaret Renfrew without looking there, and wrung her hands. "What's to be done?"

"I'll show you."

Flora nearly screamed when he left them again. He hastened to Lady Cork's boudoir. After knocking, he twisted the knob—which always opened or closed with a loud snap—and went in.

Lady Cork drowsed in the armchair, by the dying fire, her frilled cap sagging, her hand on her stick. Even the macaw's eye was closed. But, at the snap of the lock, she reared up and rolled round her head.

She was a sharp-witted old lady. Something of Cheviot's errand must have showed in his face.

"What's amiss, lad?" she demanded, getting to her feet. "Come; I've eyes in me head! What's amiss?"

"I regret to tell you that your niece, Miss Renfrew—"

"She's no niece o' mine!" said Lady Cork, her face hardening. "Or kin either, for that matter. What's she done now?"

"Nothing. She has met with an accident. To be quite blunt, she is dead."

"Dead," Lady Cork repeated after a pause, and seemed to go white under the eyes. Then her eyes narrowed. "Accident, ye say?"

"No. That's only a police formula for softening a blow. She was shot through the heart from the back, and is lying out in that passage. That, madam," Cheviot caught and held her gaze, "is where I ask your assistance. As a police-officer, I must not have a great number of people trampling over that passage until I have properly examined it. Will you be kind enough to assist me by detaining your guests in the ballroom, with a speech or the suggestion of another dance or what you like? Detaining them for ten or fifteen minutes, without telling them (as yet!) that anything is amiss? Can you, will you, do this?"

"Ay!" retorted Lady Cork, striking her stick on the floor. "I can and I will. And there's ten dowagers in there, as chaperones, who'll help me!"

She bustled forward. Then she stopped, lips pursed up.

"Shot," she said flatly. "Who did it? Her lover?"

This time Cheviot's face betrayed nothing.

"Then Miss Renfrew had a lover, Lady Cork?"

"Pah! Don't tell me! To be sure she had!"

"His name?"

"How should I know? The jade was too close-mouthed. But couldn't ye see it in her eyes?"

"I saw something, yes."

"Pride and shame, at the same time? Tetchy and savage, for fear somebody'd read it in her face? When it was printed there for all to read, with rouge and lip-salve? And where was the need for·that, at thirty-one? Pah! These nowadays non-conformist consciences!"

Anger moved across her old face, like dough with water bubbling underneath.

"That's what I misliked, and I don't deny it. Sly, curs't sly! Lawks! Did she think I'd mind?" Lady Cork suddenly cackled, either with laughter or something else. "In my time, lad, a gel wasn't a gel unless she'd had half a dozen before she was twenty. If ye want to find Peg's macaroni, he's in the ballroom there. But *she* denied she had one.—And now she's dead."

"Lady Cork!"

The latter had bustled past him and was almost at the door. "Hey?"

"Am I correct in assuming, as I have assumed for some time, that it was Miss Renfrew who stole your jewellery? Or, at least, you believe she stole it?"

The music stopped.

It left a great void in the old, musty house. There was a spattering of applause from the ballroom, but this sounded merely polite. It was evident that momentarily exhausted guests, male and female, desired large quantities of food and drink.

"Yes, Lady Cork? Did you suspect Miss Renfrew?"

"Lad, lad, make haste! Can't ye hear what I hear? Whether supper's announced or not, they'll gallop downstairs like horses for a trough. Come!"

"They can't gallop yet. I locked the doors on the outside."

"Lawks!" screeched Lady Cork, rather like her macaw. Her bearing altered. She regarded him with formal, drawn-up sarcasm. "Now that will quench their curiosity, I daresay, when you desire to keep all things dark? That will discover them rejoicing, when they find locked doors?"

"Will you answer my question, Lady Cork?"

"Young man, are you bullyin' me?"

"No, madam. Nevertheless, if you don't reply, I must assume you do suspect Miss Renfrew. And act accordingly."

She stared at him.

From her expression he was sure he had found the truth. He could have sworn she was within a hair line of barking out, "Yes," but her strange mind altered again. She sniffed, opened the door handle with a snap, and marched out.

Cheviot, in despair, could only follow.

Lady Cork paid no attention either to Flora or to Mr. Henley, who stood as they had stood before. For an instant the short, squat little figure stood blinking down at Margaret Renfrew's body.

"Poor gel," Lady Cork said gruffly.

Without another word she bustled to the ballroom doors, unlocked them, marched inside, and closed the doors. The murmur of voices changed to a ripple and then a burst of applause.

"Now!" Cheviot said to Flora. "Let's see what can be done."

He should not have allowed the body to be disturbed, of course. It was necessary to disturb it so that he, he of all people, could distract the chief clerk's attention and hide a recently fired, still-warm pistol.

But that was a minor matter. Margaret Renfrew had fallen hard. An outline of her fall, including the position of arms and legs, was printed in the dust of the carpet. Rolling her over again, he set every finger and shoe-tip into line.

Even as he did so, the full helplessness of his position swept over him.

He could not take photographs. He had no chalk, no magnifying lens, no tape-measure. But these were still small matters; he could find rough substitutes for them.

Not a modern ballistics expert on earth could identify a bullet fired from a smooth-bore barrel. Even granting Flora's innocence, and some plausible explanation of the weapon in the muff, he could never prove from what pistol the shot was fired.

Fingerprints, on which he had staked so much in his proposed experiment for Colonel Rowan and Mr. Mayne, were worse than useless here. Aside from servants like Solange, aside from himself and Mr. Henley and Lady Cork, every person in the house was wearing gloves.

His fine advantages had crumbled to ruin. He was left alone to his own wits.

"Mr. Henley!" he said, looking round and measuring distances with his eye. "In that writing-case of yours, have you by any chance a piece of chalk?"

"Chalk, Mr. Cheviot?" the other blurted, and backed a step away. "Egad, sir, what do you want with chalk?"

"To draw an outline round the body. We can't keep her there forever."

"Ah!" breathed Mr. Henley, relieved to hear sanity. "I have a stick of charcoal, if that's of use?"

"Yes! Thank you! I think the carpet is light-coloured enough for that. If you don't mind, you had better give me the writing-case. I must take sketches and measurements for myself."

For fully ten minutes, while they watched him, and Flora neared the verge of hysterics, he worked swiftly. For measuring distances he used his own big silk handkerchief. He prowled back and forth, from the body to the walls, and then to the rear of the passage.

Louder and louder grew the clamour of voices from the ball-room. Again Cheviot feared invasion. His pen scratched on bad paper; ink flew wide. There was no damned blotting paper; he forgot the sand.

"That's all, I think," he concluded, handing back the writing-case and waving the paper in the air to dry it. "Mr. Henley, I dislike making this request. But you have a horse here. Will you go and fetch a surgeon? Any surgeon, but by preference a good one."

"Mr. Cheviot! The lady's dead! A surgeon can't bring her back to life."

"No. But he can probe for the bullet, and tell me the direction of impact."

"S-sir?"

"Now listen to me!" said Cheviot, fixing the chief clerk's rather large and cow-like brown eyes with his own. "We agree, don't we, that Lady Drayton fired no shot?"

"Ay! That there I do!"

"You will further observe," Cheviot insisted gently, "that Lady Drayton carries no firearms of any kind?"

"Ay again!"

"Very well." He did not dare look at Flora. "But there's no weapon in the passage. I've just finished searching. Next remark the position of Miss Renfrew's body. She was shot in the back. We all saw that; we all know it. She lies, as you see, in the middle of the carpet, facing the stairs, and well ahead of any door opening on this passage."

"Ah! Then it means—"

"It means, as a possibility, that one of those doors might briefly have opened and closed."

"But you said—!"

"I know I said it. I still believe no door was opened. Nevertheless, unless we accept this possibility, we are left with a belief in miracles or devilry or witchcraft."

"Here, sir! Steady! Pull up! There may be witches, for all they say it's lies!"

Cheviot ignored this. He took another step forward.

"You ask me what a surgeon can do. In extracting the bullet, he can say whether it was fired in a straight line or diagonally.

If diagonally, was the direction from left or right? You understand the vital nature of this? You see it will show where a
murderer, visible or invisible, was standing at the time?"

"Ah-ah-ah!" breathed Mr. Henley, and stood up straight.

"Sir," he added rather huskily, "I asks your pardon. I see now
there's much more to this detective-police business than handling
your fives, or beating the truth out of a house-breaker just because
you think he may 'a' done it. I've been wasting your time, Mr.
Cheviot; but I won't waste any more of it. I'll be off, now, to
fetch that surgeon."

With much dignity he inclined his half-bald head. He turned
round, hobbled towards the stairs, and was gone.

For a moment Cheviot stared after him.

"Handling your fives," he knew, was current slang for using
your fists. Despite all his heavy reading in political and social
history, so that he might interpret the meaning of the new Metropolitan Police, he could not hope to understand every catch-or-
cant phrase.

He could only lurch along as best he could, as in this crime,
under the bitter load which time had burdened him with.

Bending down, with one arm under Margaret Renfrew's
shoulders and another under her knees, he lifted up that dead,
heavy weight.

"Flora!" he said sharply. "We have to move her somewhere."

Flora, about to speak, changed her mind. With the muff dangling from her right hand, she ran over and opened the single
door nearer the stairs.

Cheviot, in the act of carrying the body there, hesitated and
swung round.

He could hear the babble from the ballroom. Lady Cork
couldn't hold them back much longer. It was unlikely, when they
came pouring out, that anyone would look under a hollow-based
lamp to find a pistol concealed there. All the same—

With a violent effort, the woman's body across his forearms as
he bent down, he lifted the lamp with one hand and with his
other hand he caught up the small pistol whose lozenge-shaped
gold plate in the handle bore the initials A.D.

He couldn't put the pistol in his pocket, or he would have dropped the woman's body. He nearly dropped her as it was; her cheek rolled up, grisly, against his own.

Flora moistened her lips. She was as pale as dead Miss Renfrew. Though Flora's heavy, smooth, silky hair was not at all disarranged, she made a wild gesture with both hands to her exposed ears.

Cheviot followed her quickly through the open door, which led to the dining-room. At each end of a long Chippendale dining-table, cleared and polished, stood a massive silver candelabrum of seven branches. They lit the candles, which had burnt far down, in stiffened drippings of white wax. The flames sputtered, throwing dim and fluttery cross-lights in the big room.

"Jack! What are you doing?"

"Putting her body on the table. They're not making use of this room tonight. Lock the door."

Even as he deposited that burden face-up on the table, between the sets of dim and unsteady flames, he heard another brass key chatter and tremble at a keyhole. The lock snapped shut as Flora turned it—not one second too soon.

He could hear the double-doors of the ballroom burst open. Though it was a trifle muffled in the locked dining-room, the babble rose so loudly that he could make out no distinguishable word. Afterwards it seemed to swirl down the passage towards the stairs.

Cheviot went to the far and narrow side of the table. There he faced Flora, whose back was pressed against the door. The sight of a corpse in that dim-lit place seemed to wrench her further towards a snapping point of nerves. Yet she was drawn forward, irresistibly and in spite of herself.

He did what had to be done. Facing her across the table, weighing the pistol in his hand, he raised his head and looked her in the eyes.

"Now, Flora," he said quietly.

7

"For Too Much Love
Doth Lead—"

Flora shrank back.

"Now . . . what?" she asked.

"There are certain questions to ask you, my dear. Wait!"

He held up his hand before she could speak. His head had begun to ache, and there was a dull nausea in his throat.

"Please remember that I shielded you. I would never have reminded you of this, Flora, never once thought of reminding you, if it weren't to show you can trust me.—In the past, Flora, you and I have been lovers."

"Jack! For heaven's sake! Don't say it! What if someone should overhear?"

"Very well. But wait again!" he insisted. "And for God's sake don't think me mad or drunk"—here her eyes flickered briefly—"in what I do say. When I first met you tonight, in the carriage at Great Scotland Yard, what did I do?"

"Jack!"

"What did I do?"

Flora tossed her head and turned partly away.

"You—you put your arms around me, and your head in my lap, and talked a vast d-deal of nonsense. And you said I was a picture out of a book."

"Yes. So I thought, at the time."

"You—thought?" said Flora, and backed away.

Through his brain, in a flash, loomed the vivid colours of face and gown in the folio at the Victoria and Albert Museum. "Lady (Flora) Drayton, widow of Sir Arthur Drayton, K.C.B. H. Fourquier, 1827."

"Flora, I'm no ladies' man. I could never even have touched a strange woman unless actually, somewhere at the back of my mind, I knew she was no stranger at all."

"You and I? Strangers?"

"I didn't say that. All this evening I have had a belief growing to a certainty. Somewhere, maybe in another existence, you and I have been just as intimate as we are today."

Then Cheviot made a short, sharp gesture.

"That's all," he said curtly. "I tell you only to explain to myself, as well as you, why I act as I do. But don't lie to me. This pistol." He held it up. "How did you come by it?"

Flora, it was evident, had been through too many changes of mood that night. His new and abrupt tone, striking like a whip, carried her past exhaustion. It held her rigid, hardly trembling at all.

"How did you come by it, Flora?"

"It—it belonged to my husband."

"Hence the initials, A.D., carved in the gold lozenge?"

"Y-yes!"

"Why did you bring it here tonight?"

Her utter amazement, he decided, could not have been feigned.

"Bring it here? But I didn't! I never did!"

"Listen, my dear." He spoke gently. "Other women may have brought fur muffs to this dance. But not a woman is carrying one in the house. Why do you carry yours?"

It was as though he had asked a question to which the answer was so plain, so blatantly obvious, that she could find no words for a reply.

Instead Flora threw the muff on a Chippendale seat. She thrust out her right arm, pointing and pointing again at the gaping rent in the glove where a seam had burst across the top of the hand. Her mouth worked before she could attain speech.

"When I was waiting for you in the carriage, and you were with Colonel Rowan and Mr. Mayne, I put on these gloves. The—the seam split then. So I hid my right hand. When you said we were going to Lady Cork's, I was *obliged* to wear the muff. Did you not see how I held out my left hand to Freddie Debbitt? Or gave you the list of jewels with my left hand? Or kept the other hand hidden whenever I could?"

Cheviot stared at her.

"And that's all?" he demanded.

"All?" echoed Flora, as once before that night. "All?"

"You didn't, for instance, use the muff to conceal this pistol?"

"Oh, God, no!"

"All this, Flora, about a split seam in a glove? Couldn't you have worn the glove as it was? Or simply taken off both gloves in the house?"

Flora was regarding him with something like horror.

"Wear a burst glove in the ballroom? Or, worse still, appear there with no gloves at all?"

"But—!"

"To be sure, had you danced with me as I wished, your left hand would have hidden it and not a soul would have seen. But otherwise?" Her voice rose in a despairing cry. "Oh, my dear, what's come over you?"

Pause. Cheviot turned away.

The dying candle-flames fluttered with a watery hiss. Their broken gleams showed the cages, covered and silent, containing what Lady Cork had called birds "almighty exotic and wonderful." He could discern only outlines of the dining-room, with its big portraits and its glimmer of silver.

He hated that dim, quivery light. It made even Flora seem ghost-like. But he remembered, with a shiver, that he spoke to a woman out of another age; an age with a code of special social customs as inflexible as once were the laws of Rome.

As he turned back, they regarded each other for an instant without comprehension on either side.

"You don't believe me?" Flora asked incredulously.

"Yes! Yes, I believe you!" he answered honestly. "But how did this pistol get into the house?"

"She borrowed it." Flora looked briefly at what was on the table, and averted her gaze. "More than a fortnight ago."

"Miss Renfrew borrowed it? Why?"

"For Lady Cork, she said. You can't have forgotten that affright of burglars near a month gone? When three houses in this neighbourhood were robbed?"

"I—no."

"That odious woman said Lady Cork feared nothing at all. She said there were no men in this house except the manservants; and Lady Cork would defend herself if need be. I know nothing of such things; I hate them! But Miriam found the pistol, among Arthur's possessions, in his own chamber. There was—a pouch of bullets, and a powder-flask, and a little ramrod. That horrible woman went away with them. And now, she's dead."

"Flora, what I am trying to understand . . ."

"And not believing me!"

"Yes! I believe you. But I want to understand how the pistol came to be concealed in your muff, and dropped out immediately after—"

"Dearest, dearest, it was not the pistol that—that killed her!"

"Why not?"

"Because it had been fired long before she died. It had been fired when I found it."

"What?"

"I found it in the passage. That's true!"

Whereupon Flora nerved herself for a pleading of effort.

"Jack, don't be vexed with me. I've been awfully patient. I'll tell you what you like." Her voice was high. "But I can't endure longer to be questioned with that woman there before me. With her eyes and mouth open, as if she still wanted to bite."

Half-blinded with tears, Flora ran for the door. She could not see the key. Her fist beat helplessly at the door.

Without a word Cheviot circled round the table and was beside her. Shifting the pistol to his left hand, he put his arm round

her. Flora, relenting even when she sobbed, nestled her head
against his shoulder.

"I had not thought," he said. "The passage should be empty
now. We can go to Lady Cork's boudoir. Gently, now."

He unlocked the door. They slipped out, Flora moving away
from him. Cheviot relocked the door from outside and pocketed
the key.

And straightway they came face to face with someone else.

Along the passage, from the direction of the stairs, hurried a
girl whom he had seen somewhere before, and recently. She was
carrying, rather clumsily, a large plate high-piled with cold
meats and also a glass of champagne.

The girl's silk gown was of dark blue, the skirts swaying wide
as she moved. Forget-me-nots were twined in her thick light-
brown hair. When she raised startled eyes, which were hazel in
colour and set wide apart above a short nose and wide mouth,
he recognized her.

She had been dancing with the arrogant Captain Hogben
when the two of them collided with Cheviot in the ballroom. She
was the girl who . . .

Clearly she had not expected to find Flora here, and she
stopped short. Flora sharply turned her back on both of them.

"You were not downstairs," the girl in blue blurted out. "I
had thought to bring you . . ."

She glanced down at the plate and the glass, which suddenly
clattered together so that the champagne splashed over.

"My papa-says-I-talk-too-much-and-indeed-it's-true-though-I-
have-no-wish-to-intrude-my-company-where-it-is-not-desired-oh-
dear."

All this rattled out, naïvely, as though in one breath. The
girl in blue thrust plate and glass at him, so that he was compelled
to take them whether he liked it or not.

"It was most kind of you, Miss—Miss—?"

There was no time to return her curtsey with a bow. Blurt-
ing out, "You-have-forgotten-me-oh-dear-Hugo-Hogben-will-be-
furious," she left him and went scurrying away down the stairs,
her brown curls flying out.

Cheviot, now laden with a plate of cold meats and in his other hand a champagne-glass, with a pistol hanging on one finger by its trigger guard, contemplated the stairs in a way the girl might not have understood.

She had been struck with consternation only when she saw Flora. Presumably it was not usual for men to walk about openly carrying firearms at a ball. Yet the girl in blue had first looked straight at the pistol; and she had shown no surprise.

No surprise at all.

His professional instincts, possibly, were overdoing it. He might see meanings where there were no meanings at all. But he would have pondered the matter, when he joined Flora in Lady Cork's boudoir and closed the door, if he had been given any opportunity to ponder at all.

For Flora whirled on him, her beauty heightened and coloured by blazing rage.

"Did you do this most deliberately?" she asked in a suppressed voice.

"Do this? Do what?"

"As if you didn't know!"

"Flora, what in hell are you talking about?"

"Do you try to make me jealous? And sting and hurt me for-ever and forever?"

"I still don't under—!"

"Not a ladies' man," she mimicked, flying in. "No! If you mean you don't ogle and strut and wear scented whiskers like some of them, I grant it. But what's your reputation, pray? Even that horrible Renfrew woman, for one. And now little Louise Tremayne. Her!"

"Louise Tremayne? The girl in blue? Is that her name?"

Flora, at such apparent brazenness, was past speech. Viciously she struck up at him with her open palm. The blow had little force, but it whacked and smarted across his cheek.

Cheviot did not move. In him, born of an obscure yet fierce jealousy of a dead husband about whom he knew nothing at all, there surged up an impulse to whack her across the face in reply. If both his hands had not been laden, he might have done it. Flora saw it in his eyes, and was terrified.

"I told you once before," he said with outward calmness, "that I never even set eyes on Miss Renfrew before tonight. Why should you imagine I had?"

Flora flung away the question, ignoring it.

"Damn her!" she cried, stamping her foot. "Damn and blast her!"

Even these mild expletives, in Flora's sweet voice, sounded as incongruous as though she had uttered a string of obscenities. And she rushed on.

"Jack, how old are you? Yes; I know already. But how old are you?"

"Thirty-eight."

"And I'm thirty-one!" said Flora, as though this were middle age or even senility. Her tone changed. "Didn't you see the woman's expression? Tonight? On the stairs? When those dreadful young men ran past her? And she looked straight at you, and said—"

"But she—"

Their voices clashed. Another notion, which might have helped him much, darted through Cheviot's mind but vanished in emotional turmoil.

"I've never been unfaithful to you," said Flora. "After all that's happened between us, you know that. You can't help knowing it. No other man has ever . . ."

Her voice trailed away. She could not help taunting him and stabbing him with that provocative, alluring smile.

"Except, of course," she added, "my husband."

"Then damn and blast *him!*"

"Jack!" She spoke out in mock astonishment and concealed pleasure. "You're not jealous of Arthur?"

"If you must have it, yes."

"But, darling, that's absurd! He—"

"I don't want to hear anything about him, thanks!"

Above their voices rose an inhuman screech.

"Ha, ha, ha," screamed the macaw on the perch behind

Flora. Its coloured plumage fluttered up, like the devil in a swamp, as it rattled and scraped and tried to fly.

Back on Cheviot rushed the knowledge of where he was: in the pink boudoir, with a problem before him but also with the eternal Eve to put her arms round his neck and distract him. He set down plate and glass on the tortoise-shell table beside Lady Cork's wing-chair.

But he kept the pistol, transferring it to his right hand with his finger round the trigger. The fire in the grate had gone out. The room was growing cold.

"Flora, this must stop."

"What must?"

"Don't pretend. You know perfectly well. Sit down there."

Flora sat down in the wing-chair, though her fingers tightened hard on its sides.

"Oh, Jack, must we—?"

"Yes. We must. You tell me Miss Renfrew borrowed this weapon, on behalf of Lady Cork, over a fortnight ago. Did you see it, or hear anything of it, between that time and tonight?"

"Good heavens, no! Anyway, I've only seen the wretched thing two or three times in my whole life."

"Tonight, you say, you found it in the passage. When and where did you find it?"

"Well! You sent me," Flora retorted, with an accusing note on "you," "to procure a list of all Maria Cork's jewels from Solange. Solange is terribly clever; she could remember every one; but she can't read or write, so I wrote the list. Afterwards I returned and gave it to you without coming into this room. Don't you recall?"

"Yes? And then?"

Flora threw out her arms, but again gripped the edges of the chair.

"Afterwards," she said, "I sat down in one of those teakwood chairs by the little tables, and awaited you. Just as I said I should do."

"Which chair? Which table?"

"Oh, how can I remember? Stay, though; I do! It was the

same chair by the same table where later you—you hid that pistol under the lamp with the hollow base."

"Good! Go on!"

"I had nothing to do but worry and perplex my head. You caused it. I'm not stupid and I'm not a rattle, you know. You would speak of nothing but the ridiculous bird-seed; yet all the time you were apprehensive, all of a dither. You asked questions about money, jewels, thieves. You ordered me to get that list of jewellery, but wouldn't say why you wanted it. Darling, I knew something dreadful had happened, or would happen."

"Go on!"

"Well! Presently I glanced down on the carpet, just under the table. I saw something golden. It was shining. I thought it must be a bit of jewellery, or the like. But, when I bent down to look closely, I saw what it was."

"You recognized the pistol?"

"Yes! Oh, God, yes! With Arthur's initials on that diamond-shaped plate?"

"What did you do?"

"I daren't touch it. I was afraid it was loaded and might go off. I pushed it out from under the table with my foot."

"And then?"

"I saw it had been fired. Look at it now! The hammer is down. Look at those burst bits of metal and paper under the hammer. That's what you call the percussion-cap, isn't it? Yes! And I saw it had been fired, and couldn't hurt anyone."

"What did you do then?"

Flora braced herself and looked up at him.

"I picked it up," she said clearly, "and hid it inside the lining of the muff."

"Why did you do that?"

"I . . ."

Her voice, hitherto so sweet and clear and firm, died behind shaky lips. She looked down at the pink-and-green-flowered carpet, and hesitated.

"Why, Flora? That's the whole crux and point of what happened— No, hold on! When you picked up the pistol, how did you pick it up? Can you show me? If you're afraid to touch it, I won't press you."

Again she looked up.

"No, of course I'm not afraid to touch it!"

"Then show me."

He held it level, gripping the trigger-guard underneath. The palm of Flora's hand went over the top, across the fallen hammer and part of the barrel, her fingers gingerly holding the wooden stock underneath. She held it for an instant; then drew back.

"Thank you, Flora. When you held it like that, was the barrel (that's this part) was the barrel warm?"

"Warm? No. At least, it didn't seem so through my glove." Though she could not read his mind, she could sense his every mood. "Jack! What's the matter?"

"Nothing at all. Afterwards you put the pistol inside the muff?"

"Yes. And held it with both hands."

"How long was this before the murder?"

"Oh, how on earth can you expect me to tell? I was too distraught. Finding someone had shot a pistol in a house where there was trouble. It may have been minutes and minutes; I can't say. All I know—"

"Yes?"

"—is that I jumped up and stood facing forward. I stood there. It seemed I couldn't move. Presently I heard the lock click (it always does) on the doors of this room. You and that lame man came out, muttering to each other. I didn't look round; I wished no one to see my face. I heard you say something like, 'She's not telling the truth,' or 'the whole truth'; I can't swear to the words. I thought you meant me."

"You thought . . . what?"

Flora's gesture stopped him.

"My knees began to tremble, all up over me. I couldn't have moved. Then that awful Renfrew woman walked out of Maria Cork's bedroom, up towards the ballroom. But she altered her mind, and went towards the stairs. She was well ahead and to the left of me. I felt a wind, or kind of whistle or the like, past my arm. She went on a little and fell on her face. I can't tell you more."

"And yet—"

"Please, dear!"

"But I'm bound to ask, Flora, if only between ourselves: *why*? Why did you conceal the weapon to begin with?"

Flora's rounded chin grew firm as she looked up. Her eyes were deep and steady; the long black lashes did not move.

"Because," she replied, "it was bound to be all my fault."

"I beg your pardon?"

"When Arthur was alive," she said with passionate intensity, "everything that went wrong was my fault. Or I was suspected of it. Now that the poor man is dead, and that's over two years, it's worse. I can do nothing, nothing in this world, without all odious people thinking and saying the worst of me.

"It's not vanity, Jack, to know I'm not ugly or a frump. Can I help that? Yet I can't drive round the Ring in my carriage, I can't smile or even nod to any man, without seeing the eyes and hearing them whisper. 'Aha!' they whisper. They think I'm deep when often I don't even think at all."

Suddenly Flora darted out her arm and again touched the pistol.

"That belongs to me," she said. "Or, anyway, it belonged to Arthur and that's the same thing. Before there had been any— any murder, when there were only hints of thieves or jewels and intrigue, someone fired a weapon that was mine. My only instinct was to hide, hide it, hide it, before anyone could suspect me of anything. Perhaps that seems silly. Perhaps it is silly. But can't you understand?"

There was a silence.

Cheviot nodded. He put his hand on her shoulder, and she pressed her cheek against it, with a warmth of vitality flowing between them. Then he moved away, looking vaguely at the crowding of pictures and miniatures on the pink walls.

Yes: every word of Flora's story could well be true.

Cold reason told him how counsel for the prosecution, in

court, would jeer at it. "Come, gentlemen! Surely this is just a little thin? Can we credit . . .?" And so on. But Cheviot, whose business was to probe witnesses' minds and touch the pulse of guilt, felt her words ring with the uttermost conviction.

The macaw, silent on its perch, studied them first with one wicked eye; then craned its neck round in an attempt to study them with the other.

If that macaw screeched again, Cheviot decided, he would wring the damned bird's neck. Meanwhile . . .

"You are saying, Flora, that two shots were fired in the passage?"

"Dearest, I am saying nothing except what happened."

Cheviot shut his teeth.

"I am bound to tell you something. When I took up the pistol from the carpet, and hid it under the lamp, the barrel was still warm."

"Warm? Warm?" she repeated after a pause. "Why, to be sure it was warm! It had been inside the silk lining of a muff, and grasped in both hands, for minutes and minutes and minutes!" She faltered, and spoke incredulously. "Do you—do you still doubt me?"

"No. I don't doubt you. You are to trouble your head no more."

Flora closed her eyes.

"And now," he went on briskly, "you must go home. You are in a highly nervous state of mind; you must not so much as speak to anyone else. The footman will call your carriage."

"Yes, yes, yes!" She sprang up eagerly. "And you shall go with me." She hesitated. "You will, won't you?" she asked.

"No! I can't!"

"And why not, pray?"

"This affair can't be kept secret any longer. It mustn't be kept secret. On the contrary, I must question every guest and every servant in this house."

"Yes, yes, I daresay! But afterwards?"

"Have you any idea how many people there are here? It may take all night."

"Oh. Yes. So it may."

"For God's sake, Flora, don't you see I can't?"

As she moved away from him, he reached out to seize her. But Flora, with a motion as quick and graceful as a dancer's, eluded him and went to the door. There she turned, her chin lifted and her shoulders back.

"You don't want me," she said.

"Flora, you're mad! That's the thing I want most of all on earth!"

"You don't want me," she repeated in a higher voice. The tears filling her eyes were less of fury than of reproachfulness. "If you can't be with me at the time I have most need of you, then there's no other explanation. Very well. Take your pleasure with Louise Tremayne. But, if you will not be troubled now, you really need not trouble to see me again. This is good night, Jack; and I suppose it's also goodbye."

Then she was gone.

8

Certain Whispers in a Coffee-Room

Dawn.

It was far past dawn, hidden behind a grey and chilly October sky, when Superintendent Cheviot at last left number six New Burlington Street, closing the front door of a house already astir with servants cleaning up the mess of last night.

Cheviot had passed the point of being over-tired. He had reached a state of mental second-wind where the brain seems very clear, very alert; and, treacherously, is not. His black depression, his nerves, all showed it.

He tried to put out of his mind what had happened when he tried to question a mob of guests. It was a humiliation he would not soon forget. He would have chucked the business altogether, he thought, if it had not been for the help of Lady Cork, of young Freddie Debbitt, and that Louise Tremayne of whom Flora had been so unreasonably jealous.

Flora . . .

Oh, damn everything!

Flora, surely, had flown into a tantrum only because she was overwrought?

In his pocket, wrapped up, he now had the bullet which had killed Margaret Renfrew. Curious evidence, much of it concerning Flora, had been provided by the surgeon whom Mr. Henley brought not long after Flora had gone.

Cheviot could not forget that scene, anyway. It was in the dining-room, with fresh wax-lights in the silver candelabra, and the dead woman's body rolled over on the table for the surgeon's examination.

Mr. Daniel Slurk, the surgeon, was a little, bustling, middle-aged man, with a professional grave air of wisdom but a knowing eyelid. On the table he put his bag, which was only a small carpet-bag, rattling with instruments inside. Examining the bullet-wound, he pursed up his lips, shook his head, and said, "H'm, yes. H'm, yes."

"Before you begin, Mr. Slurk," Cheviot had said, "may I ask a quite private and confidential question?"

The little surgeon took out of his bag a probe and a pair of surgical scissors, neither of them very clean.

"You may ask, sir," he said, with a sinister look.

"I observe, Mr. Slurk, that you are a man of the world?"

The surgeon became more amiable at once.

"Even in our studious profession, sir," he said portentously, but with a suspicion of a wink in the left eyelid, "we learn a little of the world. Oh, dear me, yes. A little!"

"Then does the name 'Vulcan' mean anything to you?"

Mr. Slurk put down his instruments, and stroked his black side-whiskers.

"Vulcan." His voice was without expression. "Vulcan."

"Yes! Could he be a pawnbroker? Or perhaps a money-lender?"

"Come, now!" Mr. Slurk spoke dryly, with a hint of suspicion. "You also, I take it, are a man of the world. And, as Superintendent of our new Law Enforcement, you tell me you don't know Vulcan's?"

"No. I confess it!"

Mr. Slurk eyed him, and cast a quick glance round. They were alone; Cheviot, deciding he must deal with the case on his own, had sent the chief clerk home. Again Mr. Slurk almost winked.

"Ah, well!" he murmured. "No doubt Law Enforcement can be blind when it likes. I hear (I say I *hear*) that in the neighbourhood of St. James's there are above thirty fashionable gambling-houses—"

"So!"

"And Vulcan's, it may be (eh?), is among them. Should you care for a fling at rouge-et-noir or roly-poly—"

"What's roly-poly?"

"Tut! My dear sir! Officially it is called roulette. A French name; a French game. Need I tell you how it's played?"

"No. I understand how it's played. Then if a man lacked money to play there, he could always find it by pledging or selling a valuable piece of jewellery?"

"It is often done," replied Mr. Slurk, even more dryly. "But (excuse me) that's none of my business. My scissors, now. Dear, dear! What have I done with my scissors?"

The scissors snipped and sheared cloth. There were no undergarments or stays. Mr. Slurk probed. He cut, brutally but quickly, with a far-from-clean knife. He extracted the bullet with a forceps, wiped the blood off on a handkerchief from his pocket, and tossed the bullet to Cheviot.

"You wish to keep that? Well, well! I daresay the coroner of the parish won't mind, when I tell him. They'll fetch her away tomorrow. Meanwhile, as to the direction of the wound—"

It was over soon enough. By what the surgeon told him, and by comparison of the bullet with Sir Arthur Drayton's pistol, Cheviot could be sure of one fact.

Flora was completely innocent. If necessary, it could be proved. The bullet in the victim's heart, though small, was just too large to fit into the pistol-barrel at all. Evidently its powder-blackening had been wiped away with the blood; it had not struck bone, and was unflattened; a dull leaden ball you could roll on the table.

True, this new evidence only made the problem more baffling. Hitherto there might have been some way in which a woman could be shot to death before the eyes of three witnesses, by a hand nobody saw. Now, apparently, there was no way.

Cheviot raged. He still raged when he sat down, methodically, to write a report which took nearly three hours to compose and occupied nine closely written foolscap pages. A footman, heavily bribed, engaged to deliver it at Great Scotland Yard so that it should be in the hands of Colonel Rowan and Mr. Mayne that morning.

"There's something wrong here," he told himself as he wrote. "It's here, in this report, as plain as the nose on Old Hookey's face. And I can't see it."

But Flora was innocent.

Such was his state of mind, which he believed clear, when he left Lady Cork's house and felt the fresh wind on his eyelids.

His conscience still nagged at him badly, and wouldn't be still. For the first time in his life he had put falsehoods in a police report; or, at least, he had suppressed truths. He had said little of Flora, except naming her as a witness and quoting the parts of her statement which seemed apt or relevant. The pistol, now tucked away in his hip pocket, he had not even mentioned; after all, whoever had fired a shot with it, it had killed nobody. He simply stated he could find no weapon whatever.

The report was done now; it couldn't be recalled.

Cheviot's skin grew clammy, and not from chill morning air, when he thought what would happen to him if anyone had seen him pick up that firearm from the carpet and hide it under the lamp. Fortunately, he told himself, nobody had seen him.

"Forget this business for a while! Look where you're going!"

In New Burlington Street, at a quarter to eight in the morning, the gas-lamps were still burning. Every chimney smoked against the dull sky, sifting soot-drizzle into the mud of the roadway. But the houses, red brick or white stone, looked trim and furbished and clean. Nearly every private house bore, on its front door, a polished brass plate engraved with the name of its occupant.

"I had forgotten that," he reflected, "though it's in Wheatley, of course. What I'd give for Wheatley's three volumes of topography! And also—"

Yes. As he turned to the right along New Burlington Street, left into what was then called Savile Street, and right again down

Clifford Street, he saw the street signs were also brass plates affixed to the houses at corners.

Still a broad double-line of gas-lamps stretched ahead. If in fact he occupied rooms at the Albany, as Colonel Rowan had said, this was his shortest way home. In Bond Street a full bustle and stir of life burst over him.

Most shop windows were yellow with gas glare. Cheviot saw the crossing-sweepers busy with their thick-bundled brooms in the mud. He saw the red coat of a postman. But mostly he saw the white, horribly shrunken faces of the very poor, who had no work and nothing to do. They shuffled past, or stared unseeingly into windows full of Chinese shawls, of gold brocade, of those many-hued silk turbans, called *turcs,* which placards in French said were the height of fashion for ladies.

Turning down Bond Street towards Piccadilly, Cheviot passed the lights of an hotel. A glass-panelled door, marked "Coffee-Room," reminded him of his ravenous hunger.

While he was hesitating, the keeper of a shop next to the hotel—its curly lettered sign proclaimed it that of a gunsmith and arms-maker—unlocked his premises. The gunsmith, an elderly man with clear silvery hair and no side-whiskers, gave him a casual glance; then a quicker, harder glance.

Cheviot hastily opened the coffee-room door.

Inside, in a hush of deep carpet under gilded ceiling cornices, a row of oaken booths, or boxes with bare tables inside them, stretched along either wall. At the rear of the coffee-room, an immense and full-length mirror reflected back his own image.

A side-mirror, over the chimney piece in the left-hand wall towards the back, gave him a sideways glimpse of two gentlemen eating breakfast in a box opposite it, and having a heated if low-voiced argument.

Both men wore their hats as they ate, so Cheviot did not remove his own hat as he slid into a box nearer the door and sat down.

On the table lay a small and stained newspaper. Beside it were a bill of fare and a small glass of toothpicks. He snatched up the newspaper and looked at its date.

The date was October 30th, 1829.

The gas burned yellow-blue in brass brackets. There was no sound except the low, insistent voices of the two men in the far booth.

One of them said distinctly: "Get rid of the rotten boroughs, sir! Reform, sir! A vote for every householder, according to a uniform plan."

The other said: "No Whiggery, sir! Let us have no Whiggery, if you please."

Desperately Cheviot wanted to question Flora. But, apart from the fact that he did not even know where she lived, Flora might still be enraged or too horrified about the proprieties if he burst into her house at eight o'clock in the morning.

With powerful, irrational conviction he felt that Flora, if only unconsciously, held the secret of how and why he had been shut into a past century.

Even in time-trickeries there must be a how and a why. He could not have slipped through a chink and appeared here, for instance, as one of his own ancestors. His forefathers were all West Country squires; not one had lived in London for eight or nine generations.

Everybody appeared to recognize and accept him. All night Lady Cork had been referring to him as "George Cheviot's son." But his father's name was—

Was—what?

And Cheviot couldn't remember.

He sat very still, holding the newspaper. Here, this was idiotic!

Even last night his memory had been perfect. He could still see, as plainly as the rather smeary type of the newspaper, the pages of one of the text-books they used at Hendon Police College in the old days, and the section devoted to muzzle-loading firearms. Some of the candidates jeered at this, didn't trouble to study it, and got themselves pipped in an examination.

In imagination, too, he could see the faces of his father and his mother. Here was a simple test: what was his mother's maiden name?

That had gone, too.

"Yes, sir?" enquired a voice at his elbow.

The voice spoke in an ordinary tone. But it sounded like thunder. Cheviot looked up at an aproned waiter, with an inquisitive nose.

"Yes, sir?" the waiter repeated.

Cheviot ordered fried eggs, broiled ham, toast, and strong black tea. When the waiter had gone, he wiped sweat off his forehead.

His memories seemed to be slipping down and down, as though into water. Was it possible that in hours, or days or weeks, the waters would close over them and leave him submerged too?

He shut his eyes. In his old life he had lived (good!) in a flat off Baker Street. What was the address, the number of the flat? A sharper-piercing recollection went through him. Was he a bachelor, or had he been married? Surely, of all things on earth, he could remember that. Well! He was—

"Jack, old boy. Hal-lo!" cried a hearty if weak voice.

Beside the booth, swaying a little but reasonably sober, stood young Freddie Debbitt.

"Rather thought," he said, lurching and sitting down on the other side of the table, "rather thought I should find you here. Usually do come here, don't you?"

Freddie's high beaverskin hat, its nap rubbed the wrong way, was stuck sideways on his bright brown hair. His button nose was red, his round face pale, from a long night's carouse. Collar, neckcloth, and frilled shirt were all rumpled and dirty.

Cheviot shut down the lid on panicky thoughts.

"Where have you been, Freddie?" he asked. Bitterness rose in his voice. "Didn't you—er—disappear with the others?"

Freddie gulped, as though he wished to bring up some of his liquor and couldn't.

"Some of us," he said, "went on to Carrie's, you know. Got some new gels, Carrie has. Mine was r-rather good, too."

"Oh. I see."

But Freddie would not meet his companion's gaze.

"I say, though!" he added suddenly. "It's about last night. That's why I'm here. Wanted to see you, dash it. Had to see you."

"About what?"

"Well . . ."

This was the point at which the waiter reappeared, sliding platters of food across the table, arranging a silver tea service with immense cup and saucer, and doing a twinkling conjuring trick with silver cutlery.

"Breakfast, Freddie?" suggested Cheviot.

The boy shuddered. "No, thanks. Stay, though! Pint of claret and a biscuit."

"Pint of claret, sir. Biscuit, sir. Very good, sir." The waiter again melted away.

Cheviot poured tea and pitched in, trying to conceal his voracity.

"Jack!"

"Yes?"

"Last night." Freddie cleared his throat. "When you said Peg Renfrew was dead, and asked leave to question all of us, and proclaimed slap-out you were a p'leece-officer—"

"Freddie, I must thank you and Lady Cork and Miss Tremayne for what efforts you made to help. But the others? They did not even trouble to refuse answering questions. They ignored me altogether, and marched out of the house as though I were the scum of the earth."

Freddie writhed.

"Well, old boy; damme, Jack!—no offence, but they were right!"

"Oh?"

"Peelers *are* the scum of the earth, you know."

"Does this apply to Colonel Rowan? Or Richard Mayne? Or Mr. Peel himself?"

"That's different. Peel's a Cabinet Minister. The other two are Commissioners. But the rank and file?" Freddie meditated, plucking a toothpick from the glass. "Deuce take it, I was struck all of a heap! Why didn't you say you were a crossing-sweeper? Or a body-snatcher, even? They'd have taken it better. A Peeler! A *Peeler* put questions to an officer of the Guards, like Hogben?"

Cheviot stopped with his knife and fork above the plate.

But he said nothing; he knew his difficulty; he knew this boy, sixteen or seventeen years younger than himself, was trying to aid him. And he went on eating.

"You!" said Freddie, jabbing at the table with a toothpick. "You! A Peeler! Still! At least (or I hope, old fellow?) it's not too late?"

"Too late?"

"You haven't gone and joined 'em, I hear? Put your fist to a bit of paper, or the like?"

"No."

A ripple of relief went over Freddie's pale face and small red nose, agitating the bright brown side-whiskers. He put down the toothpick and spoke quietly.

"You must drop it, old boy. Then they'll all see the joke and laugh with you."

"Joke?"

"It's your own rum notion of a joke, a'n't it? But drop it. Devilish sorry; capital hoax; but you must. If you don't—"

Freddie moistened his lips. It was difficult for him, standing in so much awe of his companion as a sportsman, to stare back. But Cheviot suddenly realized that in Freddie Debbitt there were more force and strength of character than he would ever have suspected.

"Jack! A lot of us—well, dash it, we like you! But if you won't drop this . . ."

"Yes? If I won't drop it?"

"Then, damme, we'll make you drop it!"

Cheviot put down his knife and fork.

"Now just how do you propose to do that?"

Freddie had opened his mouth to retort when two persons arrived together at the table. One was the waiter, with Freddie's claret and a plate of biscuits on a salver. The other was an officer of the Guards, in full parade uniform.

This officer was a fair-haired, fair-complexioned young man in his middle twenties. His high bearskin cap, with its red short plume on the right to mark him as of the Second or Coldstream Regiment of Foot Guards, towered up as he held himself unnaturally straight.

His eyes were sharply intelligent, his manners formal and courteous, though he had the same lofty and languid look as so many of his tribe.

"Your name is Mr. Cheviot, I believe?"

"Yes?" said Cheviot.

He did not rise to his feet, as the officer seemed to expect. He merely eyed the newcomer up and down, without any favour at all.

"You will not be surprised, sir, when I tell you that I am here on behalf of my friend Captain Hogben, of the First Foot Guards."

"Yes?"

"Captain Hogben begs to express his opinion that your behaviour last night, on at least two occasions, was of such an insulting kind as no gentleman can endure."

Freddie Debbitt moaned a whispered oath. The waiter bolted away as though devil-pursued.

"Yes?" said Cheviot.

"However," continued the newcomer, "Captain Hogben requests me to add, considering your present somewhat inferior position as a member of the so-called police, that he is prepared to accept a written apology."

Cheviot slid along the oaken bench and rose to his feet.

"Now damn his eyes," Cheviot said quite pleasantly, "but what makes him rank the Army above the Metropolitan Police?"

The other man's hard, intelligent face grew expressionless. But a slight flush mounted under his high cheek-bones.

"I bid you take care, sir, or you may have another challenge on your hands. I am Lieutenant Wentworth, of the Second Foot. Here is my card."

"Thank you."

"However, sir, I have not yet done."

"Then have done, sir, by all means."

"Failing the tender of a written apology, Captain Hogben begs you to refer me to a friend of yours, that we may arrange a time and place of meeting. What is your answer, sir?"

"The answer is no."

Amazement flashed briefly in Lieutenant Wentworth's eyes. "Do I understand, sir, that you refuse this challenge?"

"Certainly I refuse it."

"You—you prefer to write an apology?"

"Certainly not."

It was deathly still in the coffee-room, except for the faint whistling of the gas-jets.

"Then what reply am I to take to Captain Hogben?"

"You may tell him," Cheviot said almost tenderly, "that I have work to do and that I have no time for adolescent foolery. You may further tender to him my hope that in due course his mind will grow to maturity."

"Sir!" exclaimed Lieutenant Wentworth in a human and almost likeable tone. This instantly changed to stiff-jawed grimness. "You understand the alternative? You know what Captain Hogben may do with this?"

"What he may do with it, sir, I trust I need not put into words. Good day, sir."

Lieutenant Wentworth stared back at him.

His left hand dropped to the hilt of his dress-sword. He was too well-mannered to sneer. But the edge of his lip lifted, with very slight contempt, above the chin strap of his bearskin cap. He returned Cheviot's bow, wheeled round, and marched out of the coffee-room.

The two men in the far booth, who had stood up to look, hastily sat down again. Cheviot saw his own disgrace mirrored in Freddie Debbitt's eyes as he continued, with outward quiet and inward boiling rage, to finish the eggs and ham and toast.

"Jack!"

"Yes?"

"You?" blurted Freddie. "A shuffler? A coward?"

"Is that what you think, Freddie? By the way," and Cheviot

pushed aside his plate, "you were about to tell me how you would force me to resign from the police."

"And now this! My God! Hogben'll horsewhip—"

"How, Freddie? How will you force me to resign?"

"I won't," retorted the other, who had swallowed most of the claret. "But everybody will. When this news gets about, damme, you won't be received anywhere. You'll have to resign from your clubs. You can't go to Ascot or Newmarket. As a Peeler, they won't even admit you to a gambling-house. . . ."

"Not even," said Cheviot, "to Vulcan's?"

"Why Vulcan's?" Freddie asked quickly, after a pause.

"No matter. It doesn't signify."

"Dash it, Jack, you're not the same man I saw a fortnight ago! Is it Flora Drayton? Or her influence? Or what?" Due to that last pint of claret, Freddie had become maudlin and half-tearful. "But she can't have wanted you to turn into a dashed Peeler. Last night all you'd do was go on about Peg Renfrew and jewellery and what not. Why, I could have told you—!" Abruptly he stopped.

"Yes," agreed Cheviot. "I rather thought you could."

"Eh?"

"A while ago, Freddie, I thanked you for the help you gave me. You, and Lady Cork, and Louise Tremayne. But you didn't in fact give real help. Lady Cork was too stubborn; Miss Tremayne too fearful of Lord knows what; you too overawed by your friends."

"Not overawed, curse it! Only—"

"Wait! Even before I questioned you downstairs, it was plain from what Flora and Lady Cork said that you knew a deal of the business. Your high spirits, your sense of humour, persuaded Lady Cork to hide her jewels in the seed containers. You were hovering everywhere."

"Only fun, you know!"

"Granted. But did Margaret Renfrew steal Lady Cork's jewels, as Lady Cork thinks she did?"

"Yes!" answered Freddie, with his eyes on the table.

John Cheviot drew a secret, deep gasp of relief. But his countenance showed nothing.

"Margaret Renfrew," he muttered.

"What's that, old boy?"

"I see her." Cheviot made a gesture. "A vivid brunette, with a high colour and a noble figure. She would have been beautiful, appealing, except for what? Hardness? Defiance? Shame? She's the one person whose character I can't grasp."

Freddie began to speak, but altered his mind.

"Listen!" urged Cheviot, seeing that gleam in the blurred young eyes. "She was shot to death, Freddie. She's the centre of the maze. We shall be nowhere unless we understand her."

Whereupon Freddie Debbitt, his expression far away, muttered words which for him were surprising and even startling.

" 'Fire burn,' " he said, " 'and cauldron bubble!' "

"What's that?"

"I say!" Freddie emerged from his trance. "D'ye know Edmund Kean? The actor fellow?"

"I have never met him, no," Cheviot answered with truth.

"H'm. Just as well. He's finished now. The drink's done for him; lost his memory; all that. Though, mind you, he's shifted to Covent Garden and he still plays."

"Freddie! I was asking you—"

"Little bit of a fellow, no mor'n a dwarf," insisted Freddie. "But with a big chest and a voice to break the window panes. When Kean was a lion in the old days, my father says he'd seldom go into society. 'Damn 'em!' says Kean. Now that he's done, so weak he can't more than stagger from Covent Garden to Offley's, there's no hostess'll receive him except Maria Cork.

"Stop, stop, now!" said Freddie. "One night, month or so gone, Kean was at Maria's. Saw Peg for the first time, I think. Gives a start like What's-his-name seeing the Ghost. Stares at her. And—

" 'Fire burn and cauldron bubble!' Damme! Out it came, in a voice to make the footmen's hair stand on end. Can't say what he meant. Full of brandy-negus, to be sure."

Those words, in the gas-lit coffee-room, sent a shiver through

Cheviot. Behind Miss Renfrew's painted face, her curling lip, what went on in her mind and heart and body?

"Freddie! Will you say what you know of her? And especially this mysterious lover of hers?"

The other hesitated.

"If I do," he said with sudden and youthfully intoxicated cunning, "will you drop your tomfoolery of being a Peeler? Hey?"

"I can't promise that. But it might affect my conduct in the future."

Freddie glanced left and right, carefully. Then he beckoned with both hands.

"Listen!" he whispered.

9

The Innocence of Flora Drayton

Colonel Charles Rowan, standing by the table in his office with Mr. Mayne beyond him and Mr. Henley behind the desk in the corner, was rigid with pride and pleasure.

Yet little of this showed in Colonel Rowan's long, undemonstrative face.

"Mr. Cheviot," he began, "may I have the honour of making you known to Mr. Robert Peel?"

The fifth man in the office, who had been staring out of a window at the nearly denuded tree and bushes in Great Scotland Yard, with his hands clasped behind his back and his under-lip upthrust, now wheeled round.

Mr. Peel was a big man, shock-headed, imperious of presence. He wore a long brown surtout with a high black-velvet collar and frogged buttonholes. At forty-one he was growing florid of face, though with large and curiously sensitive eyes. Cheviot, from reading of him, had imagined him as cold and pompous; certainly Mr. Peel's speeches in the House walked on stilts and unreeled yards of Latin quotations.

Nothing could have been more different from his manner now.

"Mr. Cheviot," he said, smiling broadly as he gripped Cheviot's hand, "you've won me over. You've got it."

"Sir?"

"The position, man! Superintendent of the Home Division!"

"Mr. Peel," interposed Colonel Rowan, tapping the many

and well-thumbed sheets of paper on the table, "has been much impressed by your report."

"Best report I ever read," Mr. Peel said briefly. "They send you out—on what? A theft of bird-seed. You prove (like that!) it was a jewel-robbery. You demonstrate where the jewels were hid. You surmise who stole them, and virtually lure Maria Cork into admitting you're right. That's as neat, concise a bit of mathematical reasoning as anybody could want.—Mathematician, Mr. Cheviot?"

"No, sir. Mathematics was always my poorest subject."

Up and down went the eyebrows.

"H'm. Pity. You surprise me. Now *I'm* a mathematician. I'll tell you more: I'm a Lancashire man, a practical man. If one thing won't do, use the opposite measure and stay in office: that's practical politics. Never mind what they call you, if you know you're right. They'll call you names in any case, as they call me."

Mr. Peel began to pace up and down, like a great wind in a small room. Though the office of Colonel Rowan and Mr. Mayne was not in the least small, the Home Secretary's tall presence made it seem so.

Then the florid face and the shock head turned on Cheviot.

"Thus, sir, concerning *you*. You are Superintendent of this division. All the same! We can't run the risk of wits such as yours being knocked out in a street brawl."

"But, sir—!"

"I am speaking, Mr. Cheviot."

It was three o'clock in the afternoon, with a nip in the October air. Watery sunlight, streaming past what few yellow leaves remained, poured through the red-curtained windows and hovered above a red Turkey carpet sprinkled grey with tobacco-ash.

Nothing had changed here since last night. Even the medium-weight pistol, with its silver handle and its hammer at half-cock as a sort of primitive safety-catch, lay undisturbed under a light-less red lamp.

To Cheviot—bathed, shaved, and in freshly fashionable new

clothes—his position already seemed less strange. It seemed less outlandish that he should occupy chambers at the Albany, where a young and dull-witted manservant assisted him with the hot tub and set out the garments he wore.

If he reflected on these circumstances, they might have been terrifying. But he did not reflect; the Home Secretary kept his eye hypnotized.

"I am speaking, Mr. Cheviot!" the Home Secretary repeated.

"Your pardon, sir."

"Granted, granted." Mr. Peel waved his hand. "Most of your nominal duties, therefore, will be assumed by the senior Inspector. You will not wear a uniform, even with gold lace round the collar to show your authority. You must remain in coloured clothes, as you are now."

("Now why didn't that occur to me?" Cheviot was thinking. "'Coloured clothes' merely means plain clothes, as I ought to have guessed from what the cabman said.")

"There can't be any 'detective police' as yet," announced Mr. Peel. "More than one man in coloured clothes would make the cry of 'Spy!' even worse. But we can have him," and he nodded towards Cheviot, "as a whole detective police under one hat. Are you a mathematician, Colonel Rowan?"

"Mr. Peel," courteously began Colonel Rowan, "I have some elementary—"

"Are *you* a mathematician, Mr. Mayne?"

The young barrister, his eyes and his round cheeks bulging from the black circle of side-whiskers, was compelled to check the torrent of words he would have poured out. Mr. Mayne writhed, pop-eyed, and shook his head.

Mr. Peel chuckled.

"Ah, well," he said. "You needn't be. Merely jot down the rewards we're obliged to pay these cursed Bow Street men. For taking a house-breaker: forty pounds. For taking a highway robber: forty pounds. For taking a murderer: forty pounds." Again he nodded towards Cheviot. "You see the amount of money we save with *him*?"

"Oh, doubtless," Colonel Rowan said gravely.

"Well?" demanded Mr. Peel, and looked full at Cheviot.

There was a brief silence.

"Yes, sir? What?"

"I must be off to the House. I can't stop here. But one thing I must know."

Here Mr. Peel retreated to the table, where he struck his big knuckles on the sheets of Cheviot's report.

"Who killed Maria Cork's niece, this woman Margaret Renfrew? And how the devil was it done?"

Now Cheviot understood why four pairs of eyes bored into him.

It was curiosity, a curiosity simmering almost beyond endurance even in Mr. Peel.

The Home Secretary's lips were drawn down. Mr. Mayne openly stared. Behind the desk in the corner, Mr. Henley had propped himself upright on an ebony stick. Colonel Rowan, though better concealing his feelings, slapped and slapped with his white gloves at the white trousers below the scarlet coat.

"Sir," Cheviot answered, "as yet I can't tell."

"You can't *tell?*" echoed Mr. Peel.

"No, sir. Not yet. This morning I obtained very helpful information from Mr. Frederick Debbitt, which is not in the report. But—"

"Here's a man," exclaimed Mr. Peel, incredulously appealing to the others, "who takes but one glance at the evidence before him, and tells us nearly all of what has happened. Yet he can't explain a detail like this?"

Cheviot's heart sank.

After his work last night, work which would not even have earned him a word of commendation from the Deputy Commander in his past life, these people were so impressed that they expected miracles. And miracles they meant to have.

There was more. This old house, much enlarged at the back to form a whole police-office, today stirred and was alive despite its unfinished confusion. The four Inspectors of the division, with short silver lace at the neck, and the Sergeants, with metal collar-numerals from one to sixteen, were present and correct. Sixty-five constables, he had been told, awaited his inspection on a small parade-ground at the rear.

They were a hard lot, ready to snarl or grow sullen under a Superintendent who could not handle them. Even when he entered he had sensed hurrying footsteps, smelt a whiff of brandy, heard the *whack-whack* as two humorists struck in vicious mock-battle with wooden truncheons.

In more senses than one, he was on trial.

But Cheviot, who had been compelled to control his temper since early morning, did not fail to control it now.

"Mr. Peel," he said coldly, "I ask you to consider the difficulties here. For instance! You have read my report, I understand?"

"Yes. Every word of it."

"You have also seen my sketch-plan of the upstairs passage where the crime was committed?"

Without a word Mr. Richard Mayne dug among the sheets of the report, found the plan, and held it up.

"All this," complained Mr. Peel, "is surely unnecessary? I have many times seen the passage you describe."

"And I," said Colonel Rowan, with his gaze on a corner of the ceiling.

"Forgive me," said Cheviot, "but it is not at all unnecessary. Finally, I call your attention to the surgeon's findings and the direction of the bullet."

He paused, surveying each of the auditors in turn.

"The bullet that killed Miss Renfrew," Cheviot added clearly, "was fired in a dead straight line. You mark it? A dead straight line."

It was as though Mr. Peel had retreated a little, merely watching and weighing with those large, sensitive eyes. Both Colonel Rowan and Mr. Mayne, the Commissioners, edged forward.

"I see what you imply, Mr. Cheviot," replied Colonel Rowan. He took the sketch-plan from his companion and tapped it. "In this passage, facing the stairs, we have two single doors on the left, and one set of double-doors (to the ballroom) on the right. Therefore none of these doors could have opened. Else, with this

—this poor lady's body lying well to the front of them, the bullet would have taken a diagonal course and not a straight."

"Exactly! And then?"

"Why, damme," Mr. Mayne burst out at last, "it's as plain as a pikestaff!"

"Is it?" Cheviot asked.

"The bullet," said Mr. Mayne, "was fired from the rear of the passage. Somewhere very near the place where you and Henley were standing. You allow it?"

"Apparently. Yes."

"We must grant," continued Mr. Mayne, regaining his barrister's dignity, "that neither you nor Henley is guilty. You would have seen each other. But what of the double-doors just behind you? Eh? What, I say, of the double-doors to Lady Cork's boudoir?"

"Well?"

"Your backs were turned to those doors. *They* could have opened, I daresay?"

"In theory, yes."

"In theory, Mr. Cheviot?"

"Yes. But not," retorted Cheviot, "without a snap and crack of the lock as loud as a light pistol-shot. As I pointed out in my report, the lock snaps whenever you open or close the door. We should have heard it; but we heard nothing. Second, is it likely that someone fired a pistol behind my shoulder, or Henley's, without either of us feeling the sting of the powder or the wind of the bullet?"

"Likely, sir?" repeated Mr. Mayne, with rich courtroom politeness. "Likely? My dear sir, that is what happened."

"I beg your pardon?"

Despite himself Mr. Mayne shot out a pointing finger.

"Wherever the place from which the bullet was fired, you have acknowledged it must have been close to you? Yes. And yet, you tell us, you heard little and felt little and saw nothing?"

"Are you calling me a liar, Mr. Mayne?"

"Gentlemen!" interposed Colonel Rowan, very stiffly. Mr.

Robert Peel, hugely amused, glanced from one to the other and said nothing.

"As for—er—impugning your veracity, Mr. Cheviot," the barrister told him with dignity, "I do no such thing. I am a lawyer, sir. I must examine evidence."

"I am a police-officer, sir. So must I."

"Then be good enough to do so." Mr. Mayne snatched the sketch-plan from Colonel Rowan and held it up. "In this admirable plan of yours, I note, we have the arrangement of all the doors."

"We have."

"Good! At some time before the murder, for example, could someone have slipped out of the ballroom unobserved by any of the other dancers?"

"Not while Lady Drayton was waiting in the passage, no."

"Ah, yes! Lady Drayton," said Mr. Mayne in a musing tone. His eyes, round and black and shining, rolled up suddenly; Cheviot felt a twinge of fear. "But we dismiss her, for the moment. Lady Drayton, as I understand it, was not sitting in the passage for the whole time before the murder?"

"No. She had gone downstairs to fetch a list of Lady Cork's jewels."

"Pre-cisely!" agreed Mr. Mayne, teetering on his heels. "Precisely! Therefore I repeat: could an assassin, he or she, have slipped out of the ballroom unobserved by any of the other dancers?"

"Yes; quite easily. When I myself glanced into the ballroom, the dancers were so absorbed that none so much as glanced at me."

"Ah!" said Mr. Mayne, teetering again. "I put to you, Mr. Cheviot, a feasible supposition. The assassin, let us imagine, slips out of the ballroom. He, or she, crosses diagonally to the door of the dining-room. We have here," and he held up the plan, "evidence that there is a door from the dining-room to Lady Cork's bedroom, and another door from her bedroom into her boudoir."

Here Mr. Mayne dropped the plan on the table, and stood teetering with his dark eyes shrewdly shining.

"I put it to you, Mr. Cheviot," he continued, "that the murderer could have been lurking in Lady Cork's bedroom. As soon as you and Henley leave the boudoir, closing the double-doors, the assassin moves across and opens one leaf of the doors behind you. Under cover of the noise, he fires a shot past you below shoulder-height. He then closes the doors and departs by way of the bedroom. I put it to you"—again Mr. Mayne's finger shot out automatically—"that this is quite possible?"

"No," said Cheviot.

"No? And pray why not?"

"Because," Cheviot retorted, "Lady Cork was in the boudoir the whole time."

"I fail to—"

"Do you, Mr. Mayne? Consider! When I entered the boudoir a brief time afterwards, Lady Cork was dozing beside the fire. But one snap of that lock roused her instantly."

"Well?"

"Well, sir! Do you imagine the murderer could have crept into the boudoir, opened that cracking door, fired a pistol, shut the door again and moved away, all without our notice or Lady Cork's? Or do you suggest Lady Cork as an accomplice in the crime?"

There was a strained, polite silence.

Mr. Peel nursed his chin, fingers hiding a smile. Colonel Rowan's handsome face, the grey-blond hair swept up above the temples, was apparently not there at all. Richard Mayne remained poised, though the dark eyes sparkled with wrath.

"You prefer an impossible situation, Mr. Cheviot?"

"To your solution, sir, I do."

"There is, to be sure," the barrister said thoughtfully, "an alternative and very easy explanation. But I hesitate to suggest it."

Cheviot merely lifted his shoulders and made a gesture for the other to go on.

Richard Mayne's round face softened. At heart, as he had proved in the past and was to prove in the future, he was a kindly and very efficient man. But his bouncing energy, at thirty-three, sometimes drove him at problems as though with his fists.

Still hesitating, he strolled over to the nearer window. Mr. Mayne drew back one side of the red curtain. He looked out at the soft mud of the yard, churned with wheel-tracks and enmeshed in dead leaves. He glanced at Mr. Peel's sober but luxurious carriage waiting there, at the dead bushes, at the one tall and crooked tree with a few yellow leaves still clinging to its branches.

Then Mr. Mayne's mouth tightened. He stalked back to the table, and tapped the sheets of Cheviot's report.

"Mr. Cheviot," he said in a hard voice, "why are you shielding Lady Drayton?"

Behind the desk in the corner, the pen dropped from Mr. Henley's hand and rolled clattering across until the chief clerk seized it.

Cheviot's heart jumped into his throat.

"Is there anything there," he demanded, "to say I am shielding Lady Drayton?"

Mr. Mayne made a gesture of impatience.

"It's not what you say. It's what you *don't* say. Come, man! Here is your most important witness, yet you scarcely speak of her. By your own account Lady Drayton was standing only ten or a dozen feet behind the victim. And, a most unusual circumstance, she was carrying a muff indoors. Are you a student of history, Mr. Cheviot?"

"Fortunately for myself, I am."

"Then you will be aware," the barrister said dryly, "that as early as the late seventeenth century, in the so-called and preposterous 'Popish Plot,' ladies were accustomed to defend themselves by carrying a pocket pistol in a muff."

Here Mr. Mayne drew himself up.

"It would be a pity, Mr. Cheviot," he continued with bursting politeness, "if our association began in a quarrel. But (forgive me!) we know so little of you. You are a well-known athlete, they say. Yet can you dominate the hard-bitten crew you purpose to command? Last night you boasted that any of us might take a pistol—yes, that pistol on the table now!—and fire at the stuffed bear by the mantelpiece, and you would tell us who had fired it. Have you fulfilled that boast? I think not. Instead—"

Abruptly he stopped.

He stopped, and turned towards the windows, because no one could have ignored the voice from outside.

The voice clove through October air now turned from watery yellow to dull grey. Cheviot knew whose voice it was. It belonged to Captain Hogben, and had no trace of a lisp. Harsh, strident, it beat at the house in a fury of hatred and triumph.

"Come out, Cheviot!" it screamed. *"Come out, shuffler, and take what's coming to you!"*

10

The Battle in the Yard

Cheviot took three strides to the nearer window, and, like Mr. Mayne, flung back the curtain at one side.

There were three of them, not thirty feet away from the house. They stood in the mud, motionless, under the tall and crooked tree with the few yellow leaves.

Captain Hogben and Lieutenant Wentworth were both in full parade uniform. Against their scarlet coats the white cross-belts stood out vividly in the grey air, as did the white duck trousers for daytime wear. From each man's left hip hung the long sabre in the gold scabbard, as straight as the top-heavy bearskin cap on each head. In fact, except for the short white plume on the left of Hogen's tall cap, and the short red plume to the right of Wentworth's, you could not distinguish the First Foot Guards from the Second.

But there were other differences.

Captain Hogben stood crookedly, under the high and crooked tree above him. His face showed red, his mouth split for yelling above the chin-strap. His left shoulder was up and his right humped down, white-gloved right hand gripping the stock of the horsewhip trailing out snakily behind him.

Lieutenant Wentworth remained straight and rigid. Between them, shivering, stood Freddie Debbitt.

Then Hogben's eyes caught Cheviot's through the window-glass.

"Come out, coward!" he screamed. *"Come out here now, or—"*

And Cheviot's temper, so long restrained that day, blew to pieces with a crash all the more violent for being inaudible.

He spun round. On his face was a smile so broad and murderous that for a second his four companions did not recognize him as the same man.

"Excuse me for a moment, gentlemen," he said in a voice he scarcely recognized himself.

And he ran for the door and threw it open.

Just outside, in the passage, there was already a clump and clatter of hurrying footsteps. Down the stairs poured tall hats of reinforced leather, and tight-fitting blue coats with lines of metal buttons. From the rear of the passage stalked a tall Inspector, with short silver lace at his collar, holding back the staring and straining men behind him.

When they saw Cheviot in the doorway, every man stopped dead.

Just in front of Cheviot stood a shortish but very broad man, marked as a sergeant by the metal numeral 13 on either side of his collar. He had a red face and a good-humoured eye, though his hard glance appraised the new Superintendent even when he stiffened to salute.

"Orders, sir?"

Cheviot did not speak loudly. Yet his voice seemed to penetrate to every corner of the house.

"There are no orders. Let every man stay where he is. I deal with this myself."

The sergeant's eyes gleamed. From under the back skirts of his coat, where it hung hidden, he whipped out the long baton of that very hard wood called lignum vitae.

"Truncheon, sir?"

"Now what need have I for a weapon? Stand aside!"

Cheviot ran for the front door. It was a large, heavy door. When he turned the knob and flung it open, the knob bounced and rebounded against the inner wall.

Every sense strung alert, eyes moving left and right and forward, he jumped down into the mud. Some dozen paces to his left, far out from the brick wall of the house, Mr. Peel's large carriage waited, with two footmen up behind and a sleepy coachman on the box. One of the horses suddenly stirred and whinnied.

Captain Hogben uttered a yell of triumph. Right hand back, he charged forward across the yard.

According to every rule, Cheviot should have stood still and taken his lashing. He should even have cowered, arms protecting his face, as befitted one who had refused a challenge to a duel. This always happened in books; Hogben, Wentworth, Freddie Debbitt firmly believed it happened in real life.

But he did nothing of the kind.

Instead, left arm slightly lifted and right arm a little below, Cheviot raced forward to meet Hogben in the middle of the yard.

Too late Hogben saw they must collide. Too late he recognized he should have stood off and lashed. But he could not stop his charge, and there was still time to use the whip. His right arm swung forward, the thin black whip curling out.

Cheviot stopped short. Hogben did not. As his right arm flew forward, the fingers of Cheviot's left hand gripped hard round the Guardsman's wrist. Cheviot braced himself hard on his right foot, turned slightly sideways, and yanked with all his strength.

Captain Hugo Hogben, nearly six feet tall and weighing eleven-stone-ten, pitched headlong over Cheviot's left shoulder.

His sword-scabbard rattled and flew. He landed head down, his tall bearskin cap squashing and turning under him to spare concussion of the brain. His body landed with a shock and thud which drove the breath from his lungs and the wits from his head.

Cheviot jumped over that motionless figure, sprawled in scarlet and white against the black mud. He tore the horsewhip from Hogben's hand. Coiling it up as best he could, he threw it far away among the bushes.

Then he jumped back again.

"Now get up!" he said.

A carriage-horse whinnied loudly and reared up. The coachman, down off the box, soothed the horse and muttered words nobody heard. A *whush* of chilly wind swept the bushes. A dead leaf spun off the tree, fluttered lazily, and floated down.

Almost instantly Captain Hogben twitched hard and was on his feet.

His gloved left hand ripped the chin-strap upwards. With both hands he slowly lifted the top-heavy cap from his head, and threw it aside. From uniform to face he was one spatter and smear of mud, except the clear patch over the forehead and eyes and round the ears where the cap had protected him, and a mudless space beneath his right eye.

His eyes were bleared. He was none too steady on his feet. But he had guts enough for ten men.

"Swine," he said.

And his gloved right hand whipped a vicious round-arm blow at his opponent's face.

Cheviot slipped under the blow. He seized Hogben, and spun him round backwards by his own front cross-belts. The dart was so unexpected that Hogben's shoulders and arms momentarily fell loose.

Instantly his right arm was gripped by the wrist, and locked up high behind his back. By instinct Hogben thrashed out towards the man behind him. He was just able to bite back a cry of agony.

"If you do that again," Cheviot said clearly, "you'll break your own arm. Now be off with you before I throw you in the cells. And don't make threats about horsewhipping people until you're sure you can carry 'em out."

Lieutenant Wentworth, still motionless, spoke in a high voice.

"Release him!" said Lieutenant Wentworth, with so superior and commanding an air that Cheviot's rage boiled again. "Do you hear, Peeler? Release him, I say!"

"With pleasure," snarled Cheviot.

He dropped Hogben's arms. Both hands flashed down nearly to the small of the Captain's back. Again all his strength went out in one catapult-shove.

Hogben staggered forward for three long paces, reeled, and

just saved himself from falling on his face. He bent down, one knee touching the ground, while you might have counted six.

Then he straightened up and turned round, breathing hard. The white mudless patch under his right eye gave that right eye a singular appearance: tip-tilted, distorted, devilish.

"God damn you," he whispered.

His left hand jerked the sword-scabbard to one side. There was a rasp of steel as he whipped out the straight sabre and charged again.

There could be no foretelling the result if Hogben, all but on top of his adversary, had lunged out for a thrust with the point. A simultaneous yell of warning, rising from many throats of people Cheviot could not see, burst like a war-whoop over the yard.

But it was not necessary. Captain Hogben flung back arm and shoulder for an overhand cut with the edge. In the split-second he was off balance, Cheviot leaped in at him.

Mr. Robert Peel, Colonel Charles Rowan, Mr. Richard Mayne, and Mr. Alan Henley, all unashamedly fighting each other to look out of one window, had long found their view obscured.

Officers as well as constables, disregarding orders, poured out of the house and lined up against the walls to watch.

Mr. Peel, for instance, saw the sword-blade whirl high in the air. It dropped, point downwards, and stuck upright in the mud not four feet in front of Lieutenant Wentworth. Mr. Peel could not see how Cheviot's hands altered their grip.

But Captain Hogben seemed to sail out in the air, feet forward and back parallel with the ground. They saw the soles of Hogben's boots, kicking towards the house, before he landed on his back and head, and lay still.

It was different, very different, in that deadly little circle of emotion round the fallen Hogben.

Cheviot, the breath whistling in his throat and sweat running down his body, strode forward. With his right hand round the hilt, he jerked the sabre out of the ground. His left hand fastened round the blunt edge. There was a sharp *crack* as he broke the blade across his knee. The two pieces he tossed away.

"Oh, God," whispered Freddie Debbitt.

Lieutenant Wentworth's fair complexion had gone chalk-white. He moistened his lips. Though he spoke clearly, it was with a kind of horror.

"You have broken the sword of a Guards officer," he said.

"Indeed?" gasped the unimpressed Cheviot. "Now just who the devil," he added, almost pleasantly, "do you Guardsmen think you are?"

Lieutenant Wentworth did not reply. He could not. It was as though Cheviot had asked the King who the devil he thought *he* was, or perhaps put the same question to the Deity Himself. Again Wentworth was merely bewildered.

"Mr. Cheviot, I—"

For the first time Cheviot raised his voice.

"Now look here," he shouted, dragging out his watch, opening it, and glancing at the fallen Hogben. "I'll give you just thirty seconds to take that—that specimen away from here. If you don't, I'll collar the lot of you and charge you with assaulting a police-officer. Take your choice."

"Jack, old boy!" bleated Freddie.

"Ah, my dear Freddie!" Cheviot said with rich politeness. "You professed to be a friend of mine, I think? What do you do in the camp of the enemy?"

"Dash it, Jack, I *am* your friend! I tried to prevent this! Ask Wentworth if I didn't!" Here Freddie paused in alarm as he looked sideways. "Hogben! Stop!"

For the indomitable Captain Hogben had again struggled up to his feet.

"No!" Lieutenant Wentworth said curtly.

Stalking towards Hogben, he seized his friend's left arm and held him back. Freddie, with surprising strength and firmness, dived and held Hogben's right arm.

"No!" Wentworth repeated. "If you use your hands against him, like a ploughboy, he'll make a fool of you every time. Be still!"

"Ten seconds," murmured Cheviot.

Wentworth drew himself up formally.

"Mr. Cheviot! You don't really mean to arrest—?"

"Don't I?" asked Cheviot, with a broad smile. "What do *you* think?"

"I am informed, Mr. Cheviot, that you are a gentleman despite your profession. A while ago, in the excusable heat of the moment, I uttered words of which I am heartily ashamed. Sir, I apologize." Wentworth slightly ducked his bearskin cap. "Nevertheless, matters have gone too far. You *must* meet Captain Hogben in the field—"

"With pistols?" Cheviot asked sardonically. "Fifteen seconds!"

"Yes, with pistols! You must meet him, I say, or he will have the right to shoot you down in the street."

Cheviot, about to answer contemptuously, caught sight of Freddie Debbitt's face. Inspiration came to him from the sort of moral blackmail Freddie had attempted to use that morning. He saw now what he stood to gain.

"Agreed!" said Cheviot, and shut up his watch.

"You will meet him?"

"I will meet him."

"You would have done much better," said Wentworth, drawing a deep breath, "had you said so earlier today. To whom do you refer me as a friend?"

"To Mr. Debbitt there. He will arrange matters with you, at any time and place you like." Cheviot replaced his watch. "You will, Freddie, won't you?"

"I . . . I . . . curse it, yes!"

"Very well. But, before our formal meeting, I shall insist on one condition."

Lieutenant Wentworth's back stiffened.

Cheviot, staring out at the cool grey air, went hot-and-cold all over. He was trying, in an abstract way, to remember the appearance of the flat in which he had lived (where?) in his old life as Superintendent of C-One.

He could recall nothing. Slowly, relentlessly, his memory was being submerged. Yet he could now remember the appearance, the numbers, even the smell and atmosphere, of places he did not even believe he knew.

"Joe Manton's shooting-gallery," Cheviot snapped, "is at number twenty-five Davies Street? Yes, yes, I am aware Manton is dead! But his son still keeps the gallery, and the gunsmith's at number twenty-four next door?"

"Well?"

"Before our formal meeting," said Cheviot, "Captain Hogben and I shall try our hands against each other, six shots each at a wafer, and for any wager he cares to name."

Lieutenant Wentworth was scandalized.

"Two principals," he cried, "to practice together before a meeting? That's imposs—!"

"Stop! Wait!" croaked out Hogben.

Hogben was now pretty steady on his feet. He jerked his arms loose. His face, under mud-stains, was paper-white between the black side-whiskers and feathery black hair. Though he drew his breath with difficulty, he bit at mud-caked lips and spoke again.

"*Any* wager, ye say?" And greed moistened his lips.

"Yes!"

"A thousand guineas? Hey?"

"Done!" said Cheviot.

"You fancy yourself, I hear," sneered Hogben through panting breaths, "at pistol-shootin' at a wafer. It'll be different when you face fire in the field, I promise you. Still! You do fancy yourself when there's no danger. What odds d'ye give?"

This time Cheviot drew a deep breath.

"All odds," he retorted in a loud voice. "If you outshoot me, in the opinion of judges to be agreed upon, I pay you a thousand guineas on the spot. If I outshoot you—"

"Hey? Well?"

"On your word as a British officer, you shall tell all you know about the late Margaret Renfrew. And so shall your friend Lieutenant Wentworth. That is all."

Once more the wind went stirring and rustling in the bushes. Mr. Peel's carriage, with its still-restive horses soothed by the coachman, had clopped up to a point almost behind them and towards their left.

"Wait!" said Wentworth, with an indecipherable expression on his face. "I again protest against—"

Hogben silenced him, still holding himself upright without swaying.

Captain Hogben was not an articulate or an intelligent man, as Lieutenant Wentworth clearly was. For Hogben, at all times, courage alone sufficed. And yet, as he rolled round that one vivid tip-tilted eye, it held a look of such malicious and delighted cunning that Cheviot ought to have been warned. He should have sensed fanged dangers in ambush, an unseen stroke to crush him forever.

"Done!" Hogben said softly.

"I tell you, the code—" began Wentworth.

"Damn the code. Be quiet, Adrian, and fetch my cap!"

Lieutenant Wentworth hurried to pick up the muddied bearskin cap, slapped at it to clean it, and fitted it slowly down on his friend's head as he adjusted the chin-piece. Hogben winced slightly with pain, but held himself straight. He did not even glance at the pieces of the broken sword.

Freddie Debbitt ran out into Whitehall. Putting two fingers into his mouth, he whistled shrilly. A large and wide open carriage, drawn by two black horses and with its rather grimy silk upholstery in white as though to match the plume of the Grenadier Guards, came spanking into view.

Behind it, almost too close, rattled another open carriage: more severe, but better kept from its red wheels to its glossy dapple-grey mares.

In this latter carriage sat a fat and purplish-faced gentleman with a velvet-collared surtout over his coat, and a majestic hat. Beside him, on the near side, Louise Tremayne leaned out and looked straight at Cheviot.

Young Louise wore one of the fashionable turbans in blue silk; a white cloak, with blue-striped cape to it, was clasped round her neck. Her hazel eyes, very intense in the pretty, immature face, conveyed a message as plainly as her wide mouth moved without sound.

"I must see you immediately at—"

The fat gentleman, observing the turn of her head, touched her shoulder. While Louise shrank meekly inside her cape, the fat gentleman—obviously father or uncle or close relative—raised his thick black eyebrows so outrageously high that it might have been a gesture of pained astonishment on the stage.

"You, fellow!" sneered Captain Hogben.

Cheviot shifted his eyes back. All hatred rose again.

"Manton's?" asked Captain Hogben. "Nine o'clock tomorrow morning?"

Cheviot nodded curtly.

"And afterwards, hey, the meetin'?"

Again Cheviot nodded.

Ignoring him, Captain Hogben swung round and moved towards the first carriage. His step faltered; Wentworth and Freddie Debbitt held his arms on either side. But he had gone only two steps when he whirled round again.

The venom of the one eye had a tint and taint of the demoniac.

"May Christ help you," Hogben said, not loudly, "when I get you at the end of a duellin' pistol!"

Lieutenant Wentworth jerked at his arm. He and Freddie hurried Hogben forward, assisting him into the first carriage between them. The driver's whip cracked; the black horses swept the carriage away up Whitehall. A lighter flick danced over the dapple-grey mares of the second carriage. While Louise kept her eyelashes demurely lowered, and the purplish-faced gentleman took a pinch of snuff from an ivory box, the carriage rattled after Hogben's past the grey courtyard of the Admiralty across the road.

Superintendent John Cheviot stood motionless, his head down.

His high collar had wilted; its points ceased to stab him under the chin. He was cooling off, both in mind and body.

He had beaten Hogben hands down. But he was far from sure he had not made a fool of himself. There, in the mud, lay the two pieces of the broken sword. Cheviot, a little ashamed, bent down, picked them up, and weighed them in his hand.

Still with his gaze on the ground, he walked slowly and heavily towards the house.

Then he raised his head—and stopped short.

For he saw what he had never expected to see.

Every man of the division's sixty-five constables stood motionless, in a double rank on either side of the door. Just in front of them stood the sixteen sergeants, eight on either side to mark the path to the door. And, in front of these, the four Inspectors stood two on either side.

They stood rigidly at attention, their shoulders so far back as to threaten the cloth of the blue coats. Their hands were straight down the trouser-seams. Their eyes were fixed straight ahead, in a sightless and glassy stare, though any observer could have seen that each man's lungs were all but bursting to cheer.

Still silence, while only the wind stirred.

It was the greatest tribute they could have paid him. Cheviot knew it. To his heart it drove the blood of pride and pleasure; it straightened his own back, and made his head sing. But he sensed how he must deal with it, to avoid embarrassment.

So he marched straight up, and stopped before the cleared path to the door. There he ran his eye slowly to the left along those motionless lines, and then slowly to the right, as though in careful inspection.

"Which of you," he asked curtly, "is the senior Inspector?"

The tall and lean man, whom he had seen before and who had a nose like the as-yet-uncreated Mr. Punch of the magazine-cover, took two stiff paces forward and saluted.

"Sir!" he said. "Inspector Seagrave, sir."

"A good parade, Inspector Seagrave. I congratulate you."

"Sir!"

Cheviot glanced down at the two pieces of the sword in his left hand.

"I have here," he added, "a small trophy for our first trophy-room. It belongs to all of you. Take it."

Abruptly he threw the pieces to Inspector Seagrave, who

caught them neatly in one hand with a sharp clash of steel. The short, slight gesture of the Inspector's other hand indicated, "No cheering!" to the men behind him, though the lines of tall hats wavered and an explosion hovered close.

Once again Cheviot glanced slowly left and right.

"Stand easy," he said.

And, smiling for the first time, he sauntered between the ranks, up the step, and through the open door into the house.

He did not even hear the outburst behind him. Cheviot had the bit in his teeth; Mr. Richard Mayne was attacking, and there was one who must be kept from any danger, if he must outface the Home Secretary too.

Striding to the door of Colonel Rowan's office on the right, Cheviot opened it without the formality of knocking. He closed the door behind him.

Then he looked slowly round at Mr. Robert Peel, at Colonel Rowan, at Mr. Alan Henley again behind the desk, and above all at Mr. Richard Mayne.

"And now, gentlemen," he began briskly, "as we were saying before this unseemly interruption? Mr. Mayne, I believe, was accusing Flora Drayton of having committed murder?"

11

Louise Tremayne—and Dear Papa

"But, damme, man," exclaimed Mr. Mayne, removing his hands from under his coat-tails, "I never said any such thing! I only said—"

Colonel Rowan held up a hand for silence.

The Colonel, who had clipped and lighted a cigar, was pacing restlessly. He stopped in front of Cheviot, with his large nostrils distended.

"Superintendent," he said, taking the cigar out of his mouth, "the First or Grenadier Foot Guards are the oldest regiment in the British Army. Your conduct was infamous; I must rebuke you severely. Er—consider yourself rebuked," added Colonel Rowan, and put the cigar back in his mouth.

"Yes, sir," said Cheviot.

Mr. Peel, not a man much addicted to mirth, uttered a great gust of laughter. Then his large eyes narrowed with cold shrewdness.

"For myself, Mr. Cheviot," he said, "I should give much to know whether you merely lost your temper, or whether you did that deliberately to impress your men. Well, you impressed 'em. And by gad, sir, you impressed me! But you've landed yourself in trouble all the same."

"With Captain Hogben, sir?"

"Hogben? That lout? The other officers of the First Foot won't even speak to him; that's why he needed a Coldstreamer

for support. No! I meant the Duke. The Guards are the Duke's
pets. To talk to him, you'd think no other regiments were even
present at Waterloo—"

Here Colonel Rowan grew rigid.

"—and there'll be a fine mess if *he* hears of this. Further,"
mused Mr. Peel, with his chin in his big hand, "I wonder what
you and Hogben were discussing so formally just before he left?"

"A purely private matter, sir. It does not concern us."

"H'm," Mr. Peel said thoughtfully.

Cheviot advanced to the table.

"But what does concern us," he drove at them, "is Mr.
Mayne's statement that I failed in my duty and that I shielded
Lady Drayton."

"I said as much. Yes!" Mr. Mayne retorted with drawn-up
dignity.

"On what grounds?" Cheviot struck the table. "With your
permission, sir, *I* will repeat the argument. You are suspicious,
you state, on the grounds of what I 'do not say.' I have never
heard, in law, of a man being condemned for perjury because of
what he does not say."

"You are twisting—!"

"I am stating. Your only so-called evidence, which you term
an 'unusual circumstance,' is that Lady Drayton carried a muff
indoors. Had you read this report, however," and Cheviot lifted
the sheets and dropped them, "you would have seen it was not at
all unusual. Lady Drayton had split her right-hand glove wide
open, as everyone can testify; and, like other ladies, she wished
to conceal it. Where is your evidence that any pistol was in the
muff or existed at all?"

Mr. Mayne's dark eyes glittered.

"Evidence? I mentioned none. I but suggested a line of inquiry
which you seem to have neglected."

"Sir!" blurted out a hoarse, heavy voice behind him.

Alan Henley leaned out with his thick hands on the desk.
Though it was only five o'clock, the grey sky had grown so dark
that these people loomed up like the ghosts they might have been.

A grease-soaked wick flared up; again, with a loud pop, Mr.

Henley kindled the broad green-shaded lamp on his desk, as opposed to the red-shaded one on the table. His big head, with the reddish side-whiskers, was thrust out with great earnestness.

"Sir," he continued, addressing Colonel Rowan, "she didn't!"

"Oh? Didn't what?" Colonel Rowan spoke mildly, removing the cigar from his mouth.

"The lady," insisted Mr. Henley, "hadn't got a pistol. I was there, sir. I saw. As for the Superintendent being negligent—why, sir, it was the first thing he thought on."

"Ah?"

"He thought (begging your pardon, Colonel) the lady might have fired a shot. I knew she hadn't; I watched her. She no more had a weapon than me and the Superintendent had. But he asked her to show and turn out her muff, case she might have fired through it. And she hadn't."

Mr. Henley's honesty, since he really believed every word he was saying, carried conviction.

And all the time, in imagination, Cheviot had been seeing Flora: Flora's jealousies or rages lasted only for a moment, though why could she have been jealous of Margaret Renfrew? All day she would have been waiting for him at her house in Cavendish Square; and he had not called there. He would only have to mutter that it was his fault, and she would pour out frantic cries that it was all her fault, and run into his arms. . . .

Here Cheviot checked his thoughts, with a clammy shock over his body.

How did he know Flora lived in Cavendish Square, if she did? How did he know how she always behaved after a quarrel or misunderstanding?

But he must wrench back his mind. Mr. Henley was still doggedly speaking.

"—so you see, sir, *I* didn't read the Superintendent's report. Or hear about it till a while ago. All the same, this surgeon says the bullet was fired in a dead straight line. Well! Anybody can tell you Lady Drayton was standing behind the poor woman a good two or three feet to the right of her. So she'd have had to fire a shot diagonal-like, now wouldn't she?"

Mr. Richard Mayne lifted his shoulders.

"Then you are all against me, it seems," he said.

"No, sir, Mr. Mayne, we're not!" Again the chief clerk, with heat, appealed to Colonel Rowan. "One word more, Colonel?"

Colonel Rowan smiled and gestured assent with his cigar.

"*I* think," said Mr. Henley, "Mr. Mayne's right about a shot from inside them double-doors behind us. Noise!" he scoffed, with puffed cheeks. "You're not put off by snapping locks or even light shots. Me and the Superintendent (eh, sir?) were too pre-occupied by what Lady Cork had just said. That's what puts you off. If you ask me, somebody could have let off a blunderbuss behind us and we shouldn't have heard. There!"

" 'For this relief,' " murmured Richard Mayne, " 'much thanks.' "

"Mayne!" Colonel Rowan called softly.

"Eh?"

"You and I," smiled the Colonel, "have been joint Commissioners without any disagreement so far. Let's hope there will never be one. Still! You are engaged to be married, I believe, to a very charming young lady?"

"Indeed and I am!" declared the other, adjusting his cuffs with pride.

"But a lady who, quite rightly, has strong moral and religious views?"

"We all know, Rowan, your own loose views concerning—"

"Tut!" said the Colonel, waving away cigar-smoke. "Now confess it, Mayne! Confess it! In your heart haven't you been suspicious from the first of Cheviot and Lady Drayton merely because Lady Drayton is (how shall I put this delicately?) his *belle amie?*"

Mr. Mayne was too honest a man to deny this completely. He took a turn back and forth from the table, flapping his coat-tails behind him.

"You may be right," he said. Then he struck the table. "But come now! To business! We have heard what the Superintendent does not say. What *does* he say? Mr. Cheviot, who killed Margaret Renfrew?"

Cheviot moistened his lips.

A wind was getting up and prowling round the house, tugging at the window-frames. In this red, weapon-hung room, lighted by a green lamp, there was a hush more tense than seemed to befit mere investigators.

"In my opinion, sir, she was killed by her lover."

"Ah!" Mr. Mayne touched the report. "This mysterious lover at whom you hint so much? What is his name?"

"I can't yet tell you his name," Cheviot answered with honesty. "Even Freddie Debbitt, who knows every bit of gossip in London, couldn't tell me that. But I can describe him."

"Then pray do so."

"He is a man," said Cheviot, weighing facts, "of good birth and presence, though not wealthy and chronically hard up. He is physically attractive to women, though rather older than Miss Renfrew. He is a heavy gambler. He—" Cheviot paused. "Tell me, gentlemen. Has either of you ever met Margaret Renfrew?"

Colonel Rowan nodded, his blue eyes regarding a corner of the mantelpiece. Mr. Mayne inclined his head without enthusiasm.

"Very well," said Cheviot. " 'Fire burn and cauldron bubble!' "

"I beg your pardon?" murmured the barrister.

Cheviot threw out his hands.

"Here is a beautiful woman," he said, "of thirty-one years. Outwardly she is cold and imperious, though of the fierce inward temper she displayed. She rages against her position as a poor-relation, but attempts not to show it."

"Yes?" prompted Colonel Rowan, slowly blowing out cigarsmoke.

"When a woman like that falls in love, she is apt to explode like a cannon. According to Lady Cork, she *does* fall in love. Fiercely she denies, of course, that this man even exists. She is so passionately in love with him (or in lust, if you prefer the term), that she lies for him, steals jewels for him so that he may gamble at Vulcan's. . . ."

"Did Lady Cork," smoothly asked Mr. Mayne, "give evidence that Miss Renfrew stole the jewellery?"

"Not quite to me, as you know. But to Freddie Debbitt—"

"Hearsay evidence, my dear sir."

Cheviot looked at him.

He was not deceived by the barrister's courteous expression, his round face and interested dark eyes. Mr. Mayne was more than an honest man; he was clever, subtle-minded, if more through instinct than through reason. Firmly he had got into his head the notion that Flora Drayton was guilty of something, of anything. The whole powder-barrel would blow up if Cheviot's hand slipped, or Mr. Mayne learned of the facts about Flora which his Superintendent had concealed.

So Mr. Mayne waited, his arms folded. And, metaphorically, Cheviot hit him again.

"Hearsay evidence?" he demanded. "Good God, what else can I use? I remind you, sir, that we are not yet in court."

"There is no need for heat, Mr. Cheviot. What do you propose to do?"

"Tonight I visit Vulcan's gaming-house," said Cheviot, "at number twelve Bennet Street, off St. James's Street. If necessary, I shall play high at the tables—"

"With whose money?" suddenly demanded Mr. Robert Peel, towering up. "Not with the Government's, I warrant you! Not with the Government's!"

Cheviot bowed, touching his pockets.

"No, sir. With my own. That, I regret to say, is why I was late in arriving here today. I was obliged to visit my bankers in Lombard Street."

"Your own money?" breathed Mr. Peel, much impressed. "Egad, man, but you're a razor at your work!" He mused. "I've heard much of this Vulcan's, I'm bound to say. It is one of the few houses in St. James's where ladies are admitted."

Mr. Mayne raised his eyebrows.

"Ladies?" he repeated. "Oh! I see. You mean prostitutes."

Mr. Peel loomed up with the cold arrogance he assumed in the House of Commons.

"No, young man, I do not mean prostitutes. I refer to ladies, and ladies of quality. They are protected by male servants, and never molested. The worst rake in town, when he sits down to cards or roulette, has no eye for anything save his winnings. At least," Mr. Peel added hastily, catching Colonel Rowan's eye, "so I have been told." He turned to Cheviot. "But what's your scheme, man?"

Colonel Rowan was as deeply fascinated as the Home Secretary.

"Yes! What's the plan?"

"Well—"

"Not a raid, I hope? That's difficult. There's always an iron door at the top of the stairs."

"No, not a raid. I mean to go in alone—"

"Damned dangerous," said the Colonel, shaking his head. "If they've learned you're a police-officer—"

"I must risk that. Besides, with your permission, I shall in some sense be protected."

"But what'll you *do*?"

It was Cheviot's turn to pace the smoky, dusky room.

"This morning, at the coffee-room of a hotel," he went on, peering out of the window, "Freddie Debbitt drew me a sketch of Vulcan's house, including his private office."

"Well?"

"By Lady Cork's testimony, a very valuable piece of jewellery was pledged, that's to say pawned, at Vulcan's office. This is easily distinguishable: a diamond-and-ruby brooch shaped like a square-rigger ship. Since it was pawned and not sold, it will still be there. It's unlikely the brooch was pledged by Miss Renfrew; her hatred of gaming was well known, and she would never have been so indiscreet. No! It was done by the man. Let me lay my hands on that brooch, and we can force Vulcan to disclose his name."

"And this," Mr. Mayne asked rather sarcastically, "will prove he killed Miss Renfrew?"

Cheviot turned from the window, went to the table, and looked down into the barrister's eyes.

"Legally, no," he admitted. "But if you are resolved to have proof of a man's guilt before we even know who is guilty, then all investigation stops forthwith. I have only a strong belief, based on more experience than I care to tell."

"In short, a guess at hazard?"

"A belief, I say! That this man will be trapped when we know his name."

"You—you may be right. But, whatever your private beliefs are you sure of your conclusions?"

"No! No! No!" Cheviot's face was rather pale. "Is any man, except a star-led maniac like the late General Bonaparte, ever sure? Are you? Is Colonel Rowan or Mr. Peel? I can swear only that it's the likeliest thing. This matter is too perplexed. For all I am sure of, the murderer may even be a woman."

"A woman?" echoed Mr. Peel.

This was the point at which there was a sharp rapping on the door to the passage.

It was opened by the short, but very broad and burly, sergeant with the collar-numeral 13, whose red face and expression Cheviot had liked very much. The Sergeant addressed Colonel Rowan, but his stiff salute was directed toward Cheviot alone.

"A lady to see the Superintendent, sir."

"A lady?" Colonel Rowan, distressed, considered the tobacco-spattered disorder of the office. "That's impossible, Sergeant Bulmer! We have no place to receive her!"

Sergeant Bulmer remained stolid.

"Name of Miss Louise Tremayne, sir. Says she has important information about a Miss Renfrew. But won't speak to anybody except the Superintendent, and speak to him alone."

Colonel Rowan extinguished his cigar on the edge of the table, amid a shower of sparks, and threw the cigar into the china spittoon underneath.

"Mr. Peel," he said to the Home Secretary, "you have matters of great moment on your mind. We—we cannot entertain this young lady in my living-quarters upstairs. But Mr. Mayne and I can withdraw there, while Mr. Cheviot sees her here. Doubtless, sir, you would wish to leave us?"

Carefully, like a Roman emperor, Mr. Peel placed his tall beaverskin hat on his head.

"Doubtless, Colonel Rowan, I should wish to withdraw," he intoned. "But I am hanged if I will. This accursed drawing-room game, of who-killed-who-and-how, has made me forget my duties to the nation. I account you responsible; but I accompany you."

In three seconds the Colonel had led them away. In the dim passage still lurked Sergeant Bulmer and the long figure and Punch-like nose of Inspector Seagrave. Holding the door slightly ajar, Cheviot whispered to them.

"Inspector! Sergeant! Are your duties free enough so that you can assist me tonight, say between ten-thirty and one o'clock, for a small mission among the blacklegs?"

It was not merely that the men agreed; eager assent radiated from them.

"Good. Can you also free six constables from their duties too? Good!"

"Any special sort of men, sir?" whispered Inspector Seagrave.

"Yes. I want climbers. Men who can go up over a roof or among chimney-pots as quickly and quietly as house-breakers."

"Got 'em, sir," whispered Inspector, after casting up his eyes as though counting. "Just the men you want. Between ourselves, I shouldn't like to say they haven't *been* house-breakers, at one time or another."

"Better still. A word in your ear later. Now admit the lady."

With his arms Cheviot fanned ineffectually at the air, to dispel tobacco-smoke. He raised one window; but, since there was no window-stick to prop it up, he had to lower it again. Then Louise came in.

Her age he had already put at about nineteen or twenty. In her blue turban, with the white cloak with the blue-bordered short cape outlining the puffed sleeves of her dress as well as its wide skirt about three inches from the floor, the hazel-eyed girl was so charming that she might have turned Cheviot's head if he had been a dozen years younger.

As it was, since he preferred more mature women with skill at conversation as well as other skills, he at first treated her with an avuncular air which she instantly sensed and resented. He sensed it in turn and became very gallant, which vastly pleased her.

"It is the greatest of pleasures to see you, Miss Tremayne," he said, slapping with his immense handkerchief at a purplish-padded armchair, and only raising more dust. "Will you have the kindness to be seated?"

"Oh, thank you!"

"Er—the room, I fear . . ."

Louise did not in the least mind the dirt or disorder; indeed, it appeared, this was only what she expected to find. But she kept her eyelashes lowered from him, and cast frightened glances at the window.

"Pray do forgive my boldness, Mr. Cheviot. But it was most imperative to see you. I was even obliged to deceive Papa. Mr. Cheviot, *why* is one's papa always in such a fearful wax about something?"

Cheviot restrained the impulse to say it was because they ate and drank too much at that age, and had it all their own way in the home.

"I have never discovered, Miss Tremayne. But they always are, aren't they?"

"Indeed mine is. As we were driving through Westminster, dear Papa went on awfully about a tailor—"

"About a what?"

"A tailor in Westminster. Dear Papa says the tailor will fire a house, or begin a riot or something, about Reform. We were—well! We were following Captain Hogben's carriage, because Captain Hogben wished us to see him horsewhip you. It didn't happen quite like that, did it?"

Here Louise turned her head, lifted her clear hazel gaze, and looked him straight and unashamedly in the eyes.

"*I* think it was wonderful," she said.

Cheviot, feeling as though he had been struck by an amorous bullet, swallowed hard. He was not yet used to the way of women in this age. But he liked it very much.

"Er—thank you."

Louise instantly blushed and looked away. But, now that she felt more confidence, she was going on in her usual rush of speech.

"Dear Papa was furious. But, in his way, I own he was just. 'G.d. the fellow,' he said; wicked words, you understand, about you; 'I've seen wrestling all me life, but I never saw a wrestler like that, and g.d. me,' he said, 'if I can tell how the b.h. that fellow did it.' You see, Papa was cross because he wishes me to marry Captain Hogben—"

"And will you marry him, dear Miss Tremayne?"

"Not if *I* know it!" cried Louise, flinging up her small chin in defiance. "But I was saying. Dear Papa was so vexed he must stop at his club, and leave me sitting outside. I ran away in the carriage, and told Job to drive me here."

"You had something to tell me, I believe?"

"Yes, yes, yes! Oh, dear. I must tell you two dreadful things. I desired to tell you last night, but at one time Flora Drayton was there—" She stopped.

"Yes," said Cheviot, looking at the floor.

What he felt now, flowing from the slender girl in the blue turban and white cape, were fear and uncertainty. Worst of all, which he could not understand, the fear and uncertainty were about him.

"What I wished to tell you," she continued, trembling but speaking in a clear voice, "was about—about *the man*."

"Man? What man?"

"Peg Renfrew's man," answered Louise. "They say she positively adored him. She adored him so much that sometimes she hated him. Can you understand that?"

"I think so."

"Well, I vow I can't. But they say," Louise went on with shattering frankness, "Peg stole money for this man, stole jewels so that he could gamble. But she was in a terribly difficult position: a poor-relation, dependent on Lady Cork. If Lady Cork ever discovered it, she thought, she'd be turned from the house. So, a few days ago, she changed."

Cheviot nodded without looking up.

Louise's slender ankles, in their French-silk stockings, trembled too. Her shoes, of blue Moroccan leather, were muddy from walking across the yard.

"Peg was hard, hard, awfully hard! She told him, they say, that she'd never steal another penny or another jewel. If he used force, she said, she'd tell of him to Lady Cork and everyone else. And this man (oh, dear, I'm only repeating gossip!) has a most abominable temper."

Louise was rising in spite of herself.

"And he said, if she ever spoke a word to anyone, he'd kill her. He'd shoot her. And that's what happened. Isn't it?"

Again Cheviot nodded without looking up. He felt she was casting him quick and furtive looks, her broad innocent mouth open.

"Again last night, you see, I t-tried to tell you when you were putting questions at people. But there were so *many*, all listening! I could do no more than hint."

A sweat of excitement stood out on Cheviot's forehead. He might be closer to finding the murderer than he thought. He stood facing Louise, head down, his left hand gripped round the burned edge of the table.

"Yes, I know," he said. "So did Lady Cork. But your hints were so mysterious, all of a jumble, that I could read no meaning into them until Freddie Debbitt explained it this morning in a coffee-room. Louise! All this has been common gossip. Yet I never knew it?"

"Well! Papa and Mama have spoken of it. I always listen, though they think I don't."

"But listen to me. *Someone* must know the name of this lover who threatened her! Have you heard it?"

"Haven't—haven't you?"

"No; how should I, with all mouths closed? Who do they say he is?"

"C-can't you guess?"

"No, no! Who do they say it is?"

"Well!" murmured Louise, keeping her eyes lowered. "Some say it was *you*."

There are some shocks so unexpected and fantastic that they take a little time to seep into every corner of the brain before they are understood.

Seconds passed. Cheviot, resting his whole weight with the left hand on the table, suddenly found his palm growing moist. He slipped, and nearly stumbled forward.

"To be sure," flattered Louise, "*I* knew it couldn't be truth!"

But she wasn't quite sure; she was terrified of him, despite all the trouble to warn him; her voice pleaded for a denial.

"Although, to be sure," she went on in a rush, "you are sometimes a *very* heavy gambler. But that is only when you have been drinking quite heavily, and you are never seen the worse for drink in public."

They were almost the same words Colonel Rowan had used last night.

Louise stopped. She saw his face as he looked up.

"Louise," he said hoarsely, "do you imagine *I* would take money from a woman? Or that I should need to? I'm not hard up!"

"No, no, no! But—but often people say they're not, don't they, when they are? And some wonder, if you had so much money, why you should take this odious place as a police-officer."

Cheviot controlled himself. He could see the dangers opening all round him, amid dumb-faced people who would neither affirm nor denounce. And *he* had tried to question *them* about the murder!

Did Flora know all this? She must know some of it, at any rate. And that would explain . . .

"Will you believe me," he asked, "if I tell you I never met Margaret Renfrew before last night? In fact, she said as much herself before other persons!"

"But—but she would say that, wouldn't she? And Peg always declared she could fall in love only with an older man, who had," Louise shied away from some word as being improper, "who had been in the world. Once *I* can recall how she remarked (oh, so very negligently, touching her bonnet) how well you carried yourself on horseback."

"Listen! The first time I ever heard that woman's name—!" Cheviot stopped abruptly.

As shocks can stun the emotions, so they can open the brain to facts hitherto observed yet never properly understood. He saw his own words printed in his mind, and the fact they represented. Another fact followed, then another and another.

He could not see them before. He had been blinded by his feelings. Standing beside the table, his gaze wandered down. There, beneath the unlighted red lamp and beside his own report, he saw Colonel Rowan's medium-bore pistol with the polished silver handle.

If only, last night, he had performed that simple fingerprint test to see who fired a pistol, he would have seen through to the heart of truth. Instead—

"Smoke!" he said aloud. "Smoke, smoke!"

Louise Tremayne jumped up from the chair and backed away.

"Mr. Cheviot!" she breathed, extending lilac-gloved hands and then hastily dropping them.

"I have not told you," she rushed on, "the most dreadful circumstance of it all. It concerns both you and—and Lady Drayton."

Cheviot flung away speculation. "Yes?" he demanded, rather too roughly. "Yes?"

Louise moved still farther towards the window. Evidently she was torn between fear and tenderness; a hatred of being hurt, yet an obscure desire to be hurt by him.

"Hugo Hogben and I," she said, "were dancing together. That must have been just after . . . after . . ."

"After Miss Renfrew was shot. Yes?"

"Well! We—" Now it was Louise who paused, twitching her head round.

She was more alert than he. Cheviot had not heard heavy, fat footsteps squelching towards the house, or a port-winy voice upraised in addressing the door.

"It's Papa," said Louise. Her short nose and wide mouth seemed to crumple up, like a child's. "He'll beat me. He's a dear, good, kind man; but he'll beat me if I don't think of some fib. I can't stay; I can't!"

She flew to the door, which opened and slammed behind her.

Cheviot was after her in a moment, but he was too late. Except for a constable examining a number of dark lanterns under a hanging petroleum-oil lamp, the passage was empty and the front door closed.

He could hear the domineering male voice upraised above the creak of hooves and carriage-wheels as the vehicle drove round. He and Flora walked amid still taller dangers; Louise could tell him. But she and her dear, good, kind papa were gone.

Cheviot went to fetch his hat. He did not communicate with those waiting upstairs, in Colonel Rowan's living-quarters. Instead, after brief orders to Inspector Seagrave and Sergeant Bulmer, he hastened out.

At the top of Whitehall he found a hackney cabriolet. After what seemed an interminable drive, through muddy streets beginning to glimmer with gas-lamps, he got down at number eighteen Cavendish Square.

Flora's house was of whitish stone, untainted by smoke. But it was without light or sound, every window closely shuttered. Though he hammered at the door, and nearly broke the bell-wire in pulling at its brass knob, there was no reply.

At half-past ten that night, after dinner and after dressing himself carefully, Cheviot stood back waiting in a dark doorway of Bennet Street, off St. James's Street—looking across towards Vulcan's gaming-house, and what awaited him there.

12

The Black Thirteen

Two faces, one lower down and the other higher up, shone in the gloom of the doorway on either side of him.

Cheviot, in full evening-dress, wearing over it an ankle-length black cloak with a short cape whose collar was trimmed with astrakhan, and the most glossy of heavy hats, stood between them.

"Got yer rattle, sir?" whispered Sergeant Bulmer, on his right.

"Yes." Cheviot felt in the small of his back. "The tails of my coat hide it. You can't see it even with the cloak off."

"*And* yer truncheon?"

"No."

"No truncheon, sir?" demanded Inspector Seagrave, from his right side. "But a pistol, surely?"

"Pistol?" Cheviot rounded on him. "Since when have the C.I.D. been permitted to carry firearms?"

"The—the what, sir?"

Cheviot pulled himself up. He kept swallowing and swallowing, because he was nervous.

"Pardon me. A slip of the tongue. Now listen, I don't think it'll be necessary for either of you, or any of the others, to enter the house. But if it should be necessary, and any man-jack of you is carrying a pistol, get rid of it. Do you understand me?"

Sergeant Bulmer, he had discovered, was stout-hearted but

happy-go-lucky. Inspector Seagrave, though hard and capable, was a constant worrier.

"Sir!" said the latter, his long figure formally drawn up. "Begging your pardon, Superintendent, but there's a great store of pistols and cutlasses at number four. On special occasions, Mr. Peel says, we're allowed to use 'em."

"This isn't one of the occasions. Look there!"

It was a fine, cool night; no moon, but a bright crowding of stars.

Bennet Street, a short and narrow lane lighted by only one feeble gas-lamp, was the first street on the right as you turned down St. James's Street from Piccadilly. Cheviot, with his companions, stood in the doorway beside the dark premises of Messrs. Hooper, the coach-builders. Bennet Street was as deserted as a byway in Pompeii. But, through the thick and unsavoury mud in St. James's Street, a stream of gigs, curricles, berlines, hackney coaches or cabs went with a rattle and clop-clop up and down the hill.

Cheviot nodded towards them.

"The time will come," he said, "when those people—all people!—will regard you as their friends, their protectors, their guardians in peace and war. It is a high honour. Remember it!"

Sergeant Bulmer was silent. Inspector Seagrave grunted a short laugh.

"Reckon it won't be in *our* time, sir."

"No. It will not be in your time. But it will come," and Cheviot gripped his arm, "if you behave as I tell you. No swords or firearms; your hands and your truncheons if need be."

"I'm with you, sir," said Sergeant Bulmer. "I can't pitch away the barker in the street. But I can unload it."

"Sir!" said Inspector Seagrave. "You've been at Vulcan's before this?"

"Yes," lied Cheviot.

"You know what to expect, then, if they twig it you're an officer?"

"Yes."

"Very good, sir!" said the Inspector, saluting and then folding his arms.

Fumbling through the cloak with a white-gloved hand, Cheviot drew out the double-cased silver watch, with the silver chain, as befitted evening-wear.

"Just ten-thirty," he said. "Time to go in. Oh! One question I forgot to ask. This 'Vulcan.' What does he look like?"

Sergeant Bulmer's astonishment breathed out of the gloom.

"You've been to the place, sir? But you never saw him?"

"Not beknown to me, at least."

"He's a big cove, sir," muttered Sergeant Bulmer, shaking his head. "Taller than you, and broader-like. Got a bald head without a single hair on it, and one glass eye: I disremember whether it's the left eye or the right. Got the airs and speech of a gentleman, too, though I can't say where he picked 'em up. If you mean to talk to him—"

"I mean to talk to him. You already know that."

"Then look sharp, sir! You can't hear his step, and he moves like lightning. If he tumbles to anything, don't let him get behind you!"

"Why do they call him Vulcan? It can't be his real name?"

"Dunno his real name." The Sergeant brooded. "But a gentleman, a eddicated gentleman it was, he tells me the story. It's in the Bible, I think."

"Oh?"

"Yessir. Vulcan, he's the god of the underworld; and his wife's the goddess Wenus. One day she's up to her games with Mars, who's the god of war, and Vulcan catches 'em at it. Well! It happened the same with *this* Vulcan, across the road."

"Oh? How?"

"Well! He's got a wife, or a mort, maybe: a handsome piece but a spittin' firebrand. One day he catches her in what you might call an embarrassin' position, no clothes there weren't, with a Army officer. *This* Vulcan pitches *this* Mars out of a two-pairs-o'-stairs window.—He's a hard nail, sir! Look sharp!"

"Yes. Well, you have your instructions. Good luck."

And Cheviot stepped down and sauntered across the dim street.

Everywhere, all over London, trembled that shaky noise of hooves and wheels: vast, unfamiliar, yet one he could never get out of his ears.

Vulcan's was a trim brick house three floors high, the top storey smaller than the others. Not a chink of light gleamed anywhere, except that the front door was set a little way open, and a tiny glow shone inside the entry. This was common to all gambling-houses, he had been told, as a sign and invitation of what they were.

Cheviot put his foot on the first of the stone steps leading to the front door, and looked up.

Yes; he could admit he was nervous.

But that, he knew in his heart, was because he could not find Flora. During those desperate hours when he searched and inquired after her, he had come to recognize one truth. Flora was more than a woman with whom he believed himself to be in love. She was necessary to him, entwined in his life and soul; and, though he would never have dared to say aloud such hideously banal words, he could not live without her.

Well, you think that. But live you must. And he must live in this lost London, so strange and yet so vaguely familiar, which was Flora's.

If—

Cheviot woke up, his foot on the stone step.

A smart gig with bright lamps, driven by just as smart a manservant, came bowling along from the direction of Arlington Street. It swerved across the street and drew up at Vulcan's door.

Down from the gig, swiftly assisted by the manservant, alighted a gentleman of about Cheviot's own height and dressed exactly as he was. But the newcomer was younger, with a dissipated eye, long red nose, and luxuriant brown side-whiskers.

Together he and Cheviot mounted the few stone steps, silently assessing each other, until they reached the partly open door.

"After you, sir," said Cheviot, politely standing aside.

"Not at all, sir!" declared the newcomer, who was slightly drunk and elaborately courteous. "Come, come! Shouldn't dream of it! After *you*."

This sort of exchange might have gone on forever if Cheviot had not pushed the door wide open, and with mutual bows and smiles they both went into the small, den-like entry. Facing them was another door: heavy, very thick despite its black paint and gilt-work, with an oblong closed spy-hole at eye-level.

With another elaborate bow of excuse, the amiable stranger with the luxuriant side-whiskers leaned past Cheviot and dragged at a brass bell-pull. Immediately the panel of the spy-hole was shot back. First the stranger, then Cheviot, were given careful scrutiny from a pair of sharp, rather disturbing eyes.

A heavy key turned. Two bolts thumped back. The door was opened by a footman in sombre red-and-black livery, lightened by white at neck and wrists and (seemingly) gold shoe-buckles. Like other footmen he wore hair-powder, though otherwise hair-powder had been a dead fashion for thirty years.

Any experienced policeman, after one look at that footman's seamed and shut-up face, would have seen his quality and been on the alert.

"Good evening, my lord," the footman said very deferentially to the amiable one. Then, only a slight shade less deferentially: "Good evening, Mr. Cheviot."

Cheviot murmured something inaudible. His nerves, twitching momentarily at a smell of danger, quietened again as he realized he must be well known here.

Deftly the footman removed the cloak of my lord, whoever he was. But, since my lord made no move to take off his hat, Cheviot left his own hat on his head when the footman twitched off his cloak.

"Ha ha ha!" suddenly chuckled my lord. His eyes gleamed, and he rubbed his white-gloved hands together as though in anticipation. "Play good tonight, Skimpson?"

"As always, my lord. Will it trouble you, gentlemen, to walk upstairs?"

The marble foyer at Vulcan's was large and high, though of

a sour and stuffy atmosphere thickening through a faint scent of flowers. A journalist, describing the foyer, had written that it was "full of tubs containing the choicest blooms and exotic plants."

A red-carpeted staircase ascended to a closed door above. Though its hand-rail was of rather fine wrought-iron scrollwork, it was spoiled by being brightly gilded. My lord grew even more affable as he went up beside Cheviot.

"New to Vulcan's, sir?" he inquired.

"*Rather* new, I confess."

"Ah, well! That don't signify." My lord's face momentarily darkened. "I've dropped two thou here, I'll acknowledge it, in a few days. But the play's fair, and that's the thing." His amiability brightened again. "And my luck's in tonight. I feel it; I always feel it. What's your fancy? Rouge-et-noir? Hazard? Roly-poly?"

"I fear I have little knowledge of rouge-et-noir."

Abruptly my lord stopped, and swung round unsteadily with his back supported by the iron hand-rail.

"Not know rouge-et-noir?" he exclaimed, his eyes opening wide in amazement. "Come! Damme! What a Johnny Newcome you must be! Simplest game there is. Here, I'll show you!"

My lord threw out his white-gloved hands.

"Here's the table," he explained, indicating a long one. "Here's black, that's the noir, on my left. Here's red, that's the rouge, on my right. In the middle sits the croupie—"

He broke off to utter his neighing chuckle; then became very solemn.

"Apologize," said my lord, with a bow. "Been so long with these sportin' blades (good fellers, very!) I begin to talk like 'em. I mean the croupier, of course."

"Yes. I think I understand."

"All right. The croupie, with six packs of shuffled cards, deals first to the left for black. The idea is to make the pips of the cards reach thirty-one, or as close to it as you can. Suppose the croupie deals thirty-one. He says, 'One!' Then he deals to the right, for the red. Got it so far?"

"Yes."

"All right. This time suppose he deals an ace (that's one), a court-card (that counts ten), a nine, another court-card, a five, a deuce—" My lord stopped, puzzling and pursing up his lips. "I say! How many does that make for the red?"

"Thirty-five."

"Ah, that's bad! The croupie cries, 'Four! Black wins.' Simple: you lay your wager on black or red, that's all." My lord hesitated. "True, there's always the chance of an *après.*"

"And what, if I may ask, is an *après?*"

"Ah! That's when both red and black make the same number. Thirty-one, thirty-four, what you like. Fortunately, it don't happen often." My lord frowned a little. "In that case, the bank rakes in all the money."

"*The bank rakes in . . .*" Cheviot was beginning, astounded in his turn, when he caught himself, coughed, and nodded.

"Simple, ain't it?" inquired my lord.

"Very. Shall we go on up?"

On the landing they faced a door which clearly was of thick iron, without any peep-hole. Cheviot, who was reflecting, hardly saw it.

Rouge-et-noir was not only simple; it was simple-minded. With six packs of cards being dealt, the same number for red and black would come up more often than the punters, obtuse in their lust for play, seemed to imagine; and then the bank won all. The bank, in fact, took no risk whatever: the punters were merely betting against each other.

"Now *my* game," exulted my lord, "is roly-poly. I'll break 'em tonight; you see if I don't. Besides, there's always an attraction at the roulette-table. Kate de Bourke."

"Oh, yes," Cheviot agreed, as though the name were well known to him. "Kate de Bourke."

My lord winked.

"She's Vulcan's property," he said, "but she's anybody's woman. Always at the roulette-table, you'll have remarked. If her name wasn't first Katy Burke, then mine's not—well, never mind. Hair like a raven! Plump as a partridge! Dusky as—"

He paused. Some signal by bell-wire must have been sent by the footman below.

Without noise, without any sound of its felt-covered bars inside, the four-inch-thick iron door swung open. Another footman stood there: Cheviot found himself looking at dead eyes and a face-scar covered with powder.

Out of the broad, high gaming-room stirred a breath of thick, stuffy, almost unbreathable air, heat-laden and foul. The room must occupy the full width of the house.

There were no windows. Curtains of yellow velvet, with looped pelmets in scarlet, muffled most of the wall-space down to a deep-piled scarlet carpet with yellow rings for its pattern. In the wall towards his left, Cheviot saw a marble fireplace where a too-large fire roared and shimmered. Against the other wall, towards his right, white-draped tables bore silver platters of sandwiches or lobster-salad, bowls of fruit, and long ranks of bottles.

But, most of all, he was conscious of the fever pulsing here, as high crowns of wax-lights shone down on the gaming-tables.

Two tables—each one eighteen feet long, rounded at the ends, and covered in green baize with bright markings for the stakes— were set with their long sides longways towards the iron door.

The nearer table they had marked out for rouge-et-noir, with large red triangles at one end and large black triangles at the other. A little obscured from Cheviot's view, the far table resembled an ordinary modern roulette-bank except that the wheel appeared of cruder design.

At each table, facing him, one croupier sat in the centre. Beside each stood a second croupier, holding a long-handled wooden rake.

"By-by!" said my lord, waving to Cheviot and moving soundlessly away on the thick carpet. His voice seemed to ring loudly.

For there was silence here except for the mutter of a croupier's voice, the slap of cards upturned, the skitter of the ball in the wheel, or the rattle of the rake drawing in ivory counters.

Cheviot, his eyes moving to spot Vulcan's blacklegs and bruisers, approached the table. It was pretty well patronized, mostly by men in flawless evening-clothes, wearing their hats, and sitting close to the table in flimsy imitation-Chippendale chairs.

The croupier, sweeping his glance along to see that both red and black were covered in white ivory counters stamped from five pounds to a hundred, dealt rapidly for black.

Cheviot moved close to the table as the cards flicked over.

"Six!" muttered the croupier. "Deal to red."

A young-old man, who looked about forty but was more probably twenty-one or -two, breathed hard and drew his chair closer.

"Got it already!" he whispered. "Red's bound to get under that! Bound to! I'll wager another—"

"Sh-h!"

The croupier dealt to the other side. His wrist turned quickly, but not so quickly that anyone failed to see the pips of the cards.

He dealt the queen of diamonds, the knave of clubs, and the ten of hearts, each counting ten. He hesitated, and then turned up the eight of clubs.

"Seven!" he said. "Black wins."

The young-old man, his face sagging as though pulled down from under the eyelids, muttered something and started up from his chair. Beside him a stoutish, bluff-looking man, with the air of a retired naval officer and the whitest of linen shirt-frills, reached up gently and pulled him down again.

Cheviot circled round the table and approached the roulette-bank. The fire popped and spat, its shifting light reflected in the rows of bottles across the room.

There was a little cry from someone at the roulette-table as one play ended. The counters rattled under the rake. This table was crowded. Footmen moved soundlessly over the carpet, carrying salvers and offering claret, brandy, or champagne.

As he neared the roulette-table, Cheviot stopped and glanced up. All along the back wall, about fourteen feet up and a little back from the roulette-bank, ran a narrow gallery whose hand-rail also resembled gilded iron scroll-work, but was more probably gilded wood. This gallery, with its own set of yellow-velvet curtains and scarlet pelmets, had a narrow staircase curving down at each end to the gaming-room floor.

"That's it," he thought.

The yellow curtains did not conceal three doors facing out on the gallery. The middle one was of heavy polished mahogany, bearing the gilt initial V.

"Vulcan's private office. If he's thrifty, and Freddie's description was accurate, and my plan has any value . . ."

He looked down again at the thronged roulette-table. Two women sat there.

One of them, from my lord's description, must be that Kate de Bourke who belonged to Vulcan.

She sat at the right-hand end of the table, her back towards the white-draped ledges of sandwiches and lobster-salad. Kate was smallish, handsome, and surly. Her shining black hair was drawn back, exposing the ears and terminating in a long coil. No flash lit up her vivid eyes, of strong whites against dark-brown iris and dead-black pupil. In her right hand she held a pile of counters, absent-mindedly dropping them one atop another on the table. She dreamed sullen dreams, her thick lips compressed.

The other woman . . .

Cheviot's glance ran along the far side of the table, to a chair just to the right of the first croupier.

The other woman was Flora.

"Lay your wagers, ladies and gentlemen." Thin, automatic, sing-song: the croupier. "Lay-your-wagers; lay-your-wagers; lay-your-wagers."

Flora had been conscious of his presence long before he was conscious of hers; perhaps from the time he entered. She sat with eyelashes lowered, in a dark-blue velvet gown bordered with gold: low-cut, but with shoulder-straps and, as with most evening-gowns, having at the shoulders short blue-and-gold cloth projections like narrow epaulettes.

A little pile of ivory counters stood on the green-covered table before her. Flora's heavy yellow hair was dressed as it had been the night before, and as Kate's was now. Just behind her chair,

watching, on guard every second, stood her liveried and muscular coachman.

Briefly, she raised her eyes towards Cheviot.

Contrition, apology, appeal were in that glance. As soon as
they looked at each other, it was with an intimacy as great as
though they were in each other's arms.

"What are you doing here?" her glance said, with a little of
apprehension.

"What are *you* doing here?"

Flora looked down again, disturbed, touching the counters.
The coachman recognized Cheviot and drew a breath of relief.

Carelessly Cheviot strolled round the side of the roulette-table,
where many persons were snatching glasses from the footmen
before placing their bets.

The gambling-fever, rising all about him, did not touch him
at all. He could never understand the strange minds of those
who, of an evening, would occupy themselves with cards when
there were books to be read. True, there were other temptations.
Except for his self-discipline, he could easily have gone to the
devil with drink and women.

In fact, as a very young man during another life now gone,
he very nearly had done so. When he came down from Cambridge, some girl raved and refused to marry him because of his
determination to enter the police instead of reading law. He was
too stubborn to yield, but he had gone on a drinking-bout of
dangerous duration. The girl had said—

Cheviot's mind wavered and grew dark.

Memory submerged; he could not even remember her name
or what she looked like.

The foul air, the roaring fire, the movement of guests who did
not even play but strolled slowly round the yellow-hung room,
darkened his eyesight and made his head spin.

He counted to ten, and his sight grew clear. So long as he
could remember police-work, it didn't matter. If that failed him
too—

He found himself on the other side of the roulette-table, sauntering past it. There was the board, in yellow squares with black or red numbers on either side of the clumsy wheel. It had—

His wits jumped to complete alertness.

When the roulette-ball fell into the number marked zero, the bank won every stake on the board. This wheel had not only a zero, but a double-zero. There was something else too.

"Lay your wagers, ladies and gentlemen! Lay-your-wagers; lay-your-wagers-lay-your-wagers!"

Cheviot edged into the group, his thigh against the table, between Flora and the first croupier. The coachman bowed respectfully and stood aside.

Cheviot did not speak to Flora. Gently he put his hand on her shoulder. The flesh was warm and damp, and the shoulder trembled slightly. Again she gave him only the quickest of backward looks. Flora's face was a little flushed and moist where the rice-powder had run beneath the heat of melting wax-lights.

"Good evening," Cheviot said loudly, to the nearer of the two croupiers, and to draw attention to himself.

The croupier looked up to nod and smile, showing decayed teeth. He said, "Good evening, Mr. Cheviot," and returned to his sing-song whisper as punters thrust out counters on the table.

Cheviot leaned past to address the second croupier.

"To begin with," he said, even more loudly, "let me have a modest two hundred. In fifty-pound counters, if you please."

From his hip-pocket he took out the money he had drawn from Groller's Bank. A thousand pounds, in five-pound notes, makes a sizeable lump of money.

Instantly a dozen pairs of eyes slid round towards him; slid round, then grew opaque or filmed.

At the rouge-et-noir table he had already spotted nine of Vulcan's blacklegs or bruisers. There were at least four among those who lounged in the room and watched. With the twelve at the roulette-bank, on both sides of an eighteen-foot-long table with the wheel in the middle, that brought the number up to twenty-five.

There were probably more, say four or five: thirty among a hundred and twenty guests.

The second croupier, who had before him an immense heap
of notes and gold as well as piles of counters, merely nodded.
Shoving the rest of the money into his hip-pocket, Cheviot prof-
fered forty five-pound notes and received four counters stamped
fifty each. He was careless or clumsy in receiving them.

One counter slipped out of his hand. It fell on the carpet
beside the first croupier, who presided over the wheel. Bending
down to get it, Cheviot took a quick look at the croupier's right
foot beside the imitation-Chippendale chair.

Then he straightened up.

"Tonight," he declared in a ringing voice, "I am inspired."

And, remembering Sergeant Bulmer's collar-numerals, he
reached out and planked down a hundred pounds on the black
thirteen.

This time there was a sharp stir round the whole table.

"Jack—!" Flora began, in instinctive protest.

Again he pressed her shoulder, reassuringly.

It was as he had hoped. Whenever a man shows supreme self-
confidence in backing a number against ruinous odds, there is
a rush to follow him.

Faces were thrust out, reddened with claret or brandy. Hands
scrabbled among ivory counters. The character known to Cheviot only as my lord, his nose fiery with more drink, tossed a
twenty-pound counter on the black thirteen. So did a stout
young man with yellow side-whiskers, at the far side of the
table, whom Cheviot vaguely remembered seeing at Lady Cork's
ball.

Others, more cautious, backed red or black, odds or evens,
above the line or below it. At most they quartered four numbers,
with the exception of a very tall, lean young gentleman who
stood up with the black-browed air of a man playing Hamlet
and dropped counters totalling sixty pounds on the red six.
Then, his hat jammed over his eyes, he sat down again.

The board was laden, the game heavy; and the croupier's
drone changed.

"The game is finished!" he said, standing up and speaking

almost clearly. "Nothing-more-goes; nothing-more-goes; nothing-more-goes."

With one hand he spun the red-and-black wheel in one direction. With the other he tossed the little ivory ball in the direction opposite.

Dead silence, except for the skittering noise of the ball.

It fell into the wheel, bounced out again, and swirled round the outer ebony rim. It hesitated, running backwards and forwards on the rim. It began to slow down.

As it did so, Detective Superintendent Cheviot was again apparently careless with his two remaining counters. One dropped on the carpet. He bent to retrieve it; looked quickly at the croupier's right foot; and straightened up.

The ball stopped, as the wheel slowed down to a shade of motion. The ball swayed a little, and then bounced with a click into zero.

Round the table ran a hiss of indrawn breath, a murmur like one stifled groan, the intense swallowing of oaths and curses.

That was the point at which Cheviot sensed the presence, behind him, of someone watching.

Just under the shadow of the high gallery above, against yellow curtains with red pelmets, stood Vulcan himself.

13

The Gathering of the Damned

But he dared show no curiosity. He did not even turn his head round. Only a blur, at the corner of his eye, gave him the impression of a very big and broad man, with a shining bald head, and in immaculate black and white.

Smiling, self-assured, Cheviot faced the table.

As the long-handled rake darted out to sweep in all the counters, there were many persons who looked daggers at him: concealed daggers, thumb on the blade.

But my lord, his flushed face expressionless, merely shrugged his shoulders and drew out a red-silk purse. Beside him sat an obvious blackleg, a powerfully built man with a piebald wig to hide head-scars, who whispered encouragement in my lord's ear.

Equally expressionless was the stout young man, with the yellow side-whiskers, who had danced last night at Lady Cork's. Beside him, too, a blackleg breathed flattering encouragement; this was a bony middle-aged man with a lined face and false teeth which tended to surge forward when he talked.

"Jack!" whispered Flora, who had loyally staked fifty pounds on the black thirteen. "Don't you think it time to . . .?"

"I do indeed, madam." Cheviot's gallantry was of the heaviest sort. He glanced towards the white-draped ledges of food and wine, well beyond the far end of the table, and threw his two remaining counters on the green cloth. "Some refreshment, I think?"

"Yes, yes, yes!" Flora rose up, and he drew back her chair.

"Our luck will be better afterwards," Cheviot added, addressing the muscular coachman. "In the meantime, will you hold Lady Drayton's chair and guard our stakes?"

"Yes, Robert, do!" urged Flora.

"I will," said the coachman, nodding grimly. "Depend on it, sir and madam: I will."

In looking at the far end of the table, Cheviot could not help seeing Kate de Bourke.

Alone, aloof, speaking to nobody, Kate sat with her elbows on the green cloth and toyed with ivory counters. She wore a light-green gown, emphasizing into relief her broad-fleshed charms. Only once, when Cheviot made his bet, had she lifted her eyes for a speculative look at him. Afterwards she toyed with the counters again.

Click, click, click-click, went those same counters, as Cheviot sauntered past under the gallery with Flora on his arm.

Round swung Kate's dark head, for a short, hard appraisal of Flora, before returning to her dream.

Flora's golden head was just above the level of his shoulder. In her dark-blue gown bordered with gold, in elbow-length white gloves and a gold-dusted reticule in one hand, her beauty dimmed the tawdry room.

But she kept her head down, gaze on the carpet, and spoke softly.

"Jack."

"Yes?"

"Last night," Flora burst out, still softly, "you were so patient. And I was so hateful and odious and spiteful. How shamed I was afterwards! Shamed and shamed and shamed!"

"My dear, don't agitate yourself. We are consulting together. But we must have an understanding now. Last night, for instance, I had heard no gossip about—"

"—yet nevertheless," Flora interposed in exactly the same tone, "you might have visited me today."

"Visit you? I did! I nearly broke the bell-wire. But no one answered."

Flora's tone was almost airy as she lifted her head.

"Oh, as to that! I had gone deliberately to see my aunt at Chelsea, and told the servants not to answer if you rang. But you might at least have put a note through the letter-slot, to show you'd been there."

Cheviot stopped and studied her.

"Good God, Flora, must you always be so perverse?"

"Perverse?" The blue eyes widened and sparkled; they melted his anger even as she began to be angry. Then Flora herself was stricken. "Perverse," she added in a whisper. "Yes. I own I am. Dearest, dearest, what am I doing *now?*"

"Nothing at all," he smiled, "except using women's weapons. In this age—"

"In this age?"

"You have no rights, little freedom, no privileges. What other weapons can you use? But don't, I beg, use them against me. There's no need. Flora! Look at me!"

They were standing by the buffet.

Cheviot, who long ago had doffed his hat and thrust his white gloves into the opening of his waistcoat, set down the hat on a white-draped table. He held out a silver platter of sandwiches, with stale bread and ham cut enormously thick. Flora took one, still without looking at him.

Along the tables stood silvery buckets, cold-wet outside, from whose tops projected the necks of open bottles above melting ice. Drawing out one dripping bottle, of a brand of champagne unknown to him, he filled two glasses. Flora accepted one, still not turning her head.

"Let me repeat," he said, "that last night I had never even heard any of this gossip about—about Margaret Renfrew and myself. You had heard it, I imagine?"

"And pray who has not?"

"Have you heard anything else about it?"

"No. Is there so very much else to hear?"

"Flora! Look at me! Look up!"

"I won't!"

"Then had you heard," he asked sardonically, "as a part of

the same gossip, that she stole money and jewels for me, and I accepted them?"

Up lifted Flora's eyes, filmed with tears, her lips parted in dumbfounded astonishment.

"But that's utterly ridiculous! *You?* Do that? Why, it's the silliest . . . it's . . . I wonder what awful woman *dared* to say it?"

"And yet it's a part of the same gossip, you know. If you believe one, you must believe the other. Do you?"

"I—"

"Aren't you only using women's weapons, Flora? Don't you know, in your heart, this Margaret Renfrew was never anything to me, or I to her? Don't you know that?"

There was a silence. Then Flora nodded quickly.

"Yes," she said. "That is, I knew—if you were with me, you couldn't very well have been with her." She flushed, but regarded him steadily. "It's my horrid *thoughts*, that's all. I can't help it."

"Then need there ever be any misunderstanding between us?"

"Never! Never! Never!"

He lifted his champagne-glass. Flora touched the rim of her glass to his. Both gulped down the champagne in quick swallows, set away the glasses, and, with mutual instinct, put aside the sandwiches neither of them could eat.

And Flora held out her hands to him.

He couldn't, physically, couldn't tell her of the worst danger they both faced. He could not tell her of Mr. Richard Mayne's suspicions, hovering and swooping. If anyone had seen the pistol fall from Flora's muff, or seen him hide it under the hollow-based lamp, they might both stand in the dock on a charge of murder.

But of one thing he must warn her quickly.

He drew her closer and spoke in a whisper.

"If you trust me, my dear, then you must do as I ask. You must leave here, and leave immediately."

"Leave?" He felt her start. "Why?"

"Because of Vulcan's blacklegs. There are too many of them. I can smell trouble."

"Blacklegs? What are they?"

Once more Cheviot studied the room while not seeming to do so.

"In the vernacular, they're extra-flash-men hired by the house at two or three guineas a night."

"Yes? Don't stop there!"

"They lure in the pigeons and the Johnny Newcomes to play high, and encourage 'em again when they lose. The blacklegs, of course, only make dummy bets against each other; they must return their winnings to the house before the bank closes about three in the morning. If the pigeons grow suspicious—well! It may be hushed up. If not hushed up, the blackleg is a bruiser or a knife-and-pistol man."

Again his gaze roved among the men against the yellow curtains.

"I tell you," he added in a fiercer whisper, "there are too many of them! There's too much noise and talk; can't you hear it? And the tension's too high; watch the corners of their eyes slide round to each other."

"I can't see anything!"

"Perhaps not. But I can. They're waiting for something to explode."

"To explode? What?"

"I'm not sure, but . . . Flora! Why did you come here tonight?"

"I—I was hoping to find *you*. I—I thought . . ." She stopped.

"You thought me again gambling heavily and drinking even more heavily, lost and out of my wits? As you suspected I was last night?"

"I don't mind that! Really and truly I don't! Only—"

"Well, observe that I am in no such condition. All the more reason why you should leave here before the boiler blows up. Go; cash in your counters; Robert will see you home safely enough."

He was so close to her that he could have bent over and kissed her mouth. He felt emotions through her body rather than saw them in her face; and he felt her mood change in a flash.

"Oh, God," Flora whispered, "is this to happen again?"

"Again?"

"As it happened last night. You promised, on your honour. I awaited and awaited you, with the rush-light burning." She did not speak in anger, but in desperate curiosity. "Does it give you pleasure, Jack, that I should tumble, and toss, and weep and bite my pillow, until the dawn comes up and I am drained of tears or any feeling at all?"

Cheviot nodded towards the gaming-room.

"Tonight," he said, "you're in danger. And so, in some very small degree, am I. But it is my duty to remain here. My work—"

"Yes." He felt her shiver of disgust. " 'Your work.' I'll be honest with you. That's what I hate."

("And you, too, Flora?")

"Danger?" she said in a low voice. "Why, all true men must face danger; so much is natural; as they must drink and gamble and—!" She swallowed. "If you were an officer of the Army or the Navy, and war came, I should be fearful. But I should be pleased and proud too. Proud!" Her disgust, showing now in her face, trembled through her. "But these police! Filthy gaol-birds better back in prison! Can you ask me to suffer this? We are not married. Have you the right to ask it?"

"No," said Cheviot, and dropped her hands.

"Jack! I did not mean—!"

Cheviot picked up his hat from the table.

He was so long-schooled in hiding his thoughts that even Flora, who knew him or believed she knew him, could not read the fury and bitterness behind his placid face.

"Why, then," he replied almost agreeably, "to the devil with this police-work! Let us forget it. I accompany you home, and I shall be there for as long as you please."

"Jack!" A slight pause. "You mean that?"

And for the time being, in his bitterness, he honestly believed he did mean it.

"What's the good?" he was raging silently to himself. "Can I, single-handed, conquer prejudices established since Cromwell's time? Why should I batter my wits, and endure only humiliation, to convince fools that one day the police will mean only fairness and law? Better strong love with Flora than a smashed skull in an alley, which most of us will come to. What matter? Who cares?"

He fought down the thoughts.

"You may be sure I mean it," he declared, with what he swore was sincerity. "And we must go now."

"Yes, yes, yes!"

"Have you a cloak or a pelisse?"

"Yes, downstairs. In the foyer!"

"Then we can collect the value of our counters and be off. My arm, Flora?"

And, as they walked along the rear wall, under the gallery and past the length of the roulette-bank, he could feel Flora's exaltation and pride flowing through her finger-tips. He himself was buoyed up, his senses all too conscious of her presence.

The second croupier at the roulette-table, scarcely taking his eyes from a board on which play now ran very high, changed their counters for notes and gold. The wheel spun again. Intent gamblers, eyes fixed and shining, did not even glance up.

And yet . . .

As he took Flora across to the door, the coachman following, Cheviot had the feeling that many heads were turned and that eyes bored into his back. It was an animal-like sensation; animal-like, he stiffened to it.

The footman, with the dead-looking eyes and the powdered-out face-scar, stood by the iron door with its two felt-covered bars. It seemed he hesitated very slightly before drawing the bars back without sound, and opening the door.

And then, behind Flora and Cheviot, spoke out a soft, deep, cultivated voice.

"Come, Lady Drayton!" it said. "Come, Mr. Cheviot! Surely you are not leaving us so soon?"

Behind them towered up Vulcan. Beside him stood Kate de Bourke.

Seen close at hand, Vulcan was some two or three inches taller than Cheviot. He was correspondingly broad and thick, though much of this lay concealed under admirably tailored clothes. Some of the bulk might be fat, though Cheviot doubted it.

The man was too cat-footed of step, his neck too thick and firm in carrying the immense bald head. He had scarcely any eyebrows. The glass eye was his right; it gave the only staring, rather sinister touch to a manner of charm and grace. But he kept it as much as possible from the light, using his good left eye. His age might have been forty-five. Vulcan, with infinite toil and patience, had through long years got himself up to resemble someone in the Peerage—and then spoiled everything by wearing one emerald and one ruby ring on his left hand, and a single large diamond ring on his right.

He glanced down at Kate. This charmer, with her broad gipsy allure in the light-green gown, plainly adored him. Vulcan had brought her to the door, Cheviot suspected, only to feed his vanity.

"I believe, Lady Drayton," Vulcan went on in his big, soft voice, "this is the first time you have honoured us with a visit?"

"I—I believe so."

The iron door was wide open. Flora cast a glance towards it over her shoulder. The coachman, Robert, stood behind her with his eyebrows drawn down.

"In that event," smiled Vulcan, "may I make you known to my wife? Kate, I present you to Lady Drayton."

Kate was so obviously a woman of the streets that Cheviot marvelled. Vulcan's tutoring must have been long, careful, even savage. Gone was Kate's sulkiness or fierce brooding. Her inclination of the head matched Flora's in manners; she murmured polite words in a contralto voice whose pronunciation was like Vulcan's own.

"Mr. Cheviot!" said Flora in a formal tone. She indicated the open door. "Don't you think it's time to . . ."

"Alas!" said Vulcan.

He turned up the palms of his big hands, so that the green, red, and glittering-white rings flashed and sparkled.

"As a good host," he went on humorously, "I can but speed the parting guests." His tone sounded faintly hurt. "But you, Mr. Cheviot! In you, I confess, I find myself surprised."

"Oh? How?"

"I have never known you, sir, to fear high play. Or, indeed, to fear anything else."

To anyone else the words would have sounded like an idle compliment.

But, as he said this, the big man swung down on Cheviot his lifeless, staring glass eye. The stare of the glass eye, even while Vulcan smiled, turned those words into a challenge and even a jeer.

That was the point at which Cheviot knew he couldn't leave here.

He couldn't! He must have been insane, under Flora's spell, even to think of such a thing.

He had a job to do. He could hardly desert Inspector Seagrave, Sergeant Bulmer, and the six constables posted at his instructions. Once before, for Flora's sake, he had betrayed his duty; and it had haunted him ever since. He couldn't do this for her or for any woman on earth. He looked at Vulcan.

"Come!" he said, snapping his fingers. "I thank you for the reminder. There *was* one small matter of business I wished to discuss with you."

Vulcan spread out his hands in assent and welcome.

Cheviot turned to Flora.

"I think, madam," he smiled, "it would be better if you left us, after all. You will be safe enough in Robert's care."

Flora had gone very pale, clutching her gold-dusted reticule in both hands.

She was no fool, Cheviot knew. She would guess the reason

why he felt he must stay. But would she understand it, or at all sympathize with it? A faint sweat stood out on his forehead.

"Madam, we have an appointment tomorrow," he said, appealing with his eyes in the intense dumb-show that he meant tonight, tonight, tonight. "If I am one minute later than one o'clock, you may disown me."

Flora's answer was without inflection.

" 'Disown'?" she repeated. "Can one disown what one has never owned? Good night, Mr. Cheviot. Robert, follow me."

She swept through the doorway, Robert shambling after her. The iron door closed; its felt-covered bars shot soundlessly into their sockets.

"And now," thought Cheviot, "and now, as the ghost said in the story, we're all locked in for the night."

Vulcan's big face wore a look of faint distress.

"Mr. Cheviot, Mr. Cheviot! This business-matter!" His hand moved towards the inside pocket of his coat; then it dropped, embarrassed. "Pray forgive me. But if it should be a momentary lack of funds, you can always be accommodated."

"Oh, it's not money." Carelessly Cheviot took the wad of banknotes from his pocket, and replaced them. "No, not at all!" He looked up at Vulcan, at one good eye and one lurking in ambush. "It is, as I say, a business proposition from which, I think, both you and I can derive profit."

"Ah?" murmured Vulcan.

"Is there somewhere, perhaps, we can speak in private?"

"Oh, by all means. My office. Kate, my dear, will you accompany us and kindle lights? If you will follow us, my dear sir."

Cheviot followed them, over the soft carpet, again in the direction of the buffet.

His pulses had jumped at Vulcan's words. Vulcan *was* thrifty. He kept no lights burning in an office when he was not there.

But there was no need for his heart to beat faster than it already did. As soon as he had felt those eyes boring into his back, he had known that all this tension was fastened on him: on him alone.

They knew.

Every blackleg in the room knew he was a police-officer, and waited for the kill.

Again he sauntered past the gamut of eyes. He was conscious, as through the pores of his skin, of all small details: the smell of Macassar oil on the men's hair, the shifting of a chair on the carpet.

Vulcan, with the flary wax-lights polishing his skull, making broader and thicker his massive figure, bent down to speak to Kate.

"Fond of me, little one?"

"Yes!" Kate said in a low voice. She enlarged on this with a stream of passionate obscenities so picturesque that Cheviot was forced to admire. If it had not been for Vulcan's bishop-like decorum, Cheviot felt, she would have tried to jump up and bite the lobe of his ear.

Vulcan's vanity expanded and purred.

"Ah, here we are!" he said.

They had passed the place at the buffet where Flora and Cheviot had been standing. Only a few feet away was the right-hand staircase of the two ascending to the narrow gallery above.

From a saucer on the table Kate snatched a long waxen spill out of a bundle there. But she did not light it. Indeed, except for the fire at the opposite end of the room, there was no place at which she could have lighted it.

Cheviot moved forward, a little too hastily, and stopped. At all costs he must be first up those stairs. But Vulcan, stepping back, made it easy for him.

"After you, my dear sir," he said, with a stately bow and a beam from his good eye.

As Cheviot mounted the narrow stairs, he found his guess had been right. Stairs and gallery were made of wood. Even the handrail, gilded to resemble iron scrollwork, was of old and flimsy wood. This would be no pleasant place in the event of fire.

There could be no mistaking the centre door to Vulcan's office. A bracket on either side, a little way out from the yellow curtains and holding a candle in a parchment shade, threw light on the deep red mahogany and brightened the gilded letter V.

Vulcan was just behind him, with Kate following. Cheviot glanced over the hand-rail. Below was the long roulette-table. The room had grown eerily silent after too-loud talk. He could feel the blacklegs' unspoken glee.

Cheviot leaned casually against the left-hand frame of the door. Taking from his waistcoat pocket a key-ring with two keys, one short and the other long, Vulcan unlocked the door and swung it inwards to the right.

"Again after you, my dear sir," Vulcan said.

Kate was already raising the waxen spill to light it at the candle burning on the right.

"Thank you," said Cheviot.

He entered with the appearance of blundering, as a man does in a dark room. As though to make way, he immediately moved along the wall towards the left.

Then, with blinding swiftness, he made the move which might win or lose his life.

14

Flash-and-Fraud

About four feet along the wall, projecting from it, was the brass knob of a bell-pull communicating with the only bell-wire in the room.

Cheviot's fingers encountered it.

He had about twelve seconds to accomplish what must be accomplished.

If the gleam of the waxen lighting-spill fell into the room before he had finished, he was finished too.

His hat fell softly on the carpet. From his waistcoat pocket he jerked out the object for which Sergeant Bulmer had searched over half the town before finding one at a spectacle-maker's: a very tiny screw-driver, less than an inch long.

Cheviot's forearms no longer trembled. His fingers were cold and quick and rapid. Working in darkness, by a sense of touch alone, he found the microscopic screw on the projection of the knob, which held the knob to the bell-wire as such a screw holds a knob to the spindle of a door. The edge of the screw-driver fitted in. . . .

"And pray what takes you so long, my pet?" That was Vulcan's soft bass.

"Ah, ducky, but blast your bloody eyes—!" That was Kate's refined contralto.

"I have warned you before, my pet, against using unseemly language."

The tiny screw fell into Cheviot's hand, just as the waxen spill flashed into flame from the candle outside the door.

As it did so, Cheviot's heart jumped into his throat for fear the bell-wire would clatter down inside the wall, or the knob fall off inside the room.

But the wire, from long fixture in that position, remained as it was. So did the knob. There was just time for Cheviot to slip both screw and screw-driver into his pocket. He was well out from the wall, bending over to pick up his hat, when the glow of the waxen spill sent a wavering light out across the carpet.

"Now here, Mr. Cheviot," Vulcan's rich voice went on, "we have what the newspapers are wont somewhat vulgarly to call my sanctum sanctorum. Kate, be good enough to light both lamps."

Cheviot could dimly make out the lines of the good-sized if low-ceilinged room. Its walls were papered, after a French Empire fashion long dead, in vertical stripes of orange and green. Two smallish windows, heavily muffled in orange-plush curtains, were in the rear wall opposite the door.

"Observe the table," Vulcan suggested rather smugly.

There was little furniture. Cheviot had already noted the table.

At first glance, in gloom, it appeared to be a roulette-table. It was eighteen feet long, set longways to the windows, and a roulette-wheel had been let down into the middle.

But this was decorative. The table, on either side of the wheel, had a top of polished mahogany. Some distance out, on either side, stood a solid-looking china figure: each one about a foot high, tinted in natural life-colours and with a high, hard glaze. Beyond these, at both ends of the table, loomed up a lamp in a cut-glass orange-coloured shade.

"Observe again!" said Vulcan, as Kate tilted the shade and lighted the lamp on the right.

An orange glow, dull and rather menacing, filtered through a room whose windows had not been raised in years.

The figure to the right of the roulette-wheel represented the popular notion of Vulcan: black from the forge, stooped and yet broad and powerful, a hammer in one hand and a net in the other.

"Yes," agreed Cheviot. "I see. And the figure on the left—" He stopped.

Pop went the wick on the other orange cut-glass lamp, as Kate moved quickly to the other end of the table and lighted it.

The other figure, nude, represented Venus rising from the sea. So much power or skill had seldom been breathed out by the potter, the fire-glazer, the painter, in what appeared living sensuality.

"In classical mythology," pursued Vulcan, "Venus or Aphrodite is usually represented as being fair-haired. You, Mr. Cheviot, were perhaps thinking of . . ."

He paused, coughing delicately.

"But *this* Venus," he went on, and even his glass eye seemed to gleam, "is dark. See how the black hair streams down over her shoulders. Her eyes are half-closed; her arms straight down at her sides, hands turned outwards. You do see?"

"Very well. It is admirable, if unorthodox."

Vulcan laughed his soft laugh. Kate de Bourke, her thick lips drawn down, had been standing above the second orange-gleaming lamp. She ran along the line of the table to the right of the room.

Against the right-hand wall stood a large and deep cabinet of painted Chinese lacquer, with double-doors. Before this background Kate posed and poised, chin up, eyes half-closed, arms down at her sides with hands turned out.

"It's me," she said, dropping the refined speech. "I'm proud it's me! Ah, so-and-so, why pretend?"

"*Kate!*"

Kate ran at Vulcan, greedy-mouthed, and threw her arms round his neck.

"Give us a kiss, ducks. 'Tain't as if—"

With sudden violence Vulcan's shoulders twitched. He flung her off, so that she staggered backwards. Her spine and head banged against the edge of the Chinese-lacquer cabinet on the wall to the right of the open door.

But Kate only laughed, delighted. This time she sidled toward him with a coyness which, despite or perhaps because of her beauty, was almost grisly. It flashed through Cheviot's head that this was a deliberate imitation of Flora Drayton.

"And yet, dearest, may I not remain while you speak with this gentleman?"

"No. This is business. Leave us!"

Vulcan, his hand at her back as he turned her towards the open door, recovered his mantle of benevolence.

"Come, Mr. Cheviot, I neglect you! Pray be seated—there."

His gesture was so quietly commanding that Cheviot looked round behind him.

Against the wall to the left of the door, not far beyond the brass knob in the wall, stood a large and weighty flat-topped desk of Regency design. Its polished top was inset with green leather; on either side, two tiers of drawers had metal handles with the metal design of a lion's head on each.

At either side of the desk, sideways, stood outwards a wide-backed armchair upholstered in green plush, with green buttons to indent its bulges.

Then Cheviot's eye caught something else. Propped against the far edge of the long table were two of Vulcan's famous collection of walking-sticks. One of them, twisted like a corkscrew, was of very heavy black wood with a silver top. The other, its handle curved, appeared to be much lighter.

A remembrance of advice tapped out a warning:

Don't let him get behind you! Don't let—

But Vulcan was some distance away.

The thick mahogany door closed with a slam as Cheviot swung round. Vulcan, using the longer key from his ring, carefully locked the door.

"Merely a precaution," he explained, "against intruders on our privacy."

"Of course," Cheviot agreed, and sat down in the far armchair his host had indicated.

Vulcan replaced the key-ring in his waistcoat pocket.

His air of self-satisfaction seemed almost to burst his evening clothes. He towered up as he approached, a massive shadow of him spreading out behind on the orange-and-green walls.

"Is it not strange?" he asked in a musing tone. "Strange, I say, that a man—a man, I again explain, with so few natural advantages—should yet hold a compelling fascination for so many women? Even women (I do not mention Kate, though I am fonder of her than any), even women of high birth and re-fined tastes?"

Here Vulcan glanced down over his white shirt-front, his im-maculate cuffs, the rings a-flash on his fingers.

"Yet I know such a man," he added, and almost smiled.

"Oh, yes," said Cheviot, without looking at him. "So do I."

Vulcan stood very still, beside the desk and in front of the other armchair.

It was as though an arrow had struck home, with mysterious effect, as Cheviot meant it to strike.

"May I offer you a cigar, Mr. Cheviot?"

"Thank you."

Most of the cigars he had bought and smoked in this age were the vilest of weeds. This one, offered from a thin deep sandalwood box on the desk, was the finest Havana. With the cigar-cutter in his right-hand waistcoat pocket, at the end of the chain which ran to his heavy silver watch in the other pocket, he snipped off the end.

Vulcan took a cigar, and did the same.

"A glass of brandy, my dear sir?" he beamed. "Tush, don't hesitate! This is the Napoleon *cru,* of admitted excellence."

"I can't resist that, I thank you. I have never tasted true Napoleon brandy."

Vulcan unstoppered a cut-glass decanter, on a silver platter amid glasses. He poured the brandy into two glasses, without moving them. Cheviot rose to his feet and moved across. There, apparently, he stumbled, slipped, and bumped straight into Vul-can with a heavy thud.

"Come, I do beg your pardon!" Cheviot blurted, disengag-ing himself. "It was unpardonably clumsy of me!"

"Not at all," said Vulcan.

Taking the glass of brandy, Cheviot sat down again. Vulcan, still standing, whisked an inch-long metal rod across the base of a gold-and-silver toy pagoda. Oil-soaked flame curled up. Vulcan carefully lighted Cheviot's cigar, moving the flame back and forth.

Next he lit his own cigar, took up the glass of brandy, and settled his weight back comfortably into the green-padded arm-chair.

"As we were saying—" Cheviot began, drawing smoke into his lungs.

A brief smile, like a shark opening its jaws, flashed across Vulcan's face and was gone.

"Yes," he said, "it really was clumsy when you pretended to stumble against me. It was to test my weight, was it not? And you found me solid enough, I think?"

Cheviot did not reply.

"And now, Mr. Superintendent Cheviot," said Vulcan, with absolutely no change of tone, "what do you really want of me?"

Cheviot's voice remained just as detached.

"As I told you," he answered, blowing out smoke and study-ing it, "a fair business-bargain. An exchange . . ."

"Of what?"

"Information. It will benefit both of us, believe me."

"Forgive my frankness, sir," Vulcan said dryly, and shook his big head, "but I think you have very little to offer. However! Speak on."

"You've heard, I suppose, of the murder of Margaret Renfrew at Lady Cork's house last night?"

Vulcan looked shocked.

"My dear sir! Who has not? The columns of the *Morning Post* were full of it."

"Well! A diamond-and-ruby brooch, shaped like a full-rigged ship, was pledged here at your establishment by a person we be-lieve to be the murderer. Four other pieces of jewellery, of which I have a list here," and Cheviot touched his breast-pocket, "may have been pledged too."

"It distresses a gentleman to say so. But I have a fully legal pawnbroker's licence."

"These jewels were stolen."

"And was I to know that?" inquired Vulcan.

For a moment he sipped brandy and drew at his cigar.

"If they were stolen," he continued, mighty in virtue, "they shall be returned. But think of my difficulties! What was it you said? A diamond-and-something brooch, shaped like a ship? Have you any notion how many such trinkets pass through my hands, or those of my chief croupier, in the course of a year? Yet you ask me to remember one of them?"

"Oh, come off it," Cheviot said vulgarly.

"I beg your pardon?"

"I said come off it," retorted Cheviot, finishing his brandy and setting down the glass on the desk. "You don't issue pawn-tickets, I understand. You keep account-books, with a description of the article set down opposite the name of the person who pledged it. Yes or no?"

"Yes." Vulcan spoke after a pause. "I keep account-books. What, exactly, do you wish to know?"

"The name of the man who pledged that brooch."

"And what do you offer in return?—One moment!"

Vulcan lifted the hand which held his glass. He sat up straight. The sheer force of his personality, apart from any size or weight, seemed to dwarf Cheviot and pin the latter in his chair.

"Let *me*," he suggested, "tell *you*. Any offer you make must concern my gaming-house here. True, to keep a gaming-house is illegal. But the law is seldom enforced. Why? Because you cannot convince any man that gambling is a crime, provided the play at the tables be fair. As mine, notoriously, *is* fair.

"So I will give you three good reasons," he continued, "why you cannot help me; still less hurt me. First, if the new police meditated any attack on my premises, I should be warned beforehand."

Cheviot nodded.

"Oh, yes," he said. "I was aware of that."

Again it was as though a driven arrow had struck home.

The force of Vulcan's personality did not alter. His tone did not change. But his glass eye, in the orange light, remained dead; his good eye took on a glitter of malice.

"Second," he said, "you could never find witnesses to testify against me in the box. The high-born, fearing scandal, would not testify. The—shall we say medium or even base-born?—dare not testify—"

"Because they would be bribed, intimidated, or beaten within a gasp of death by your blacklegs?"

"I don't like your tone, Mr. Cheviot."

"Nor I yours. May I hear your third reason?"

"Willingly!" said Vulcan, softly putting down his cigar on the edge of the table and his glass beside it. "Third, your police could not get in. You took note of my iron door, which is four inches thick in a thick wall. By the time your police could force that door, with axes or what tools you like, it would take twenty minutes or even half an hour. You agree?"

"Yes."

"By that time, dear sir, no evidence of gambling would remain. My guests, or such as wished to do so, would have disappeared. The intruders would surprise only quiet talk in a gentleman's drawing-room."

Cheviot laughed.

It was a jarring sound, as he meant it to be.

"Vulcan," he said, "you disappoint me."

There was no answer. The cut-glass bowls of the lamps seemed to grow dull and darken their orange light.

"Forgive my frankness," said Cheviot, in mockery of the other's voice, "but you are like any other householder, in any other street. You make your front door so strong, so impregnable, that no intelligent bur—housebreaker would think of attacking it. Then, like another householder, you completely neglect your back door."

Cheviot nodded to the two windows, closely muffled in orange curtains, in the rear wall.

"Outside those windows," he said, "two steeply pitched tile

roofs slope down to a back wall in a mews. When I visited the mews very late this afternoon, the back door was wide open for air. It gives on a scullery and kitchen. These lead, left and right, to a ground-floor supper-room and dice-hazard room."

Still Vulcan did not move or speak.

"When I visited the mews late this evening," Cheviot went on, "your back door was still on the jar. Vulcan, Vulcan! If I had fifty constables outside that back door at this minute, they could be up into your gaming-room within twenty seconds."

Then Vulcan moved.

Amazingly, in so vast a man, he bounced to his feet like an india-rubber cat. He darted behind his chair. His right hand shot out towards the brass knob to the bell-wire, seized it, and pulled hard. The knob came away in his hand.

"No," said Cheviot. "You can't summon your blacklegs like that."

The knob dropped on the carpet with a faint thud. Without speaking, without smiling, Vulcan moved across to the mahogany door.

His big fingers fished in his waistcoat pocket, fished again, then flew across to his other pocket. . . .

"No," Cheviot told him, "that won't do either."

Reaching into his side pocket, he drew out Vulcan's key-ring with the two keys.

"I greatly fear," he said, "that I picked your pocket when I bumped into you. Was *that* so very clumsy, do you think?"

Vulcan's bald head turned slowly round. His good eye gleamed and burned.

"It is true," Cheviot added, "you can always hammer on the door and scream for help. And yet, since you are known to be alone with only one unarmed man two or three stone lighter than yourself, I think you would be ashamed to do it."

"Yes," Vulcan agreed, "you are right. But what need have I," and at last he smiled, "when I can always take the keys from you myself?"

Cheviot considered this.

"Now I wonder if you could?" he mused. "But reassure yourself. There are no constables outside your back door."

"If this is a lie, or a piece of bounce—!"

The latter term, which in after years would come to mean bluff, stung Cheviot far worse than he had stung Vulcan.

"I never lie," he said, "and I never use bounce. I despise those who do." He controlled his voice. "Besides, you have talked a great deal. You haven't even heard what I offer in exchange for a murderer's name."

"Very well. Speak."

Cheviot leaned across and carefully put down his half-smoked cigar on the silver platter of the decanter. He stood up, bracing himself on his right foot.

"Your roulette-wheel is rigged," he said. "And I can prove it. If I do, it will ruin you."

Only Cheviot's next words, sharp-pierced with common-sense, stopped Vulcan's charge at him.

"Gambling?" Cheviot said. "What matter to me if you fleece a thousand young blockheads, provided I can avenge one human life? Human life means little to you? By God, it means all to me! I want no violence, no fight, if we can make terms. Nor do you. Shall I demonstrate how your wheel downstairs is rigged?"

Without waiting for an answer he backed away. He backed past his chair, round the left-hand side of the table where the two walking-sticks were propped up, and behind the roulette-wheel with his back to the curtains.

In the wheel lay a small ivory ball. Cheviot picked it up.

Whereupon, without even glancing at Vulcan, he went down on his knees against the thick green carpet. His fingers explored the carpet to the right of where a croupier's chair would have stood. They ran along the carpet to the left.

Cheviot stood up.

Vulcan was looking at him from just across the table, two and a half feet wide.

"Yes?" prompted Vulcan.

"This table is not rigged. But I can show you the principle.

It is so old, so old and primitive, that no one would use it in any modern—" Cheviot stopped.

"*Yes?*"

"The croupier's right foot," returned Cheviot, "controls four (yes, four) very small buttons under the carpet. These, connected by taut wires, lead to rods up the legs of the table and inside it. A very slight pressure sets in motion three separate coiled springs driven by compressed air. You are acquainted with the principle in your—our time. But the full weight of each spring must never be uncoiled at once. If it did, it would explode mightily."

Cheviot paused.

All of a sudden, as he spoke, his gaze seemed to fix on the cigar-smoke rising from the desk at the far side.

"No, no, never!" he breathed, as though fighting his own senses. "A very slight touch; the air must be preserved, in touches, for use all night!"

"And what end, may I ask?"

"Follow this!"

Cheviot gave a whirl to the silvered pivot of the wheel, which flashed into a red-and-black-blur. Next he tossed in the ball.

It bounced down; jumped, and, as always, went whirling and spinning round the outer ebony rim. Presently, while the clicking grew more soft and only Vulcan seemed to breathe, it slowed down.

"And to what end, I repeat?" demanded Vulcan.

"Look at it!"

"I see nothing!"

"As the ball slows down, it is certain at one revolution or other to roll somewhere near the zero or the double-zero, set side by side. A touch of the croupier's foot, heel or toe, can control three of the hidden springs at once. It does not matter where the ball is; the wheel is quartered. A touch tilts up three sides of the wheel: slightly, invisibly. If this wheel could tilt up . . ."

Cheviot leaned forward, his fingers darting out.

"By the Lord, it does tilt up!"

Cheviot's fingers could only flick lightly at the sides, far less effectively than a simultaneous mechanism. The tilting of the wheel, swaying as it rotated towards a stop, could not even be detected. But the ball slid down and dropped with a click into double-zero.

Vulcan's shaven jowls bore not even any side-whiskers. A bright drop of sweat appeared on each cheek-bone.

"*I* tried it only once," said Cheviot. "How many weeks or months has your croupier practised it?"

"I—"

"It's finished," said Cheviot, looking up straight into his eyes across the table. "Don't you think your own number's up, Vulcan?"

15

The Rites of Venus

How he wished he could dent the hard expressionless look, the placidity, of Vulcan's face! But he couldn't.

"Don't you think your own number's up?" he repeated. "If you compel me to expose this—"

"Dear sir, you will never leave this room to expose it."

"No? I can leave this room," Cheviot said, "at any time I please."

"Lies? Lies again?"

Cheviot moved back to one window, and partly twitched open an orange-plush curtain.

"I told you truthfully," he said, "there were no constables at your back door. But outside these windows, on the roof-slope, are six constables and two officers. I have only to raise a window and spring my rattle, or even smash a pane. They will be over the sill and inside before you can even touch the door." He drew the curtain wider. "Vulcan, do you challenge me?"

"Drop the curtain! Close it!"

Cheviot complied. The two stood watching each other with deadly wariness from opposite sides of the table. But Vulcan remained agreeable.

"Mr. Cheviot, what are your terms?"

"You've heard them. The diamond-and-ruby brooch, and your account-book with a certain man's name written opposite its description. In return, we let you alone."

"We-el!" murmured Vulcan in his soft bass. "After all, I am a law-abiding man. And already you have the key."

"Key?"

"On the key-ring you were deft enough to steal, the shorter key will open any drawer of my desk. The left-hand tier of drawers contains my collection of jewellery; thrown in higgledy-piggledy, I regret. The two top right-hand drawers contain my account-books. *Voilà tout.*"

Vulcan's cigar was acridly burning the edge of the desk. He went back to take it up in one hand, his unfinished brandy-glass in the other hand. As though to show his entire detachment, he strolled along the side of the table.

Towards the door? Yes; but he did not even glance at the door. Passing the big Chinese-lacquer cabinet, he moved round towards Cheviot's side of the table.

Cheviot slipped away to the right, round the other end of the table, and up to the desk.

One eye peered over his shoulder, keeping watch on Vulcan. Vulcan had stopped about the middle of the table, putting down glass and cigar on what was now the far side, and apparently studying the roulette-wheel.

Compelled to look away, Cheviot slipped the smaller key into the lock of the top drawer in the right-hand tier. The key turned easily. He pulled open the drawer.

Vulcan had not lied about this, at least. Inside lay four account-books. They were big ledgers, bound in thick stippled cardboard, the topmost bearing a pasted white-paper label with the inked figures, *1823–1824.*

The ledgers were so big that he must work each ledger side-ways out of the drawer before he could find the one he wanted. He must—

Don't let him get behind you! Don't let him . . .

With the sole of his shoe Cheviot pushed back the armchair, to have free play on either side. Unseen, shielded by his body, he slipped out his watch of bright polished silver like a mirror, and propped it up tilted at the back of the drawer.

He could see reflected, over his shoulder, any attack which came close.

Then he eased out the first ledger, and put it on the desk with his eyes on the polished surface of the watch. The second ledger, disconcertingly, was dated 1822–1823. He wormed it out and pitched it on the desk.

Underneath lay the account-book for 1828–1829.

Got it!

Cheviot could not see Vulcan dart along the left-hand side of the table behind him. He could not see Vulcan snatch up, by its silver head, the very heavy black cane twisted like a cork-screw.

But he saw a black shape loom up in the watch-mirror. He saw the flash of the diamond-ring as Vulcan's arm whipped back. Just before the cane lashed over, in a blow to smash his skull, Cheviot leaped sideways and to the right.

It would have missed his head, missed even his shoulder and arm, if—

The watch, jerked out of the drawer by its chain, lodged under the top edge of the drawer. There was only a breathing-space before the chain yanked loose the cigar-cutter from Cheviot's other pocket.

The blow, meant for the back of his head, caught him glancingly on the side of it over the thick hair, missing arm and shoulder as Cheviot dodged.

But it was bad enough. He felt that flying weight crack the side of his head. The wave of pain went out in eerie tuning-fork noises to dim his eyesight.

He heard Vulcan grunt as the cane whacked and tore green leather, sending a spasm of agony through Vulcan's wrist. It was all the time Cheviot needed. Though his head felt swollen and throbbed with pain, his arms and legs were steady.

Catching up the light and curved-handled cane—of no earthly use to anybody except as a blind—he ran round the table and stopped beyond the roulette-wheel. There he steadied his swimming eyesight, sweeping from the table an empty glass and a dead cigar.

Vulcan had turned round, showing his teeth. The heavy cane was in his hand as he moved, cat-footed, again with the width of the table between them.

Both spoke only in murderous whispers.

"If you touch that curtain—" This was Vulcan's whisper.

"I won't. Unless you touch the door."

"This is between ourselves?"

"Yes!"

Instantly Vulcan lunged and lashed out, across the width of the table, at Cheviot's head.

Cheviot didn't attempt to parry with the light cane; it would only have smashed to flinders. Instead he jumped to one side. The crooked stick, missing widely, struck with a *crack* against the far side of the table. It gashed and scarred mahogany. It made the orange lamps jump and quiver, the china statues rattle.

But Vulcan, never off balance, was instantly back on his feet. Cheviot could only face him with silent derision. He dared not try for a judo-hold, against such strength and quickness, unless—

Unless he could madden Vulcan into lunging off balance.

Vulcan watched, moving right and left. Cheviot approached and stood against the edge of the table, daring him.

Crack!

Vulcan lashed and missed again, so widely that Cheviot's derision grew broader.

Slowly Vulcan drew back from the table. Slowly he moved towards the left, behind one of the china figures. He had only one eye, Cheviot's look seemed to imply; his measuring of distance would be poor.

Vulcan knew that, and it infuriated him still more. He drew farther back, as though about to turn away. Cheviot, on the contrary, pressed against the edge of the table and leaned partly across it.

Vulcan whirled back, ran in, and struck. Too late he saw where the blow must fall; but he could not stop his arm. The crooked weight smashed full down on the half-smiling Venus, with her black hair over her shoulders. The china figure burst to pieces, all but disappeared, as the cane hit the table.

Still nobody spoke. Vulcan stood motionless, his good eye wide with horror. His pale face grew paler. In a paralysis he whispered the only words of human feeling Cheviot ever heard him use.

"Kate," he said. "My poor Kate."

Whereupon fury caught him. The blood surged up in his cheeks, leaving only his skull white. He raced along the table to the middle, Cheviot following him. Seeing that hated face, Vulcan lunged far and struck—completely off balance.

Cheviot had already thrown away his useless cane. As Vulcan's right arm shot across the table, the fingers of his left hand gripped the wrist as he had gripped Captain Hogben's. He jerked that Leviathan bulk across the table and past the roulette-wheel.

For a second Vulcan's neck rested on the other edge of the table, as in the collar of a guillotine. The edge of Cheviot's right hand, like a hatchet, chopped down across the back of the neck. Then he yanked Vulcan fully over, setting a-spin the pivot of the roulette-wheel.

Vulcan landed sideways, quivering, and rolled over on his back. His eyes were glazed; the eyelids fluttered and closed. He did not seem to breathe.

The roulette-wheel, at first wildly spinning, steadily slowed down and came to a stop.

And Cheviot, sweating with fear at what he might have done, stared down at Vulcan.

A blow like that, in the proper place, could kill and not stun, as he intended. But *had* he intended merely to stun? *Had* he struck in the place to stun and not kill?

That whole battle, except for four whispered words and the crack or thud of Vulcan's stick, had gone in dead silence.

Silent now, horribly silent, Cheviot searched for his watch to see whether breath would cloud the glass. His watch was gone. He bent down and felt for a pulse. He thought he felt one beating, but he could not be sure. Tearing open Vulcan's shirt, ripping down the thin silk undervest beneath, his fingers sought the heart.

And the heart was beating, thinly but steadily. Vulcan was only knocked out.

Cheviot lurched to his feet. The act of bending over threw a dazzle of pain through the left side of his head. He steadied himself against the table. After a moment or two he hurried round to the desk. He took out the account book for 1828–1829, and put it on the desk. He retrieved his watch, chain, and cigar-cutter. He took the shorter key out of the lock, replacing the key-ring in his pocket.

Then, listening for any noise below, he hurried across to the windows. There was much trouble in opening the windows; they were stuck fast. He wrenched one of them up, cracking a pane in the glass. His hands hammered and bumped at the other until that went up too.

To gulp the cold night-air was heartening, soothing. Drawing together the curtains behind him so that no noise could be heard inside, Cheviot took out the rattle from under his coat. Its noise tore and splintered out against the night sky.

He walked back, stepping over a Vulcan now breathing stertorously beside the crooked stick, and went to the far end of the table nearest to the door and the Chinese-lacquer cabinet. Now that the shock of the fight had passed, he was again strung to alertness and anticipation.

Through the drawn curtains, like demons in a pantomime, leaped Inspector Seagrave on one side and Sergeant Bulmer on the other, their truncheons drawn. They moved aside. Six constables, wearing duty-armbands and with truncheons drawn, flowed over the sills and spread out in a line.

"Orders, sir?" demanded Inspector Seagrave.

"First, clap a pair of darbies on that sleeping beauty. He'll wake up at any moment."

Sergeant Bulmer whipped the handcuffs from under his coat, and clicked them shut on Vulcan's thick wrists. But his eyes bulged out as he did so.

"Gord!" blurted Sergeant Bulmer.

"Quiet!" said Cheviot.

"But what did you do to the cove, sir?" insisted Bulmer. "We couldn't see or hear a thing, 'cept what sounded like a fight. You've got a nasty lump on the side of your head, too. Couldn't have been easy, downing old Vulcan."

The always-worried Inspector Seagrave silenced him with a glare and remained wooden.

"Orders, sir?" he repeated.

"The same as our original plan. I was to come into the house and find the device, packed cards or a rigged wheel, Vulcan employed to fleece his guests. If I found it, I was to use it as a weapon to get his account-book and the diamond-and-ruby brooch."

"And—and you've done that, sir?"

"Yes, by luck. Look for yourself! His account-book for 1828–1829 is over on the desk there. The left-hand tier of drawers, four of them, is packed with his collection of jewellery. Here!"

Cheviot took the key-ring from his pocket and put it on the edge of the table.

"The shorter key," he said, "opens any drawer. The only reason why I called you in here is that we must make great haste. Four of you will each take one of the drawers and go through it. Get the brooch alone; that will do as evidence; but get it quickly before we're discovered."

"And after that, sir?" insisted Inspector Seagrave, who wanted to have every detail right in his head.

"After that, we release Vulcan and go down over the roofs. We don't touch Vulcan or his house. I made a promise, and I'll keep it."

"Begging your pardon, sir," spoke up a hoarse and dogged voice from one of the constables, "but ain't there to be any fight?"

Cheviot, who had moved back almost to the armchair where he had been sitting, wheeled round.

"Fight? Can nine of us meet thirty blacklegs, probably half a dozen more in the footmen down there, and most of 'em armed?"

A stir went through the line along the opposite wall.

"Thirty? Maybe thirty-six?" cried Sergeant Bulmer. "Sir, that's twice the lot of legs that Captain Whimper and the Black Dwarf used to stuff the house and make sure they cut Billy Hench's throat!"

"Well, Vulcan packed the house against me. He knew I was coming. Somebody warned him beforehand. But never mind that! Hurry! Don't you see, with the evidence we have, we've won the game? We've completely—"

He stopped.

There was a woodeny, rattly kind of flap and crash. Cheviot, staring at Bulmer across the room, saw its effect reflected in his men's eyes before he turned.

The double-doors of the big Chinese-lacquer cabinet had been hurled open as though by the hands of a maniac, which was very nearly true.

Inside the cabinet, crouching, stood Kate de Bourke.

Her glossy black hair was torn down over her shoulders, torn by her own fingernails, just as they had ripped down the bodice of her green gown. The lips were drawn back over her teeth. Her eyes seemed swollen lumps of fury.

"She's been there all the time," flashed Cheviot's thought. "I never actually saw her leave the room. Vulcan keeps a witness for everything. She's heard every word, and seen her image smashed, without daring to help. She—"

Then Kate screamed.

The screams went piercing up, and must have been audible to everyone in the big gaming-room downstairs. Kate's wide skirts billowed out of the cabinet. She was nearly blind from being so long in the dark. But even dim eyes saw the gleam of the keys lying at the edge of the table just in front of her.

Kate seized the keys, tottered round, and ran to collide with the mahogany door not three paces away, just as the paralysis lifted from every man.

"Bulmer! Grab her!"

Cheviot raced for the door as Bulmer and Seagrave did. They were too late.

In fact, they overshot the mark. Cheviot never knew by what miracle Kate found the lock, instantly unlocked the door, and flung it open.

As he and Bulmer crowded together in the doorway, he threw out his arm and held Bulmer back. After all, he could hardly collar the woman like a felon. She had done nothing.

But Kate, flying out on the narrow balcony, momentarily stopped to look back. He had a glimpse of her face over her shoulder, past the tangled hair. He saw the mouth drawn up at one corner, and the terror in her eyes.

She must many times have peeped out of that cabinet. What she saw, blurred, was the face of the man who had thrown her unbeatable Vulcan across a table and knocked him senseless with a blow across the neck.

In a space only while you might have counted two, Cheviot was conscious of men jumping to their feet in the big yellow-hung room below, of faces upturned, of three great chandeliers, dazzling with candles, about on a level with his eyes.

"Stop!" he said. He tried to speak gently, but his voice seemed to thunder out. "We mean you no harm. We won't hurt you. But stop, or you'll hurt yourself!"

What Kate heard was the frightening voice of the man who—

She screamed again. She ran blindly to the right. Once more she tried to look over her left shoulder. Her eyes saw only the blaze of yellow candlelight from the chandeliers. And her wits dissolved along with her sight.

She turned and ran straight for the wooden handrail in front of her.

The crack of tearing and splintering wood, as her body struck gilded and flimsy scrollwork rotted through, was not as loud as the crack of Vulcan's cane on the table. But it seemed to go on longer.

Kate turned in the air and fell face down. She fell fourteen feet, her hair lifting from her shoulders, and her body as limp as a dead woman's because she had fainted. That dead-weight landed on the right-hand side of the long roulette-table just below.

Under such an impact one of the table-legs, underneath the same side, broke off completely. The other, wavering, splintered and broke as well. The opposite end of the table, eighteen feet long and covered with green felt, grotesquely jerked up and tilted into the air.

Ivory counters, banknotes, gold coins rolled over and spilled down to the right. But that was not what drove a stamp of silence on every mouth.

With a ripping and twanging noise, two long taut wires tore the carpet underneath the table. Those wires ran to the two good table-legs on the left. They glistened as they surged up, tearing the carpet still further and exposing a metal plate with four black buttons.

Then it was as though the table, endowed with life, went mad. Machines do go mad, when you smash them. Few understood the exploding hiss of compressed air. But they saw the roulette wheel itself jump up as a coiled spring emerged at one side, crawling and expanding like a metal snake. Another uncoiled spring shot up as though to attack the wheel.

Every man down on the floor there, punter or blackleg, stood up or ran to look. All stayed motionless, hats falling off or eyeballs glistening, when they saw.

Cheviot alone, at the broken handrail, was looking at Kate de Bourke.

She had slid down the table, her skirt dragged above her knees. He could not see her face. But her outspread arms moved. Her fingers clutched at the green baize. Slowly, dazedly, she lifted her head and blinked round.

Nobody heard Cheviot's strangled gasp of relief.

He had given the wrong order—"Bulmer! Grab her!"— which might have sent a half-crazed woman to her death. It turned him sick when he saw her fall.

And yet, as so often happens, she had fallen as flat and limp as a jockey or a drunken man. Far from being dead or bone-smashed, the woman was not even hurt.

Hardly two seconds had elapsed since she fell. But every one of his eight men, despite his frantic gesture, had run out into the gallery and lined up on either side of him.

They were trapped here amid thirty-odd blacklegs, whose eyes were beginning to move up to the gallery.

They were trapped here, that is, unless . . .

The bursting hush still held. Vividly Cheviot was conscious of four persons standing up at the far side of the roulette-table. The tall young man addressed by the footman as my lord, he of the luxuriant brown side-whiskers and the red nose, was stricken cold sober. Beside him stood the thick-set bruiser in the piebald wig, hand threateningly half-raised towards him.

Beyond the wheel, staring at it, was the stout man with the yellow side-whiskers, whom Cheviot had seen at Lady Cork's. Beyond *him* loomed the lean, bony blackleg with the lined face and the false teeth.

"*Yes!*" Cheviot shouted.

A quiver went through them all. All of them looked upwards: seeing uniforms, seeing truncheons, seeing only Cheviot in evening-dress and empty-handed.

His voice rang out again.

"That is how they fleeced you," he said, pointing down to the roulette-table.

From across the room, at the rouge-et-noir table, he heard the click as the hammer of a pistol was drawn back to full-cock.

"Yes, we are the police," Cheviot said. "But on whose side do you stand: on the side of those who robbed you—or on ours?"

One, two, three, four . . .

"My lord" whirled round to the bruiser in the weird wig. My lord's high, harsh voice rose up.

"You damned cheating leg," he said, almost in surprise.

His left fist swung and drove into the bruiser's fat stomach. His right came over to the head. Taken completely off-balance, the breath squeezed from his lungs, the bruiser sat down hard on a chair which broke under him.

At the same moment the expression altered on the face of the bony man with the false teeth. A knife slipped out of his sleeve. He had no time to use it on Yellow-whiskers beside him. Snatching the rake from the hand of the second croupier, Yellow-whiskers lunged with the head of the rake and smashed the false teeth down his throat.

At the rouge-et-noir table, two punters ran in together at the croupier, pulling him over backwards by the neckcloth and flinging him on the carpet under a rain of cards from six packs. Somebody threw a bottle. Somebody else raised a war-cry. The battle boiled over.

At each end of the gallery above, a small staircase led down to the floor. Cheviot ran to the head of his men on the right-hand side. Catching sight of Inspector Seagrave on the extreme left end, he raised his hand high, singled out the three behind him, and snapped his fingers.

"Now!" he said.

And empty-handed he led three constables down into the brawl on the right stairs, while Inspector Seagrave led four men down into it from the left.

16

"I Kissed Thee Ere . . . They Killed Me"

The clocks were striking three in the morning when a hackney cab turned into Cavendish Square towards Flora Drayton's house.

The passenger inside, despite his uneasiness, was jubilant. He almost sang.

Outwardly he looked respectable enough. Neither his cloak nor his hat had entered the brawl at Vulcan's. The cloak was worn closed and fastened at the chin, the hat jolted on the seat beside him because the head-bruise ached.

Cheviot's jaw felt very sore on the right, but it did not seem to be swollen. He scarcely felt his body-bruises, though they would be stiff enough next day. On the seat at his right lay two account-books, and Cheviot's handkerchief, tied up in a knot, containing five pieces of jewellery.

"Ta-ti-ta!" sang Superintendent Cheviot, who was not very musical.

If only it were not for Flora's wrath . . .

The cab slowed from a trot and drew up at the door of her house.

Cheviot glanced out of the window. The house would be dark and sealed up; he must, of course, find some way of breaking in. He looked. Astounded, he looked again.

A gleam of gaslight illuminated the fanlight over the front door. Though the shutters were closed inside the windows to the left of the door, they bore tiny star-shaped openings; and the room was lighted too.

Gathering up hat, handkerchief, and account-books in a bundle, Cheviot hastened to jump down and pay the cabman who opened the door. By this time he had discovered that you did not tip cabbies in the way he knew it; the jarvey stated from three-pence or sixpence more than his actual fare, and you paid that.

He ran to the door. He had hardly touched the bell-knob when the door was opened by a middle-aged, almost stately woman, rather stout, in a lace cap and long lace apron. She resembled a housekeeper rather than a maid.

"Good evening, sir," she said as casually as though they were meeting at seven in the evening, and not at three o'clock in the morning.

"Er—good evening."

"Your hat, sir?"

"Thank you. But not," he said hastily, "the cloak or—or these other things."

"Very good sir," said the middle-aged woman, who was now beaming at him.

"Er—is she—Lady Drayton—is she—?"

The woman merely curtseyed gravely, indicating closed double-doors at the left of the marble-floored foyer.

Flora made no pretence that she had not heard wheels stop in the street outside. Still fully dressed in her dark-blue gown bordered with gold, she was sitting up straight at a round table near the fire, her fingers pressed hard on the pages of the leather-covered book she had ceased to read.

A petroleum-oil lamp burned on the table. Gaslight flickered yellow from a bracket on either side of the white-marble mantel-piece, and there was a good blazing fire. All these brought out the delicate hollows under her eyes.

When Cheviot opened and closed the doors behind him, she still sat rigidly: her slender neck upright, her eyes searching him in fear that he had been hurt. When he seemed uninjured, she uttered a little cry.

Hastily Cheviot put down the account-books, the handkerchief-wrapped jewellery, on a chair of cherry-covered velvet. For Flora ran across to him, throwing her arms round him with such violence that he tightened his shoulders against the pain of body-bruises. Flora put her head back. He kissed her so hard and in such a complicated way that after some seconds he thought it better—let us say more delicate—to hold her a little away from him.

His voice was husky. But he tried to assume a light tone.

"May I observe, my dearest, that of all the women on earth you are the most utterly unpredictable?"

"What a pretty compliment!" Flora almost sobbed. She really thought it the highest of compliments. "You can bandy words fairly, when you like."

Whereupon she must put on a grand-hostessy and haughty air, drawing back from him even while she clung to him.

"Foh!" said Flora, in pretended disgust. "You have been smoking again."

"Certainly I have been smoking. But you needn't make it sound as though I had been smoking opium or hashish. After all, it's only tobacco."

"Which," declared Flora, drawn up even with tears in her eyes, "is a filthy and repulsive habit, not permitted in any well-bred house. If a man must smoke, he goes upstairs and smokes up the chimney."

"He—*what?*"

"He sits on the hearth," here she grandly indicated the hearth of the fireplace not far from her, "and puts his head inside and lets the smoke go up the chimney. Of course," Flora added hastily, "there mustn't be any fire."

Cheviot was in a mood which combined desire, hilarity, and the knowledge that he was beginning to understand her at last.

"I sincerely hope not," he said with a grave face. "If I were obliged to stick my head up the flue over a fire, I might find my whiskers a trifle singed before I had finished the cigar."

"But you haven't got any whis—oh, stop! You're quizzing again! I hate you!"

"Flora, look at me. Do you honestly mind the smoking?"

"No. Of course I don't. Kiss me again." Then, after an interval: "I allow I was cross with you tonight—"

"You had cause."

"No, no! I was furious," said Flora, dropping her grand airs and becoming natural, "because I was so frightened. Do you imagine I had heard nothing of Vulcan? Or his reputation? And there he was, daring you to remain. And there you were— oh, no matter! But there *was* trouble, was there not?"

"A little, yes. Nothing to speak of."

"Thank God," she said breathlessly. "Darling! Come and sit down and tell me. Let me have your cloak."

"No, no! Not the cloak!"

But Flora had already unfastened the catch and slipped off the heavy astrakhan collar. When the cloak fell into her hands, she leaped back and stifled a shriek.

His collar and neckcloth were gone. His shirt was crumpled, dirty, and in two places spotted with dried blood. His trousers, split at both knees, were as dust-patched as the torn coat. In this coat, slewed back round as well as possible when he had washed his hands and face at a pump, the right sleeve showed the black-burned rent of a bullet-hole.

"I—I see." Flora spoke in a low voice, swallowing. "I remark it. There was but little trouble; nothing to speak of."

She began to laugh, and went on laughing.

"Flora! Enough of that! You must not give way so!"

Her laughter ceased as he spoke. Pressing the cloak hard against her breast, she looked up with such intense tenderness that he could not meet her gaze.

"Nay, that was no nerves or megrims, Jack. It was honest laughter for the comical. But it came from the heart, which must hurt a little too. Now I will tell you what I determined, and determined this night."

She moistened her lips, pressing the cloak more tightly against her breast.

"To be open with you, my dear, there is much I don't understand. Of you. Sometimes you might be a man from another world. I don't understand why you insist so much on 'your work.'" Perplexity made her bite her lip. "A gentleman does not work, or at least need not. Never, never, my father said! No, don't protest!—For why need I understand?

"Shall I be a silly woman," she cried, "as so many are silly? And fancy that affectations are realities? I was stupid last night—yes, I was!—and again tonight. You won't find me stupid another time, if you love me. And, if you are so devoted to this cause of the police—why, then, so am I! That is no merit in me. It is because I love you, and I would not have you other than as you are."

Still Cheviot looked down at the carpet. He did not raise his head. There was a lump in his throat, and he did not look up because he could not.

Flora had moved closer. He reached out; and, as she shifted the cloak to her left arm, he lifted her right hand and pressed his lips to it.

And then, as complete understanding came to them and wrapped them round in a warmth which seemed never to be broken, there rose up from somewhere at the back of the foyer the clank-jangle-rattle of the front door-bell.

Flora drew back from him and stormed.

"At this hour?" she exclaimed. "No! I'll tell Miriam to admit no one. They shan't take you away from me tonight!"

"You may be sure of that." He spoke grimly. "No power on earth could compel it."

There was a light, discreet tap at the door; then a long pause; then the door was opened by the stately housekeeper.

"My lady—" she began in some hesitation, and paused. "I should not have disturbed you, as well you know, save that . . . it is Lady Cork."

"Lady Cork?" Flora spoke blankly.

Cheviot's begrimed white gloves, adhering with dried blood to the knuckles inside, cost him pain as his fists clenched.

"We had better see her," he muttered.

"You—you are sure?"

"Yes. This afternoon, Flora, I began to see the solution of the problem."

"Of Margaret Renfrew's murder?"

"Yes. I had been blind. But I saw who committed the crime; and tonight, at Vulcan's, I realized how it was done. Barring one detail, and one question which you and Lady Cork alone can answer, my cause is complete."

Flora drew a deep breath. "Miriam, please beg Lady Cork to come in."

As the door closed, Cheviot spoke again in that same rapid mutter.

"You are not to be alarmed at what I say. All is well. But this morning Mr. Richard Mayne, one of the Police Commissioners, did his best to make out a cause that you had killed the Renfrew woman and I had shielded you. No, I beg: don't start or put your hand to your mouth!"

Cheviot glanced at the closed door and spoke still more quickly.

"At any time," he said, "I could have cleared you. But only by confessing that both of us had told lies and suppressed evidence, which would have been more dangerous still. My only hope lay in showing how this murder was done. And that I think—I say I *think*—I can now prove to the full."

He held up his hand for silence. Catching the cloak from Flora's arm, he draped it round himself and fastened the collar as Miriam announced the Countess of Cork and Orrery.

They heard Lady Cork's sniff, and the tap of her crutch-headed stick, before the little, stout-bodied, vigorous old woman stumped in.

Lady Cork did not wear her white frilled cap, but the white poke-bonnet with long sides gave much the same effect as her shrewd eyes probed out of its shadow. Her white gown was the same, under a grey fur pelisse rucked up round her.

The eighteenth century, with all its train of ghosts, crowded in round her and fluttered the gas-jets with their presence.

"Lawks, girl!" she said to Flora, with a hint of apology even in her defiant tone. "I'd not ha' been so troublesome to you, at this time, if I hadn't seen lights burning on the ground floor." There was a very slight emphasis on the word "ground."

Even two or three days ago, Flora might have been in agitated confusion. But she was all coolness and graciousness, smiling.

"You are most welcome, Lady Cork. But surely you are up late?"

"I'm always up late. I don't sleep." Lady Cork craned her neck round. "No, no, wench, I'll keep me hat and coat. Don't fuss me!"

This last remark was addressed to her pretty young maid, Solange, hovering in the doorway. Solange's soft and liquid brown eyes peered out from the hood of a green cape, herself in confusion at seeing Flora.

"Sit down there," Lady Cork told Solange, pointing with her stick at a far chair, "and be vanished. My visit's a brief one."

"As is mine," murmured Cheviot, touching his cloak.

"Is it, George Cheviot's son?" Lady Cork asked sardonically. Her eyes moved to Flora and back to him. "Is it? Bah! Tell the truth and shame the devil!"

"A practice, madam, I strongly recommend to yourself."

"Hey? D'ye say I don't tell the truth?"

"Sometimes, madam. But seldom directly."

Nor, as he knew, would she approach any subject directly. Lady Cork snorted. She peered round the room, papered in silvery grey, its chairs and sofa and ottoman upholstered in cherry-coloured velvet.

Snorting, she hobbled over and plumped herself down in Flora's armchair, under the lamp and beside the fire, with the little round table at her elbow. On the table lay the book, opened, which Flora had been reading when Cheviot entered.

Lady Cork blinked at the pages. It was as though the very sniff of printer's ink set her off.

"D'ye know where I've been this night? No? Well! I've been a-dining with John Wilson Croker," Lady Cork said ferociously, "and a parcel of other red-behinded Tories. Can you imagine what Croker has the impudence to propose?"

"Yes," returned Cheviot. This was the only way to keep her from flying off at a tangent. "Mr. Croker proposes to edit and annotate a new edition of Boswell, which may take him two years or more. No doubt he wished for your reminiscences?"

"Ay; so he did. Why, curse his dem—"

"Have no fear, madam."

"Hey?"

"Young Mr. Macaulay, who writes such admirable articles in the *Edinburgh Review,* hates Mr. Croker worse than cold boiled veal. In due time he will dust Croker's jacket so thoroughly that future generations may remember it."

"Ay, so Rogers prophesies." Lady Cork brooded, her hands folded on her crutch-headed stick. "But what does it matter? I've given 'at homes' for all the cursed literary lions in recent years, from Washington Irving to young Ben Disraeli, when he made the town stare with that novel *Vivian Grey.* But the wit's gone. The light's gone. All's gone."

"Not the wit, I protest!" exclaimed Flora. "Is Mr. Disraeli, for instance, in town at the moment?"

"Lawks, now!" sneered Lady Cork, rearing up her thick neck. "Who don't know he's tourin' the Continent, and says he'll stand for Parliament when he comes back?"

"He will make his mark, madam." Cheviot spoke gravely. "He will make his mark, I promise you that."

"Ben Disraeli? And what are you grinnin' at?"

"I was only thinking of *Vivian Grey.* One of the imaginary characters is called Lord Beaconsfield. Mr. Disraeli, in his youth, never dreams that one day he himself will be called—"

"Well, lad? Don't stop as though you'd bitten your tongue through! Called what?"

"To another sphere, I was about to say."

A large sofa was drawn up straight towards the fire, sideways to Lady Cork's armchair. Flora sat on the sofa nearer her guest, and Cheviot beside her.

But a change had deepened wickedly in Lady Cork when he

said those words. She leaned over her stick, her jowls flattening, and said abruptly:

"I heerd something else at Croker's, too."

"Oh?"

"Yes. A footman came up and whispered it in John Wilson's ear, about half-past twelve. I heerd," said Lady Cork with much deliberation, "that Superintendent George Cheviot's son, with only eight Peelers, bobbed up like a flash o' magic at Vulcan's. The devil knows how they got in. But they beat the blacklegs, and rolled every one of 'em down the front stairs, in seven minutes by somebody's watch."

Cheviot sighed.

"That is not quite an accurate account, madam."

"Then what did happen?" the old woman asked truculently. "Eh, lad? What did happen?"

Cheviot looked back at her steadily.

"The story," he answered, "must wait for some other time. It will suffice to say this: that the swell yokels—"

"The—the what, please?" asked a bewildered Flora.

"I beg your pardon. A swell yokel is a gay or dashing fellow. I referred to the gentlemen, the honest punters. They were enraged by a rigged or false roulette-wheel. They turned on the blacklegs, at least eighty per cent of them, and fought on our side. As a result, we so far outnumbered the blacklegs that it was hardly a fight at all. They were overcome in five minutes, not seven."

Brushing this aside, he still kept his gaze fixed on Lady Cork.

"But I don't imagine, madam, you came here at past three in the morning to seek details of a broil at Vulcan's. Could it be some interest in a brooch belonging to you?"

Lady Cork's eyes wavered and fell. All her feigned ferocity dropped away.

"I'll not deny it," she muttered. " 'Twas a wedding-gift, ye comprehend. The first ever I had. Four other pieces of jewellery *may* have gone to Vulcan. He may keep 'em, for all I care; they don't signify. But the brooch—!"

Cheviot rose to his feet. He went to the chair near the door.

On top of the two account-books lay the bag formed by his tied-up handkerchief.

Returning to Lady Cork, he put the bag into her lap. He untied the knot and opened it. Under the flicker of gaslight, under the glow of the cherry-and-grey-coloured lamp, burned a shifting litter of precious stones.

"Permit me," he said gently, "to show you all five."

Lady Cork looked down. She did not exclaim or even speak for some time. She pressed her withered hands against her lips, palms upwards, and rocked her stout body in the chair.

Presently she seized only one of them, a little ship of diamonds and rubies, pressing her mouth to it, and then her cheek, and crooning a sing-song which was of sixty years gone by.

Flora turned her head away. After a moment Lady Cork cleared her throat and peered up.

"Nowadays, lad," she said, "they don't make many men like you."

"But I did little or nothing!" He told her this sincerely; he believed it. "If you would praise anyone, praise Seagrave, Bulmer, my six constables. By God, madam, they were magnificent. In my report, already sent to the Commissioners, I have given them the highest possible commendation."

"While you, I dessay," Lady Cork sneered, "stood by and did nothing?"

"I—"

"Enough!" said Lady Cork, in a voice of really impressive dignity. She sat up. "Mr. Cheviot. I cannot say or express how much I am beholden to you. But I'll write to Bobby Peel. Ecod, I'll write to the Duke!"

"And yet I had rather you didn't."

"Eh?"

"If you wish to show any gratitude, madam, you have only to tell the truth."

The dark shadow was back again.

The brooch fell from her hands into the other jewellery. A thin singing of gaslight, a clenching of Flora's hands, reminded them they were still in the presence of a dead woman shot through the back.

"Last night," continued Cheviot, "you told me a certain story. You said that four of your best treasures, including the brooch, you hid in the seed-containers of the bird-cages in your own bedroom on Tuesday night."

"But I did! So I did! You said as much yourself!"

"True; I don't gainsay it. However, what of Thursday night?"

Lady Cork opened her mouth, shut it again, and looked away.

"On Thursday night, madam, you told me you set a snare for the thief." Cheviot reached down, and picked out the only ring amid the pieces of jewellery. "You said that you put a ring, which you called 'worthless,' into one of the seed-containers of the canary-cages in the passage? Yes?"

Again Lady Cork began to speak, and hesitated.

"You then stated," Cheviot went on, "that you succumbed to temptation and swallowed laudanum. You drank the laudanum, and did not see the thief after all."

"I—"

"Forgive me, but I found that flatly impossible to believe. You were all in agitation, all aghast. You *must* learn the identity of the thief, even if you only suspected it. This ring you hid, for instance."

Cheviot held it up. Its single large diamond flashed back malevolently.

"In Vulcan's account-book it is pledged (pawned, not sold) for a hundred guineas. Hardly worthless, as you stated? You must set good bait for your thief. Is it reasonable to think you would drink laudanum before you could possibly see the thief? No." He paused. "You saw the thief, did you not? And recognized her as Margaret Renfrew?"

"Yes," said Lady Cork, after a pause.

"Would you so testify in the witness-box, madam?"

"I could and I would!" retorted Lady Cork, lifting her head. Then she mused for a time, her old eyes wise and shrewd.

"I saw her," Lady Cork added suddenly. "In bare feet, and

a thin night-shift, carrying a light. Ecod! Peg was never a prude; I always guessed that, though I well knew," the eyes twinkled, "her choice was not *you*. But—egad! Until I saw her there in the night, with her mouth open and her cheeks afire, groping for the ring, I never felt in me bones how much of that gel was the world, the flesh, and the devil."

" 'Fire burn,' " muttered Cheviot, " 'and cauldron bubble!' "

"Eh, lad? What d'ye say?"

"Forgive me." Cheviot was contrite. "Only a quotation I have several times applied to her. The fire burned too high. The cauldron bubbled over. Whereupon she stayed herself; she became again her quiet, shut-in self, with a conscience."

"Oh?" said Lady Cork in a very curious tone.

He dropped the diamond-ring back among the other jewels in Lady Cork's lap.

"There is but one more question, madam; then I have done. It concerns a letter you wrote on the night of the murder. It even concerns Lady Drayton here."

"It concerns *me?*" Flora cried.

Cheviot smiled. Above the fireplace, between the gas-jets, hung a full-length portrait of Flora herself, painted three or four years ago by an ageing Sir Thomas Lawrence, who seldom accepted commissions now that he was President of the Royal Academy.

All the time Cheviot could not help glancing from the pictured Flora to the real one, who in more than the pictured sense was more alive. With his gloved hand, openly, he tilted up her chin as she sat on the sofa. Even through the glove he could feel the softness of her chin and cheek.

"You?" he repeated. "My dear, when Mr. Richard Mayne was driving at me with questions this afternoon, I was in fear lest he remember a certain letter. I should have had no answer for him."

Standing straight on the hearth-rug, he turned back to Lady Cork.

"Last night, the night of the murder, you wrote a letter to Colonel Charles Rowan at Scotland Yard?"

"Ay; and what of that?"

"You sealed it conspicuously, and in yellow wax? Yes. Why, if I may ask, did you despatch it to Colonel Rowan and not to both Commissioners of Police?"

"Lad, lad, Charles Rowan comes often to my house. He was even acquainted with poor Peg."

"I see. Flora!" He looked down. "If you recall, you were waiting outside the police-office in your closed carriage. A footman rode up with the letter. You stopped him, and asked to see the letter."

"Oh, dear!" Flora sat up straight. "So I did! I had forgotten."

"So, fortunately, had Mr. Mayne. Why did you ask to see the letter?"

"As you say, it had a conspicuous seal in yellow wax. I saw it by the light of the carriage lanterns." Flora paused, her face growing crimson. "All the world knew," she added defiantly, "I should be with you. And all knew where *you* were going that night. I thought the letter might be for me."

"You took it then. Did you break the seal?"

"Good heavens, no. It was addressed to Colonel Rowan. Besides, the seal was already broken."

Cheviot stared at her.

"Good!" he exclaimed. "Better still. And now, Lady Cork, if you please! To whom did you give this letter when you had written it?"

"Why, to Peg Renfrew, of course! I was upstairs in me boudoir, and—"

"To whom did *she* give it?"

"To the footman downstairs. Who else?"

"The seal," he muttered, staring at the fire, "was broken when it came into Colonel Rowan's hands. Then the likeliest person to have broken it was Margaret Renfrew herself." He slapped his hands together. "Yes! She interpreted (pray forgive me, madam) your customary oblique approach about stolen birdseed. She knew the police would be there. Lady Cork! Did you remark her manner afterwards?"

"Ay." The old woman nodded grimly. "I remarked it."

"Hard, defiant, ashamed? Yet ashamed mainly because . . . stop! Under all that hard surface, couldn't you discern a clamor of conscience? If I had pressed her sharply with questions at that time, might she not have confessed?"

"She might," agreed Lady Cork, with a snap. "I'll say more: I thought she would. Else I might ha'—bah, no matter! Who can say what goes on in the heart of a lonely woman? She might, or she might not. But . . ."

"Yes. The murderer stopped her mouth."

Still contemplating the fire, its heat fanning his eyelids and its crackle dim in his ears, Cheviot saw the pattern take form.

"He shot her. He shot her in cold blood. And all because he must not be exposed. And all for a handful of jewellery. And all for a wad of flimseys—I beg your pardon: I mean banknotes—"

"Jack!" Flora interrupted. "Where on earth did you learn all these dreadful terms? 'Extra-flash-men.' 'Swell yokels.' 'Flimseys.' And a dozen more. Where did you learn them?"

Cheviot stood very still. "I—I am not sure."

"I ask," Flora persisted uncertainly, "because some of them are in that book. The book I was reading when you arrived."

"Book?" he repeated, jerking his head towards the round table.

To the astonishment of both women, he moved over and snatched up the leather-covered book. He opened it and glanced down the title-page.

"This," he said, "was published five years ago. I may well have read it, and partly forgotten or never finished it. But it hardly seems your sort of reading, Flora. *The Fatal Effects of Gambling exemplified in the Murder of Wm. Weare, and the Trial and Fate of John Thurtell, the Murderer, and His Accomplices, with—*"

Flora intervened hastily.

"No, not that part! The second part of the book. Look lower down!"

"*The Gambler's Scourge,*" he read aloud, "*a complete ex-*

*posé of the Whole System of Gambling in the Metropolis;
with . . ."*

There was more print, but he did not read the rest of the
title-page. Quickly he turned to the back of the book, flipping
over the pages. Again Flora protested.

"No; you've passed the gambling part. That's the appendix.
It's about a horrible man named Probert, who was concerned
in the murder of Weare, and what he testified after he was re-
prieved." She broke off. "Jack! What's the matter?"

For Cheviot, paler of face than she had ever seen him, was
holding the open book under the lamp in hands that trembled.

He had reason to behave as he did. On the four hundred and
eightieth page, there had jumped up at him a dozen lines in
type which seemed even more heavily leaded than it was. He
read the lines slowly. He read the next page, and the following
three, without enlightenment. Then, at the top of the next page,
six lines stung out like an adder.

"Come!" growled Lady Cork, peering past the side of her
poke-bonnet and looking disquieted. "What sort of behaviour's
that, now? What d'ye call it?"

"I call it finality," said Cheviot.

"Finality?"

"Yes." He closed the book. "I did not really need this. Yet
it is confirmation. It tells me where to find what I want." He
smiled a little. "You spoke of the murderer, madam?"

"I didn't, but—"

"I have him," Cheviot said without expression. "I have him,"
and he closed the fingers of his right hand, "here."

"Ecod," bellowed Lady Cork, hammering her stick on the
floor and all but spilling the jewels from her lap, "but who *is*
this murderer? And how was the dem thing done?"

"I am sorry, madam. I must keep my own counsel as yet."

"You won't tell me?"

"I can't."

"Well! Here's more fine manners! In that event, I'll take my
jewels (thanking you very much) and be off."

Upset, angry without quite seeming to know why, she began

fumblingly to tie together the edges of the handkerchief when
Cheviot intervened. Putting down the book on the table, he
bent down and finished tying the knot. Then he took the jewels
away from her as gently as he could.

"Much though it distresses me, Lady Cork, I cannot allow
you to keep the jewels just yet. They must be used in evidence."

A stricken look crossed Lady Cork's face.

"Not keep 'em? Not even the brooch? Not even the wedding-
gift?"

"Madam, I am sorry! They will be returned to you, of course.
I will write you a receipt now, if you like."

"Receipt!" cried Lady Cork, as though this were the greatest
outrage of all. "Receipt!"

She pushed herself to her feet on the crutch-headed stick,
jerking the fur pelisse round her shoulders.

"Good night to ye, ma'am," she said to Flora. And: "Come
with me, girl!" to the olive-skinned Solange, who had been sitting unobtrusively in a corner, ankles crossed, all eyes. Solange
hastened across to open the double-doors. Lady Cork marched
towards them like a man-o'-war.

"The coachman'll be cold, and so am I," she snorted. At
the open doors she half turned, glaring at Cheviot.

"Hey-dey! I'd not ha' thought to see you so pale. And your
hands tremble! You'll find yourself nobly fit, I dessay, when
tomorrow you meet—"

Glancing at Flora, she bit at her under-lip and stopped. Into
her face, instead of anger, came a certain shame.

Cheviot, staring back at her, wondered how she seemed to
know everything. Freddie Debbitt, probably; you could not shut
Freddie's mouth. But tomorrow, after shooting against the man
for a wager, he was engaged to fight a duel with Captain Hugo
Hogben. And he had completely forgotten it.

Lady Cork, upreared in the open doors with her hand on her
stick and a glimmer of gaslight behind her, bit her lip and
changed again.

"Mr. Cheviot! I—I ask your pardon, sir, for the vapours of
a cross-grained, bad-tempered old woman. I have a fondness for

you; you know it. I am much your debtor; that you know too."
Tears glimmered in her eyes. "Good luck, lad. God speed your
aim."

The doors closed behind her. They heard a murmur of voices,
then the closing, locking, and bolting of the heavy front door.

Flora, who had risen when Lady Cork did, now sat down on
the far end of the sofa, near Cheviot as he stood and looked at
the door.

"Jack, what did she mean? About—speeding your aim?"

"Nothing! At nine o'clock tomorrow morning I have a prac-
tice-match at Joe Manton's gallery. That's all."

"Oh."

Still he looked at the closed doors. He had never practiced
with their accursed pistols. He was not even sure of the weight,
the balance, the throw of the bullet. He might never see Flora
again.

A burning log exploded in the fireplace, showering out sparks.
Cheviot turned round. He bent down and gathered Flora
quickly, violently, into his arms.

17

Six Shots at a Wafer

The pistol-shots, exploding in that long brick room against a thick iron-back wall, set up a din as loud as cannonading in a battle.

The smoke of black powder had thickened to such a haze that even Joe Manton the younger, who was used to it, could hardly see the face of his customer—critical, without any other expression—as Cheviot threw out his arm for the final shot.

Whack! Lead smote on iron. The flattened bullet rattled down to a stone floor.

So great a stillness crept out in the gallery that you could hear, through an open door to the gunsmith's shop, a big white-faced clock ticking on the wall there. It was ten minutes to nine. Superintendent Cheviot had been practising, alone, since twenty minutes past eight.

Joe Manton the younger moved along behind the grilled iron railing, a little less than waist-high, which separated the visitors from the thirty-six paces to the target-wall. There was a creaking of rope as he tugged at the pulleys of the big skylight, tilting it to let out smoke.

The brick walls were whitewashed; they needed a fresh white-washing every fortnight or so. In the right-hand wall was a many-paned window, already pushed partway up. Through it the smoke slipped, curling with furtive eddies as it billowed out up the skylight.

Black-powder stings the eyes; it makes the nostrils and lungs ache. But, as the haze lifted, Cheviot's face emerged. Both their faces were powder-smudged.

"You can do it, sir," said Joe, coughing. "You can do it." Inside himself, a protest squirmed and struggled. "But, begging your pardon, Mr. Cheviot, you do it all *wrong*."

"I know."

"But, sir—"

On the shelf above the iron-grill partition lay one medium-bore duelling-pistol.

Cheviot had tried as many as a dozen pistols: from the murderous twelve-bore, all but useless because its jump threw the bullet too high, to a small pocket-weapon not unlike the one belonging to Flora's late husband.

Each time, after he had fired, Joe the younger would deftly slip the pistol aside, flick off the burst percussion-cap, rapidly clean the barrel with rod and greased rag, and hang it back again in the long racks of pistols along the left-hand wall.

Cheviot still remained motionless, studying the effect of his last shot. There seemed nothing to study. The iron wall was powder-dark, in some places scarred or uneven, spotted over with what looked like bits of white paper.

Joe the younger fidgeted down to his toes. He was a thick-set, sandy-haired young man, with high cheekbones and earnest eyes. His face was as powder-black as a goblin's. He wore a dark coat, a brown waistcoat, and mulberry-coloured breeches with dark gaiters. He had not yet attained the polite manners yet the shatteringly frank speech of his famous father, gunsmith since 1793.

"Here!" Joe was thinking. "Here, now!"

He wished this new gentleman, with the broad shoulders and the light-grey eyes, would smile or laugh or crack a joke as the others did.

This Mr. Cheviot, except for spotless white linen, was dressed all in black: even a black waistcoat.

"Why?" thought Joe. "There isn't going to be a duel, is there?

He says it's only a match. Besides, they'd fight a duel early in the morning."

"Begging your pardon, sir—!" he began aloud.

"I know," Cheviot repeated. He turned his head and smiled. "But I can't do it, Joe. Not, that is, if I want to score a hit."

"Sir?"

"This is how you would desire me to stand, isn't it? Sideways to the rail: thus? Right foot pointed forward, left foot sideways?"

At each movement Joe nodded eagerly.

"Whereupon," said Cheviot, illustrating, "I bring my right arm down and over, like this, stiffly stretched out towards the target? Isn't that the manner of it?"

"Sir, that's the only manner of it! I bet you," exclaimed Joe, inspired, "I bet you even my *pa* wouldn't think of another way!"

"Oh, but there is. You've seen it. You're thinking of form and not effect, aren't you?"

"Sir?"

"Some of the best pistol-shooting (I don't say all, but some) is done as you saw it. You don't consciously aim. It's like—like throwing out your hand and pointing with the forefinger. It can be done very quickly: like this! It's (what shall I call it?) a gift, a knack, a trick. You possess it, or you don't." Cheviot paused. "Is there anywhere I can wash?"

Joe the younger seized with pleasure at what he could understand.

"Just there, sir! Water laid on."

In the left-hand wall, outside the rail and beside the door to the shop, there was a brownish stone sink, with a tap above it and a short metal pump-handle beside it. The small mirror above had been polished, the thin towel on the nail was clean.

Cheviot washed his hands and face with yellow soap, pumping up the water in gushes at a time.

The beaverskin hat fitted well on his head, since the bump had begun to go down. But his body-bruises, tightening now, hurt badly when he bent over the sink.

And the worst part, he was thinking bitterly, was that this

duel—somewhere, anywhere; at some time; he didn't know!—
need never have been undertaken at all.

He had accepted Hogben's challenge only to draw Hogben
on, to make it part of a shooting-match and a wager. If he shot
better than Hogben, then Hogben and Wentworth would tell
him all they knew about Margaret Renfrew. But he need learn
nothing more about the dead woman; his case was finished.
What mattered was the duel.

If he lost Flora, after last night . . .

After last night, this morning, a few hours . . .

If he lost Flora, because of a foolish challenge and a bullet
through his brain . . .

Could that, perhaps, be the meaning of a brief but terrifying
dream?

The big white-faced clock in the shop went on ticking. It
was four minutes to nine.

Hanging the towel back on its nail, refusing to face the possibility of Flora being carried irresistibly away from him as
though in dark water, he went back to the iron rail with its long
shelf.

"Joe! If you please, Joe."

Joe the younger, who had cleaned, polished, and hung up the
last weapon used, scurried back. From the floor Cheviot took
up the green-leather case, like a writing-case with a handle, he
had brought with him from the Albany.

It was in fact a writing-case, though he had cleared out its
contents for all the exhibits he meant to display that day, if
he lived to show them. Putting the case on the shelf, he opened
it and took out the small pistol with the lozenge-shaped gold
plate let into its handle.

"Joe, have you ever seen this before?"

"Well, it's a Manton." Joe was pleased again as he examined
it. "That's our mark: you see? Before my time, but then I'm
very new. 'A.D.' Specially made, I bet."

"Yes. For a man now dead. If you have a bullet to fit this,
will you load it for me?"

"Got to clean it first, though. Look at the inside of this barrel!"

"Very well, clean it. Then load it. But make haste!"

Cheviot tapped his fingers on the shelf as he looked behind him. Not Captain Hogben, not Lieutenant Wentworth, not even Freddie Debbitt had appeared. Freddie might at least have let him know the time and place of the actual duel: and, more important, the distance.

The front of the shooting-gallery, with a large bow window on either side of the door, resembled an ordinary shop. Through the panes, each oblong set in frames of white-painted wood, he could see out into Davies Street. He could see its long lines of stone hitching-posts, as everywhere else, and its iron tethering-rails. Nothing else.

The flighty October weather, alternately dazzling with sun or dark with cloud, floated its flash and shadow over the skylight. A smell of decaying earth clung to the gallery and to the street.

Joe, by the left-hand wall, was loading the small pistol. He poured in powder, to an exact measure, from one of the sealed metal flasks. He greased and dropped in the tiny pellet, from one of the various-sized bullet-boxes on the wall. Using a small wad torn from a newspaper, Joe carefully folded it, pressed and tamped down with a ramrod.

"Where shall I put up the wafer, sir?"

"This time, Joe, I need no wafer. I am only firing anywhere at the wall."

The hammer clicked back. There was a light, stinging crack. Instead of studying the iron back-wall, Cheviot leaned over the barrier and seized Joe's arm.

"This is not large," he indicated the pistol. "But you smelled smoke? There's still a sharp and distinct smell of it?"

" 'Course there is!" cried Joe. His voice went up. "There allus is!"

"Good. Now fetch me the bullet, please."

"Sir?"

"The bullet I just fired. Bring it to me."

Joe clumped back to the target-wall. His feet rattled among

fallen and misshapen bullets. He studied them, picked up one, and returned.

"Take care, sir. It's still hot."

Cheviot did not care if it burnt his fingers. The explosion of powder had burnt black that twisted pellet, driving its grains into soft lead and covering it. He nodded, putting away the bullet in the writing-case, and taking out a leather-covered book.

"Joe, I am neither mad nor drunk. I have cause for what I do. Be good enough to read a dozen lines: here. And another six lines: here."

There was a pause, under the swift-moving, lightening-and-darkening sky.

"Well, sir," said Joe, "what's o'clock? It's plain enough."

"But the weapon? In my stupidity, at first, I never thought it had yet been invented."

"Not invented?" exclaimed Joe. "Why, Mr. Cheviot, we've had it for years and years and years! Didn't you see the King's coronation procession eight—no, nine—years ago?"

"No. I—I was from home."

"Well, *I* was only a nipper. But it put my father in poor spirits for days. I was no better, though I couldn't tell why. Crowds in the streets, everywhere, but not a cheer for the King. All quiet."

"Yes?"

"The state-coach was beautiful. Like a dream. I never saw the King before or since, 'cos he won't come to London. But he was so big and bloated you couldn't believe him. He kept his eyes half-shut up, as though he didn't care. He did care, though. He would shift round and round, angry as fire, 'cos people didn't huzza. Anyways! Don't you remember the bullet-hole in the glass of the state-coach window? And, first off, nobody could tell how it had come there?"

"Yes! I seem to have read . . . no matter. Go on."

"Not invented?" exclaimed Joe, annoyed and ashamed of himself for having been so much impressed. "Why, sir, I've got one of 'em here!"

"You've got one? May I see it?"

Suddenly assuming his father's air, Joe opened a little gate in the barrier and marched out.

"Be pleased," he said, "to step into the shop."

The white-faced clock ticked more loudly there. The atmosphere, of oil and wood, was pleasant to breathe amid the gunracks. Though there were some few rifles, most of them were single-barrelled sporting-guns, their barrels polished and their wooden stocks a new, glossy brown. Joe reached up among them . . .

Bang!

Cheviot had been too preoccupied to hear horses in the street. What he heard then was the heavy slam of the street-door to the shooting-gallery, as three men strode in.

"Put it back!" Cheviot said quickly to Joe Manton. "Put it back in the rack!"

In the open doorway to the shop stood Captain Hugo Hogben.

Like Lieutenant Wentworth, a little way behind him, Hogben did not wear his uniform. He wore black with white linen, a hat stuck on rakishly, and a cloak over his arm. The other two wore ordinary clothes, though Freddie Debbitt's waistcoat would have shamed the rainbow. Hogben's little eyes turned away.

"The fellow's here," he said to Wentworth, over his shoulder. "Been practising, I see."

Not once did he look directly at Cheviot, or speak to him, even when they stood full-face. Hogben's expression, between the feathery black side-whiskers, was impassive except for a very slight sneer.

"Hullo, Joe," he said. "It's a match for a thousand guineas. Now where's the fellow's money?"

He swung round and strode back into the gallery.

Freddie, moving past him and past Wentworth, came hurrying into the shop. He nodded towards Manton the younger, indicating that Joe should go on into the gallery, and Joe did so. Freddie, in something of a dither, addressed Cheviot in a low voice.

"Dash it all, Jack! Where have you been? Looked everywhere for you. After all! Got to tell you the terms of the—meetin', haven't I?"

"Where is it?"

"Just beyond old Vauxhall Gardens. T'other side the river, by Vauxhall Bridge. North-east there's an imitation Greek temple, and a flat space with trees all round it. Know the place?"

"Yes," replied Cheviot, who didn't. "At what distance do we fire?"

"Twenty paces." Freddie gulped a little, eyeing his companion, because this was much shorter than the usual distance. "Agreed?"

"Agreed. The time?"

"Five o'clock this evening."

"In the *evening?*" That took him aback; for some reason Cheviot drew out his watch and opened it. He looked out of the shop-window. "I never heard of a meeting in the evening. Besides! Let's see: today is the thirty-first of October. . . ."

"All Hallows' Eve," said Freddie, trying to make a small joke. "Eh? When ghosts walk, and evil spirits ride the wind."

"At five o'clock, Freddie, it will be nearly dark. How are we to see each other?"

"I know, I know!" Freddie sounded querulous. "But those are Hogben's terms: conveyed through Wentworth, of course. Never been done before; but nothing in the code against it. We looked to see. Deuce take it, Jack, why are you worried?"

"Did I say I was worried?"

"No, but—" Incautiously, Freddie's voice soared up. "Damme, man, you're the better shot!"

From the gallery adjoining, addressed to empty air, Hogben's voice called out.

"Let the fellow come in here," it sneered, "and try to prove that."

"Steady, Jack!" cried Freddie.

And Freddie was right. He must never again lose his temper with this Guards officer: not a fraction of an inch. Cheviot loosened his tense shoulders, nodded, and followed Freddie into the gallery.

There, looking out of one of the big bow windows towards the street, he saw Flora sitting in a carriage drawn up at the kerb.

The bay horses were harnessed to an open carriage: low-built, of gilded dark lacquer and white upholstery. Flora, in a short fur jacket, her hands in a muff, an uptilted bonnet white-framing her hair, caught sight of him.

Flora pressed her fingers to her mouth, then threw them out towards him. Her eyes and lips said the rest.

Cheviot lifted his hat and bowed, hoping to return the message with his gaze. He dared not look at her for more than a second or two, or it would have unsteadied his aim. He had not expected her; it was a shock from which he turned away.

The preparations, under Hogben's loud-voiced orders, were nearly ready.

Joe Manton had loaded six duelling-pistols, setting each down on the shelf just two feet apart. It was impossible to compare them in any way to modern revolvers; the round bullet weighed about two ounces. Then Joe took up the box of "wafers."

These wafers, of the heavy material which afterwards they would call cartridge-paper, were white in colour, round, and something over two inches in diameter. On the back of each was a light coating of glue.

Carrying a wet rag in one hand and the wafer-box in the other, Joe went to the black target-wall. He wiped the wall clean of paper-bits. Turning back and forth to measure distance, he moistened the backs of six wafers. He banged them with his fist to a wall as thick as Vulcan's iron door. Like the pistols, they were each two feet apart, shoulder-high.

As Joe returned, those wafers became white and staring spots on the black. But, at thirty-six paces, they looked very tiny.

"Now, then!" said Hogben, stamping his feet as though about to begin a race. He addressed Lieutenant Wentworth. "A thousand guineas. Where's the fellow's money?"

Wentworth, whose appearance out of uniform seemed even odder than Hogben's, stood straight in astonishment. Finally he saw his companion was serious.

"Hogben," he said, "permit me to tell you that I'll not suffer such behaviour much longer. There's no need for this. In any wager, no gentleman is expected to—"

"Where's the fellow's *money?*"

Without a word Cheviot went to the left-hand edge of the shelf, behind which Joe Manton was standing almost against the wall. Mainly in banknotes, but with a number of gold sovereigns and some silver, he counted out the money beside Joe's elbow.

Still without speaking, he returned to stand beside Freddie with his back to the window.

Hogben cast off his cloak and threw it aside. For the first time he looked at Cheviot.

"Now, fellow!" And he jerked his head towards the shelf. "Shoot first."

Suddenly Cheviot took a step forward. Freddie, seeing the look on his face, leaped in front of him.

"Toss a coin! That's fair. Toss a coin!"

"As you please, Mr. Debbitt," agreed Wentworth, fishing a florin out of his waistcoat pocket. "Hogben, you were challenged to this match. It's your call: cry it."

"Heads," said Hogben, as the coin spun high in the air.

"Tails," Wentworth announced, bending over it as it rattled down. "What's your will, Mr. Cheviot?"

"Let *him* shoot first."

Hogben, unruffled, settled his hat on his head. He took up the first pistol on the left-hand end. There was a muffled melodious click as he drew back the hammer to full-cock. He turned sideways, setting his feet into position.

The clock in the shop ticked loudly. No one must move, no one must utter a word of congratulation for a good shot or a word of condolence for a bad.

Hogben did not swagger. With his mind on the money, he was quiet and prudent. He took his time, which he could never have done in a duel. His right arm lifted, lowered, and straightened. He waited until the skylight grew bright on that tiny wafer.

Whack!

A streak of fire, a report echoed back in iron concussion. The wafer, struck dead-centre, flew to pieces or disintegrated in flame.

In a leisurely way Hogben put down the first pistol and moved on to the second.

His second shot clipped the upper edge of the wafer; it split, with tearing edges, but still stuck to the wall as the bullet clattered down and rolled.

His third shot was a complete miss.

The flattened bullet freakishly bounced back and bumped along the floor halfway towards those who watched. Hogben stood for a moment with his head down, the black hairs at the back of his neck bristling over the collar, but still unruffled. Acrid smoke-haze thickened round them; he waited until it had lifted.

With his fourth bullet he got more than an edge of the target. His fifth and sixth shots were straight on the wafer. In fact, the sixth wafer flashed into flame as it vanished.

Hogben put down the last pistol, straightening his shoulders still more.

"There!" he said jauntily, with one eye on the notes and gold. "Beat *that*, fellow."

It was first-class shooting. Everyone knew it. But no one said anything, as Hogben washed his hands and face at the sink, and Joe Manton jabbed and scratched with his wet cloth to clean the target-wall. He put up six new wafers.

Whistling between his teeth, Captain Hogben lounged with arms folded. Joe began the business of cleaning and reloading the six pistols. It seemed to take an interminable time, while the clock ticked and Hogben whistled "A Frog He Would."

"Your turn, Mr. Cheviot," said Lieutenant Wentworth.

Cheviot's throat felt dry. He did not look out at Flora. Freddie touched his arm; he hesitated, and walked to the barrier at the left-hand side.

Whereupon Freddie, despite the rules, jumped and cried aloud to his Maker.

Whack!—Whack!—Whack!—Whack!—Whack!—Whack!

Cheviot, in fact, was not moving and firing as fast as it seemed to his startled companions. But the stunning concussions rolled back. The black-powder smoke, spurting and clouding, blotted out heads, faces, and the barrier as well. Six shots were fired in as many seconds.

In the street, bay horses stirred and clattered. Cheviot put down the last pistol and joined Freddie in the window. Smoke presently lifted, gushing out of skylight and window.

Each of the six wafers, shot squarely in the middle, had burnt or disappeared. Except for a few white adhering bits, and a few bits floating up with the smoke, the target-wall was as clean as when Joe had last wiped it.

The earnest-minded Wentworth, who had been regarding Hogben in a thoughtful way, spoke very politely to Freddie.

"I think, Mr. Debbitt, there can be no doubt your principal has won the match?"

"N-no! N-no! Deuce take it, none at all!"

"Very well." Wentworth turned to Cheviot. "Sir, we agreed to give you certain information—"

But Cheviot, coughing smoke out of his throat, stopped him.

"Sir, this information is no longer necessary to me. I absolve you from giving it."

"That's good. That's damn good!" said Hogben, and laughed. "Because you wouldn't have got it anyway."

Wentworth's fair complexion flushed red.

You might have thought such shooting would have taken down the gallant Captain a little. At very least it meant that a duel at twenty paces would be fatal to them both. But Hogben remained as loftily superior as ever.

"Oh, I keep my promises," he said, plucking up his cloak from the floor and throwing it round his shoulders. "You've made the mistake, fellow. I said I'd *give* information. I didn't say who I'd give it to, remember? I didn't say to *you*."

Here he opened his eyes wide, pleased at his own cunning, and laughed again.

"I'll give it fast enough to your superior officers, What's-their-names, at Whitehall Place. I say, Wentworth. You've arranged with Debbitt for the time and place of the meeting?"

"Yes."

"We're usin' my pistols?"

"Stop!" said Freddie, seizing at his own smudged face. "I forgot to mention—"

"Any pistols," Cheviot interrupted curtly, and went over to wash at the sink.

"Then that's settled, fellow," grinned Hogben, "and *you're* settled." He shouldered towards the door. "Coming, Wentworth?"

"No."

"Coming, Debbitt?"

"Yes, yes! That's to say, not with you. Got no horse. 'Nother appointment. Jack, old fellow! Congratulations, and shake hands. There!" Freddie lowered his voice. "No doubt about this evening. You'll wing him. Meet you there. Goodbye!"

Outside the window, Flora was standing up in the carriage and contemplating Cheviot uncertainly. He waved and smiled at her as he finished washing.

The door slammed as Hogben strode out. He mounted a white horse and galloped south towards Berkeley Square. Freddie followed him. Stopping only to lift his hat, bow deeply to Flora, and pay her (it seemed) flowery compliments, he hurried north towards Oxford Street.

With no notion of the thunderbolt to fall in the next few seconds, Cheviot paid the modest charges asked by Joe for the use of the gallery, and received Joe's compliments. Leaving Joe sweating with relief, he retrieved the green writing-case from where he had left it below the barrier.

Lieutenant Wentworth had also drifted towards the sink, examining a grimy face in the looking-glass above. Cheviot, murmuring something polite to him, opened the front door.

"Good day, sir!" called Joe Manton the younger. "I thought, for a while, there'd be trouble here. So help me Harry, I did!"

Abruptly Wentworth yanked down the metal handle. Water splashed into the sink, and out over his clothes. His face, reflected in the mirror, was twisted into a look nobody would have cared to see.

"Mr. Cheviot," he said, with his countenance smoothed out again, "may I have a word with you on a matter of the most vital import?"

18

The Trap by Vauxhall Gardens

The door was partly open. The air, though tinged with autumn decay, was mild and mellow. Cheviot held the door open.

"Yes? What is it?"

He turned back with reluctance. Flora, whose fear of the proprieties would not let her step down from the carriage and enter a shooting-gallery, made a mouth of impatience. Cheviot's head ached; he had had less than half an hour's sleep, and a terrifying dream.

"Sir," said Lieutenant Wentworth, "it may be that I betray a trust. Or doubt a friend. But it is my duty to speak out. Did you mark nothing strange in Hogben's manner?"

Cheviot made a gesture with the writing-case.

"Frankly, sir," he said, "I grow weary of Captain Hogben. Even if we kill each other in the duel, as seems likely—"

"In my opinion," said Wentworth, "there will be no duel."

"*What?*"

They were now alone in the gallery. At first mention of that word "duel," flat and ominous, Joe Manton slid out from the gate in the barrier and disappeared into the shop.

Wentworth splashed water on his face, dried it without troubling about soap, and moved closer. Out of uniform he seemed less a soldier than, say, a student: correct, formal, yet far less haughty, like a man who has gained much experience overnight.

"What do you tell me?" Cheviot demanded. "No duel? No—no danger?"

"I did not say that. There may be very great danger. For you."

"But Hogben . . .?"

"Oh, Hogben will risk nothing. There are many who will tell you that he never gives fair play."

Flora had said that. Cheviot looked out of the window. Flora stood holding at her hat, the wind whipping her skirt against her knees, while her lips formed the words, "What is it? Why do you stay?"

"But what can Hogben do?" Cheviot insisted. "You yourself will be there, I take it? And my own second?"

"Yes, if Hogben is there. I can tell you no more, sir; I don't know; I only suspect. I have tried to be the man's friend, but it won't do. If we are not there—"

"Yes?"

"Someone else may meet you in the twilight. And Hogben is much desirous of your death."

Cheviot, realizing he had forgotten his cloak, fetched it from the ledge of the bow-window. The open door creaked and swayed. Hogben's image rose up, grinning, still with all the honours and an ace of trumps up his sleeve.

"Someone else may meet you in the twilight." The twilight of All Hallows' Eve.

"Lieutenant Wentworth," said Cheviot, twining the cloak round him and with his hand again on the knob of the door, "I thank you deeply for your warning."

He bowed, closed the door after him, and hurried across to Flora.

Even while he sprang up the step, and Flora made room for him to sit down, neither of them would speak what was uppermost in both their minds. True, Flora began: "What time did you leave me this morning?" but swallowed it back after four words as she noted the stolid back of Robert, the coachman. There were no footmen up behind.

"I have heard," she said instead, "you were an expert pistol-shot. I loathe to watch even practice. But how you showed it against Captain Hogben!" Proud, intensely happy and yet uneasy, she added: "There—there was no quarrel with him, I hope?"

"None whatever, as you saw."

"But I heard nothing, dearest! Except the shots."

"There was little else to hear."

"I thought," Flora said eagerly, and nodded towards a wicker hamper on the floor, "we could go for a drive into the country, if it pleased you? There is food and wine in the hamper there. And we could be from London all day?"

"Yes! I must visit Scotland Yard, but only briefly. What should you say, Flora, to somewhere past Vauxhall Gardens?"

"The very place!" Flora's eyes shone. "To be sure, the Gardens are closed for the season. And none but the vulgar people have gone there since my grandparents' time, though they still have fireworks and balloon-ascents."

"Flora, don't use those words!"

She was appalled. "Don't use . . . what words?"

" 'Vulgar people.' It is time we understood—!" He gulped and checked himself.

"Jack! Have I offended you?"

"No, no! You could never do that; I spoke from vapours; pardon me. There is a Greek temple, I think, north-east of the gardens?"

"Oh, there is!" She lifted her voice. "You heard, Robert?"

"My lady," said the coachman. "I heard."

The carriage clopped away towards Berkeley Square, with the mild air in their faces under a changing sky. From under the short brown fur jacket, its seams outlined in blue-and-white, Flora slipped her arm through Cheviot's. Because she wished so much to speak of themselves, as he did, she would not do it.

"To Scotland Yard, you said?" she went on with unnatural brightness. "I daresay it's all those people you captured at Vulcan's. You never told me, you know. But all sorts of rumours are going round, and the most tremendous praise for you."

"For *me?*"

"Well, and for your police too."

"Ah, that's better! That's what I hoped!"

"But do tell me! If the police attack a gaming-house, aren't the punters supposed to be as guilty as those who keep the house? Aren't they arrested too?"

"In theory, yes."

"And yet they say you didn't arrest any of the punters! You shook them by the hand, and congratulated each on his prowess as a warrior, and assured them their names would never be mentioned in the affair. Is that true?"

Cheviot laughed. It loosened his taut nerves to roar with laughter.

"My dear, could I arrest those who had assisted me?" he pointed out. "Besides, it gave me a helpful suggestion. You should have seen Inspector Seagrave and Sergeant Bulmer in that broil. As one blackleg after another went down under a truncheon—"

"Not *all* of it, please!"

"—then Seagrave or Bulmer would haul the leg up to a sitting position, and cry, 'Here's Jimmy So-and-so; he's wanted for housebreaking,' or 'Here's Tom Crack-'em-Down: highway robbery, arson, God knows what.' I should have seen it before then: Vulcan had drawn in half the fraud-and-flash world to pack the house. When we rolled 'em downstairs into wagons—"

"Don't laugh! It is not funny!"

"Darling Flora, but it *is* funny. I was able to assure the punters this was no gambling raid, but the biggest haul of known criminals in years. Which it was. B, C, and D Divisions had to open their cells to accommodate 'em all. That's why I was so late."

"Yes. You were late."

The carriage had swept through Berkeley Square, where nursemaids in fantastic tall caps pushed perambulators in the garden under foliage still yellow-green. It had rattled down Berkeley Street, and left into the tumult of Piccadilly.

Flora, deep-dreaming, spoke again.

"Vulcan!" she muttered. "Vulcan and that woman of his! Jack, what . . .?"

"That was not pleasant. He's in a cell now."

"Then I don't wish to hear a word of it. No; stop; tell me all the same."

"The woman we released. But Vulcan had been—well, put to sleep, in handcuffs, in his office upstairs. By the time I found the key to the jewel-drawers (Kate de Bourke dropped the key-ring in the gallery), Vulcan was up and trying to destroy his ledger even in handcuffs. I never guessed he was carrying a pistol."

"And that's where you got the bullet-hole in your sleeve. *Isn't it?*"

Cheviot's mirth had left him.

"That's not important. No," he repeated, "I never guessed he was carrying a pistol. He never tried to draw it when we fought across the table. Vulcan, in his own twisted way, is a sportsman. But Hogben—!"

"What *of* Hogben?" Flora asked very quietly. "There is something more, as I well know. Surely it would be easier for me if I heard?"

"Don't trouble your head about Hogben. He has some ace of trumps up his sleeve, or thinks he has. I wish I knew what it was. That's all."

He would say no more. The carriage turned down the slope of the Haymarket at its junction with Piccadilly, left into Cockspur Street, and down Whitehall.

"Flora, may I give an order to your coachman? Robert! Be good enough to stop at number four Whitehall Place. Don't drive into the yard; pull up at the gas-lamp outside it."

"Very good, sir."

And then, to Flora, as he got down from the carriage outside the red-brick house:

"I shall not be a long time. Afterwards, I hope, we can both laugh."

But he was a long time. Flora, cradling her muff, felt the minutes as hours as she waited. The coachman's back was straight and unmoving. All about the carriage a rumble and rattle of wheels, the shouting of those who drove them, beat against a woman torn between intense happiness and intense apprehension.

It was, actually, more than an hour before he returned: apologetic but grim-faced as he climbed into the carriage, and gave the signal for Robert to go on.

"I am afraid," he said, "you must stay by me until this evening."

"But what else?" Flora cried. "That is no penance. Are we to—to laugh?"

"No, unfortunately. I should not keep you by me, yet perhaps that may be best. You see, I have promised to deliver Margaret Renfrew's murderer by eight o'clock tonight."

The carriage, with its deep upholstery, swayed and rattled faster.

"And," he added, "I am excused one duty. Should there be any riot outside Pinner's, I need not command the division."

"Jack," a stifled voice answered him, "I beg you to cease speaking riddles. Riot?"

"There is a tailor, it seems, named Pinner. I think that yesterday," and he pressed his hands over his eyes, "someone mentioned a tailor with a taste for making inflammatory political speeches. I've just heard of him from Colonel Rowan and Mr. Mayne. His shop is in—Parliament Street, they said."

So far as confusion mattered, he was in a worse state than Flora.

As the carriage rapidly bowled south, gone was every vestige of Whitehall as he seemed to recall it in his other life.

Ahead loomed up a triangular wedge of buildings, smoke-clouded from piled chimney-stacks, dividing it into two streets. The right-hand street, he decided, could only be King Street since the left-hand one, along the river, must be Parliament Street.

He was right. Robert reined the horses left, where there were few wheeled vehicles and the house-fronts showed ancient, darkened, of stone or brick crumbling away. Most were shops—a

tallow-chandler's, a mirror-maker's, a butcher's—amid some
private houses which bore no brass plates or polished bell-han-
dles.

"A crazy ruin," he muttered. "Look there!"

Across Parliament Street a small crowd had gathered round
a small man, with a big chest and a shock of white hair, who
was standing on a wooden box outside the door of a shop lettered *T. F. Pinner, Tailor and Cutter* above its window.

A policeman sauntered on the left-hand side of the street,
eyeing the crowd but not interfering. The little man with the
big chest and the white hair, a bottle of gin stuck in the pocket
of his surtout, had worked himself into a fury.

"Don't you want the Corn Laws repealed?" he was shouting.
"You can't argue with starvation. *They* can't argue with it. Is
there one man among you," his arm went up, fist flourishing,
"who hasn't starved or seen his family starve?"

A voice yelled, "No!" The crowd, small enough indeed, moved
and shuffled. It spilled out across the roadway. Robert's back
stiffened; his whip-hand drew back and up.

"Drive on!" said Cheviot, standing up in the carriage. "Don't
touch anyone. Drive on!"

"Then the only way to get it," bawled the orator's voice,
"is by a Reform Bill and a Reformed Parliament. The facts, the
true facts . . ."

They clattered past, the voice beginning to fade. Someone
screamed at them; no more.

"But, Jack," protested Flora, who was surprised rather than
distressed, "this happens every day. Where is our concern in it?"

"Not today or tonight, at least. All the same—"

He was still standing up in the swaying carriage, holding the
handrail behind the driver. He could not go on speaking, because he was gripped uncannily by that past of which he was a
part.

On the right, serene beyond antiquity, rose the towers of the
Abbey. On the left, beyond Westminster Bridge, he saw another
tower: squat and square, beside a huddle of carved and painted
buildings stretching towards the massive stone of Westminster

Hall. In five years all of this on the left, except Westminster Hall, would be gutted by fire, and perish. He was looking at the old Houses of Parliament, with a flag flying from the square tower to show Parliament was sitting.

And, glimpsed past Westminster Bridge and the square tower, flowed the Thames: too close without embankments, brown-coloured from mud and sewage, the kindly river that would yet bring the cholera.

"Jack," said Flora, "what on earth are you gabbling about?"

He had not known he was speaking at all. He sat down beside her and took her arm.

"Forgive me. That drunken tailor, I daresay, seemed to you oafish and ridiculous? And yet he's right. It will come about."

"You? Preaching reform?"

"Flora, I preach nothing. I only regret the unhappiness I have caused you, and may still cause you, because of what I cannot explain. Meanwhile, we go to the country. For God's sake, if we can, let's forget all else."

It seemed that they did forget. When they crossed Vauxhall Bridge, iron-built and comparatively new, the Surrey side of the river opened with a drowsy beauty of autumn. No life stirred in Vauxhall Gardens: the winding walks, the bandstand, the two statues of Apollo and one (a strange companion) of Handel.

But it was pleasanter to be alone. The carriage presently reached an open space, surrounded by trees. Against the trees at the back of it gleamed the thin white marble of a small semi-circular temple with a statue inside. Since the temple was after the Greek fashion, the statue must be given her Greek name of Aphrodite.

Robert swung the horses round and came to a stop near the temple. He wound the reins round the whip-stock, put on the drag, and climbed down to make Flora a formal little speech.

Her ladyship, he said, doubtless would not require him for an hour or two. Near the entrance to Vauxhall Gardens, he said, there was a public-house, the Dog and Vulture, and might he beg leave of absence for a time?

Flora made a little speech meaning that he could. They hardly heard his footsteps in the grass as he went away.

"And now, sir," declared Flora, with a mock-prim air but a deadly coldness at her heart, "you will be kind enough to expound all the hints you have been giving. Do you wish to drive me mad? I . . . What's wrong?"

Cheviot had been looking at the sky.

"The time," he answered without thinking. "It must be well into the afternoon. Later than I thought."

It would have been easier to look at his watch. But he dared not do it.

"The time?" Flora echoed indignantly. "Does the time matter?"

"No, no, of course not! Except—"

"Do you wish to eat or drink?" asked Flora, haughtily tapping the hamper with her foot. "There is much here, if you find my company so tedious."

"Stop that! Don't coquette. This isn't the time for it."

"Oh, I know! But last night, or rather this morning, was so—so—"

"Yes." He spoke with some violence. "It was perfect and complete. Perfect and complete, I say again. That's why I must ask you: Flora, have you and I ever been married?"

"*Married?*"

"Yes. I am quite serious."

"Well, really! What a question! If—if we ever have," cried Flora, "I must have made vows at the altar in a dream. Besides, you—you never asked me."

"You're sure of that? *You* never thought it? Because I did. When I crept downstairs this morning, and let myself out without rousing the house, I wondered . . ."

"What *I* wondered," she said, "is how you could have left without awakening me. I always wake when you do. I put out my arm, and you were not there. It was dreadful. It seemed as though you had gone forever."

"Flora, stop! Say no more—just for a moment!"

He lowered his head. Beside the wicker hamper stood the

green writing-case. But he was not thinking even of that. The trees, which yet retained green in tattered foliage amid yellows and reds, whispered faintly round the Greek temple.

"No," he said in a baffled kind of way, "it can't be true. You are a prisoner in this age, and have always been of this age. Whereas I . . ."

"Yes?"

"Listen! Only three nights ago I promised to tell you all. I must do so, and yet you will not credit me. Just as at Lady Cork's, you will shrink back and think me mad-drunk though my eyes are clear and my speech unstumbling. . . ."

"If you told me *what?*"

"Still I must say it," he insisted, without seeming to hear her, "because there are dreams and premonitions inside the mind, perhaps even inside the soul. And I think, Flora, that soon we shall be separated from each other."

"No!"

Then she was in his arms, but not in the way of love-making. As he held her, it was more like a whispered and desperate quarrel.

"But what could separate us? You mean—death?"

"No, my dear. Not death. And yet, in a fashion, something like that."

Flora cried out in protest. Whereupon, while he clung to her even more fiercely, there ensued one of those endless, aching scenes in which each person misinterprets the other's words; and it cannot be set right. Flora maintained he said he was going to die; and he retorted that he hadn't said anything of the kind. On and on it went, while the shadows deepened and heart-sickness grew.

"Then be pleased," Flora sobbed, "to say what you do mean!"

"Only this, as I have tried to explain. At some hour soon, at what seems an hour of victory and triumph, the dimension called time will move and change. All will dissolve. All! What is it about 'the unsubstantial pageant'? Never mind! But on this occasion it won't be easy. It will be terrifying."

"I don't understand! I don't!"

"A dream I had—"

"Oh, dreams. Everybody knows dreams go by contraries!"

"One day, my dear, they will make dreams rather more complicated than that. No: perhaps I shouldn't have said a dream." He drew his breath in deeply. "Very well. You had better hear the truth. When you once said I seemed like somebody out of another world, that was truer than you knew. I *am* . . ."

"My lady! Sir!"

Those two, locked away in their own world, had failed to hear the loud fit of coughing which had been going on at a distance for some seconds. When Robert the coachman felt that his tact would only strangle him, he gave a respectful hail instead.

Both of them lifted heads from a world lost.

A light, dazzling into Cheviot's eyes, made him blink and stare round. The light was lowered. But shadows were so heavy that he could scarcely see Robert, with a lantern in his hand.

The air felt misty and damp. The lines of the Greek temple glimmered white.

"Forgive me, my lady," Robert called respectfully. "But I thought you'd wish me to return. It's twenty-five minutes past five."

Cheviot's hand went to his watch-pocket. "Past *five?*"

"Yes, sir. Much more than that, too. That was the time I left the Dog and Vulture, and it's a bit of a walk from there."

This was the point at which they heard hoof-beats on the road by which Robert had come from the pub. Horses, more than one and at the gallop, pounded hard and pounded closer. He thought there were three of them. The wink of a swinging lantern, held in the right hand of the leading horseman, brushed greenish-yellow foliage.

Then Hogben would be here, after all. The other horsemen must be Lieutenant Wentworth and Freddie Debbitt. On the other hand, if Hogben had sent someone else . . .

"Robert," he said quietly, "please get up on the box and drive Lady Drayton home as soon as may be."

"Robert," said Flora in a high but calm voice, "you will do nothing of the sort. We remain here."

The leading horseman swept into the clearing, with the others behind him. They rode lathered horses, blowing through the nostrils. As the first horseman held his lantern high, Cheviot saw what he had never expected to see.

True, the third horseman was Lieutenant Wentworth. But the second was Sergeant Bulmer. The first was Inspector Seagrave, with the silver lace glinting at his collar.

"Sir," croaked out Seagrave, holding the light, "can this coachman of yours drive fast? He'll need to."

"What's this?" Cheviot demanded. "What are you doing here? I expected to meet Captain Hogben. I—I have an appointment for five o'clock."

Seagrave and Bulmer exchanged glances.

"Then *that's* it!" the latter blurted. "Well, sir, Captain Hogben made another appointment for five o'clock. As like as not, to be sure you'd be here and out of the way. His appointment was with the Colonel and Mr. Mayne at Scotland Yard."

"With . . .?"

"Sir! He's denounced Lady Drayton for murdering Miss Renfrew, and you for helping her. He's done that already, he and a Miss Louise Tremayne. They say they saw Lady Drayton fire; and the pistol fell out of her muff; and you hid it under a lamp. And they've got Mr. Mayne mor'n half convinced!"

Cheviot stood up in the carriage. His mind went back, vividly, to that passage at Lady Cork's house on the night of the murder. He remembered his impression that one of the orange-and-gold doors to the ballroom had opened and closed, with what might have been black hair in the opening . . .

He had been seen. He had been seen after all, and by Hugo Hogben.

19

Counter-Stroke

In the Whitehall Place office of Colonel Rowan and Mr. Mayne, at a quarter past six, question and answer had reached their height.

"You are prepared, Captain Hogben," asked Mr. Mayne, "to sign the statement of which two fair copies are now being made by our clerk?"

"I am."

Mr. Richard Mayne showed neither satisfaction nor dissatisfaction; he was a lawyer; but his voice almost purred. He sat behind the scarred table, with the red-glass lamp burning in the red weapon-hung room. Colonel Rowan, however, stood by the table with a faint angry flush under his cheekbones.

"Be very sure, Captain," he said curtly. "Both Mr. Mayne and I are magistrates. This is a deposition under oath."

Hogben, in front of the table with his arms carelessly folded, eyed him up and down. It was evident that he did not think much of a Colonel who had commanded the 52nd Light Infantry. Hogben's face showed as much.

"What's the good of the clack?" he asked, opening his little eyes wide. "I said it, didn't I?"

"And you, Miss Tremayne?" Colonel Rowan inquired with much politeness. "You are prepared to sign a statement, too?"

Louise Tremayne, in a padded chair well back from them all and towards the windows, had come to a state not far from hysterics. After all, she was little more than nineteen. Clasping a muff of silver-fox fur against a silver-fox jacket, she raised a pale face in which the hazel eyes seemed enormous.

Even her turban, of dove-grey silk, added to that child-like appearance. And yet something stubborn and tenacious, something perhaps inherited from him she called her dear, good, kind papa, kept her from giving way to her feelings.

"I vow to you, as I have vowed before," Louise told them, without blurring a syllable, "that I did *not* see Lady Drayton . . . well! I did not see her fire a shot."

The last three words horrified her, as though she could not imagine herself speaking them.

"Not that, no!" she insisted. "Hugo saw that. The rest of it I saw with my own eyes, and I vow it. Indeed, I tried to tell Mr. Cheviot yesterday. But I did not see Lady Drayton k-kill anyone."

"Careful, m'dear!" Hogben dropped his arms and spoke threateningly. "You said to me—"

"I didn't!"

"Captain!" And Colonel Rowan snapped it like an order. Hogben stiffened by instinct, then sneered when he remembered. "If you please," Colonel Rowan added, "we will not have this young lady intimidated."

Mr. Mayne, seated at his ease and very bland, held up a deprecating hand.

"Come, my dear Rowan," he said. "There has been no intimidation here. We have seen to that. But there is evidence, I fear; yes, a great deal of evidence. Do you now so greatly favour our own Mr. Cheviot?"

"We have not heard his side of it."

"True. True. But he lied to us, my dear Rowan. Can you doubt it? Do you imagine Captain Hogben and Miss Tremayne have spun this story out of whole cloth, especially since every word they say confirms what I have already suggested?"

Colonel Rowan hesitated, and Mr. Mayne went on.

"Not one word did *he* say about that pistol or any other pistol. He lied to us, in the most serious matter which can affect a police-officer. As a barrister—"

"As a barrister, then, you already prejudice the case."

"Pardon me, Rowan. It is you who prejudice it. You like Mr. Cheviot because he is of your own sort and kind. He is well-mannered. He is quiet. He is modest—to you. He never strikes until first he is struck; and then, I grant, he strikes back quickly and hard."

"Another English principle," Colonel Rowan said politely, "which I commend to your attention."

"*But*," replied Mr. Mayne, tapping the table, "he is a man of notoriously loose morals. Either he shielded his mistress, Lady Drayton, who is known to have hated Miss Renfrew; or else, being himself entangled with Miss Renfrew and wishing to be rid of her, he himself planned the whole crime."

Here Mr. Mayne spread out his hands.

"I say this with evidence, Rowan. When we have fair copies of the statement—" Hearing a pen scratch, Mr. Mayne scowled and craned round. "Tush, tush, Henley, have you not yet finished making the copies in longhand?"

The green lamp was burning on the desk of the chief clerk in the corner. Behind it Mr. Henley lowered his pen.

"With all respect, sir," Mr. Henley answered in his hoarse, heavy voice, "it's not easy when my hand shakes like what it does. And, again with all respect to the Captain and his lady, this can't be true."

"Henley!"

"Mr. Mayne," said the chief clerk, "I was there!"

Alan Henley could be unobtrusive when he liked. But he could seldom hide his strong, forceful personality. The heavy face with the thick reddish side-whiskers, the brown eyes glowing, was thrust out past the lamp.

"If I was there, which I was," and the pen seemed small in his fist, "I should have seen it. If a pistol dropped out of the good lady's muff, and Superintendent Cheviot hid it under a lamp, wouldn't I ha' seen it?"

"No." Hogben, the inarticulate, got out his words fast enough.

"And I'll tell you why, clerkie. Your back was turned. You were shifting a dead 'un over on her back, face up. Weren't you, fellow? Yes or no?"

"Yes or no, Henley?" Mr. Mayne asked without inflection.

Beads of sweat glimmered on Mr. Henley's forehead.

"It may be," he said, "I shouldn't ha' seen that." He nodded towards the half-fainting Louise Tremayne. "But, as the young lady tells you, Lady Drayton fired no pistol from her muff. Why, I watched her! And the muff had no bullet-hole. And she couldn't ha' done it."

"Not even," Mr. Mayne inquired quietly, "by turning the muff quickly sideways, thus," his hands illustrated, "and firing through the opening at one end, so that there would be no burns of powder?"

"I—"

"On your oath, Henley, do you swear that could not have occurred?"

Mr. Henley began to prop himself up on his thick ebony stick. He stumbled and almost fell. His gaze shifted away and dropped.

"Well . . ." he said uncertainly.

"Then you cannot swear it?" Mr. Mayne demanded.

"No, sir, I can't swear on my oath as—"

"Then your testimony is valueless. You have only half a dozen lines to write. Sit down, my good Henley, and complete them."

A slight smile twisted Hogben's mouth, ineffable and superior, as the chief clerk slumped down and picked up the pen. It was Colonel Rowan who suddenly held up his hand.

"Listen!" he ordered.

For five or six seconds nobody spoke. There was no noise except for the dogged scratching of the chief clerk's pen. Louise Tremayne put her face in her hands. Perhaps only Colonel Rowan's quick ear had caught the faint roaring sounds very far away. In any case, he plucked up a hand-bell from the table and rang it with loud clangour.

The door to the passage was instantly opened by a sergeant, with the numeral 9 on his collar.

"Sergeant!" said Colonel Rowan. "What's the latest report from that—that small disturbance in Parliament Street?"

"Sir!" said the newcomer, saluting. "No rioting yet, sir. But the crowd's a-getting bigger. The pint is . . ."

"Yes? Continue?"

"Well, sir, it's not only that tailor-cove, Pinner. They've got more'n half a dozen speakers. As soon as our lot persuade one of 'em to shut his potato-trap, another bobs up in another door with people holding torches all round him."

"Who is in attendance, Sergeant?"

"Inspector Blaine, sir. Sergeant Crossley, too, and his constables ten to nineteen. There's complaints from the 'Ouse of Commons, sir."

Mr. Mayne interposed. "I tell you, Rowan, we can spare no more men!"

"Not from our division, perhaps." Colonel Rowan smiled coldly. "But with your permission, Mayne, C and D divisions have provided eighteen more. Sergeant! They may join the others. No violence unless it be unavoidable."

"Yes, sir."

"Sergeant!" Mr. Mayne called in a different tone. "As you do this, will you be good enough to step out into the street and fetch in two witnesses for a deposition? Any passers-by will do."

"Very good, sir."

As the harassed officer opened the door to go out, there were sounds of hurry and turmoil in the passage. Evidently the police were active that night. Not a minute later they heard, through closed window-curtains, a carriage smash at a gallop into the yard and pull up.

Nor was it long before the sergeant, number 9, ushered in two witnesses. One was a seedy man in a battered white hat, the other a shrunken elderly gentleman on his way to the Athenaeum Club. Both were far from sweet-tempered.

"Gentlemen, gentlemen," protested Mr. Mayne, soothingly, "I shall detain you but a moment. (You have finished, Henley?

Good.) I humbly beg you, my dear sirs, merely to affix your signatures as witnesses to two copies of a document. Captain Hogben?"

Hogben scratched his signature with a bold flourish. So did the others. The copies were sealed and attested, the witnesses bustled out with as little ceremony as they had been bustled in. Mr. Mayne beamed.

"Though it is scarcely essential," he continued, "may I ask, Miss Tremayne, whether you will give Captain Hogben your muff?"

"My muff?" cried Louise.

"If you will. And let him show us how Lady Drayton held the muff, sideways, so as to fire the shot?"

"Yes!" struck in a new voice. *"By all means let him show that."*

The voice was not loud. If anything, it was quiet; too repressed, too quiet.

In the open doorway stood Superintendent John Cheviot.

His face was pale, his jaws clenched hard except when he spoke. Under his cloak he wore black, as Hogben did, except for soiled white linen and a gold watch-chain with seals. He carried by its handle what resembled a green writing-case.

But the effect of that quiet, almost agreeable, tone was so sinister that it left in the room a faint chill. Louise Tremayne repressed a scream.

Just behind him stood Flora Drayton; and, beyond her, Sergeant Bulmer. Cheviot bowed for Flora to precede him into the room. In dead silence he pushed out another padded chair, not far from Louise. With a slight nod to all the others, Flora sat down. She was more pale than Cheviot; but just as composed, her head up.

Cheviot made a slight and cryptic gesture to Sergeant Bulmer, who nodded and closed the door. Cheviot softly crossed the room to the table behind which sat Mr. Mayne. Amid the drift of papers there still lay, a sardonic reminder, Colonel Rowan's silver-handled pistol.

With a look of distaste, without speaking, Cheviot transferred it to the desk of the chief clerk. In its place he put down the green writing-case.

The eerie silence was broken at last by Mr. Mayne.

"You come rather late, Mr. Cheviot," he said.

"Yes, sir. That is true. A certain person," Cheviot answered, "took the most elaborate precautions to make sure I should not be here at all."

He turned briefly, and glanced at Hogben. Hogben laughed in his face. The laugh, behind closed teeth, clashed badly against the quiet and the hard courtesy of the two Police Commissioners.

"Surely, Mr. Cheviot," remarked Mr. Richard Mayne without expression, "it was rather brazen of you when you promised to deliver to us the murderer of Miss Renfrew by eight o'clock tonight?"

"Sir, I do not think so." Cheviot removed his cloak and hat, putting them carefully in a chair. He returned to the table. "After all, it is only a quarter to seven."

"Mr. Cheviot!" interposed Colonel Rowan, with an almost pleading note in his voice. "Captain Hogben has made a statement, now copied and attested. . . ."

"I was aware of it, sir. May I see the statement?"

Mr. Henley handed over a copy.

There was a small fire burning in the grate of the mantel-piece, beside the big moth-eaten stuffed bear with one glass eye. Nobody spoke while Cheviot slowly read the statement through. Flora Drayton, still with her head up, looked from Colonel Rowan to Mr. Mayne and to Captain Hogben; she did not look at Louise.

"I see," remarked Cheviot in the same cold, calm voice. He put down the pages on the desk. "Captain Hogben, of course, is ready to answer questions concerning what he has testified?"

He faced Hogben. Hogben, arms again folded, looked in his eyes with calmness changing to surprise.

"Questions, fellow? From *you*, fellow? Damme, not likely!"

"I fear that won't do," Colonel Rowan said quietly.

And Mr. Mayne, for all his prejudices, was iron-fair.

"Indeed it won't do!" he agreed, and rapped his knuckles. "You have accused Lady Drayton and Mr. Cheviot of a conspiracy to do murder. Pending further notice, he is still the Superintendent of this division. Should you refuse to answer his questions, your deposition becomes suspect."

"*That* fellow?" demanded Hogben, and then controlled himself. "Ask away!" he said.

Cheviot took up the statement.

"You state, here, that you saw Lady Drayton fire the shot?"

"Yes! Disprove it!"

"You further state that the weapon was a small pistol, with a lozenge-shaped plate in gold let into the handle, and bearing some initials? You saw this, you say, when it fell from Lady Drayton's muff, and I picked it up?"

"Yes!"

Cheviot unfastened the writing-case, took out the pistol belonging to Flora's late husband, and gave it to Hogben.

"Is that the pistol you saw?"

Hogben's eyes narrowed, fearing a trap.

"You need not hesitate," Cheviot said in the same bleak tone. "I acknowledge it as the pistol in Lady Drayton's muff. Do you identify it?"

"Yes!" Hogben said triumphantly, and handed it back.

"Did you smell smoke? Either at the time of the shot, or afterwards, did you smell powder-smoke?"

"No!" Hogben blurted. "Funny thing. I—" He stopped, shutting his mouth tightly and warily.

"Did you hear the shot?"

"I . . ."

"Since you refuse to answer, we will ask others who were present. Miss Tremayne: did *you* hear the shot?"

"No!" said Louise, startled. "But, to be sure, the orchestra was . . ."

"Mr. Henley! Did you hear the shot?"

"N-no, sir. As I said. But, as this young lady tells you . . ."

Cheviot turned to the two Commissioners of Police, putting the small pistol on the table.

"Mark it, gentlemen. No sound of the shot; and, which is far more important, no smell of powder-smoke. The latter fact, in my density, I failed to note at the time."

A convulsion of creaks and cracks went through Mr. Mayne's straight chair.

"Mr. Cheviot!" he said, lifting his hand. "Do you *admit* Lady Drayton killed the deceased woman with this pistol here?"

"No, sir."

"But you admit the pistol was in Lady Drayton's muff? That it fell to the floor? That you hid it under a hollow-based lamp?"

"I do, sir."

"Then you lied? You suppressed evidence?"

"I did, sir."

"Ah! And in that event," Mr. Mayne asked in a silky voice, "may I make so bold as to ask why?"

"Because it would only have misled you, as it has misled you now." Cheviot's voice, so repressed that the nerves ached for it to grow louder, was having an uncanny effect on them all. "Because that pistol had nothing whatever to do with the murder of Margaret Renfrew. Permit me to prove as much."

With no change in his expression he went to the closed door, knocked once on it with his knuckles, and returned.

The door was opened by Sergeant Bulmer, ushering in a small, bustling man, in a brightly coloured waistcoat and with dark bushy side-whiskers. His knowing eyelid gave him a man of the world's appearance, yet his pursed-up mouth indicated that never, never would he say too much on any matter.

"Mr. Henley," said Cheviot, "can you identify this gentleman?"

"Why, sir," the chief clerk returned, with a grimace, "that's the surgeon I fetched three nights ago, when you desired to have the bullet removed from the poor lady's body. That's Mr. Daniel Slurk."

Mr. Slurk gravely removed his hat and approached the table.

"I am rejoiced to see you, gentlemen," he said to the two Commissioners. He did not sound rejoiced; his tone was guarded and irritable. "Superintendent Cheviot, I may observe, has

summoned me from home at a most devilish inconvenient time.
I—"

Cheviot's gesture stopped him.

"Mr. Slurk. Three nights ago, the twenty-ninth of October,
did you go to number six New Burlington Street, and in my
presence extract a bullet from the body of Miss Margaret Renfrew?"

"I extracted a bullet from a woman's body. Yes."

"Did this bullet cause her death?"

"It did. The post-mortem examination has since proved—"

"Thank you. Could you identify the bullet?"

"If I saw it," replied Mr. Slurk, stroking his bushy whiskers
and letting droop a knowing eyelid, "yes."

Cheviot opened the writing-case again. From a piece of
paper, wrapped up and marked in ink, he took out a small pellet of round, smooth lead. It shone under the light of the red-
glass lamp as Cheviot held it out in his palm.

"Is this the bullet?"

Pause. Then Mr. Slurk nodded and handed it back.

"That's the bullet, sir," he declared, preening his whiskers.

"You are sure?"

"Sure, sir? The bullet did not strike bone; it is unflattened,
as you may remark. There is the scratch, rather like a question
mark, made by my probe. I observed it at the time. There is the
distinct marking left by my own forceps. You would wish me to
swear to it? I am cautious, sir; I must be so. Yet I would swear."

"Mr. Mayne!" said Cheviot.

Catching up the gold-mounted pistol and the small bullet, he
thrust them across the table under the barrister's nose.

"You need be no authority on pistols, Mr. Mayne," he continued. "In fact, you need never have touched one. But take
these, sir; thank you! Now try to fit the bullet into the muzzle,
as I myself did three nights ago."

Mr. Mayne instinctively jerked back. But, challenged, he
took both of them. After a pause he cleared his throat.

"This—this won't do!" he cried, with a wavering sound in

his tone. "The bullet, small as it is, is much too large to fit into the barrel of the pistol."

"Consequently," Cheviot demanded, "the bullet could not possibly have been fired from Lady Drayton's pistol?"

"No. I allow it."

For the first time Cheviot raised his voice.

"And therefore," he said, pointing to Hogben, "that man has been telling a pack of lies under oath?"

It may only have been the tension which held them, like a drumming in the ears; yet it seemed to some of them that they could hear, distantly, a very faint roaring noise. Both the women had stood up from their chairs.

Hogben, dropping his arms, glanced quickly at the open door. Sergeant Bulmer stood in the doorway, his lips drawn back from his teeth.

"One moment!" interrupted Colonel Rowan.

Throughout this Colonel Rowan, who had moved back from the table, had been listening with a look of satisfaction on his thin, handsome face. Now, however, he was frowning and biting on his lip.

"I entirely agree," he remarked, as a hush fell on the room again, "that the bullet could not have been fired from that weapon. But . . . may I see the bullet, Mayne?"

Mr. Mayne passed it to him.

"You seem to be a person of some reflection, Mr. Cheviot," the barrister said. "And, as for myself, I—I appear again to have been too hasty. Mark you, sir! This does not in any way lessen the charge against you of suppressing evidence, or . . ."

Once more Colonel Rowan interrupted.

"In my opinion," he announced, "we have here more than a question of a bullet fired from Lady Drayton's pistol. This bullet was not fired from any weapon at all."

"Oh yes, it was," said Cheviot.

Colonel Rowan drew himself up.

"I may say, I think," he replied with suave courtesy, "that I have had *rather* more experience with firearms than even yourself, Mr. Cheviot. This bullet," he held it up, "is smooth and unblackened by powder-burns."

"Exactly, sir. So I found it three nights ago."

"But any bullet, fired from any pistol," said Colonel Rowan, "is burnt black by powder grains into soft lead by the time it leaves the muzzle of the weapon!"

"Again I praise your correctness, sir," Cheviot declared in a ringing voice. He dived once more into the writing-case, and held up a tiny, flattened, black-crusted pellet. "Here, for example, is a bullet I fired from that pistol at Joe Manton's shooting gallery this morning."

"Then may I ask, with all restraint, what the devil—?"

Cheviot replaced the flattened missile in the case.

"But it is not so, Colonel Rowan, with *every* weapon," he said.

"You mock me, Mr. Cheviot!"

"No, sir. I should not mock one who has ever stood my friend. Consider, Colonel Rowan! No noise! No smell of powder-smoke! Finally, no bullet burnt black by the powder! What sort of weapon alone could have fired the shot that killed Miss Renfrew?"

Colonel Rowan stood motionless. As illumination came to him, his pale-blue eyes turned slowly. . . .

"You have it!" Cheviot said. "I confess myself blind and obtuse to it until last night, when I exposed a rigged roulette-wheel at Vulcan's gaming-house."

"Vulcan's?" asked a bewildered Mr. Mayne.

"Yes, sir. In the midst of exposing it, I realized what might also be done by the impact of a powerful spring released by the immense force of compressed air."

"Powerful spring? Compressed air?"

Cheviot took from the writing-case a leather-bound book. He flipped over its pages.

"Allow me to read two very brief passages from a volume entitled *The Fatal Effects of Gambling*—and so on, published by the firm of Messrs. Thomas Kelly, etc., in 1824. It deals with the clumsy crime of John Thurtell, who killed a blackleg named

William Weare by quite literally punching out his brains with the muzzle of a pistol. This, or the part dealing with false gambling methods, need not interest us.

"But here, in the appendix, is the testimony of a rogue named Probert. True, or false, Probert's words are illuminating. Thurtell, he says, had also intended to murder a man named Wood. Remember it: Wood!"

"But I still demand to know—" began Mr. Mayne.

Cheviot, finding his place in the book, swept on.

" 'Probert,' " he read aloud, " 'was to go home early at night, and keep the landlady and her daughter drinking belowstairs after Wood was gone to bed; and when he was supposed to be asleep, John Thurtell, disguised in a boat-cloak, was to enter the house by means of Probert's key of the street door, proceed to Wood's room, and shoot him through the heart with the air-gun.' "

The stillness in the room, despite the faint distant tumult, was like a cloying physical presence.

"An air-gun," muttered Colonel Rowan, and snapped his fingers.

"Wait!" said Cheviot.

" 'He was then,' " Cheviot went on reading, " 'to place a small pistol that had been discharged, in Wood's right hand, so that it might appear as if he had shot himself.' "

Cheviot lowered the book.

"Crime, or intended crime," he asked, "surely does go on repeating itself, does it not? Afterwards, Thurtell could have found himself an alibi."

And Cheviot snapped his fingers towards Sergeant Bulmer in the doorway.

"Now what, exactly, does an air-gun of this age look like? We find the answer on page 485. Permit me to read again!"

Over flickered the pages.

"Here we have it! 'The air-gun,' " Cheviot read, " 'resembled a knotted walking stick—' "

"A—a what?"

" 'A knotted walking stick,' " Cheviot read inexorably, " 'and

*held no less than sixteen charges. It was let off by merely press-
ing one of the knots with the finger, and the only noise was a
slight whiz, scarcely perceptible to any one who might happen
to be on the spot.'"*

Cheviot closed the book and dropped it.

"Sergeant Bulmer!" he cried. "Show us what you have found,
in the place where it must be."

Bulmer's hand reached outside the doorway. He entered the
room carrying an object which drew all eyes, and Mr. Mayne
jumped to his feet.

Cheviot pointed to it.

"We sought the explanation of an apparently impossible
crime. But there never was an impossible crime. The assassin
fired his shot in full view. With my own eyes I saw him lift the
weapon to fire, when I thought he meant only to point. If you
accept my innocence, he was the only person standing in a dead
straight line to the victim."

Drawing the breath deeply into his lungs, Cheviot faced the
two Commissioners of Police.

"The murderer, gentlemen, is your own chief clerk—Mr.
Alan Henley."

20

The End of Death-in-Waiting

To Flora Drayton, standing up on trembling legs with her hands moist from being inside the silk lining of the muff, the staring faces before her seemed to swim in a murk of red and green light.

She could not see Cheviot's face, and was glad she could not.

But clearly she saw the face of Mr. Alan Henley. Mr. Henley, his fleshy lips open and his brown eyes bulging, had turned a sickly colour from terror. He tried to prop up his stocky figure on the thin ebony stick; but he stumbled, and nearly fell face down across the desk.

Cheviot's voice, dominating them all, still rang out.

"I will offer further proof. When I first met Mr. Henley in this room three nights ago, I marked him (without suspicion, I allow) as something of a ladies' man, a dasher, a lover of good food and wine. He had bettered himself from his original beginnings, and he strove to fly higher.

"He limped, as he limps now, on that same thin ebony stick. The walking-stick-cum-air-gun, which you see in Sergeant Bulmer's hands and which was found in Mr. Henley's own locked cupboard in this house, he never dared carry at his duties here. Colonel Rowan, an experienced Army man and a sportsman as well, would at once have recognized that thick knotted cane for what it is.

"Three nights ago, when I was bidden to visit Lady Cork's

house on what seemed a matter of stolen bird-seed, he was ordered to accompany me as a shorthand writer. Had he not been so ordered, he would have suggested the same excuse to go.

"But what followed, and to which Lady Drayton herself can testify—"

Briefly Cheviot swung round towards Flora.

She could not bear to see him. He seemed coldly inhuman, the light-grey eyes wide and hard. To Flora, in her cosy and sheltered and gaslit life, it was as though someone had squeezed her heart with fingers; she could not bear to look on.

But Cheviot had turned back.

"As Lady Drayton and I left this house," he went on, "Mr. Henley was already on horseback. He must ride on well ahead of us, you see. But first he stopped by our closed carriage. Very conspicuously, in the light of a carriage-lantern, he permitted me to see the thick and knotted cane he had exchanged for his ebony one.

"If *I* recognized the disguised air-gun for what it was, his plan would have been frustrated at the beginning. But, clearly, I recognized nothing. God help me, no! With its iron ferrule-cap fitted on, as you see it now in the hands of Sergeant Bulmer, I did not even recognize it when he boldly and cynically allowed me to examine it just after the murder.

"But, to return to the time when he sat on horseback by Lady Drayton's closed carriage, and he gave me a certain warning. I marked his uneasiness then, as I had already marked the sweat that ran down his head (why?) when Colonel Rowan had been saying that the clothes of someone shot at a fairly short distance would bear powder-burns.

"Sitting on horseback, Mr. Henley said to me, *'Look very sharp when you talk to Lady Cork. And to Miss Margaret Renfrew too. That is, if you do talk to her.'*

"It was the first mention, in this affair, of Miss Renfrew's name. Why?

"And how did Mr. Henley come to know so much of Lady Cork's household? When he was there, I noted, he was treated almost as a servant. He was scarcely noticed. Lady Cork did not know him. Miss Renfrew herself did not seem to know him. But recall this:

"When Flora and I entered Lady Cork's house, we were greeted by Miss Renfrew on the stairs. Her mood was strange, wild; it seemed unreadable. But all agree it was defiant—and it was *ashamed*.

"On those stairs, and in this humour, she spoke certain words with great intensity. She spoke them after a group of young men had passed her and gone up.

"*'What puppies they are,'* said Miss Renfrew. *'How little amusement they provide! Give me an older man, with experience.'*

"She was not looking at me. No. Her eyes, with a most strange and cryptic look, were fixed at a point past my shoulder. Much as it may distress you, Lady Drayton, I beg you to speak. Who was standing just behind me on those stairs, and followed us up?"

At first Flora, through dry throat and lips, could form no words. She too was remembering that scene on the stairs.

"It—it was Mr. Henley," she faltered out. "But I had forgot him."

Cheviot swung back.

"We all forgot him," he said. "Yet look at him, even now! He is likeable, as none can deny. He has much virile charm. He has raised himself, doubtless from what you would call low beginnings, to the position of chief clerk to the Commissioners of Police.

"When or where he first became acquainted with Margaret Renfrew: this I cannot prove or even say. But is it remarkable that a lonely and pretty woman—denied affection, denied love to her passionate nature by some mysterious repulsiveness which all could feel yet none define—is it remarkable she should have fallen victim to an older man who had learned the craft of flattery?

"More! Does it surprise you that *his* head was turned?

"He was bettering himself, as he strove to do. This infatuated woman, for a time at least, would steal money for him. She

would steal Lady Cork's jewellery for him. And why? So that
he could line his pockets, so that he could win money across Vulcan's gaming tables; and become in his own eyes the 'true gentleman' he wished to be.

"Nevertheless, there was a matter on which he had not reckoned.

"He had not reckoned on Miss Renfrew's soul, as deeply and
damnably snobbish as any about her. Offend snobbery, and you
are undone. Recall her, all you who knew her! Physical passion, the balm of compliment and flattery, would hold her en-
thralled for a while. But then . . .

"Then she would become ashamed of having robbed Lady
Cork. But this only in part. Most of all, she would be horrified
at having taken as a lover someone whom she could never
proudly display. A crude man, in her eyes. A man of uncertain
grammar and manners as clumsy as his walk; in short, a man
of low origins. *That* was why she was ashamed. *That* was why
she had become ready to betray him, as well he saw and knew.
And so, to protect his own fierce respectability, he shot her with
the air-gun before she could speak."

Cheviot paused.

Mr. Alan Henley, behind the desk with the green-shaded
lamp, uttered a bubbling kind of cry. He had not uttered a
word. But he jerked his right hand, with the head of the stick
in it, and papers flew wide.

"Stop!" said Mr. Mayne.

As though emerging from a kind of mesmerism, Mr. Mayne
rubbed his forehead and thrust out a round face.

"You speak with persuasion, Mr. Cheviot," he said. "But this
man," he nodded towards Mr. Henley, "has served us faith-
fully, according to his lights—"

"Agreed!" said Colonel Rowan.

"And the evidence against him must be complete." Mr.
Mayne struck the table. "Your producing of the air-gun, there,
is legal proof which may be taken into court. Always provided
this unburned bullet *is* an air-gun bullet—"

Mr. Daniel Slurk, who had been tapping the brim of his hat against his teeth, allowed one eyelid to droop still further.

"Sir," he said to Mr. Mayne, "I could have told you it was fired from an air-gun. As a surgeon, sir, I have some small experience of bullets."

"But you did not so tell Mr. Cheviot?"

"I am a cautious man, sir. I was not asked."

"Very well!" And Mr. Mayne stared at Cheviot. "But it is little of legal evidence to say, 'A woman looked thus.' 'A man spake thus.' Have you any proof that Miss Renfrew stole Lady Cork's jewels, or that Henley ever laid hands on them?"

"Yes!" said Cheviot, and opened the writing-case again.

"Here," he went on, "is a letter written by Lady Cork, and delivered to me by hand at the Albany early this morning. It contains the substance of a conversation I had with her late last night. Lady Cork actually saw Miss Renfrew steal the diamond ring which appears in a list I produce. Lady Cork knew Miss Renfrew was prepared to confess; she is willing, as you see, to testify in a court of law."

Once more he attacked the writing-case. A handkerchief, knotted round some objects within, he untied and flung out; glittering jewels rattled and rolled across the table under Mr. Mayne's eyes. Beside them Cheviot thumped down two account-books.

"Here," he continued, "are the jewels themselves. Any of my men can tell you I found them at Vulcan's gaming house; and Lady Cork has identified them. Now look in these accounts!" He riffled the pages, pointing. "See whose name is written opposite the description of this, and this, and this, and this. All five of the stolen pieces. The name, in every case, is Mr. Alan Henley."

"This," said Mr. Mayne, after a pause of examining, "would seem—"

"Complete," said Colonel Rowan, and swallowed.

"And you divined all this, Mr. Cheviot," demanded Mr. Mayne, lifting his eyes, "from the very beginning?"

"No, sir. No, as I have been attempting to tell you! My eyes were opened, only yesterday afternoon, by a remark made by Miss Louise Tremayne."

"*I* made such a remark?" cried Louise. "*I?*"

She drifted forward towards him, all hazel eyes and broad quivering lips, as though she would put her hand on his arm.

Flora flung her muff into the chair behind her. At that moment she hated Louise and quite seriously believed she could kill her.

"You were suggesting," said Cheviot, not without sardonic humour, "that *I* might be Miss Renfrew's lover."

"But I never truly thought—"

"Never, Miss Tremayne?" he suggested gently. "In any case, I denied it. I said something to this effect: 'Listen! The first time I ever heard that woman's name—'

"And there I spoke no further. I remembered when I first *had* heard her name, and who had spoken it: Mr. Henley. Past events, in their true shape, took form clearly. At the same time, I was looking straight down at this table and at Colonel Rowan's silver-handled pistol. That particular weapon, I see, has been put on Mr. Henley's desk at the moment. . . ."

(Alan Henley stiffened. None saw this except Cheviot.)

". . . and I recalled, with much distinctness, there had been no powder-smoke in the passage when Miss Renfrew was shot. There had been no noise, no powder-mark on the bullet. I did not think of an air-gun until Vulcan's spring-and-compressed-air mechanism exploded in the roulette-table.

"But the sequence of events on the night of the murder must now be clear. This small pistol," and Cheviot took up the weapon with the gold lozenge set into the handle, "was only intended as a dummy and a cheat.

"Who borrowed the pistol from Lady Drayton? Officially Lady Cork; but, as we know, it was Miss Renfrew who in fact borrowed it and kept it. Mr. Henley, as we also know, arrived at the house nearly half an hour before Lady Drayton and myself.

"It would not have been difficult for him to steal the small pistol from the room of a half-distracted woman who was ready to confess. Wherever he killed Miss Renfrew, none must suspect his thick and knobbed cane of being an air-gun.

"There must be a dummy pistol, fired, to account for the death. It is the same device, you will note, which the late John Thurtell meant to use in the murder of Wood. I doubt that Henley fired a shot inside the house. More probably it was in the garden, into soft earth. He then had time to go back into the house, hide the pistol under a table in the upstairs passage near Lady Cork's boudoir, and sit down quietly in the foyer.

"Lady Drayton, before the murder, found the discharged pistol. For good reasons which she explained to me, but on which I need not dwell, she concealed it in her muff.

"In the boudoir, while I was questioning Lady Cork in the presence of Miss Renfrew and Mr. Henley, matters all but boiled over.

"By the Lord, you should have seen Miss Renfrew's demeanour then! You should have seen how often and how furtively she glanced at Henley, who was (apparently) unconcerned and busy at his shorthand. But, again, you should have seen her demeanour when she marched out!

"He knew he must kill, and kill quickly. The opportunity was provided.

"I think, Colonel Rowan, you would have seen the truth in our positions in the passage if Mr. Mayne had not so persistently suspected Lady Drayton and myself. Consider!

"Henley and I left the boudoir, closing the double-doors behind us. We turned round. Lady Drayton was standing about a dozen feet ahead of us, well to our right, her back turned. Miss Renfrew opened the passage-door of the boudoir, and came out.

"Now what happened? Two seconds earlier, Henley had lifted his cane as though to point. I did not see him remove the ferrule-cap. Probably he meant no harm—until he saw Miss Renfrew. I thought nothing of it; why should I?

"Miss Renfrew walked across diagonally, as though to the ballroom. She turned, and in the middle of the passage she walked towards the stairs with her back to us. If you had listened to the testimony of Lady Drayton, which I included in my report, you might have seen the truth. What was that testimony?"

Flora herself could not remember. Her mind was too confused. But Cheviot, putting down the small pistol on the table, spoke clearly.

"Flora Drayton," he said, "told me this. *'She,'* meaning Miss Renfrew, *'was well ahead and to the left of me. I felt a wind, or a kind of whistle or the like, past my arm. She went on a little and fell on her face.'* "

At last Flora remembered, and all too vividly. The terror of the night was returning.

"In other words," said Cheviot, "she felt the bullet pass her on the left. Henley, with a direct-sightline to his victim, pressed the knob of the cane. Any noise was hidden from me by the loud waltz-music. That small bullet, which at a longer distance would not even have been deadly, struck Miss Renfrew through the heart. She took two steps and fell dead.

"It was the last act," Cheviot said. "But it was not the last link."

"Not, you say," Mr. Mayne asked in an unexpectedly high voice, "the last link?"

"No," Cheviot suddenly pointed. "You think Alan Henley has been your faithful servant?"

"Yes!" Mr. Mayne and Colonel Rowan spoke at once.

"He is not." Cheviot shook his head. "Though I did not stress it in my second report, so much was evident from my visit to Vulcan. Someone had warned Vulcan I should be there, else he could not have packed the house with so many blacklegs. Who warned him?"

"Well?"

"I—I counted it strange," Cheviot muttered, "only a coincidence perhaps, that there should have been so many resemblances between Vulcan and Alan Henley. Both are self-educated men: though Vulcan, save for his rings, has achieved near-perfection of manner. Both have a physical disability caused by accident: Mr. Henley a lame leg, Vulcan a glass eye. Both are inordinately vain, especially of their power over women.

"Vulcan, in his study or office, could not help mentioning this. He remarked on the strangeness that some men, even with natural disadvantages, should have this power. He added, meaning himself, that he knew such a man. And I, with my eye on the two walking-sticks propped at the far end of his private roulette-table, said, 'So do I.'

"He is quick-witted. He guessed I meant Mr. Henley. It was as though an arrow had struck home.

"In fact, he tested me by referring to it later. Should the police make any attack on his gaming-house, he said that he would be warned beforehand. And I replied, without surprise, that I was aware of it.

"Then Vulcan knew. He knew I meant the chief clerk to the Commissioners of Police. Again the arrow struck home.

"Your faithful servant? No, I think not! Mr. Henley had assisted Vulcan far more than in pledging jewels there. How far he may be associated with the owners of other gaming-houses, a matter at which I only guess, it will be your duty to inquire. But faithful? Never!"

Again, from Alan Henley's thick throat, issued a wordless cry.

He did not deny; he did not speak. His left hand reached out, in a tentative way, as though he would seize the medium-bore silver-handled pistol and turn it on himself. But he could not do it.

In his staring eyes was reflected the image of the hangman. He pressed his hands over his face. The ebony stick clattered to the floor. He fell headlong across the table, amid flying papers, in a dead faint.

Flora, her throat choked, saw another figure loom up. Captain Hogben, his cloak over his right arm, was backing against Mr. Henley's desk. Hogben's body was partly obscured by the green-shaded lamp. His own right hand went snaking out. . . .

"Is it not ironic—?" Mr. Mayne was beginning, when Cheviot cut him short.

"Ironic?" he cried. "Have you seen no worse irony?"

Whereupon, to those who listened, Cheviot seemed to take leave of his wits.

"I, as Superintendent of C-One of the Criminal Investigation Department! I, who prided myself on my knowledge of scientific criminology? I, because I never dreamed they had been invented, was deceived for two days by a common air-gun, when any gunsmith of the year 1829 could have told me."

They were staring at him. Behind Sergeant Bulmer, who stood rocklike with the thick and knotted cane, the doorway was crowded with policemen. The other sergeant, with the collar-numeral 9, fought his way through them.

Breathing hard, Sergeant 9 straightened up and saluted.

"Sir!" he said to Colonel Rowan. "The riot's begun. That tailor, who's drunk, set fire to his own house. The devil knows why he did, but it's crazed 'em. There's six hundred men a-fighting in Parliament Street, and the truncheons are out. They've attacked our men, and spilled round into King Street. . . ."

"We shall deal with it," snapped Colonel Rowan. "Meanwhile, Mr. Cheviot, have you gone mad? What is this you speak of 'C-One'? 'Criminal Investigation Department'?"

Cheviot laughed.

"Your pardon," he said. "I could not even remember Mr. Fulford's biography of King George the Fourth; and the fact that a bullet-hole from an air-gun was found in the glass of the coach-window. That was in 1820. Air-guns must have been known long before then. But it took Joe Manton the younger to remind me."

"A biography of the King?" echoed an astounded Mr. Mayne. "But the King is yet alive! No biography of His Majesty has yet been written."

"No, sir," agreed Cheviot. "I had also forgotten that Mr. Roger Fulford's account will not be published for more than a hundred years."

"Good God!" breathed Colonel Rowan. "Mr. Cheviot! Control yourself, lest we think you a staring lunatic."

"Perhaps I am," Cheviot retorted. "But there is one more

reckoning to be settled. It is not at all concerned with Mr. Henley."

And he pointed to Hogben, whose hand still moved along Henley's desk.

"I mean that man there," Cheviot snapped. "Captain Hogben has sworn and is perjured. It was done before a magistrate. He will pay. And the penalty for that, in this age—"

This was the point at which Hogben acted, in what seemed all one movement.

Hogben's right hand swung up the silver-mounted pistol. His left hand whipped the long black cloak off his other arm. As it billowed out, he threw the cloak over Cheviot's head and into his face.

Making a dart for the door, he saw it was full of policemen. Instantly Hogben charged between Flora and Louise. There was a bursting crash of glass and flimsy wood as he dived, left arm protecting his face, through the lower part of the window.

They heard him hit the ground sideways, and roll. He was up in an instant. Carriage-horses screamed, whinnied, and reared up. But there was no horse for Hogben to take; he and Louise, like Cheviot and Flora, had come there in a carriage.

In the dim light of the gas-lamp, out there at the entrance by the crooked tree, they saw him running hard for Whitehall. Cheviot, who had disentangled himself from the cloak, whipped round to those in the doorway.

"Let every man stand where he is!" he shouted. "This is one prisoner I take myself."

Running to the window, shielding his own face against glass-edges, he ducked his head out, swung his legs through, and dropped outside. They saw him running hard after Hogben as the latter, at the entrance, turned left and south down Whitehall.

Even as Hogben had acted, Sergeant Bulmer flipped off the iron ferrule-cap of the air-gun and swung it up to fire. But he could not find, on the handle of the cane, the knob you pressed to discharge it. As Cheviot disappeared through the window, Bulmer flung down the air-gun on the floor.

"Sir," he said to Colonel Rowan, "I've never disobeyed the

Superintendent yet. But I'm disobeying him now. And *I've* got—"

His hand went under his coat to the hip-pocket. Then *he* vanished through the broken window.

Alan Henley still lay face down across the desk. The others stood motionless. Colonel Rowan, Mr. Mayne, Mr. Slurk, Louise, Flora . . .

They heard no noise except pounding footsteps as Bulmer ran hard across the freezing mud. Then even these died away. There was nothing except, very faintly and distantly, the roar of a fighting mob.

"No!" Flora cried. And, after a pause: "No!"

It was like a prevision, a rending of heart and a knowledge of what had happened when it did happen.

Very clearly, and not too far away, they heard a pistol-shot.

You might have counted one, two, three, possibly four; and, with the same clearness, there was another shot.

Afterwards, only silence.

Very slowly Colonel Rowan walked to the shattered window, put his head out, and looked down towards the left.

"Bulmer!" he called, though Bulmer could not possibly have heard him. "Bulmer!"

Far to the south, a red light of fire flickered in the sky.

Colonel Rowan, pale-faced, drew his head back from the window and turned round. In his scarlet coat, with the buff facings, his shoulders back, he returned to the desk as though in a dream.

They were all in a dream. It went on and on, but it could not last. Mr. Slurk's hat dropped from his fingers and bounced on the floor. Louise Tremayne had cowered down in the chair. Only Flora stood straight, her chin up and her eyes as though very far away.

Presently they heard footsteps returning. The person who returned, with dragging steps, was Sergeant Bulmer. Nobody urged him; nobody called from the window; nobody dared.

Silently, his face dumpling-dull under his tall hat, he fought his way through the group in the hall as he entered by the front door. He appeared in the doorway, not quite seeming to understand. In his hand, loosely held, was a pistol stamped with the crown and broad-arrow. Its reek hung in their nostrils.

"Yes?" asked Colonel Rowan, clearing his throat. Anger burnt him. "What happened? Where is—where is Superintendent Cheviot?"

Bulmer seemed to ruminate heavily.

"Why, sir," he said, "the Superintendent's not back."

"I know that! Where is he?"

Sergeant Bulmer lifted his head.

"What I meantersay, sir," he said heavily, "he's not ever a-coming back. What I meantersay: he's dead."

Again the eerie silence coiled round the red and green lamps.

"I see," muttered Colonel Rowan.

"Hogben," said Sergeant Bulmer, with a violent effort, "Hogben never meant to run far. Hogben, he stopped and turned. And you know the Superintendent. Went for Hogben, he did, with empty hands. So Hogben up with the pistol and fired in his face."

Once more Sergeant Bulmer made a violent effort to speak.

"Well," he said, "I wasn't far behind. The Superintendent told me never to carry a loaded barker. I swore I wouldn't. But I had one. I leaned close, so I couldn't miss. I shot that bastard Hogben between the eyes. And, by God, I'm proud I did."

Nobody spoke until Mr. Mayne burst out.

"It was Cheviot's own fault," he cried, with the wrath of shaken nerves. " 'Fire burn and cauldron bubble!' He always quoted that, about Margaret Renfrew. He never knew, he never guessed, it applied far more to himself." Then Mr. Mayne was stricken. "Lady Drayton! I ask your pardon! I never meant . . ."

His voice trailed off.

Flora, still standing motionless, did not look at him or speak. Only her lips quivered, and began to quiver uncontrollably, as the roar of the mob rose and flames were painted bright in the sky.

EPILOGUE

"O Woman! in Our Hours of Ease—"

When Cheviot saw Hogben turn round, black against the line of fire and struggling distant men, he knew what would happen as soon as light glinted on the silver mounting of the pistol.

He said one word—*"Flora!"*—as Hogben pulled the trigger.

Something struck him very hard in the head. Or so it seemed, though he saw no fire-flash and heard no report. The single notion left in his brain was that it seemed odd to be falling forward, instead of backwards, if you ran into the impact of a heavy bullet.

Then darkness; nothing more.

How long the darkness lasted he could not tell. There were movements, tremors, ripples at its outer edges. There were sensations through his muscles, in his heart and nerves. A thought crept into his brain and astonished him.

If he were dead, surely, he could not think. And certainly he could not hear.

"Superintendent!" said a voice.

Cheviot raised his head, which ached badly and blurred his sight. He was kneeling, oddly enough, against the door of some cab.

"I couldn't 'elp it!" a voice was saying over and over, a little distant. "'Ow could I see, in the sanguinary fog, if a car comes smack out o' them gates and smack across me incarnadined front bumper?"

"That bullet!" Cheviot said. "It must have missed me!"

"What bullet?" asked the voice close in his ear. And he recognized the voice.

He raised his head still further, in the open door of the taxi. All about him was white October mist. His hat was a soft hat, a modern hat. Through the mist gleamed the lights of a pub on the left.

Ahead of him, as he peered round, towered up the tall iron gates—open arches—of the western entrance between Scotland Yard Central and Scotland Yard South. Locked with the front of his taxi loomed another car atop which ran the glowing panel with the black letters POLICE.

"Don't you see the sign there?" the police-driver was demanding of the taxi-driver. "Don't you know no public vehicles are allowed beyond this arch?"

"Steady, Mr. Cheviot!" said Sergeant Boyce, who assisted Inspector Hastings in the Night Duty Room at the back of Scotland Yard Central.

"Er—yes."

"You had a bad knock on the head," Sergeant Boyce went on. Like all the night-duty force, he was of the uniformed branch. "You had a bad knock on the head when the cars hit and your head struck the door-handle. But the skin's not broken; it's only a bump. Take my arm and step down."

Cheviot took his arm and stepped down on a solid pavement. Time had slipped back; time had slipped into place.

"I didn't dream it!" Cheviot said.

"No, no, 'course you didn't. By the way, your wife 'phoned half an hour ago, and said she'd be here to pick you up and take you home in the car. Don't frighten her! She's in the office now, and—"

"Didn't dream it!" said Cheviot.

"Easy, Superintendent!"

"The murder mystery was all solved," Cheviot went on, still dazed. "All solved in every detail. But the rest of it, in many parts, I'll never know and I can never learn. I did live in 1829.

The past does repeat itself! I never even saw an engraving of the old Houses of Parliament—"

"Now listen, Superintendent."

"—I never read a description of Joe Manton's shooting-gallery, or knew its number in Davies Street. Parts of my real life here, and parts I never dreamed, are all confused together. I can never sort them out. If only she . . . she . . ."

Light footsteps rapped across the pavement from the Night Duty Room, hurried out under a smaller arch, and a woman's figure loomed up.

"All right, sir? Here's your wife."

Cheviot's wits cleared. And so, with a kind of inner cry, did his heart.

A woman's arms went round him as he seized her in turn. Through the mist looked up the same blue eyes. The same mouth, the same fair complexion, the same golden hair under a modern hat, were just as they had seemed before they faded.

"Hello, darling," said Flora.

Notes for the Curious

1.

First, as proof that the book quoted by Cheviot is not imaginary, permit me to present a photostatic copy of its title-page. It is greatly reduced in size, or it would not have fitted into any book like this. However, it appears on the following page.

It is now necessary to show that the air-gun was well known in 1824, which you see to be the date on the title-page. This is five years before the action of this novel is made to take place.

Further, as demonstration that even then they had an eye for neat, baffling methods of murder, here are the two passages which Cheviot is made to read aloud in the story. First:

> pointed him out to me at the Inquest. The air-gun resembled a knotted walking stick, and held no less than sixteen charges. It was let off by merely pressing one of the knots with the finger, and the only noise was a slight whiz, scarcely perceptible to any one who might happen to be on the spot.

And again, for a full description of the weapon used in *Fire, Burn!*, we have:

> was gone to bed; and when he was supposed to be asleep, John Thurtell, disguised in a boat-cloak, was to enter the house by means of Probert's key of the street door, proceed to Wood's room, and shoot him through the heart with the air-gun. He was then to place a small pistol that had been discharged, in Wood's right hand, so that it might appear as if he had shot himself, and he was quietly to leave the house, and sleep in the city. Probert was afterwards to have gone up stairs, and found Wood in this situa-

Indeed, the air-gun existed even earlier. Nearly every biography of King George the Fourth, from the contemporary and scandalous Huish (*Memoirs of King George the Fourth,* by Robert Huish, 2 vols., London: Thomas Kelly, Paternoster Row, 1831) to Mr. Fulford's brilliant modern study (*George the Fourth,* by Roger Fulford, London: Duckworth, 1935), mentions the bullet-hole in the glass of the coach-window. This puts the invention of the weapon at some time early in the nineteenth century.

THE
FATAL EFFECTS OF GAMBLING

EXEMPLIFIED IN THE

Murder of Wm. Weare,

AND THE

TRIAL AND FATE

OF

(JOHN THURTELL, THE MURDERER,

AND

His Accomplices;

WITH

BIOGRAPHICAL SKETCHES OF THE PARTIES CONCERNED;

AND

A COMMENT ON THE EXTRAORDINARY CIRCUMSTANCES DEVELOPED IN THE NARRATIVE, IN WHICH GAMBLING IS PROVED TO BE THE SOURCE OF FORGERY, ROBBERY, MURDER, AND GENERAL DEMORALIZATION.

TO WHICH IS ADDED, THE

GAMBLER'S SCOURGE;

A COMPLETE EXPOSE OF

THE WHOLE SYSTEM OF GAMBLING IN THE METROPOLIS; WITH

MEMOIRS AND ANECDOTES OF NOTORIOUS BLACKLEGS.

" ———— Shame, beggary, and imprisonment, unpitied misery, the stings of conscience, and the curses of mankind, shall make life hateful to him—till at last his own hand end him."—*Gamester.*

ILLUSTRATED BY PORTRAITS DRAWN FROM LIFE, AND OTHER COPPER-PLATE ENGRAVINGS OF PECULIAR INTEREST.

LONDON:

PUBLISHED BY THOMAS KELLY, PATERNOSTER-ROW

MDCCCXXIV

2. Manners, Customs, Speech

It is hoped that the reader may be tempted further to explore this fascinating age, the late eighteen-twenties to the early eighteen-thirties, which has been so little used in fiction. Disgusted at the cavorting of King George and his roistering brothers during the Regency (1811–1820), society and the middle classes had already turned to a decorum of manners and elegance of speech which at times becomes painfully refined. Much of the quality called Victorianism existed long before Queen Victoria. And yet, beneath the surface of the transition, lurked a turbulence and bawdiness from the opening years of the century.

What were they really like, these people? How did they think, act, speak?

There are glimmers from the well-known official diarists, from John Wilson Croker (*The Croker Papers*, edited by Louis J. Jennings, 3 vols., London: John Murray, 1884) and from Thomas Creevy (*The Creevy Papers*, edited by the Rt. Hon. Sir Herbert Maxwell, London: John Murray, 1913).

Croker, during 1829, is so much preoccupied by his new edition of Boswell that he says little. But Creevy snarls outright at the new age.

"Well," he writes to Miss Orde in March, 1829, "our 'small and early' party [i.e., at Lady Sefton's] was quite as agreeable as ever. But I must be permitted to observe that, considering the rigid virtue of Lady Sefton and the profound darkness in which her daughters of between 30 and 40 have been brought up as to even the existence of vice, the party was as little calculated to protect the delusions of these innocents as any collection to be made in London could well be."

Tut, tut.

Creevy goes on to call the whole thing "impudent," and "barefaced." He rails at the speech and conduct of the guests, including the Princess Esterhazy and young Lord Palmerston.

But we must remember that Creevy, like Lady Sefton and the Princess Esterhazy, was getting on in years; he was forgetting what he once saw and heard. It seems doubtful that any alleged virgin of today, between thirty and forty, would swoon away at what she heard there.

As for what the women really thought, we must try *The Journal of Clarissa Trant, 1800–1832* (edited by C. G. Luard, London: John Lane, The Bodley Head Ltd., 1925). Or, on a slightly higher social plane, *Three Howard Sisters: Selections from the Writings of Lady Caroline Lascelles, Lady Dover, and Countess Gower, 1825–1833* (edited by the late Maud, Lady Leconfield, and revised and completed by John Gore, London: John Murray, 1955).

Clarissa Trant is a poppet, both in speech and appearance. She is neither a prude nor too coy, and sparkles on for more than three hundred large pages. Born in 1800, she closes her diary with her marriage in 1832. On October 5th, 1829, we are electrified to read:

"I was doomed to spend another nonsensical morning varied by the arrival of Lady T. and her three gawky daughters. As usual, she was scarcely seated before she announced her determination of not allowing her girls to marry until after her death. *Tell that to the Marines.*"

The italics are Clarissa's own.

Unfortunately, few fiction-writers would dare make a character in 1829 say, "Tell that to the Marines." Nobody would believe it. In similar case are such expressions as "lushy," meaning drunk, though you may find it in *Pickwick,* or "the gift of the gab," though George Stephenson, inventor of the famous railway-engine *The Rocket,* cried out: "Of all the powers of nature, the greatest is the gift of the gab!" (See A. A. W. Ramsay's *Sir Robert Peel,* London: Duckworth and Co. Ltd, 1928, page 368.)

Disraeli's first novel, *Vivian Grey* (1826), is an important social document because it so well reflects the times, even though in a deliberate distorting mirror of satire. Disraeli afterwards disowned it.

"Books written by boys," he says contemptuously in his preface to the edition of 1853, "must necessarily be founded on affectation."

True; his hand had not gained the cunning it afterwards achieved with *Coningsby* or *Lothair.* But there may be other reasons for disowning it.

Vivian Grey is full of libellous (and funny) anecdotes of real persons under their real names. For instance, the hero tells how Washington Irving, nicknamed "Sieur Geoffrey" from Geoffrey Crayon, always falls asleep at dinner; on one occasion they pick him up from the table at one great house and set him down at the table of another, where Sieur Geoffrey wakes up fuddled and goes on talking without noticing any difference in the faces about him. But that might have happened to anyone. And, considering Irving's description of the dinner which inspires the ghost-or-horror stories in his own *Tales of a Traveler* (1824), it is even probable.

Unlike Dickens, who made people act and talk in the way they really did act and talk, much of *Vivian Grey* is stilted and high-flown. The hero does not use a gun; he "cultivates a Manton." But we learn, as we learn from the diarists, how his contemporaries loved their delicacies of chicken patties and lobster-salad; how they kept exotic birds, as Lady Cork did in real life; how the women expressed horror at smoking, but did not mind when the men concocted drinks to make any stomach shudder.

Past us marches a monstrous parade of bumbling politicians, of fawning hangers-on, of high-born married harlots. Even then Disraeli was a master of the epigram and the *bon mot.*

"If you would win a man's heart," he advises, "allow him to confute you in argument." We can see his satiric look as he describes the plight of the young gentleman "whose affairs had become so financially involved that, in order to keep him out of the House of Correction, it was necessary to get him into the House of Commons."

3. *Scotland Yard v. the World of Flash-and-Fraud: Places and Backgrounds*

With one exception, I have set every scene of *Fire, Burn!* in a place which really existed.

We have many source-materials. There is H. B. Wheatley's *London Past and Present, Its History, Associations, and Traditions* (3 vols., London: John Murray, 1891). Open it anywhere—to a street, to a square, to a building, what you like—and you walk in the past. There is *Hone's Day Book for 1829,* a combined day-to-day history and scrapbook, of which a whole series was published. There is *Dearden's Plan of London and Its Environs, 1828,* which, though not so large or with all the coloured plates of *Horwood's Plan of London, 1792–1799,* is a map of great value.

Number four Whitehall Place, the original Scotland Yard which even then was known as Scotland Yard, is described—with an illustration—in my friend Mr. Douglas G. Brown's great book *The Rise of Scotland Yard: a History of the Metropolitan Police* (London: George C. Harrap & Co. Ltd, 1956), which also contains portraits of Colonel Rowan and Mr. Mayne. There are other histories of the police, notably George Dilnot's *The Story of Scotland Yard* (London: Geoffrey Bles Ltd., 1929) and Gilbert Armitage's *History of the Bow Street Runners* (London: Wishart, 1932). But Mr. Browne's book has become and will remain the definitive work, to which I am deeply indebted.

Vulcan, oddly enough, was a real-life character. *The Gambler's Scourge,* already mentioned, quotes a few anecdotes about him, including the reason for his nickname which Sergeant Bulmer gives. But so little is actually known of him that I have fashioned him to suit my purpose, and the reader is free to regard the character as imaginary.

Nevertheless, his gambling-house stood where it stands in the story. The premises of Messrs. Hooper, now displaying Rolls-Royces and Bentleys, are still there, though nearly the whole south side of Bennet Street was wrecked in the war. The description of the interior comes from a journalist's in *The Gambler's Scourge,* and from a copper-plate engraving which depicts a typical gaming-house of the time. Here too we learn how to play rouge-et-noir; we are told of the mechanism of the crooked roulette-wheel Cheviot is made to expose; we are taught the behaviour and idiom in the world of flash-and-fraud.

Lady Cork's house is gone too. But Wheatley and Dearden give the number, the position, the description. It was the sixth house from the western end of New Burlington Street, on the right-hand side as you enter from Upper Regent Street. And its modern premises are now overlooked by the white stare of the new West End Central Police Station. In New

Burlington Street (see Wheatley, vol. 2, p. 308) originated the custom of affixing brass name-plates to the front door.

Of Joe Manton's shooting-gallery many stories are told in Captain Gronow's *Recollections and Reminiscences, 1814–1860* (London: John C. Nimmo, 1900). There are so many descriptions of Vauxhall Gardens, and so many illustrations, that documentation is unnecessary; the imitation Greek temple, put up about 1788, was demolished in the eighteen-fifties. A hand-coloured illustration in *Pennant's London*, a rare work in three volumes, published in 1814 with only the publisher's address, number eleven Pall Mall, to show who did issue it, shows us Westminster—the old Houses of Parliament, Westminster Hall, the Abbey—from the river side.

Only Flora Drayton's house in Cavendish Square is imaginary.

4. *The Real People*

How great a statesman was Sir Robert Peel is not always recognized, either now or in his own time. He had not the winning ways of Lord Melbourne or Sidney Herbert; he had no magnetism to charm a mob. Only among his close friends, those whom he knew and trusted, could he unbend and roar with laughter or tell jokes. Even *Sir Robert Peel, From His Private Papers* (3 vols., edited by Charles Stuart Parker, London: John Murray, 1899) gives us few glimpses into his real nature. He was innately shy, as young Queen Victoria shrewdly saw (see the excellent biography of him by Miss A. A. W. Ramsay, already mentioned) and his manner remained cold and formal.

But his greatest achievement was not the invention of the police; it was his reform of the English penal system. No reader need be told how savage was this system, or the number of offences for which men and women could be hanged even into the second decade of the nineteenth century. But let Miss Ramsay speak of its grotesque irrationality.

"Men could be hanged for cutting down a tree, sending threatening letters, impersonating a Greenwich pensioner, cutting down the banks of rivers, stealing in a shop or on a navigable river, stealing forty shillings from a dwelling-house," and so on.

Juries refused to convict; they simply brought in a verdict of not guilty. This infuriated the judges, who said the country was doomed. And yet, before Sir Robert left the Home Office, he had driven his Act through Parliament and abolished the death-penalty for more than a hundred offences.

The histories and careers of Colonel Charles Rowan and Mr. Richard Mayne may be found in some detail in the 1875 edition of the *Dictionary of National Biography*. What is told of their backgrounds here is true; their characters can only be deduced from their known actions.

References to Lady Cork are scattered through many journals, letters, and biographies, from Boswell to Tom Moore. She did keep a cigar-smoking macaw, which nipped both the King and Lady Darlington; she did threaten (in a letter) to hang Reform banners from her window; and her character has been drawn as accurately as possible. There is an admirable account of her in Mr. Michael Sadleir's *Blessington-d'Orsay: A Masquerade* (London: Constable & Co., Ltd., 1933).

In conclusion, a few questions may be asked. I have just spoken of a book about Lady Blessington and Count d'Orsay, very famous figures; why is there no reference to them in this novel? Because they were still abroad; they did not return to England until 1830. Again, since railways were being used, why is there only one mention of them?

Literary critics have asked the same question concerning *Pickwick*. But the answer is not difficult. Such railways as existed were all in the North; they did not touch the Midlands, let alone London (*cf.* the *Creevy Papers*, Nov. 18, 1829, when Creevy bitterly objected to a proposed Liverpool-Manchester railway). Though *Pickwick* was written in 1836–1837, its main action is made to take place between 1827–1828.

In Mr. Hamilton Ellis's *Four Main Lines* (London: George Allen & Unwin, 1950) we see that the famous London-to-Birmingham Line was not opened at Euston Station until September, 1838, though there was a small junction-line in 1836. Dickens never bundled the Pickwickians into a train because he himself had never travelled in one.

Were there temperance societies in 1829? Yes; again see *Pickwick*. Did dance programmes exist? Of course; they are mentioned as early as in the novels of Jane Austen, who died in 1817. How extensively was gas used in lighting houses? Only in the homes of the well-to-do, and even there by those who were not afraid the house would blow up. Street lighting was widespread, since Pall Mall had first been lighted in 1807.

Finally, all descriptions of the military have been taken from Major R. Money Barnes's *A History of the Regiments and Uniforms of the British Army* (London: Seeley Service & Co., 1951). Major Barnes's fascinating text and colour-plates require close study; for example, had this novel been set a year later, the military would not have worn white crossbelts, which were abolished in 1830.

Aside from contemporary descriptions of men's and women's clothes, the furniture, decoration, and customs (the ladies journals are rich in these), I am indebted to *English Costume in the Nineteenth Century*, by Iris Brooke and James Laver (London: Adam & Charles Black, 1947); to *The Perfect Lady*, by Dr. C. Willett Cunnington (Max & Co. Ltd., 1948), which in the age under discussion calls her "The Imperfect Lady"; and to the fine colour-plates of *Costume Cavalcade*, by Henny Harald Hansen (London: Methuen and Co. Ltd., 1956).

"Fifteen years ago, I  **terrible."**

"What?" Taylor asked, capturing his face in her hands, steeled for what he might admit. "What did you do?"

He read a thousand fleeting emotions in the pretty hazel eyes trained on his face. But it was the trust he saw in them that stabbed at him like a knife. She was going to despise him if he told her the truth.

He was the first to look away. "I can't tell you, Taylor."

"Sure you can," she insisted. "Believe me, no good ever comes of keeping secrets."

Her fervent tone gave him pause. Regarding her quietly, he felt as if he was looking at a total stranger. A *dangerous* total stranger. It could only be his imagination that made her words sound as though she knew from bitter experience what keeping secrets could do to a person. Which was absurd, because Taylor was the most straightforward, least secretive person he had ever met.

Wasn't she?

KELSEY ROBERTS

THE LAST LANDRY

HARLEQUIN®

TORONTO • NEW YORK • LONDON
AMSTERDAM • PARIS • SYDNEY • HAMBURG
STOCKHOLM • ATHENS • TOKYO • MILAN • MADRID
PRAGUE • WARSAW • BUDAPEST • AUCKLAND

For my beautiful Katie Scarlett,
who will love seeing her name in a book!

Acknowledgments

Thanks so much to Don Scott and Marty Bass of WJZ-TV, Channel 13 in Baltimore, Maryland, for sharing their time and expertise with me!

Congratulations and many thanks to contest winner Larenda Twigg—I love the name you selected for Chandler and Val's baby! I would like to thank Pat Lieberman for helping me name Lorelei, and Helen from Sault Ste. Marie for helping name Kasey and Sarah.

RECYCLED PAPER

ISBN 0-373-22903-8

THE LAST LANDRY

Copyright © 2006 by Rhonda Harding Pollero

www.eHarlequin.com

Printed in U.S.A.

ABOUT THE AUTHOR

Kelsey Roberts has penned more than twenty novels, won numerous awards and nominations; landed on bestseller lists, including *USA TODAY* and the Ingrams Top 50 List. She has been featured in the *New York Times* and the *Washington Post,* and makes frequent appearances on both radio and television. She is considered an expert in why women read and write crime fiction as well as an excellent authority on plotting and structuring the novel.

She resides in south Florida with her family.

Books by Kelsey Roberts

HARLEQUIN INTRIGUE

*The Rose Tattoo
†The Landry Brothers

CAST OF CHARACTERS

Shane Landry—The youngest Landry runs the Lucky 7 ranch but may have no claim to the land considering he may not be a Landry at all.

Taylor Reese—She's been housekeeper for the Landrys for five years and about to turn in her resignation...if she can bear to part ways with Shane.

Priscilla Landry—The mother of the Landry brothers has turned up dead. What secrets did she take to the grave?

Caleb Landry—The Landry patriarch was murdered. Was it a twisted romantic triangle that led to his death and that of his wife?

Will Hampton—The Lucky 7 ranch foreman is keeping many secrets behind his quiet facade.

Luke Adams—This ranch hand has a questionable past and a tendency toward violence.

Senator Brian Hollister—He has everything to lose. But is he capable of murder?

Constance Hollister—Knows all the Landry secrets and will keep them in order to protect her marriage and place in society.

Prologue

WMON-TV, News at Eleven

"Funeral services were held at the Jasper Community Church this afternoon for Caleb and Priscilla Landry, the wealthy Jasper couple whose remains were discovered last week in a dry abandoned well on the ranch owned by the family.

"Law enforcement officials have classified the gruesome discovery as an active murder investigation. Sheriff Seth Landry, seen here with his six brothers, is currently heading the investigation, though sources close to the story have indicated that the Montana State Police are planning to take over, since the victims are the parents of the Jasper sheriff.

"Detective Fitz Rollins, chief homicide detective with the state police, said in an interview following the funeral that despite the crime happening fifteen years ago, several strong leads have been developed based on items recovered in the well along with the remains.

"Among the hundreds of mourners, many prominent

Montanans attended the services today, including Governor Greenblat, Senator Hollister and State Legislator Jack English. In the interest of full disclosure, we here at WMON also wish to express our condolences to the Landry family. As many of you may remember, Chandler Landry was an anchor here at this station for many years and we all send our sincerest sympathies to Chandler and his family during this difficult time.

"Switching gears now…"

"Turn it off," Callie groused as she rubbed circles on her very extended belly. Her feet were propped on a chair to ease some of the swelling in her ankles.

Taylor turned off the TV, then went into the office, returning with a pillow that she gently wedged into place beneath her friend's knees. "You look beat."

"No, I look like Shamu," Callie whined. "I'm huge. I'm gigantic, I'm—"

"Eight months pregnant with twins?" Taylor smiled as she went back to the towers of plastic containers lining the counter. "I've got enough food here to feed a developing country. What am I going to do with it all?"

"It's calving season," Callie said. "Pick out what you want and send the rest down to the bunkhouse. I think Sam said they hired on twenty new temporary hands. Those guys are always hungry."

"Good idea," Taylor agreed, opening the top drawer and removing a roll of freezer tape and a marker. She peeked under the lids in order to write neat labels on each container. "I hope they like macaroni salad."

"They're men," Callie reminded her. "They'll eat anything they don't have to cook themselves."

True enough. One thing Taylor had learned in her five years as the Landrys' housekeeper was that along with a Y chromosome came a healthy, hearty appetite.

Something that had been sorely lacking in the main house in the week since the bodies had been discovered. "How's Sam?" she asked.

The other woman shrugged. "You know my husband. His idea of dealing with anything is to soldier on. Then again, I think he's always suspected they were dead."

Who didn't? Taylor thought, though she felt it was better to keep that to herself.

"Cody is taking it the hardest," Callie added, "though Shane is running a close second."

"That's to be expected." Taylor continued labeling the containers as they talked. "Until they pulled the skeletons out of the old well and Cody had proof otherwise, I think he honestly believed he would find his parents on some remote island, sipping umbrella drinks. I think Shane just wanted them to come back. Understandable, since he's the youngest."

Callie sipped a glass of juice. "Maybe now this family can finally heal."

"I hope so. Think they're ready for more coffee?" Taylor asked, hearing the muffled voices of the Landry brothers, who were still huddled in the living room.

"Have you ever known a time when they didn't want coffee?" Callie remarked. "I miss coffee," she sighed. "I miss sleeping on my stomach and I miss being able to stand up with some semblance of dignity. Now I hoist myself out of a chair like bulky cargo being off-loaded from a tanker. I'm supposed to be glowing. See any glowing here?"

Taylor patted Callie's hand and chuckled. "Buck up. It's almost over and soon you'll have two beautiful babies to spoil."

Callie's pretty face brightened. "Kevin is so excited." She smiled. "Sheldon the Child Wonder is a different matter. He's already announced that the babies can't come into his new room. Ever."

"He's two," Taylor remarked. "Jealousy is normal at that age. He'll be fine." She felt confident in the advice offered, thanks to the experience she'd gained courtesy of the three afternoons a week she volunteered at the Family Assistance Center of Jasper. The center that didn't have the budget to hire her even after she had her degree in hand. The university wasn't an option, either. Their hiring freeze prevented even the hope of an opening any time in the near future.

Callie was grinning. "My friend the shrink."

Taylor struggled to smile back. Barring an act of God, she'd have her Ph.D. in six weeks—an accomplishment that should have filled her with jubilation. Instead she found herself dreading the reality of what it represented. No more excuses. Time to go out into the real world. Alone. Again. She'd think about that later. For now, she was still, by default, a part of this family. Better to make the best of it while she could. "That would be 'counselor.' A shrink is an M.D."

"Between you and Molly, we'll certainly have all our mental health needs covered."

Taylor felt a stab of pain in her heart. So much for

making the best of it. Molly was married to Chandler; she had a reason to stay. Taylor, on the other hand, had exactly five weeks and six days left in Landry Land.

Chapter One

"Tell me again why we're doing this?" Shane Landry grumbled a week later as some pencil-necked lab tech with a long cotton swab headed in his direction.

"There were stains on the towels found in the well with Mom and Dad," his brother Seth explained as he tipped his Stetson back off his forehead. "They were pretty degraded, but they might be useful, since initial testing revealed three distinct blood types."

Shane opened his mouth to allowed the tech to scrape the dry end of the swab around the inside of his cheek. When that was over, he swallowed, hoping to rid himself of the cotton taste in his mouth. "How will samples from all of us help?" he asked as the man packed up his shiny chrome case and scurried out of the office.

Seth leaned against his desk. "I'm hardly an expert on the double helix. I'm guessing that if we all give DNA samples, then the lab will use our profiles to filter out Mom and Dad's blood, hopefully allowing the crime scene guys to isolate the third sample. All I know is that Detective Rollins called and asked that we all do this. Since we don't have anything to hide, I agreed." Seth's expression darkened. "We don't have anything to hide, do we?"

A quick, guilty shiver crawled down Shane's spine, but he answered, "No."

Seth seemed to relax. "Didn't think so. Anyway, it has something to do with the fact that it will take a lot of time to extract DNA from the…bones, so this is faster. The investigation is high profile and going no-where, so Rollins is in a hurry to find something that might generate a lead."

"I'm all for that," Shane agreed. "You coming out to the ranch tonight? Taylor's making a stew. She mumbled something about it when I saw her this morning. Not that I was paying much attention to her, mind you. I've found the best way to deal with Taylor is to ignore her whenever possible." Seth smiled, prompting Shane to ask, "What?"

"Nice try."

"What?" Shane repeated, feeling defensive.

"Give it up, Shane. You're hot for the girl. And as my wife reminded me just last night, for the hundredth time I might add, you better do something before she rides off into the proverbial sunset. So no, we won't be coming to the ranch. My wife is quite insistent that you two need time alone so you'll have no choice but to acknowledge your mutual attraction. Hurry up, though, would you?"

The defensive shield evaporated, leaving a blend of fear and annoyance swirling in Shane's gut. "Hurry up and what? It isn't like she sends me anything other than the stay-away vibe."

Seth's head fell back as he laughed. "You may not be

technically blind, but you are totally dumb, bro. Taylor's perfect for you. You just have to find a way past her defenses. She's smart, she's pretty, she's funny, she's—"

"Sarcastic and she picks on me."

"Part of her charm," Seth countered. "Besides, we all pick on you because you make it so easy. Back to Taylor. Aren't you curious?"

"Physically or intellectually?" Shane countered. "The physical part is a no-brainer. Any man with a pulse would crawl over hot coals to be with her. But she's a freaking genius, Seth. She's smarter than I am, she's about to earn her third degree—a doctorate, for chrissake. I have absolutely nothing to offer her," he admitted, frowning. Saying it out loud made him feel like more of an idiot. Her IQ shouldn't matter, but to a guy who'd barely made it through high school, it sure as hell did.

"She takes verbal potshots at me. *Only* me. Has since day one, because the rest of you all have fancy educations."

Seth rolled his eyes. "That's stupid. Taylor isn't an intellectual snob. Ever think she might be sniping at you and only you because you're the one she has a thing for?"

"No," Shane admitted candidly. "In five years she hasn't dropped a single hint in that direction. You're way off base, bro."

"Have you?"

Over the messy pile of files, Shane fired a hostile glance in his brother's direction. "We're getting a little personal here."

"You're getting a little avoidance here," Seth retorted, his tone and cadence mimicking Shane's. "I'm just suggesting that you act while you still have a chance. Just exactly how long do you think Taylor will hang around after graduation?"

Shane didn't want to think about that. She had become such an integral part of his life. Every one of his days for the last five years had begun and ended with Taylor. She was as much a part of the ranch as he was. He didn't want to imagine waking up to anything other than the smell of fresh coffee wafting up to his room. Or the thrill he felt when he walked downstairs to find her working in the kitchen or sitting at the table, her pretty face buried in a book.

He slumped in the chair. Shane knew to the second just how much time he had left. In 960 hours Taylor would get her degree.

"How long?" Seth pressed.

"Doesn't look too good. She never says anything, but I know she's been sending résumés all over the country. As far away as California." Shane rubbed the stubble on his chin. "The last few weeks, with the news, the funeral and the state police crawling all over the ranch, she hasn't said much. She's got to be getting offers, though. Hell, for all I know she's already accepted a job in Outer Mongolia."

"Then give her a reason not to leave," Seth suggested.

"Like what?" Shane snapped, annoyed by the feeling of utter helplessness that settled over him whenever he thought about her impending departure. "'You know that doctorate you've spent the last five years earning? Well, instead of working in your field, want to stick around, clean my house and cook for me?' Right, that'll work."

"No, jerk-face," Seth breathed. "Give her a personal reason. Like telling her that you're in love with her."

Shane stilled. "No way."

One of Seth's dark brows arched in challenge. "Because it isn't true?"

"No, because I'm not hanging myself out there when I have no idea how she feels. Hell, try *if* she feels."

Letting out a loud breath, Seth shook his head a few times. "What's the worst thing that can happen if you go for it?"

A humorless sound gurgled in Shane's throat. "She can verbally shred me to pieces, then laugh in my face. Pass, thanks. Besides, now isn't the best time to—"

"There is no best time," Seth interrupted, mildly irritated. "Look at Savannah and me. We got together under pretty impossible circumstances."

That much was true.

"You shouldn't use finding Mom and Dad's remains as an excuse to keep living your life in neutral," Seth added.

"I'm not." *Much*, Shane amended silently. Then again, he was haunted by a demon that none of his brothers even knew existed.

"C'mon, Shane. Are you trying to tell me that you didn't suspect their being dead was a possibility all these years? We may not have talked about it openly, but I think deep down we all knew it was the most logical explanation for their disappearance."

"I know. You're right," he sighed. "I just hope the state police can find the scumbag who killed them."

"Me, too," Seth agreed, his dark eyes sparked with

anger. "It's making me nuts to be cut out of the loop. Detective Rollins isn't sharing squat about his progress. I do know he subpoenaed old bank records. Makes sense. It's what I'd do, since we've always known about the hundred grand withdrawn the day they went mis…er, died."

"I've always heard you're supposed to follow the money."

"Pretty much. Perhaps you've also heard the expression 'the heart wants what it wants when it wants it'?" Seth said, back to the other subject like a fricking bulldog with a bone.

"Um, only from girls."

He might have his hands tied about helping to solve the case of their murdered parents, but big brother Seth was doggedly hot on the trail of his baby brother's nonexistent love life. "Brat. I'm serious. Look, Shane. You've got a choice to make. You can do nothing and live a lifetime of regret. Or you can decide she's worth it and take a chance."

"Easy for you to say. You're not the one facing verbal castration." Shane blew out a breath and made a production of tightening the leather strap keeping his hair in place. Grudgingly, he knew Seth's strategy had some merit. Taylor was smart and funny. But she wasn't just pretty, she was beautiful. Stop-in-your-tracks, heart-beat-skipping stunning. She was tiny, but not the anorexic kind of scrawny. No, Taylor had curves. Soft, supple curves that even those bulky sweaters she was so fond of wearing couldn't conceal.

She was perpetual energy, with sparkling hazel eyes

and hair the color of winter wheat. She was also mere weeks from completing her graduate work.

"You're frowning," Seth remarked.

"She scares me," he admitted. "Taylor and I have lived under the same roof for five years and we've fallen into this...this...I don't know what you'd call it."

"The Country Girl."

"Excuse me?" Shane asked, meeting his brother's dark eyes.

"It's a movie. Grace Kelly was in it?"

"You're a country girl," Shane teased. "Jeez, we marry you off and now you're quoting chick flick titles. That's just wrong, Seth. You need to go out and do something manly before it's too late."

"I'm making a point, bozo. Listen and learn. In the movie, the husband is a schmuck, the wife is an actress and the director has the hots for the actress-wife. The drunk, schmuck husband gets that the director is lusting after his wife."

"What a loser."

"Whatever," Seth grumbled. "At one point in the movie, the drunk husband says the only thing worse than two people making eyes at each other is two people trying *not* to."

"And your point is?"

"You and Taylor are the actress and the director. I see the way you watch her when you think she isn't looking."

"Everybody watches her. That doesn't mean anything."

"So what are you afraid of?" Seth asked pointedly.

"Aside from the fact that she's smarter than I am?

More educated? Hasn't so much as hinted that she's interested, you mean?"

Seth nodded. "Besides all that."

"I don't have anything to offer her. What's she going to do on the ranch, show inkblots to cattle all day?"

Seth snorted. "First, you are a smart guy. Secondly, who cares what degrees she has? Thirdly, you haven't so much as asked her out on a date. Maybe you should start there."

"A date?" Shane repeated, as if the word was new to him.

"Dinner, a movie? Surely you remember how to date."

"I know how to date. You're the one who's turned into girlie, movie-quoting guy."

"I don't know if I'd cast aspersions, Shane. Not when you're celibate guy."

Shane uttered a mild curse as he left the office. Problem was, he wasn't completely sure which one of them he was consigning to the fires of hell.

"LANDRY RESIDENCE."

"Taylor Reese?"

"Speaking." Taylor couldn't tell if the voice on the other end of the phone was male or female. No response. Which was darn annoying since she was elbow deep in pastry dough. "*Hello?* Who is this?"

"Doesn't matter."

She rolled her eyes as she trapped the cordless phone between her head and shoulder in order to continue rolling out the pie shells. She didn't have time for some teenager making prank calls on a rainy spring afternoon.

"It does to me," she said. "I'm in the middle of something. FYI, pal, this is the sheriff's house. If you're so much as thinking about harassing me, forget it. But have a nice day."

"I know who you are."

Was that supposed to be scary? "I got that when you used my name." *Annoying little creep.* While she could sympathize with some poor kid stranded in what to a teenager would be the mind-numbing solitude of Jasper, Montana, she had pies to bake and deliver to the bunkhouse before leaving to make her seven o'clock class. "Bye-bye."

With flour-dusted fingers, she grabbed the phone, pressed the off button and went back to work.

Not an easy chore, since the counters at the Lucky 7 Ranch were just a bit too high. She had to get on tiptoe in order to roll out the top crust.

The century-old kitchen was a cook's delight. In fact, everything about the house appealed to her. Everything up to and including its occupant.

Shane Landry appealed to her in a lot of ways. Too many. Which was why she did her level best to keep her distance. She'd worked too long and too hard to do otherwise. She was *not* going to turn into a woman like her mother. Not going to repeat the pattern she'd learned at the feet of a master. She attacked the dough with gusto as she mentally reviewed her mother's choices. Taylor had made that promise to herself on her thirteenth birthday. Until she had created a life for herself, no man was welcome as anything more than a temporary diversion. *She'd* never be dependent.

Which was why Shane was such a dangerous temptation. *Temptation* being the operative word. It seemed unfair that one man should be given so many gifts. She frowned at her own lack of self-restraint. No good would or could come of fantasizing about him.

Though she was weeks from graduation, she hardly needed an advanced degree to diagnose the fact that she was attracted to the wrong man. She blew out a breath of frustration as she lifted the crust on top of the sliced apples and began crimping the edges with a vengeance.

"Killing it or cooking it?" Shane asked when he sauntered into the room a second later.

His large hand snaked around her, snatching a slice of apple out of the pie before she could stop him. She slapped his fingers. The quick, fraction-of-a-second contact was all it took for her pulse to kick into gear. *Damn! No touching,* she reminded herself. Thinking about him was bad enough. Physical contact with Shane made her almost forget why he was off-limits.

She nudged him back with her elbow. Did the blasted man always have to stand so close? "Stick your hands in my food again and I'll kill you *and* cook you. Not necessarily in that order. Don't you have someplace to be? Other than here?" *Where I won't smell the fresh scent of soap mingling with your cologne? Where I won't feel the warmth of your body or know that all I have to do is turn around to be in your arms?*

"I belong here," Shane reminded her. Taylor frowned again when she noticed a new bruise on his wrist as he stole another apple slice and his arm brushed hers. "You're in a particularly nasty mood today," he said cheerfully. "What happened, did they cancel *Dr. Phil?* Bummer."

"Do not mock Dr. Phil," Taylor insisted, stepping away before she turned to glare up at him. "He's a very insightful, intelligent man. Two things, by the way, you are not."

"But I'm the man who pays you, so how about something to eat?"

"Sure. Put on your shoes and socks and go to the fridge."

His crystal-blue eyes glinted with humor. "Housekeeper, Taylor. From the ancient Greek phrase meaning 'keep the people in the house happy.' This is me…" he paused and waved his hands "…not happy."

"And this is me…" she gave him her brightest smile "…not caring."

He couldn't help but watch as she put the pie in the oven, stiffened her spine and walked out of the room with all the airs and dignity of royalty departing the throne. There was the added bonus of seeing her hips sway with each step. Taylor had a killer body. She kept him awake nights. Which sucked, since there wasn't a damn thing he could do about his attraction to her. Seth's sage advice aside, Shane still didn't think he was ready to hang himself out there just to have her slice him to shreds with that sharp tongue and even sharper mind. Especially not when she'd practically just called him stupid.

Shane took a few minutes to clean up her baking mess, then rummaged around, finally settling on some cheese and crackers. There was a wonderful smell coming from the Crock-Pot, so he knew better than to spoil his appetite. In addition to her physical perfection,

Taylor was a really great cook. He tried to tell himself that he'd kept her on for that reason and that reason alone after Sam, Callie and the kids had moved out last fall.

After that, there really wasn't a need for live-in help. Not when it was just him. And Taylor.

And enough sexual tension knotting his gut to choke several of his prize bulls.

He took the same seat at the kitchen table that had been his since he'd graduated from a high chair. He cut off a hunk of cheese and slipped it into his mouth, chasing it with a long swallow of beer.

He was still sad over the recent confirmation that his parents were gone. It didn't make sense. Who would have wanted to kill them?

He took a healthy slug of his beer, enjoying the whiff of pot roast and the mouthwatering aroma of hot apple pie.

Shane had a feeling his mom would have adored Taylor. And—God—she would have loved all her grandbabies, too. It was sad to realize his parents would never be a part of their grandchildren's lives. It wasn't fair, he thought grimly.

Shane focused on being happy for all his brothers. He adored his sisters-in-law and all the little Landrys they had produced. He felt like the odd man out, though. Again.

As the youngest of the seven sons of Caleb and Priscilla, he also held the dubious distinction of being the only one who had rebelled as a teenager. The only one who had inspired the ire of their father and the protection of their mother.

Shane suffered a familiar pinch in his chest. Suddenly, the snack wasn't all that appetizing, so he shoved it nearer the center of the large oak table that dominated the room, and concentrated on his beer.

Thinking about the recent loss filled him with guilt. He knew something about the time just before their murder. Something he'd never been able to share. Not with his brothers, not with anyone. It was gnawing at his insides.

Chapter Two

Taylor liked the structure of her life. A life, she acknowledged, as she carried the heavy tray stacked with pies toward the bunkhouse, that didn't fit any of the criteria she'd so carefully defined. "How did I manage to mess up so royally?" she whispered as she trudged across the moist ground, doing her best to balance the tray and avoid a huge mud puddle courtesy of the early snowmelt.

Didn't matter. It would be history soon. She'd get back on track. She'd forget that she actually liked caring for a family—lessons learned and reinforced over and over during her tenure on the ranch. She couldn't erase the last five years. Probably wouldn't even if she could. It would mean forgetting how much she loved preparing meals, planning parties and celebrating milestones, and she didn't want to do that. But she couldn't make that her whole life, right? No. Career had to be the focus. That was the smart choice. Relationships couldn't be controlled, and had the ability to evaporate in a second. She didn't want to be one of those sad women sitting alone in some dingy apartment, pining for a man.

Men made you desperate and she'd had enough of desperate to last a lifetime.

So, while she liked her current life, Taylor knew it had to end. Time to move on. Captain her own ship. Float her own boat. "When did I become the queen of the nautical metaphor?" she grumbled, sidestepping another hazardous mud puddle.

Here she was, on the brink of checking off one of the major things on her life-goals list, and she wasn't happy. That was annoying as sin. She should be ecstatic, exuberantly anticipating her future.

A future that didn't include the large, loving Landry family. Taylor felt a chill carried on the early evening air. Within a week of meeting the Landrys, all of her preconceived notions had started to crumble. Everything, *absolutely everything,* she'd been living, breathing, believing, planning and plotting for much of her life had collapsed, crumpled, shattered. It wasn't supposed to be like th—

She screamed, nearly pitching the tray, startled by seeing two men lurking in the shadows. Her yelp of alarm brought four or five more men out of the bunkhouse, along with the attention of the shrouded figures. Her heart was racing even after she recognized one of the men.

Nervous laughter spilled from her as Will Hampton stepped into the beam of light caused by the flood lamp mounted above the front door. "You nearly scared me to death!" she chided.

"Sorry, ma'am," he replied with a tip of his tattered hat.

Will was a walking cliché, the very image of a taciturn cowboy. From the hat to his craggy, leathery face, jeans, bowed legs and scuffed boots—you name it, he had it. Along with a personality that bordered on nonexistent. He barely ever spoke, and when he did, it was in one- or two-word sentences that almost always ended in a polite "ma'am."

Smiling, Taylor acknowledged the other man. He wasn't familiar, but they were at the launch of the spring calving season, so there were any number of men drifting in and out of steady employment. "I brought you dessert." She handed the tray to Will, glad to rid herself of its weight, and smiled at the other man. "Hi, I'm Taylor."

"Luke Adams," he stated, offering her a perfect smile.

Too perfect, she thought. Ranch hands didn't normally spend that kind of money on cosmetic dentistry. Nor, she noted, did they have tattoos across their knuckles. Nor, ink marks aside, were they usually so attractive. Luke didn't have the sun-aged skin of a tenured hand. He was just shy of six feet, with neatly trimmed hair—what she could see of it beneath his hat—and light eyes. Maybe he was just what she needed to get her mind off Shane. Not the brightest approach to filling her final weeks on the ranch, but it wasn't as if she had any plans for a future here.

"Welcome to the Lucky 7."

"Thank you," he said politely.

"When did you sign on?"

"A couple of days back," Luke answered.

He had a nice voice—not as deep as Shane's—and he was definitely checking her out. "Where'd you work before?" Taylor's curiosity was, pathetically, only marginally piqued.

"Here and there," he said with a shrug of acceptably

muscled shoulders. Shane's were broad and sculpted. She knew this because she'd seen him shirtless. A half-dressed Shane was a thing of beauty.

"...Mrs. Landry?"

She shook off her Shane-brain and asked Luke to repeat the question.

"Are you Mrs. Landry?"

"I'm not," she answered quickly, hating that she hated saying it. "But there are six of them around. Can't help but run into one eventually."

"Six wives? Is this one of those pluralist families I've read about?"

"We gotta go, Luke," Will interrupted, clearly irritated by the mildly flirtatious tone of the conversation. "Ma'am."

Then again, everything about Taylor seemed to irritate Will. They hadn't exactly bonded during her time at the ranch. At first she'd tried killing him with kindness, but that didn't get her too far. Now she just settled for civil exchanges whenever the two of them shared the same space.

Taylor couldn't fathom why it was that Shane adored Will. As she walked back to the house, she recalled the countless times he had praised the foreman, who'd been working at the ranch in some capacity or another for more than forty years. She suspected Shane thought of the older man as a substitute father. Made perfect sense, considering that Will had stepped in to handle things during Shane's father's absence. Good thing, too, since none of the other brothers had any interest in the actual day-to-day running of the ranch.

She thought about the gaggle of Landry men. Sam preferred the world of high finance. Seth and Cody were in law enforcement, Seth as the sheriff of Jasper and Cody as a federal marshal. Chance was a doctor, a general practitioner in town. Clayton had a law office in Missoula, crusading to save others from the horrible ordeal that had robbed him of four years of his life. And Chandler, well, he was a big, important author now. Taylor smiled, remembering how stunned she'd been to learn of his well-hidden, secret persona.

Shane was the homebody. He adored everything about the ranch, including Will, who he obviously looked to as a friend and mentor. That alone was almost enough of a reason for Taylor to keep trying with the crusty old guy. She had a pretty good idea of what it must have been like for Shane to return to the Lucky 7 after so many years, only to find his parents gone.

Now he knew they were dead. She felt great empathy for the Landry clan. Especially Shane, since she knew precisely how he was feeling even if they never talked about that sort of thing. Actually, they never talked, period.

The concept of parental abandonment hit close to home, Taylor acknowledged as she stepped off the pathway in order to avoid another mud puddle. She knew what it felt like from firsthand experience.

That was only a minor reason why Shane was off-limits. In addition to a strong physical pull, she suspected, they had too much else in common. They had—

Taylor didn't get to finish her thought. Not when she found herself suddenly flying facefirst into a deep puddle of mud. Turning her head to the side just in time, she spat out grit, then let loose a colorful curse.

She opened one eye to see a pair of size thirteen boots inches away from her nose. "Is that any way for a lady to talk?" Shane chided.

"Are you going to help me?" she demanded, glaring up at him as she struggled to her hands and knees in the cold slime.

His face contorted in what she was sure was a very gallant attempt to keep from laughing. "Only if you ask nicely."

She glared daggers up at him, feeling the globs of mud slide down the front of her shirt and into her bra. "I would rather gnaw off my own muddy tongue."

"Suit yourself," he sighed, shifting his weight and crossing his arms over his chest.

Taylor did a humiliating *Three Stooges* thing where she'd almost make it, then lose her footing and fall again. But she refused to ask for his assistance. Arrogant and…stupid. Neither of those things normally described her, yet Shane seemed to bring them all out in spades.

With the grace and balance of a two-legged giraffe, she finally pulled herself out of the puddle and back onto dry land. She was soaked, and filthy, smelled like earth and was so cold her teeth started to chatter.

Shane mumbled something unflattering about her being hardheaded as he removed his coat and placed it around her shoulders.

"It'll get ruined," she complained.

"So will you, if you don't get out of those wet things before you catch cold."

She wrapped herself in the coat, feeling the warmth of his body transfer to hers. "You don't catch a cold from the weather. A cold is a virus and—"

"Can't you *ever* just say thank-you?" he grumbled as he took her by the elbow and led her toward the back door.

She practically had to jog to keep pace with him. Shane didn't seem to realize that their height difference meant she had to take two steps to his one. "Sure. Thank you for not helping me out of the puddle."

He chuckled softly. As always, the sound comforted her in ways it shouldn't and at a time it shouldn't.

"You're a real smart-ass, Taylor."

"One of us has to be smart," she retorted, glancing up to bat her eyelashes at him. "Get the door so that I don't have to wash the mud off it in the morning."

"A competent housekeeper wouldn't wait until morning." He reached around her and grabbed the knob, then yanked open the door.

"A competent housekeeper wouldn't work for the pittance you pay me." Which was totally unfair, she acknowledged rather guiltily. Sometimes she had to find ammunition when no ammunition was available.

"Free room," he reminded her, following her inside. "And board, tuition payments and a car. I don't see where you're so bad off."

Removing the coat, she held it out to him as if she was handing him a giant cootie. "*I* am perfect. *You* are bad off."

"Really?" Using his coat like protective gloves, he

grabbed her by the shoulders, spun her around and marched her into the hallway.

Taylor almost shrieked when she caught sight of her reflection in the beveled mirror above the highboy. Her hair was nothing but limp, brown clumps. The only part of her face not covered in mud were her eyes, making her look like some nocturnal creature.

"Not so perfect now, eh?"

"You're an evil man," she cried, twisting free and racing off to her room. She'd worry about the mud tracks on the polished wood floors after she showered and threw her clothes in the trash. Only now there was very little hope of making her class on time. That great, structured life of hers had gone to hell in a handcart rather quickly.

Ten minutes later, a freshly showered Taylor was racing around, putting on her shoes while making an attempt at maneuvering the hair dryer one-handed. It wasn't the best system, so she gave up, grabbing a large clip off the vanity and twisting her clean but soaking hair into a messy bundle at the back of her head.

At least she wouldn't be stuck in a class for three hours wearing a damp sweater, smelling like wet wool. Glancing over at the clock, she grabbed her keys and dashed toward the front door. If she ignored the posted speed limit and parked illegally, she'd only be ten or fifteen minutes late.

"I'm leaving!" she called out, skating on her towel to clean the mud off the floor as she went.

"For good, I hope?" Shane asked as he came out of the living room and leaned against the jamb.

She smiled. "Soon enough, but for now, you'd be lost without me, Shane."

His eyes met hers. "Very true."

Man, she hated it when he did that! Banter worked. Moments of genuine kindness, like sacrificing his coat and cleaning the kitchen after her pie baking marathon, did not. The man didn't play fair.

It was easier to spar with Shane than to acknowledge his good side. Well, technically, it was a great side. But she was in too much of a hurry to deal with all that right now. "N-night," she stammered awkwardly, moving in a wide arc to avoid even the possibility of making physical contact.

"Do you have pencils and paper?" he asked, moving into her path.

"It's graduate school, Shane, not kindergarten."

His dark head tilted to one side; his warm, minty breath fell across her upturned face. Taylor's pulse quickened as his fingers reached out, hovering just shy of her throat. Anticipation rushed through her system. Contradictory thoughts—*Please touch me! No, don't touch me!*—ping-ponged in her mind. She struggled to keep from betraying herself completely.

Not an easy task when she was standing in the shadow of more than six feet of absolute male perfection. His soft, cotton shirt hugged every inch of corded muscle, outlining his broad shoulders and solid torso. She tried not to notice that unlike her, his chest rose and fell rhythmically, evenly. She had to stand her ground. She knew Shane well. Suspected he would pounce at even the smallest slip in her facade.

That was her fault. She was the one who'd put that tightrope between them. The cute-banter idea had seemed safe when she'd first arrived at the ranch and felt the tingle when he'd shaken her hand. Now it was a flimsy cover barely protecting her from the intensity of his gaze. The longing churning in her belly. The need building day by day, hour by hour, second by second.

He tucked a strand of her hair behind her ear, making her shiver. "You could stay here. I'll draw some inkblots and you can analyze me."

She slapped his hand away. "Pass, thanks. I don't have time to play games with boys in men's clothing." She checked her watch, using that as an excuse to divert her eyes from the tractor beam of his gaze.

"Chicken?" His tone was low and far too sexy for her comfort level.

"No, thanks, I've eaten." She inched past him. "Good night, Shane."

"Have a good time." His voice was now laced with something that managed to be seductive and taunting all at the same, confusing time. She was glad to be making an escape and even happier to have an excuse to do it quickly.

The man was annoying. He was impossible. "He does have a great butt," she murmured as she opened her car door. That small confession brought a smile to her lips.

A smile that vanished the instant she saw the threatening note attached to her seat by the glistening blade of a knife.

Chapter Three

Knife in one hand, Taylor read the note. Dread settled in the pit of her stomach. The block printing made it impossible for her to identify the writer, but the contents and the knife made the message frighteningly clear: "SHANE DID IT. THE PROOF IS IN THE ATTIC."

OhGodohGodohGod! This wasn't possible. Shane was a lot of things, but not a killer. Sure, they had their tense moments, but she knew with absolute certainty that he was incapable of hurting anyone. Especially not the mother he worshiped and the father he revered.

Why accuse him?

Oh, God. Who could have delivered this?

Maybe it was a joke. A sick, perverted and cruel one, but some fool's idea of humor. She couldn't show Shane. Not now.

Observing him these last few weeks, she knew where he was on the bereavement scale. The initial denial stage had passed the second he'd identified his mother's wedding ring. The anger stage had passed as well, probably because he'd transferred those emotions to the fantasies of what he'd do when the killer was caught. The funeral ritual had been an outlet for the bargaining and depression stages.

Shane had now reached the final phase—acceptance. Yes, she knew it had been a sudden, unwelcome and painful journey, but she wasn't about to let some weasel with a warped sense of humor set him back to square one. Crumpling the note, she decided when and if she ever found the prankster, she'd kick him, then charge him for repairing the puncture left by the knife. "Jackass," she muttered.

Taylor heard the sound of an approaching car and hurriedly put the knife and crumpled note inside her purse. Tossing her bag on the passenger seat, she slipped behind the wheel.

Seth's marked SUV pulled alongside her sedan just as Taylor turned the key, starting the engine. With a wave of her hand, she rushed off before he noticed anything was amiss. Amiss? She almost choked. That wasn't the word for it. Amiss didn't come close to describing the protective surge of anger churning her insides.

SHANE WAS IN THE PROCESS of grabbing another beer when he heard the front door open and close. For a split second, he let himself hope that it might be Taylor coming back inside. Maybe she'd decided to abandon her class in favor of spending the evening with him. Yeah, sure. *That* was about as likely as fish learning to dance. Acknowledging that reality made him scowl.

Seth strolled into the kitchen. "Hey," he said by way of greeting. "What's with Taylor?"

Shane shrugged. "Don't know. I never know, which probably explains why we've lived under the same roof for five years and I still don't know her middle name."

"Sophia," Seth replied with a brotherly sneer as he weaved toward the kitchen. "Put us all out of our misery and make your move. Get proactive, will you?"

"Proactive? Is that from your word-of-the-day calendar? You weren't here a few minutes ago. If you were, you'd rethink your belief that she's hot for me. She thinks I'm a moron."

"You can be a moron, but that's beside the point," Seth teased. "Trust me on this, Shane. Time's a-wastin'."

"Why do you think she's interested in me?"

"My exceptional talents for deduction."

"Really?" Shane asked, smacking Seth's Stetson off his head. "Maybe you should put those skills of yours to good use by trying to figure out why the woman can barely keep a civil tone in my presence. She hates me."

"You're so wrong," Seth stated, tossing his hat onto the table. "Men are such jerks."

"First you quote movies, now this?" Shane demanded. "You are such a girl."

"No, I'm insightful," his brother said easily. "One of the many advantages of age and experience, bro."

"Do you have a valid reason for being here?" Shane asked as he watched his brother help himself to a bottle of water, tucking it into the utility belt clipped at his waist. "By *valid* I mean something more than a roadie of water and an opportunity to rag on me? Has there been a development in the investigation?"

Seth flopped into his chair. "Nothing so far. But after

our chat this morning, I thought I'd come by to see if you asked her out. Everyone is very interested in your progress with Taylor. We voted and decided it was more fun to focus on that than champing at the bit because we can't get involved in solving Mom and Dad's murder."

Shane and his brother shared a moment of reflective silence.

"Everyone?" Shane asked. "What did you do, take a poll?"

"Actually, I did." Seth smiled. "With Sam, Callie and the kids out of the house, we all think it's time you stopped dragging your heels. I swear, Shane, it took less time for Michelangelo to paint the Sistine Chapel, for chrissake."

"He had divine inspiration. I have Taylor's verbal missile defense system. By the way, I know she'd be thrilled to hear my brothers are so concerned about our love life—the one we *don't* have—that they felt it necessary to gossip and send an emissary."

"Whatever," Seth remarked dismissively before taking a long swallow of beer. "So, what's the holdup? How much longer do we all have to stay away?"

"You call this staying away?" Shane flicked a bottle cap at Seth, which he deflected easily. "Besides, what do you care?"

"We're crazy about Taylor, and speaking only for myself, it would be really, really nice if the two of you could hook up before midnight Sunday."

Shane rolled his eyes. His brothers didn't think anything was off-limits when it came to the friendly placing of wagers. "How much?"

"I bet fifty bucks that you'd admit your undying love before the vernal equinox. Make it happen and I'll split the booty with you."

"Maybe," Shane hedged. "What's the pot up to?"

"Twelve hundred. But only because we made Chandler pony up a thousand on the sixty day over-under."

Shane gave an exaggerated sigh. "Maybe I should work a deal with Chandler then."

"Before you get too chummy with him, you should know he bet the over, that it would take you *more* than sixty days to convince Taylor to accept your sorry ass."

"He might be right," Shane admitted, shoulders slumping under the weight of knowing that he wasn't exactly on the road to success. Forget the road, he hadn't even left the driveway. That could change, if he could come up with a feasible plan. Until he had one, a switch of topic seemed like a good idea. "How are Savannah and the kids?"

"Savannah is hot and my children are cuter, smarter and growing faster than everyone else's."

Shane smiled, knowing full well Seth's remark was part jest and part fatherly pride. "Speaking with complete impartiality, I'm sure."

His brother stood and launched the now-empty bottle in a perfect arc into the trash can. "A three-pointer."

"Not from that distance, girlie-man," Shane scoffed, tossing his beer bottle behind his back, around his waist, and watching it sail easily into the recycling bin with a satisfying clink. "Now, that is a three-pointer. I am the king."

"Yeah," Seth chuckled softly. "The *lonely* king."

"That was harsh." True, but harsh nonetheless.

"Buck up, bro. I'd be happy to give you some pointers if—"

Shane glared his older brother into silence. "Don't you have someplace to be?"

"Yep. Here." Seth paused and replaced his Stetson, which bore the official seal of the city of Jasper. "I'm checking on a couple of parolees you hired for the calving season."

"Anyone I should keep an eye on?"

Seth shook his head. "One did six months of an eight-month stint for bouncing checks, and the other guy's out on early release on a simple use and possession." Seth glanced at a small pad he pulled from his breast pocket. "Brian Meyer is the bad-check passer. Luke Adams is the bad driver with the bad habit. He wasn't bright enough to keep under the speed limit while he was rolling a joint on his thigh."

"Don't have to be bright to be a criminal," Shane said with an expelled breath. "I'll keep an eye on them. Thanks for the heads-up."

Seth scanned the notepad again. "I ran checks on both guys when Will sent me their names. Nothing popped in the system. I would've called if anything came up. Meyer is a first-timer, so it's worth giving him a chance. Adams has a few other busts, petty stuff. Shouldn't be a problem."

Shane shrugged. "Will's pretty good at screening them. He wouldn't hire on anyone he didn't think was a safe bet."

"I agree," Seth said. "Still, I want both of them to know I'm in the area. I'll run out to the barn and just say hi before I head home."

Shane walked with his brother to the front door. A rush of cold air filtered in and he was distracted for a minute, wondering if Taylor was dressed warmly enough. Of course not. She'd rushed out without a coat.

"Show them your gun and be sure to look mean," Shane teased.

"Good tip, thanks." Seth raised one hand and bounded down the steps two at a time. "You have fun tonight! All alone and wandering through the house like a—"

Shane slammed the door, not interested in taking any more of his brother's ribbing. It wasn't like he was ready to concede that his hands-off policy was getting harder and harder to maintain. In addition to his staggering fear of rejection, the truth was the growing intensity of his feelings for Taylor scared him. Keeping her at arm's length was a lot easier than risking everything.

Except that his patience was running out. He felt as if his life had been one big hourglass for the last five years. Finding his parents, after wondering where they were and why they'd left, gave him an odd feeling, a kind of warning bell that there might only be a few grains of sand left.

"She's going to graduate," he told himself as he wandered back into the living room and flopped down on the leather sofa, grabbing the remote control. "Get a job and leave." The thought depressed the hell out of him.

He flicked through the satellite menu without really seeing the images. They had two hundred fifty channels, but there was nothing on. Instead, his mind played visions of Taylor. In the kitchen. Working in the yard.

She was as much a part of the Lucky 7 as he was now. Thinking about her impending and inevitable departure weighed heavily on him.

Four hours and fifty-six minutes later, Shane tried again to convince himself that he wasn't actually waiting up for her. *Right?* his conscience ridiculed in a taunting little voice that was irritating as hell. Had to be that he was totally engrossed in the infomercial for the miracle herb that promised everything from increased energy to improved sexual function. Plus, if he acted now, he could get a six-month supply for the value price of only three hundred twenty-nine dollars and ninety-five cents. A veritable steal.

"Like I *need* anything for sexual function," he muttered, standing up and taking his dishes into the kitchen. "My plumbing works just fine, thank you very much. *That* isn't my problem. Sell me a magic pill to read her mind. Now *that* would be freaking worth three hundred and ninety-whatever dollars! Hell, I'd pay ten times that."

He had just put a plate with crumbs of her delicious apple pie in the sink and was about to call it a night when he heard the muffled sound of footsteps on the front porch.

A sense of excitement rushed through him as he stilled, listening to the door opening and closing, followed by the familiar rhythm of her moving in his direction.

Taylor's subtle perfume entered the room a split second before she appeared.

He knew something was wrong the second he saw

her. "Fail a pop quiz or something?" he asked, disturbed by the tension in her hazel eyes.

Damn it. Taylor had hoped he'd be asleep by the time she got home from class. She wasn't up to a verbal sparring match with Shane tonight, she really wasn't. She'd been on a razor's edge through the entire class, absorbing nothing. Anger over the knife and the note had claimed her focus for hours.

Somebody had strolled up to her car, in full view of the house, and had taken the time to open the door, stab the knife and note into her upholstery and walk away.

Who? And why make such a cruel and false accusation about a man who'd just buried his parents?

She tossed her purse on the foyer table by rote, then panicked a little—what if Shane suddenly ripped into it and demanded to know why she was carrying a knife? She shook with pent-up rage, and rubbed her arms as a diversion, trying to avoid him when he stepped farther into the hallway. "Not now, please? It's late. I'm tired." And spitting mad and…

She'd pivoted, fully intending to hide in the sanctuary of her room, when she felt his large fingers gently close on her shoulder. Fighting the urge to lean into the invitation of his touch, she stopped in her tracks. Finding the note, trying to figure out who might have sent it, sitting though a class without processing so much as a word of the lecture—all of it had zapped her energy. She was exhausted and wired all at once—that jittery, caffeine-rush kind of energy that had her stomach burning and her pulse pounding in her temples.

"What's up, Taylor?" he asked softly, the teasing tone gone from his voice.

She opened her mouth, then went mute when he eased up behind her and began to softly massage away the tension that had been holding her hostage since leaving the ranch. His fingers moved gently, subtly. Because her still-damp hair was up in the clip, she was able to feel the warm wash of his breath against her neck.

"Your shoulders feel like rocks. Come on, tell Dr. Shane all about it."

Tell the truth? Lie? She didn't know. Couldn't know, not when his touch scrambled her already taxed brain. The bombardment of sensations easily overshadowed all rational and intelligent thought. It was impossible for her to process anything beyond the soothingly familiar scent of his cologne as he continued the massage.

Warnings flashed in her mind and she couldn't ignore them. Deliberately, she turned slowly, lifting her eyes to his. Taylor noted a slight amount of apprehension in his gaze. But mostly she saw a smoldering, tightly leashed passion that threatened to turn her knees to jelly.

It was easier—not to mention smarter—to simply walk away before this went down the proverbial path of no return. That was the wise move and she knew it. Which was why she lifted her palms and placed them against his chest. She fully intended to push him away, toss out a cutting barb, then find sanctuary in her room.

Those good intentions pretty much evaporated the minute she felt the taut plane of corded muscle beneath her palms. The rapid, even pace of his heartbeat. Shane's body was as solid as a statue and as unyielding as his clear blue eyes. Her fingers fanned out, as if acting of their own volition. Her normally sharp intellect was no match for the years of curiosity that fueled the longing building in the core of her being.

The pads of his fingertips slipped slowly up, over the flushed skin of her throat. His eyes fixed on her mouth, on the way her pale, rose-tinted lips parted ever so slightly when his thumbs hooked beneath her chin. Her eyes blazed but she didn't look away. Brave Taylor. Maddening Taylor. Shane wasn't sure if that was good or bad.

He also wasn't sure what his next move should be. Or even *if* there should be a next move. She sent out mixed signals, and Shane was afraid if he read them wrong he'd be in a world of hurt. He had no idea if Taylor would verbally knock him into the next county or if he was actually seeing possibility in her steady gaze. The signals she was sending right now all seemed to indicate she was as interested and inquisitive as he was. However, she'd shot him down enough times that he was unwilling to rely on the reading or misreadings of signals alone.

"Is now a good time for me to kiss you senseless?" he asked, applying subtle pressure to properly position her upturned face.

"That would certainly level the playing field. Then we could both be senseless."

He smiled in spite of the remark, only because he felt her trembling. Though Taylor couldn't keep her sharp tongue in check, neither could she keep her body from reacting. Thankfully, that much she couldn't hide. The knowledge made him feel a tad more confident. So Shane inched his forefinger toward her mouth. He loved seeing that flash of heat in her eyes as he brushed it across her lower lip. He felt her breath rush over his hand. When she moved fractionally closer, Shane increased the pressure of his fingertip, his confidence rising.

His palm rested against her throat, allowing him to feel a hint of her response. Taylor's pulse quickened, growing more and more rapid as he dipped his head, stopping just short of making contact.

He could have pulled her against him. Lord knew he wanted to—had for what seemed like forever. He could have kissed her, tested the passion that was smoldering in her eyes. But then he would have given up *this*. The heady, powerful sense of expectation coiled in every last one of his cells.

Somehow, seeking personal fulfillment suddenly didn't seem as important as knowing she felt something. Maybe the same things he did. As strange as it sounded to his desire-addled brain, he needed her to make the move, be the aggressor. Say it out loud, clearly, without equivocation, letting him know this was what she wanted from him.

"Tell me," he prompted. "Tell me what you want."

For the first time ever, he saw something bordering on indecision pass through her pretty eyes. Not exactly encouraging, but not totally *dis*couraging either. He took it as a minor victory.

"I—I'm not sure."

It took all of Shane's fortitude and self-restraint to

step back. His body practically throbbed with need denied, but if he had any hope of changing the nature of their relationship, this was the best way to go. He hoped. "Well, until you are, I can't help you. Good night, Taylor."

She blinked up at him, said nothing, then turned and walked briskly down the hall. At first, he labeled her quick retreat as a defeat, but then he saw the way she was digging her nails into her palms as she hurried away. He smiled. So, Taylor Reese wasn't as immune as she pretended. That knowledge alone made the whole self-denial thing worth it.

Chapter Four

"You can't be serious!" Taylor stared at the burly detective standing in the foyer. "A search warrant? To find what, exactly?"

"Read the warrant, honey."

Her eyes narrowed as she glared at the man. She didn't care that he had a dozen officers in tow. Nor was she terribly impressed by the shiny gold shield clipped to the front pocket of his tweed jacket. She didn't even care that him calling her "honey" was both demeaning and dismissive and normally would have caused her to launch into a strict lecture on sexism. All of that paled badly in comparison to the dread that came in a rush.

Detective Rollins and his uniformed minions invaded the house. Unfolding the paper, she carefully read the unfamiliar wording, pausing to absorb the part about probable cause. "An anonymous tip?" she repeated.

"Yes, ma'am," the detective acknowledged. "Please stay out of the way during the search."

"Wait until I call Shane. Or the sheriff."

"Call whoever you want." He shrugged. "However, the warrant doesn't require us to wait while you do."

Damndamndamn! Taylor raced for the phone, dialing Shane's cell phone. One, two, three rings, then voice mail. "Wrong time to be ignoring your phone," she said through gritted teeth as she punched in a 9-1-1 page. Next, she dialed Seth, who was, according to his secretary, in court.

Over the din of several simultaneous conversations and the violating sound of drawers being opened and closed, she opted to try Clayton.

"Justice Project."

Relief washed over her when she heard his voice. "Thank God," she breathed, explaining what was happening. "What should I do?"

"First, calm down," Clayton counseled. "Then read me the warrant."

She struggled to keep the emotion out of her voice. The first portion cited the date and time of the tip and identified the officer taking the call. Taylor swallowed, then continued, "The caller directed officers to the Lucky 7 Ranch, primary residence of the deceased. Caller identified Shane Landry as the perpetrator and claimed there was evidence contained in said residence, specifically .38-caliber ammunition matching the ammunition used in the crime."

"Okay. There's nothing to worry about, Taylor, because that's the most ridiculous claim I've ever heard. Shane would never have killed our parents. Yes, there's always been ammunition on the ranch but it's locked up in the attic."

Her blood ran cold. "The attic?" she repeated, lowering her voice to a near whisper.

"Yes," Clayton said. "My dad was big on gun safety. He didn't want any accidents, so the ammo has always been kept separate from the guns. My parents were fanatical about it."

"Clayton, I—"

"Stop worrying," he interrupted. "Everyone in Jasper knew about the house ammo rules. I remember hearing people rag on my dad when I was a kid. Folks used to say it defeated the point of having a gun when you had no way to load it in a hurry."

"Stop!" she insisted, fairly yelling to get his attention. It worked.

"Sorry. What is it?"

Taylor's eyes darted around to find, much to her utter frustration, that several of the officers were openly eavesdropping on her conversation—such as it was. Chief among them was the lead detective, who was standing a few feet away, rummaging through the top drawer of the highboy. "This isn't right," she hedged.

"Trust me on this."

She took the cordless phone and walked out the front door, hardly noticing the cold despite her bare feet. She let Clayton drone on while she wandered out of earshot.

"...sure it is just someone hoping to collect the reward we've offered for information leading to an arrest. The state police are probably inundated with tips. Rollins has to follow up on them, it's his job. And..." Clayton paused and expelled a loud breath "...this is a high profile case, Taylor. The governor and a U.S.

senator attended the funeral. Rollins is probably getting a lot of heat on this one."

Taylor felt confident it was safe to talk when she was a good ten yards from the house. "Quiet," she snapped, her nerves frazzled. "Listen to me. I got a note. It basically said the same thing."

"When?" Clayton's tone registered instant alarm.

After telling him about the note and the knife, Taylor asked, "What should I do?"

"Where are they now?"

"In my purse, in the hall. Why?"

"Go back in the house. Do it now."

"I am," she said, briskly retracing her steps. "Then what?"

"Grab your purse and keys and go."

"Where?"

"Anywhere," Clayton answered. "Just get the hell out of there. Do you have a cell?"

"Yes, but shouldn't someone be here while they're going through the house?"

"Technically, no one has to be present. Beside, I'll handle that. You just get out of there. Call me as soon as you're off the ranch."

Motivated by fear and an intense desire to protect Shane, Taylor walked back inside and nearly groaned when she found Rollins still planted in the foyer. How was she supposed to get her purse with its damning contents, with him standing right there?

Oh hell, it didn't matter. She put the phone back on the cradle, slapped the warrant on the table and in precise, clipped syllables, said, "Excuse me."

"Yes?"

"No," she corrected. "I wasn't asking a question, I want you to move."

One bushy brow arched almost accusingly above a penetrating brown eye. "Because?"

"I don't have to be here to watch while you harass this family."

"This family?" he repeated, new interest flaring in his eyes. "I was under the impression that you were an employee."

"I—I am. A very loyal one. One that will go screaming to the press if you and your goons don't leave this home exactly as you found it when you're finished with your little fishing expedition. So, hand me my purse and I'll be on my way."

He did as she asked.

Taylor's heart was pounding as she spun and walked toward the door. She had taken two steps when Detective Rollins said, "Miss Reese?"

She stopped. So did her heart and her ability to breathe. Rollins obviously must have figured something was up. Why wouldn't he? He hadn't impressed her as a stupid man. Stupid, no. Wrong? Definitely.

That didn't change the fact that she was caught. She actually entertained the notion of pulling out the note and eating it. Not smart, but better than giving this man more evidence to bolster the flawed theory that Shane was somehow involved or responsible for the murder of his parents.

Taylor didn't trust herself not to do something rash, making it impossible for her to turn back to face the detective. Her shoulders tensed as she managed to get a single word past the lump in her throat. "What?"

"You shouldn't leave."

Her eyes squeezed shut. "Am I under arrest?"

"Um, no."

She whirled around then, trying to read his expression. No such luck. "Then why can't I leave?"

He pointed at her feet. "No shoes. Unless you make a habit of going out barefoot."

Pressing her lips together, Taylor stiffly went to her room and slipped on some flats, keeping a tight hold on her purse. Obviously, she wasn't suited for a life of crime. Not if her shaking hands and wobbly knees were any indication.

It felt like a lifetime passed before she was tucked behind the wheel of her car, speeding down the long drive toward the main highway. Once she cleared the iron archway that bore the ranch's logo, she fumbled in her purse for her phone and called Clayton back.

"What now?"

"Do you know the old Hudson place?" he asked.

"Kind of."

"Head northeast once you pass through town. It's about ten miles up on the righthand side. Park by the tanning shed and one of us will meet you there. Can you do that?"

"Sure. There's just one problem."

"What?"

"Which way is northeast?"

SHANE HAD WORKED HIMSELF into an almost blinding fury by the time he shoved open the back door. He just didn't know which thing to be pissed about first.

Detective Rollins won, mostly because he was seated in the kitchen as if he had some sort of God-given right to be there.

In my *house. Thinking* I *was involved in the deaths of my parents.* Shane saw red and stuffed his hands into his back pockets just in case he couldn't contain the very real urge to punch the guy.

"Mr. Landry," the detective acknowledged, not bothering to stand as he continued to flip through a file Shane immediately recognized. Thanks to their mother, each brother had a thick box filled with childhood mementos. Shane suspected she'd done it just to make sure each of them felt special. It was her way of acknowledging each of her boys as an individual. Priscilla had always sworn that someday they'd all thank her for her efforts. It stung to know he'd never have the chance.

Shane felt a poignant, visceral pain at the sight of the familiar handwriting on the side of the box lying open at the detective's feet. His dad used to tease his mom about her appalling handwriting—said it looked as though a fly had fallen into the ink and crawled across the page.

Ah, man… To his heart and mind his mom hadn't died fifteen years ago, but two weeks ago, and he still felt raw.

Seeing that box anywhere near this guy who apparently thought he was guilty of parenticide made Shane's eyeballs throb. Without letting the detective get further than a greeting, Shane glared down at him. "You're way off base."

"Maybe," the officer said with a shrug. "You weren't a very good student, were you, Shane? You don't mind if I call you Shane, do you?"

"Yes, you can call me Shane, and no, I wasn't a great student. But since you're looking at my old report cards, you already know that."

"Have a seat," Rollins suggested, his tone revealing nothing. "We need to talk about a few things."

Reluctantly, Shane yanked out his customary chair and joined the detective at the table. "You think I killed my parents because I got bad grades?"

"I wanted to give you an opportunity to talk. Clear up a few things."

"Like?" Shane was eyeing the man cautiously. Clayton had warned him not to speak to the cops, but Shane failed to see the harm. After all, he hadn't done anything. Well, nothing *illegal*.

Rollins closed the file, laced his stubby fingers together and rested them on top of the table. "Why would someone accuse you of the murders?"

"I have no idea. The reward, maybe?"

The detective nodded, then flipped open a small notebook. "Tell me what you remember about that night fifteen years ago."

"I wasn't here that night," Shane reminded him, annoyed that he was being asked to repeat facts he knew full well were part of the missing-persons report filed fifteen years earlier. "I moved out that day."

"What precipitated the move?"

Shane kept his gaze level, while his heartbeat faltered. "It was time," he said easily. "I was eighteen."

"You stayed away for five years. Why was that?"

"I wanted some space. Out on my own. I can give you a list of the ranches I worked during that period, and there are any number of people who will vouch for me."

An uncomfortable silence stretched out before Rollin sighed pensively and asked, "How come a guy whose family owns one of the biggest spreads in western Montana runs off to work as a hired hand for someone else?"

"That's the reason," Shane answered confidently.

"Why be the help when you can be the boss? I don't get that. Someone wanted to hand me a ranch on a silver platter, you better believe I wouldn't up and decide to do grunt work."

"I'm not sure why this is such a tough concept for you to grasp." Shane felt a whole slew of unpleasant memories churning in his stomach. "I wasn't the boss. My father was. As far as I knew, he'd continue to be the boss, so the fact that I left should be enough to convince you that I couldn't possibly have been involved."

"That's certainly one way to look at it."

Anger washed over Shane as he again was treated to an noncommittal response from the detective. "It's the only way."

"Okay." Rollins stood with a grunt, started toward the door, then glanced back. "I should ask, Shane, how did you get on with your parents?"

Guilt assaulted him. "Like any eighteen-year-old."

"Could you be a little more specific? Good, bad, what?"

Shane's mind played a series of video clips. Happy memories interspersed with some that weren't so happy. Then the chilling details of that last time he'd seen his parents alive. "More like okay. I was a pretty volatile kid. And stubborn. A lot like my father, actually."

"Really?" Rollins pried. "How so?"

Meeting the man's gaze, Shane answered, "He taught me not to suffer fools gladly. Is there anything else?"

"Not right now. Maybe when I get results back on the items we're taking. One of the officers should be in with an inventory for you to sign."

"Whatever."

"I'm sure we'll be talking again soon, Shane."

Defiantly, Shane replied, "I'll be right here."

He was right there ten minutes later when the phone rang. Shoving aside the promised inventory sheet, he grabbed the receiver with such force he sent the base unit sailing across the counter. "Landry."

"Shane!" Taylor wailed into the phone. "Are you okay? Are the police still there?"

"They're gone. But forget about the police. A note? A knife? What the hell were you thinking, Taylor? And why didn't you say anything?"

"I don't believe this! You're yelling at me?" she huffed as she raked her fingers through her hair. Hair that was blowing all over the place. Because she was outside. In the cold. With no coat. In the middle of blasted nowhere. Smelling whatever possibly toxic chemicals were leeching from the metal drums littered everywhere. Saving his butt. "You ungrateful jerk!"

"Don't even go there," he warned, his bellowed words echoing in her ear. "Details, Taylor. Right now, before Seth gets there. I don't want to hear them secondhand. Not like I had to hear from Clayton about the note and knife you got. How could you keep something like that from me?"

She was so angry she wanted to scream. Instead, she very childishly hung up on him, and in an even more childish move, she went over to a nearby, rusted-out barrel and kicked it. Hard. Which accomplished two things: her toe hurt and she had an ugly scuff on one of her favorite shoes.

When her cell phone vibrated as it played Beethoven's *Fifth,* she purposefully waited to answer until the last possible second before it switched over to her voice mail. She started to pace on the rutted surface of the unattended driveway. "Maybe I did the wrong thing, but I did it for the right reason," she declared before Shane could say a single word. "You owe me an apology."

"No, you owe me one, Taylor."

She stopped short, recognizing the muffled voice from yesterday, when she'd been baking pies. Man? Probably. Woman? Maybe. Creepy? Definitely.

"This is not a good time, either," she snapped, wishing now she'd spent the extra three dollars a month for caller ID from her cell service.

"Pay attention, Taylor. How do you think I got this number?"

She rolled her eyes. "Off the Internet, no doubt. Not

exactly a challenge in this day and age. This really isn't a good time, so—"

"Look to your left."

Annoyance gave way instantly to the rush of fear, making the hairs at the back of her neck stand on end. *Don't be stupid,* she told herself, yet she couldn't help but turn her eyes in that direction.

Nothing. Nothing but an empty field with the remnants of a stripped pickup and a few more barrels. How dare this little weasel pull a B-horror-movie thing? She was equally annoyed at herself for buying into the prank.

"I looked. Now will you get off my phone?"

She was about to hang up when the caller asked, "Do you see the truck?"

Okay, she was completely terrified now. She spun in dizzying circles. "Uh-huh." She didn't see anyone. Nothing but the rustling trees far off in the distance. How could he know where she was? Hell's bells! No one knew. No one that wasn't a Landry.

Maybe it was just a lucky guess. Yes. Good! Had to be it. The wind was strong, easily letting the person on the other end know she was outside. The truck? Also easily explained. Virtually everyone in Montana had a truck. This was just like those fake psychics. They listen, pick up audible and visual clues, then tell you what you want to hear. A cute parlor trick, but not now.

"Great, there's a truck nearby. Are we finished?"

"Keep watching the truck, Taylor, and remember, it could just as well have been you. Get him to confess. If he runs, I'll find him. If you run, I'll kill you. Then he'll have your blood on his hands, too."

"What in the—"

Pop.

It took a second for her eyes to pick up the cause of the sound. The truck rocked. She frowned. What…? The windshield of the old truck spiderwebbed. It took several seconds for the sound and the image to register in her frozen brain.

Her breath left her lungs in a rush of sheer, unadulterated fear. Someone had shot the truck.

Chapter Five

"Are you sure you're okay, honey?" Shane asked for the fifth time since she'd been practically carried into the house.

Taylor was numb. The adrenaline rush she'd experienced in the field at the old Hudson place had faded, leaving her feeling spent and heavy. Until her brain processed the fact that he'd called her "honey," something Shane never did. He wasn't about casual endearments.

"I'm fine," she insisted, willing it to be true. "I'm sure the caller just wanted to freak me out and, well, he…she…*it* succeeded."

Shane maintained a tight grip on her hands as he knelt in front of where she sat on the edge of the living room sofa. He examined her with his piercing eyes, the troubled lines etched on his face not relaxing until he'd apparently satisfied himself that she had not been injured in any way.

She glanced around, listening to the quiet of the house, then asked, "Where's Seth?"

"Went to his office," Shane replied. "He's going to see if he can track the calls or the knife."

"Shouldn't we turn that stuff over to the state police?"

He scowled. "Eventually. I'm not trying to hinder the investigation, I just need to do whatever I can to find out why someone wants people to think I killed my parents."

"How did it go with Detective Rollins?" she asked. Shane looked troubled—no, more than that, haunted, bordering on tormented. Seeing him this way tugged at her heart. Taylor slipped her hands free, placing one flat against his cheek. His dark head leaned into her touch and she heard him expel a slow breath.

Briefly, he closed his eyes, feeling some of the tension drain away after seeing for himself that she was safe. When he'd heard someone had taken a shot at her, his heart had literally stopped. "Rollins is impossible to read," he said, distracted by the faint traces of perfume she'd dabbed at the pulse point on her wrist. "I have a bad feeling I'll know soon, though. This is pretty sick déjà vu. I always thought I knew how Clayton felt when he became a suspect in Pam's murder. Believe me, it's ten times worse when you're the target."

"Maybe you're reading too much into it, Shane," she said as her small fingers caressed his cheek.

"Maybe," he agreed. Her simple gesture was both soothing and exciting. Best of all, it served as an important reminder that there was something more pressing at hand. "We've got to get you packed."

"Didn't you hear what I said?" she asked, jumping up so fast she very nearly had him toppling back on his heels. "The caller was very, very specific. Neither one of us can run."

"Seth and I talked about that and we agreed that—"

Anger flashed in her eyes. "I don't care what the two of you *agreed.* I'm not willing to risk your life."

Shane used the time it took to get to his feet to consider the possible implications of her statement. The caller's threat against Taylor had been specific and lethal, yet her argument was all about what might happen to him. What, exactly, did she mean? he wondered, confounded. Was it some sort of coded way she was admitting she had feelings for him? Or was it nothing more than Taylor being a stand-up person caught in a situation that was out of her control? Maybe he should ask.

Right. He could just hear himself now: *Taylor, are you saying you're willing to die for me?*

Ah, hell. She wouldn't just think he was a moron. She'd know it.

He lifted his head to find her standing in the center of the room, hands on her hips, fiery challenge in her eyes. If things weren't so dire, he would have been amused by her display of stubbornness. While he appreciated the power of her conviction, he also knew she was no match should the caller decide to get up close and personal with her. She had to go, so he told her as much.

"No. This is nonnegotiable, Shane."

"You're in danger."

She sent him a castigating look. "I don't believe that."

He felt anger flare in his gut. "Weren't convinced by

someone shooting at you? Christ, Taylor, what more does it take?"

"That's my point," she countered. "I was a sitting duck. Outside, isolated—a perfect target. If the... *whoever* wanted to kill me, it would have happened right then and there. It didn't, and I'd bet that's because I'm not really the target. You are."

He ground his teeth until his jaw hurt. "If I believe every word you just said—which I don't—but if I did, that's sufficient reason to send you packing. Ever hear of collateral damage? I'm not willing to risk your safety. It's not an option. Get packing."

"Get real," she retorted. "You may not like it, Shane, but I'm in this now. I fully intend to see it through."

"Why?"

That single word seemed to shake her in a way none of his earlier arguments had.

"B-because! That's what friends do for each other."

He closed the space between them in two long strides. "Is that what we are? Friends?" Holding his breath, he hoped her answer was no. Hoped she just might give him a hint to how she felt.

"Of course." she took a step back and folded her arms in front of her. "You...irritate me, Shane, but I won't let that get in the way of things. Besides, where could I possibly be safer than in among all you Landrys?"

Hardly the admission of undying love he longed to hear. Okay, forget undying love; he'd happily take a hint that she felt some affection. Lord, he was starting to seem desperate and pathetic even to himself.

Seth was right. Shane was his own worst enemy. If

he had any hope of winning her over, he needed to take the bull by the horns. He should probably start by not thinking in terms of lame clichés.

"Okay. There is some merit to your argument."

"My arguments always have merit. Haven't you figured that out in the last five years?"

Most of the tension seemed to drain from his body when he heard the humor she'd purposefully injected into her tone. "Your arguments occasionally have merit."

She scoffed before smiling up at him. "Your life would be much easier if you simply embraced the fact that I'm always right," she teased.

"In this instance—and only this instance—you might be. He could have killed you in the field but didn't."

Taylor spread her arms as if about to take a theatrical bow. "Thank you for acknowledging my superior skills of deduction. But we don't know it is a he."

"Okay, *it*," he said with an exasperated breath. "Whatever. You can stay. With conditions."

"There really isn't any need for conditions." Taylor's tone no longer had that sharp, combative edge. She braced herself, half expecting him to tell her she would be locked in her bedroom for the duration.

"Wrong," he exclaimed, his voice firm and unyielding, as were his eyes. "No more trips out to deserted fields. Or deserted anythings, for that matter. Stick close to the ranch. If you have to go out, I go with you. If I'm busy, I'll arrange for one of the hands to go. But under no circumstances—I am serious about this, Taylor—are you to leave here without protection. Understood?"

She responded with a salute. "Sir, yes, sir."

"It's getting late." He took her hand and led her from the room. "Why don't you take a relaxing bath and I'll rummage around for dinner."

Taylor tried not to think about the little shocks of electric current pulsing where his hand held hers. It was a losing battle from the get-go. She noticed everything—the calluses on his palms, the strength in his tapered fingers. Her thoughts were so distracting that she nearly stumbled as she walked a half step behind him.

Great, the guy holds my hand and I forget how to walk. Not good. Not a raging endorsement for my mental fortitude. She wanted to believe that her insistence on sticking her neck out for him was a simple tribute to her decency as a human being.

Even later, when she was drawing the bathwater, she refused to wander into the dangerous territory of the truth. It was simpler to examine the motivations of others than it was to turn the tables on herself. Particularly when it came to her feelings for Shane.

Stripping off her clothing, she slipped into the hot, soothing water. Maybe she could wash them away. Scrub off the feelings she wouldn't acknowledge, but couldn't explore. Doing so would derail her life plan.

She rested her head against the pillow at the back of the tub, letting the warm water massage her body. Though her muscles were relaxing, her brain was not.

The threatening situation offered the perfect excuse to leave. "That's what I want, right? So why didn't I take the easy out?" she asked in a whisper.

Her own words echoed off the tiled walls, almost

taunting her for the answer. "Because when all is said and done, regardless of my careful planning, regardless of my education or my degrees, I'm *her.* I'm living proof that life's bad choices are cyclical. I could have left. I should have left. I had an out but instead argued to stay. Insisted! Knowing it is the worst possible choice. Knowing it is not in my best interests. Knowing it is flaming *dangerous.* I am," she acknowledged as she started to lower herself below the waterline, "a complete idiot and very much my mother's daughter."

TAYLOR TOOK HER TIME primping, dressing, basically dragging her heels. It was never easy to admit you were on the road to heartache. "Yet here I am," she sighed as she pulled on some thick socks. Out of habit, she spritzed on perfume and fluffed her hair before venturing out.

The house smelled of bacon, and that brought an instant smile to her lips. Shane's culinary skills were limited to scrambled eggs or BLTs.

She stopped in the hallway, realizing he hadn't heard her approach. A thrilling sensation started in her belly, then spread the tingle all through her body. Shane was busy assembling sandwiches. An innocent, normal activity that was anything but.

The sleeves of his denim shirt were rolled to midforearm, but it was the way the fabric hugged his broad back and shoulders that drew her interest. Well, that and the way his worn, faded jeans outlined his narrow waist, great butt and long, powerful legs. Taylor actually shivered.

That initial tingle morphed into warmth, making her feel flushed all over. The man inspired any number of fantasies—vivid, needy desires that only made the hot flash worse.

So, of course, he had to turn around at that moment. Turn and see the unguarded passion that must have been evident on her face.

It was. He did.

At least she assumed so, since he tossed the knife on the counter and virtually issued an invitation with his gaze. Tension crackled in the air between them. Tension born and raised on years of denial.

It would be so easy, not to mention satisfying, to simply walk into his arms. Easy but stupid. She had to remember that.

Swallowing hard, she cleared her throat and said, "Smells good."

His head tilted, and she could almost hear the litany of questions racing through his mind. Questions she couldn't answer.

"Want me to set the table?" she asked as she breezed in, heading for the drawer with every intention of getting silverware.

Shane was having no part of it. Not this time. Not after seeing the hunger in her eyes. "No." For once, he was confident when he reached for her. "Not after the look you just gave me."

He caught her by the waist and pulled her against him. Her soft curves fit him perfectly. Her hair smelled of citrusy shampoo, a scent complementing her subtle, feminine perfume.

She peered up at him through her lashes as her palm

flattened against his chest. The fluttery sensation of her fingers splayed on his body caused his heart to skip a beat.

Shane spread his feet as he placed his other arm around her. It allowed him to compensate for their height difference, but offered the added bonus of settling her snugly against that part of his body that ached and throbbed.

"You feel good," he murmured, pressing his lips to her forehead.

Her breaths, shallow and unsteady, tickled his throat. Taylor's hands were trapped against his chest. Her fingers closed, grabbing fistfuls of his shirt as she leaned into him.

Her back arched slightly as she lifted her mouth to his. Shane countered, leaning back to study every beautiful inch of her face. He smiled, moving his hands up her back, deliberately counting each vertebra until his fingers tangled in her silken hair. "Ready to ask yet?"

She blinked. "Ask?" she repeated in a husky, painfully sexy tone he hardly recognized. "Why do you think I'm standing here?"

He slipped his thumbs beneath her chin, feeling the racing pulse at her throat. "That's the problem, Taylor. I never know what you think. So I need to hear the words from you. I want to know that you need me."

Stunned was the only word he could think of to describe the way he felt when she practically rocketed out of his hold. How did they go from passionate embrace to this?

"What?"

She moved back, until she was practically plastered against the wall. Nervously, she fidgeted with her hair and kept her gaze averted. And she hadn't answered. He took a step toward where she stood.

"C'mon, Taylor, we—" He was silenced by the fact that she went rigid, looking…frightened. "I don't get this," he admitted. "You walked in here all hot and bothered. Don't try to deny it, either. I saw the look in your eyes, Taylor. I felt the way you trembled in my arms. And the next thing I know, you're cowering in the corner. What gives?"

She rubbed her face, sucking in a deep breath. "It's complicated, Shane."

"Try me," he suggested, moving back to lean against the counter. It gave him something to do with his hands, something other than shaking her until she opened up.

"I don't want to start something I can't finish."

"More like you don't want to start something *period*. Why? It's because you don't think I'm your intellectual equal, right?"

"Where did you get that stupid idea?" she demanded in a pretty convincing imitation of surprise.

He wasn't buying it. "You are always making cracks about it. Just because I don't have—"

"A clue." She fired the retort at him. "My apprehensions have nothing to do with your IQ. How could you even think such a thing?"

"Because you tease me mercilessly?" he suggested.

"I tease you because it's easier."

"Easier than what?"

She met and held his eyes. "Easier than any of the other options."

"You're wrong."

"No," she said, her shoulders slumping. "It could never work between us."

"That remains to be seen."

"What does that mean?" she asked, her brow wrinkled.

"It means," he said, as he walked over and tapped the tip of her cute little nose, "that I'll have to work hard to change your mind."

Chapter Six

Taylor's restless night was ten percent delayed reaction to the scary experience at the abandoned Hudson place and ninety percent reaction to Shane's comment.

Or maybe it was more like two percent to ninety-eight percent. At any rate, it was bad. So, as had become her practice since moving to the ranch, she needed to work out her frustrations by doing something in the kitchen.

Luckily, Shane's room was on the second floor, insulated from any noise. Shane's room—the one with the huge four-poster bed and masculine appointments. Taylor didn't want to count how many times she'd pressed his pillow to her face when changing his sheets, just to smell the heady fragrance of his skin. Or how many times she'd uncapped his cologne, or lain on his bed and fantasized about how different things could be—

"Stop it," she snapped as she flipped on the switch. The reality was if she wanted sex with Shane all she'd ever had to do was *ask*. As she well knew, a man didn't have to be emotionally involved with a woman to have sex. And she'd made her decision about casual sex years and years ago. Long before she'd ever met Shane Landry.

Sex with him would be… Taylor pressed a hand to the butterflies dive-bombing in her tummy. Sex with Shane would be incredible. She knew that. Just having his mouth on hers was enough to fry all her brain cells and make her forget her promise to herself.

Never depend on a man to make you happy. She mouthed the words to herself. Reminded herself that her mother had been tempted, too. Many times. And look how well that had turned out for her mom every time she ended up caved in like a wet meringue.

"No thanks, not me." Taylor Reese was going to use the excellent brain God had given her, and parlay it into a satisfying, lucrative career. She was going to get personal satisfaction helping people who needed her. She was not—absolutely *not*—going to throw her life and happiness away on the whim of a man.

Not even a man like Shane Landry.

No matter how strong the temptation.

And, heaven help her, his attraction was overwhelmingly strong.

"Idiot." Dawn was still hours away, but she couldn't lie in bed, staring at the ceiling, for another second. So she'd tugged on her sweats, her socks, and pulled her hair into a ponytail, opting to do something mindless yet constructive.

The kitchen was cold but spotless. Shane was good about that. He never left a mess. Not even when she'd rushed through the meal he'd prepared and raced to her bedroom like the chicken she was.

She was still frowning at the thought a few minutes later

when the coffeepot coughed and sputtered, signaling it was done. Taylor poured herself a mug, warming her hands on the cup as she pondered her baking possibilities.

Deciding on what cookie to make was less complicated than trying to figure out what, if anything, to do about Shane. Or more accurately, what to do about her feelings for him.

"Which are?" she asked. Redundant question. She knew how she felt about him. She'd just gotten really adept at burying those feelings deep inside. So adept, in fact, that having them gurgle to the surface was hard to handle.

Feelings that were locked away deep in her heart or laid out raw weren't really the issue. The real problem was knowing she couldn't do anything about them. Not if she wanted to break the ugly pattern that had defined and destroyed the previous three generations of Reese women.

By the time she finished her cup of coffee, Taylor had decided to make peanut butter cookies. Going to the walk-in pantry, she nearly tripped over a box someone—Rollins's search warrant team, most likely—had shoved inside.

Irritation rose in her throat, so fervently that she could actually taste her own anger when she thought about the detective and his ridiculous suspicions. Personal vexation aside, she was instantly curious when she saw the scrawled label affixed to the box. Just a name—"Shane."

Yes, she knew it was wrong to look. It could be full of private things that were none of her business.

Knowing all that didn't seem to stop her from plopping down on the floor and lifting the lid. She justified her inappropriate prying by telling herself she was only checking to see if it contained anything that might exonerate Shane as a suspect in the murder of his parents. That was a good thing. It would get the police and the creepy caller off their backs.

"I'm a regular saint for doing this," she muttered, knowing full well her ability to rationalize her behavior didn't make it right.

The box, she realized as she scanned the neatly labeled compartments, was very personal and very organized. Hanging tabs created color-coded sections. Nestled inside each divider was a collection of folders organizing every aspect of Shane's life. There were crisp certificates of accomplishments covering everything from T-Ball participation to science fair ribbons. Yellowed, wrinkled school records were lined up in perfect chronological order.

Taylor couldn't resist the temptation, especially now that she knew he was so touchy about his intellect. Which was, she knew, absurd. How could he think he wasn't smart? Didn't he get that she understood what it took to run this place? Apparently not.

She pulled the school section out and placed it in her lap. She hesitated for a moment, reminded again that she had absolutely no right to pry. She wasn't prying; she was helping.

"Liar," she whispered as she opened the file. She smiled as she read, in great detail, Shane's less-than-stellar years in the Jasper School District. Apparently the man had never mastered the fine art of working and playing well with others. Several of his teachers noted a propensity for "independent thought"—educator code for refusing to do work as assigned.

There was a fat section devoted to invitations for conferences with the principal of Jasper High. Said principal's last few letters included discussions that caught Taylor's attention instantly. Apparently there was some concern about Shane's well-being and safety. His defiant attitude coupled with reports of frequent bruising had been red flags to the teachers.

"Was Caleb Landry abusive?" she wondered aloud, hearing her words echo in the room. That was something she'd never considered, but it would certainly explain a lot. Especially why Shane had bolted from the ranch once he turned eighteen, and then stayed away for so long.

It also might explain the haunted look in Shane's eyes whenever his father's name was mentioned.

Licking her fingertip, she quickly flipped through the file, trying to find some sort of comment, response or something to indicate his parents had reacted to the subtle but dire accusations from the principal. She didn't find anything indicating there had been a resolution.

After carefully replacing the file exactly where she'd found it, Taylor braced her hands behind her and leaned back to ponder this new information. Although she'd never heard a whisper that Caleb Landry had been a violent man, Shane's school records indicated that that might very well have been the case. This knowledge was a double-edged sword. If true, it would explain a lot about Shane's motivation for leaving the ranch, but it was also a strong motive for murder. She wondered if the school had ever contacted the authorities. Probably not; child abuse was considered a private family matter back then.

"What are you doing?" Shane asked from the doorway. Taylor gave a guilty start. No wonder. She *was* guilty. "I—I was cleaning the pantry," she stammered, pulling the prop of a dust cloth off her shoulder.

"You did that last week. How dirty does a pantry get?" he asked. His gaze flickered to the box on the floor as soon as he stepped into the room.

Shane leaned his large body against the wall and held out his hand, helping her to her feet.

"Boning up on my life history?" he queried.

A haunted look was present in the deep lines etched on his face. Compassion quickly erased her guilt as she looked at the man and, for the first time, saw the possibility of a childhood that wasn't as idyllic as she'd always been led to believe.

"I couldn't help it. You know me," she managed to murmur over the lump of emotion in her throat. "I'm not very good at minding my own business."

He offered a small smile before rubbing his hands over his face. "Rollins was going through that box when I got here yesterday. I'm not sure why, though."

"That doesn't automatically mean something bad." The pantry was small. Very, very small when filled with six feet of sleepy-eyed Shane Landry.

He cast her a sidelong glance. "I'll say again, I'm not stupid."

There was such pain behind his statement that she felt

like she had to do something. "Let's get out of here, I'm getting claustrophobia." She followed him back into the kitchen, nudging him to sit down in his chair as she poured him some coffee. Kneeling in front of him, Taylor closed one hand over his and reached out to cup his cheek in the other. "I do not think you're stupid. I never have and I never will," she said forcefully, holding his gaze.

Shane leaned forward and rested his forehead against her shoulder. She heard him sigh deeply as his face turned. His breath fanned against her throat as she stroked his head. She intended it as a comforting gesture. A harmless display of empathy for a man who'd probably spent a lot of time in deep, private emotional pain. She understood that very well. She also knew full well that child abuse led to desperate thoughts, which led to desperate acts. She didn't want to consider the possibility, but...

"I have a bad feeling about this. Rollins didn't say so, but I'm pretty sure he thinks I killed my parents."

She should have been thinking only of supporting him, but she wasn't. She was thinking about the fact that his hands were at her waist. His fingers separated, the tips nearly touching her spine. Here he was, in the midst of a personal crisis, and she was cataloging the scent of soap clinging to him, the even sound of his breathing and the firm muscles beneath her touch.

As she mentally damned herself to the fires of hell, Taylor started to inch out of his grasp. Shane resisted.

"Just let me hold you for a minute," he said in a voice she barely recognized. "Please?"

She couldn't very well say no to something she so desperately wanted herself. "Everything will work out," she promised, massaging the tight knots at the base of his skull.

"I don't think so." His pain-filled voice was muffled and her heart constricted. *Oh, Shane...*

Taylor focused off into space, silently pleading with her conscience to stop berating her as she stroked the back of his head. "There's nothing to worry about yet, Shane. Think positive thoughts until you have a solid reason to think otherwise."

"You don't understand, Taylor." His voice broke. "I *do* know otherwise. Fifteen years ago, I did something terrible."

"What?" Taylor asked, capturing his face in her hands, steeled for what he might admit. "What did you do?"

He read a thousand fleeting emotions in the pretty hazel eyes trained on his face. But it was the trust he saw in them that stabbed at him like a knife. She was going to despise him if he told her the truth. She was going to know what a jerk he'd been.

He was the first to look away. "I can't tell you, Taylor."

"Sure you can," she insisted, her palms cool on his skin as she exerted enough pressure to force him to look at her again. Her gaze was unwavering. "Believe me," she said softly, her thumb brushing against his cheek. "No good ever comes of keeping secrets."

Her fervent tone gave him pause. Regarding her quietly, he felt as if he was looking at a total stranger. A *dangerous* total stranger. Was this Taylor Reese, almost-psychotherapist, speaking? Or Taylor Reese, fantasy woman who didn't want to get too close to him, showing concern?

It could only be his imagination that made her words sound as though she knew from bitter experience what keeping secrets could do to a person. Which was absurd, because Taylor was the most straightforward, least secretive person he'd ever met.

As if life wasn't complicated enough. The day had barely started and already it was turning into a pretty intense cruel fest.

"Talk to me, Shane. Whatever you did, I'm sure it was justified. I'm sure the courts would take that into consideration and—"

"Courts?"

"If it was self-defense?" she prompted.

Stunned, he looked into her eyes as he gently set her aside. "You think I killed my own parents?"

She twisted a lock of pale hair around one finger. "There are situations, Shane. Circumstances when—"

"Jeez, Taylor!" he bellowed. "I said I did something terrible, not criminal. Don't you know me better than that?"

"We can never *really* know another person. I know you're a good man, Shane. So does everyone in Jasper. Whatever happened in the past can be fixed."

"No," he countered, "it can't." He raked his hair back off his face, incredulous that she would even entertain such a thought. "I didn't kill anyone, for chrissake."

He stood and went to the sink, looking out the window briefly before saying, "That last night, I, um, had a fight with my father."

She scrambled up and moved to the far side of the room, pacing, rolling her hands one over the other, perhaps in time with her brain. "And you exchanged words. One thing led to another. You struggled and maybe he fell and hit his head and—"

"Hey, Oliver Stone?" He would have laughed if the whole scenario wasn't so close to the truth. Well, all but the last little part. "Yes, I had a fight with my father. Yes, it got a little physical. But I was the one who ended up on my ass, not vice versa."

She paused and glanced in his direction, then went back to her pacing ritual. "Okay. So you knew your father was capable of physical violence. So…later on, fearing another altercation, you acted in a preemptive fashion to—"

"Earth to Taylor!" he called, moving over to take her by the shoulders in order to guide her to a seat at the table. "Since I'd like to stop you from trying, convicting and sentencing me, I'll tell you what happened. But first you've got to swear you won't repeat this story."

She blinked rapidly. "Wait! Maybe you shouldn't say anything. Remember what happened with Clayton and Tory? If I'm called to testify, I wouldn't have a choice."

"I'm willing to take that risk," he countered, mirroring her solemn expression even though he found himself perversely amused by her overreaction. So amused, in fact, that he lowered his voice to a conspiratorial tone and added, "If it does come to that, we can get married because, as we all learned, a wife can't testify against her husband."

Her eyes grew wide. "Okay," she agreed on a rush of breath.

He wasn't so amused anymore.

She bobbed her head as the words fell quickly from her lips. "We could do that if need be. All right. That's settled. Go ahead, you can tell me what happened."

"You'd marry me?"

"I wouldn't send you to jail," she answered. "We could use the subterfuge to fend off any court proceedings until we can figure out a way to get you off. Or…" she continued, folding her hands neatly in her lap, as if they were agreeing on the final preparations for a barbecue "…your lawyer negotiates a plea bargain."

"Or you could remember that you have a triple digit IQ and listen to me for a minute."

Her mouth snapped shut.

It was his turn to pace. Shane wasn't sure where to start. He just knew that with the investigation focusing on him, he had to tell someone. "I walked into the kitchen that night with a boulder-size chip on my shoulder. I was itching for a fight."

Taylor watched him take ten steps, turn and take an equal number in the opposite direction before repeating the pattern. Watching him wear an invisible rut into the floor allowed her to avoid thinking about the fact that in less than ten minutes, she had agreed to marry him as part of a defense strategy. *Where did that come from?* "Remind me again. How old were you?"

"Just turned eighteen," he said, his gaze focused off in the distance. "Thought I knew everything, too."

"Common adolescent mind-set."

He shrugged. "I guess."

The action pulled the well-washed cotton shirt taut against his shoulders. Taylor swallowed her errant thoughts. "So, you went into the kitchen and…?"

"I was hot and tired and pissed because he'd had me digging the new well by myself for the third straight day."

"Hard job. But necessary." Cruel of Caleb. Digging a well was backbreaking work for a team of men. What kind of vicious father would force his own son to do it alone? "The old well is the one where the…bodies were recovered?"

"Yes." Shane took in a deep breath and expelled it slowly. "Dad found out I'd broken the pump on the old well. Not from me, mind you," he admitted with more than a touch of guilt. "Which was why, instead of letting me fix the pump, he had me digging a whole new well."

"A character-building exercise," she murmured, thinking it wasn't a bad idea. The discipline seemed appropriate for the infraction. So, Caleb wasn't quite as big a creep as she'd first thought.

"I think he asked if I was finished yet, and my response was to tell him to go to hell."

"Not a good choice, huh?"

Shane rolled his eyes and sighed heavily. "He was furious. He jumped up and took a step toward me. I held up my hand, aiming for his chest, but somehow I managed to catch him in the nose. It bled, and the next thing I knew he had knocked me flat on my back."

"This? This is your terrible thing?" she asked. "You smarted off to your father. Then he raised his hand to you. That is *never* acceptable."

Shane shot her a glance. "Maybe not in perfect-parenting land. Get real, Taylor. I had height, muscle, age and attitude on him. Believe me, I deserved to be taken down a notch. Should have ended there, but it didn't." His expression grew dark.

She braced herself for the confession. "You were provoked."

"I was a teenager with a bruised ego," he snapped. "I decided to share some of that pain, so I lashed out."

"Understandable."

"I said some nasty things, Taylor. Really nasty. I guess I had stored up a lot of frustration and I just let loose."

"It happens."

"Not like that," he promised, joining her at the table and taking her hands in his. "I told him I was embarrassed to be his son. That was one of the kinder things I said."

"Shane…" she murmured, knowing full well there was little she could do to assuage the anguish in his eyes.

"It got ugly," he admitted, sadness making his voice heavy. "Mom came in, there was a big, dramatic scene. And—and…"

"What?"

Slowly, his eyes lifted and met hers. "I threatened to leave. Tossed it right there on the kitchen floor like a gauntlet. Flat-out dared him to try and run the ranch without me."

"Hoping he would be sobered at the thought of losing you and tell you how valuable you were to him and the family, and the argument would end?" she guessed.

He squeezed her hands. "Maybe. I don't know. Yeah. Probably."

"But?"

"He gave me an hour to pack up and get out."

Taylor cringed, just imagining the scene in her head. "So being a hardheaded eighteen-year-old, you left?"

"Yep. Took years for me to get the anger out of my system. Until I was finally ready to come back and patch things up with him."

But you never got the chance, she thought, her heart aching. "It was a fight. Nothing more. Why do you think that was so terrible?"

"While I was packing, I heard my parents going at it. Big time." He yanked back his hands, stood and returned to his pacing. "She was begging him to reconsider. He was accusing her of favoritism. I couldn't hear it all, but I did hear her accuse him of taking his anger out on me instead of her. Which made sense, since for the week leading up to the fight, my dad had been a real bear. There was something going on between the two of them. One minute they'd be holding each other, the next minute my father was ranting and raving."

"So they were in a rocky place. That happens in some marriages. Sounds like she was trying to get him to rethink the situation."

"Well, it didn't do any good. He yelled something back at her I couldn't hear. I stormed out of the house." Shane sat and dropped his head into his hands. "The last words I said to my father were said in anger. Now I know I can't ever make that right."

She scooted close to him, grabbing his hands. "Don't do this."

"I can't help it," he admitted, his expression and his tone dark. "I'd give anything if I could live that night over again. What if I hadn't been such a jerk, Taylor? They might not be dead."

Taylor pressed each of his palms to her mouth, kissing them in turn. "You can't know that, Shane."

"Easy for you to say. You didn't destroy your whole family."

"Now see? There you go again," she said. "Thinking you're the center of the universe. You aren't, Shane." Her hand lingered on his face. "A boy had a fight with his father. That's all. What your parents did afterward had nothing to do with you. It sounds to me as if you were a cocky kid who happened to find yourself on the edges of an ongoing argument between your parents. Hardly your fault. And rather conceited of you to think that you alone were capable of preventing a double murder, don't you see that?"

He reached up and took her palm from his face, kissing her fingers. "All that fancy education of yours is really paying off, isn't it?"

"It doesn't take a psychologist to see that this has been hurting you for fifteen years."

His guilt and pain started to fade as he reached to frame her face in his hands. "Will you kiss me better?" he asked, his voice husky as he urged her face closer to his.

"I'm offering support and all you can think of is kissing?"

"I'm game if you are."

She wanted his mouth on hers, Taylor admitted to herself, closing her eyes. Wanted to feel the warm brush of his breath on her lips, the firm pressure of his fingers tunneling through her hair.

When he tugged and brought her to him, taking her in his arms, she felt so many things all at once. The primal, womanly part of her knew kissing Shane was everything she'd ever wanted. Her rational side warned against such a foolhardy move; passion always trumped reason. Especially when every one of her senses was under the heady spell of having Shane's body pressed against her own.

Taylor memorized everything—the way his thighs brushed hers; the way his palms flattened against her back, fingertips splayed.

The need to mold her mouth against his, to finally have that first taste, was fierce and consuming. It dominated all of her thoughts and burned in her belly. She'd gone far beyond wanting it, she needed it. Soon. Now. Her body's sole reason for existing was the promise of the kiss to come. The culmination of years of vivid fantasies was at hand.

Lacing her fingers behind his neck, she pulled gently but urgently. Feeling his resistance, she met his hooded gaze. "What?"

"Savoring the moment," he said, his voice so deep and sensual it sent a thrill though her. "In a hurry?" One dark brow arched as his mouth curved into a sexy half smile.

"Actually, yes."

His warm lips brushed her forehead, igniting all the cells and adding unnecessary fuel to the embers sparking in her stomach. Breathing normally wasn't an option. Not when her whole body was little more than a cauldron of simmering need.

This had never happened with anyone. This consuming desire that pulsed, deafeningly loud, in her ears. Taylor felt as if she were under siege from every one of her nerve endings. She was on fire and he had yet to kiss her. It didn't seem plausible that the anticipation alone should have her quaking all over.

She tugged more forcefully, moving her body against his in hopes of ending the wait.

He moaned softly against her skin—a low, soft growl that made her feel powerful and feminine all at the same time. It was a heady sensation. One that fed the current electrifying the room.

The sudden sound of the phone ringing made her jerk away from him, completely shattering the moment.

"Hold that thought," Shane told her, his eyes giving her a promise as he leaned over to reach the insistently ringing phone on the counter. "It's got to be one of my brothers. They're the only ones who would dare call here so late. I swear, there are times when I hate Alexander Graham Bell for inventing this thing." He slapped a button on the base unit, putting the call on Speaker as he kept one arm firmly wrapped around her waist. "Shane Landry."

"Put Taylor on the line."

He frowned at the brusqueness of the command. "She's

a little busy right now, since it's barely dawn. Try calling back at a decent hour." Though his tone was harsh, it was tempered when he winked playfully in her direction.

"You're running out of time, Shane."

Taylor's blood stilled in her veins as she recognized the threatening, angry voice.

"Who is this?" Shane demanded.

"You need to confess. You have one week. Do it or she'll die."

"Hey, pal," Shane warned in a cold, merciless tone. "I don't know what—"

With a loud bang, the line went dead.

Chapter Seven

"That's it," Shane announced, "you're getting out of here. I'll get you on a plane and—"

"Wait!" Taylor pressed the heels of her hands against her eyes. "We have a week."

His jaw dropped for a second. "You actually trust a person who took a shot at you to keep their word?"

She nodded. "Sure, and it isn't like we have a lot of choices here. So let's figure out how to make the best use of the time we have." Taylor opened a drawer and grabbed the pad of paper she kept for grocery lists, pulled a pen out of the cup on the counter and went to the table.

Shane's lips twitched. "We're going to solve my parents' murder using a pad of paper in the shape of a kitten?"

She ignored his little taunt. "The first call I got said the evidence was in the attic." She looked into his eyes and asked, "Does that mean anything to you? Anything jump out?"

"The only time I go up in the attic is to get ammunition or holiday decorations."

"The ammo," she said as she scribbled a note. "What about the box in the pantry? Where did that come from?"

"The attic. Rollins brought it down," Shane said with a tad more enthusiasm. "Hang on." He hurried out of the room and reappeared a minute later with a sheet of paper. "This is the inventory of stuff they took after the search."

He placed it on the table, allowing them to review it together. "The gun case, one box of old bank statements and a family photo album," Shane murmured. "The box and the case were in the attic. The photo album was in the office. I'm not seeing a pattern here."

"Forget what they took," she said. "Let's focus on the things they left behind."

"Such as?"

"Well…" she hesitated as she went to the pantry "…maybe Rollins missed something."

Shane came and got the box and placed it on the table. "You want school, medical or athletic?" he asked.

"Your call," she answered, taking the stack of files he handed her and settling into the chair.

While Shane thumbed through his stack, Taylor opened the file marked Medical and silently prayed something would jump out at her. Some magic fact that would reveal the identity of the killer. However, she learned nothing from the first few pages other than Priscilla Landry had made certain her youngest child was immunized on schedule.

Nothing but common childhood illnesses, not until the age of five. "You had the mumps?" she asked, trying to decipher the handwriting at the bottom of the receipt from the doctor's office.

"No." Shane took the paper out of her hand, a smile curving his lips. "Wrong Landry," he mused. "Look at the date. This was before I was born, so the 'S. Landry' listed as the patient was Sam, not me. He never actually had the mumps. As the story goes, several of the hands had mumps and my mother was terrified that one of her boys had been exposed to the disease. I think she dragged him into the doctor's office every day for two weeks.

"Must have just been misfiled." Shane patted Taylor's hand. "God's way of punishing her for having so many sons with names that start with the same consonant."

"It is confounding to us outsiders," Taylor joked, hoping her voice sounded even because her heart rate certainly wasn't. Nope, not with his finger making those maddening circles on her skin.

A few minutes later, she came across another weird receipt in the file. "What's a platelet function test and why did you have one when you were ten?" she asked.

Setting aside the riding ribbon he'd been holding, Shane looked at the paper. "I remember that," he mused, frowning. "My mom drove me all the way to Helena to some lab. Then she bought me ice cream, a Fleetwood Mac album and a very cool die cast model of a red Gran Torino like the one in *Starsky and Hutch.*"

"So—" Taylor grinned "—you were a butterfat-craving car freak with a thing for Stevie Nicks?"

"Pretty much." Shane stroked his chin for a second. "Gotta give me points for great taste. Stevie Nicks is still one fine looking woman and that Torino was a hot car."

"You were obviously a man ahead of his time." She

snatched her hand out from under his. "But you don't remember why you were having tests?"

"I was ten," he reminded her with a small chuckle. "All I remember is that it hurt. Why?"

"Well—" Taylor pressed her lips together as she considered ways to broach such a touchy subject with him. "I saw some notes from teachers. Maybe your mother was...*concerned*."

"Not that again," he groaned. "I was not a battered child."

"But you just told me you and your father had a physical altercation," she reasoned, hoping it might make him more willing to open up to her. "Was it a pattern of behavior?"

"It was an eighteen-year-old kid getting what he deserved," Shane insisted. "Didn't your father ever put you in your place?"

"No."

It was the way she said the single syllable that caught his attention. Not sad, not angry, just flat. No effect, no emotion and not at all Taylorlike. "What's that about?"

"What?"

He scratched his head and scooted his chair at an angle so he could better see her face. "Come to think about it, what is your family situation?"

"We only have a week, Shane. Let's concentrate on this stuff before we go up to the attic."

"Oh, no you don't," he countered, tipping her head up with one finger and forcing her to look at him. "We can spare a few minutes. You're sitting here pawing through the first eighteen years of my life, so I think it's only right for you to have to share a few personal facts about yourself."

She fidgeted in the chair, something he'd never seen her do before. It only made him more determined to extract a few details. He also knew one of her few weaknesses: she could be guilted into things, because at her core, Taylor was a people pleaser. All people but him.

But that was about to change. He was not going to let her walk out that door without at least trying. Not yet. "I told you about the fight I had with my dad. Something I never told any other living, breathing soul. I confided in you." He was on a roll now. One that was working if her pinched expression was any indication. "I entrusted my secrets to you. Now I feel like—"

"Okay," she huffed, shoving her hair off her face with a vengeance. "Just remember, you asked to hear this tawdry tale."

"I did," he agreed, placing his hand on her knee, giving it a squeeze, then leaving it there as he looked into her troubled eyes. "I do."

"After giving birth to me, my mother left the hospital and went directly to a lawyer's office to file a paternity suit against the married man who was my father."

"Sounds like she was just looking out for your best interests," he offered.

"I don't think *I* entered into the equation. See, I was the means to an end. She wanted that man. The man who didn't have any desire to leave his wife, so I was the trap. A way for her to get what she wanted."

"Whoops." Shane flinched. "People make mistakes."

"That was just the first one in a long line of mistakes," she told him bitterly. "Since Mom's plan back-fired, we had no choice but to move in with my grand-mother, who was, at the time I was born, the ripe old age of thirty-six." One pale, perfect brow arched as she watched him do the math. "Yes, sir, my grandmother did almost the same thing. However, her lover wasn't married, he was selected as her ticket out of the house. That lasted less than two years.

"My grandmother wasn't too thrilled to have us around, so my mother set her sights on one loser after another. None of my 'uncles...'" she paused to make air quotes, "...lasted very long. She'd fall in love. We'd move to wherever uncle du jour could find work. The re-lationship would spiral, normally ending with blowouts that required police intervention. I think I learned how to spell 'restraining order' before my own name."

"Oh, Taylor..."

"We're not finished yet," she insisted. "When I was ten, my mother hooked up with a guy fresh out of jail. Duane Treadwell was a nasty drunk and my mother, for some sick reason, worshiped him."

"Did he hurt you?"

"Me?" Taylor repeated. "Heavens no. Duane barely noticed I was in the house. Probably helped that I spent most of my time burrowed under the covers with a book and a flashlight. They lived together for about three months when it happened the first time. It was a school night—I remember because my science project was on the kitchen table. One of those volcanoes every kid has to make?"

Shane nodded, remembering it well. "My lava didn't bubble when I added the vinegar."

"I heard screaming and thuds. More screaming and then a loud crash, so I went running out of my room."

"And?"

"Duane was straddling my mother, pounding her already bloody face. I ran to the neighbor's house—I'm not sure either one of them heard me leave—and called the police."

"I hope they locked the bastard up."

She shook her head. "Mom wouldn't press charges. So after spending half the night in the back seat of a patrol car, I ended up going back inside to find that during their fight, my volcano had been smashed to pieces."

"What about your mother?"

Taylor shrugged. "The paramedics patched her up. One of them, a nice red-headed guy, kept urging her to go to the hospital, but she wouldn't leave Duane."

"I'm sorry, Taylor," Shane exclaimed.

"Well, everyone has baggage. The police officers who responded that night alerted Family Protective Services. I was pulled out of class the next week. The caseworker tried to convince my mother to voluntarily remove me from the home. She was more than willing."

"That *really* sucks." Shane felt his body tense as he imagined the scene.

"So, off to Grandmother's I went, only she was in pretty much the same situation. Her boyfriend at the time would disappear for days on end, return smelling like cheap perfume—I'm not sure how, but he had a second woman supporting his sorry butt. He and Grandma would fight, more police. Never any charges filed, just more begging and pleading and empty promises, yada, yada, yada.

"I was shuffled back and forth depending on who had the lesser-evil man in her life at the time. Until I was thirteen."

"What happened then?"

"My mother had spent three whole months without Duane. A record, by the way. It was the first time ever, I think, I'd made it through a whole half year without changing schools. She got a job as a cocktail waitress in some dive outside the town were we lived. That's how I learned how to cook," Taylor added as an aside.

It was the only time during the story that Shane had seen a hint of anything other than pain in her eyes. "For which I am eternally grateful," he declared fervently.

"Thank you. Then one night she came in and I heard her laughing, so I knew she wasn't alone. I figured it was some guy from the bar. My mother always had her eye out for the next man she was sure would make her life whole.

"It took a minute, but I eventually recognized the voice. Duane was back. I remember sitting in my room, feeling physically ill when I realized he was back in our lives. Mom was ecstatic, welcoming him back as if all the beatings and broken bones were an acceptable price to pay for a prize like him."

"Maybe we should drop it," Shane suggested, feeling all kinds of horrible for making her relive everything.

"Why? Don't you want to know how the story ends?"

"I'm guessing not too well," he said, taking her hand in his and pressing it to his lips.

"No, not well at all. Mom quit her job so she could be home at Duane's beck and call. It wasn't long before he slipped back into the same predictable pattern of all my mother's boyfriends. He'd be charming, then snap. They'd fight, she'd forgive him."

"Duane was a pig," Shane said, holding her hand to his cheek.

"But it was *her* choice," Taylor argued fervently. "She was defined by the Duanes in her life. She didn't make a single decision in her entire lifetime that wasn't predicated on finding a man, keeping a man or pleasing a man. Even me. The only reason she had me was to try to bond herself to a man who never really wanted her in the first place."

"We don't get to choose our relatives."

Taylor smiled at him, which seemed to ease some of the torment he read in her eyes. "No, we don't. You got very lucky. I got Duane."

Curiosity got the better of Shane. "What happened to him?"

"He died."

"When?"

"A hour after he killed my mother."

Shane grimaced and squeezed her hand. "You were thirteen?"

Taylor nodded slowly, stiffly. "Yep."

"I'm assuming you went to live with your grandmother?"

"You'd be wrong," she said, pulling her hand free. "My grandmother had just met the new man of her dreams, and taking in her teenage granddaughter wasn't tops on her list of priorities. Since my mother had never identified my biological father, I went into foster care."

"That's rough."

Taylor chuckled softly. "It should be," she admitted, "but in truth, it was the best thing that ever happened to me. I lived with three families over the course of five years. When you're in the foster care system, you know everything is temporary, but I was used to that. It took me longer to adjust to family dynamics that didn't include fighting and hitting and police and..."

"What happened to your grandmother?" Shane asked.

"Last I heard, she was in Arizona living with a guy she claimed was her one true love. That was seven years ago."

Shane regarded her for a long time. "I'm really sorry for you, Taylor. No kid should grow up feeling scared and unloved."

"Like you said, we don't get to choose our relatives." She gave his arm a gentle squeeze. "Don't look so horrified, Shane. I dealt with my grief and losses a long time ago. I'm over it."

"Is that why you don't have relationships?"

"I have relationships." Her fingers fell away from his arm. "I date, Shane. More often than you, by my count."

"Yes, you date," he conceded. "But not for very long. Name the last guy you went out with more than three times."

She opened her mouth, and he grinned when she had no choice but to snap it shut. "See?"

"Don't act so superior, Shane. Ever think I might just be waiting for the right guy to come along?"

"Nope," he answered confidently. "After hearing

your story, I'm pretty sure that you wouldn't recognize the right guy if he had it tattooed on his forehead." He chuckled. "You're not aloof, Taylor, you're afraid."

"Hardly," she said. "I'm just not going to be like my mother and my grandmother. I'm not ever going to let myself *need* a man."

Chapter Eight

"I'm going up to the attic," she told him, annoyed at him, at herself—hell, even the sun slipping over the distant mountains was getting on her nerves. *Why did I have to go tell him all that personal stuff?*

"I'm coming, too," he said, his mouth curved in a wide grin.

That didn't improve her sour mood. Not when she replayed his snide little "tattooed" remark in her mind. Didn't he get it? Obviously not, or he wouldn't have been so quick to…*to hit the nail on the head?*

Taylor was chased out of the room by her inner turmoil. Someone had taken a shot at her; Shane topped a short list of murder suspects. So this was a pretty bad time to be rethinking her life plan just now.

With him on her heels, she climbed the staircase to the second floor. The fading scent of lemon oil filled her nostrils as her hand skimmed the polished banister on the way up. Except for hers, all the bedrooms were on the second floor. She often tried to pick a favorite. Not an easy chore, since each room had its own unique feel.

With the parents' bodies found, she wondered if the master suite would be redone. It hadn't been touched since their disappearance, save for dusting and vacuuming, in all these years.

It was a gorgeous room, with handcrafted furniture custom-made for the space. Decor included a rich, warm palette of corals and beiges that worked perfectly with the greens and browns of vegetation visible through the large window that dominated one wall. A beautiful stone fireplace was angled in one corner, allowing whoever was on the bed to see not only a flicker of a warm fire, but also the majestic Rockies beyond.

The bathroom was massive, but it was the only one in the house that hadn't been redone. Taylor could practically close her eyes and imagine the possibilities of a complete makeover. Polished granite vanities, updated fixtures, maybe even a walk-through shower. *Or maybe I should stop decorating a room I won't be here long enough to see!*

Accompanied by Shane, she continued down the long hallway toward the attic ladder, automatically using her sleeve to erase a palm print on the hall table as she passed. Rollins or his men, she guessed, frowning. "You should do something with these rooms," she told Shane as they passed the empty bedrooms vacated months earlier when Sam and his family had moved to their new home.

"What do you suggest?" he asked.

"Furniture would be a good start."

"Not my area," he countered, reaching around her to capture the string dangling from the ceiling at the end of the long hall. "I like to think I'm a sensitive guy, but I draw the line at fabric swatches and paint chips. You should do it."

"I can't." She backed up as he unfolded the hinged ladder that allowed access to the attic.

"Why not?"

"First, it's not my house," she said, turning and lifting her face to his. "Secondly, to do it correctly, I'd need more than four weeks when my schedule is already crazy. Even if I didn't have a threatening caller running me in circles, I have final exams to take, résumés to send out, packing…"

His expression darkened as he reached and grabbed her around the waist. He lifted her onto the second step, magically erasing the height differential.

A curious thrill danced through her when she found herself eye to eye with him for the first time ever. His head tilted ever so slightly and that sexy, crooked half smile of his ignited a little fire in the pit of her belly.

"We need to be investigating in the attic."

"Even Nancy Drew took some personal time," he countered, tucking a wayward lock of hair behind her ear.

"If you're going to confess to being a closet Nancy Drew fan now, it will really spoil the moment for me," Taylor teased, feeling the tension build in the inches separating his mouth from hers.

"Well, I have no intention of spoiling the moment," Shane said, his deep voice resonating all the way into her bones. "Kiss me, Taylor." His fingers lingered, stroking her cheek.

Curiosity that had been with her for years took on a

new character—one she could only define as raw, power-ful, urgent need. Taylor searched his face, somehow ac-cepting that something between them had changed.

Shane saw the transformation in her. It was subtle to be sure, but he recognized it instantly, instinctively. Days and nights of wanting her fortified him as he placed his palms on the sides of the ladder. "Tell me what you want, Taylor. It has to be your decision."

He rested his forehead against hers, savoring the feminine scent of her flawless, smooth skin. "I don't want to rush you, but I'm not sure how much longer I can keep my hands off you."

Watching her, he swallowed a groan when her tongue darted out to moisten her lower lip. Her mouth glistened in the pale glow of filtered light streaming in from the window.

"Please, Taylor? Tell me what you want, but do it quickly."

"I honestly don't know. I'm all confused and…" Her husky voice trailed off as her palms flattened against his chest.

Shane felt the small tremor in her touch, saw the hint of a smile on her mouth and decided that combination was encouragement enough. Wrapping her in his arms, he held her for a second, reining in his own fierce desire.

Decision made.

Lifting her off the ladder, ignoring her muffled shriek of surprise, he carried her back down the hallway. Pre-ternaturally aware of her every breath, he twined his fingers in her silken hair as he carried her to his room. He relished the feel of her soft form against his chest, vividly aware of the swell of her breasts and the taut flatness of her stomach. His body's response was intense and immediate.

It was nothing shy of a miracle that he found his way to the bedroom, given the passionate fog swirling in his brain. When his shins contacted the edge of the bed, he lowered her to the mattress.

He expected—hell, was braced for—a long and convoluted reason why they shouldn't be doing what they were doing. But none was forthcoming.

Since she wasn't protesting, and hadn't beat him about the head with a blunt instrument, Shane took it as a sign and felt free to breathe again. Laying her in the center of his bed, he slid next to her, placed one of his legs over hers, then searched her upturned face. Her hands began to skim the taut muscles of his back. When her fingertips began exploring the contour of his spine, Shane wasn't sure whether to push or pull. Every one of his greedier, baser instincts longed to surrender to his primitive desires.

His dwindling self-control wanted her begging, wanted there to be no question that her need was as great as his own. As he looked deeply into her eyes, he knew he didn't want her to merely enjoy, he wanted her pleading for his touch, totally sure and totally wild. Desperate even. Maybe then she would see the truth: nothing that felt this right could possibly be wrong.

With that singular goal in mind, he lowered his mouth and began teasing the seam of her lips with his tongue. It took immense willpower to savor the moment while harnessing his own passions in order to inspire hers.

He kissed her softly, angling her face beneath him by gently tugging the strands of her silky hair tangled in his hands. He felt her nails dig into the planes of his back as he slipped his tongue into the warm recesses of her mouth.

Deepening the kiss, Shane dropped one hand to her tiny waist and urged her against him. She complied willingly, even enthusiastically. Having Taylor in his arms, feeling her body against his, inspired a sudden clarity that had nothing to do with lust. He didn't just want her. He loved her.

That should have scared him. Terrified him even, but it didn't. It made him want her all the more.

"You taste like coffee," she said against his mouth. "Shane?"

He held his breath, afraid she'd call a halt to things. Afraid she wouldn't. "You taste better," he said, burying his face against her throat. Her heated skin tasted fresh and clean. No cologne, no perfume, just Taylor. It was a heady, alluring scent.

Taylor could hardly breathe. He was exciting, strong and solid. The weight of his leg fell across her abdomen, pressing against the core of her desire. It was becoming more and more impossible to keep her passion in check. She groaned and lifted her lashes when his mouth trailed a fiery path to her lips. He kissed her again as he shifted in order to work his leg between hers. The intimacy of the action lanced through her, forcing her to arch against him as her primal instincts responded. "Shane," she whispered, knowing full well it was now or never.

He made a strangled, guttural sound that tugged at her resolve. "Don't,' he pleaded as he lifted his dark head. The raw, blatant sensuality in his voice was almost as erotic as the feel of his hand slinking up her rib cage.

His blue eyes locked on hers. "Don't stop me now, Taylor. It will be good," he said as his mouth dipped to her throat. "So good."

"I know," she admitted, clamping her eyes shut. "That's what I'm afraid of."

He caught her face between his hands. She noted a tremor in his square-tipped fingers. "You're driving me crazy, Taylor. Do you have any idea how much I want you? How long I've wanted you?"

"I think I've got some idea," she teased, arching her body against the unmistakable evidence of his desire.

A deep, rich moan rumbled in the back of his throat. Taylor felt very powerful at that instant. It had a heady effect on her that formed an effective barrier between her conscience and her passion. She'd deal with the consequences of her rash behavior later. For now, she slipped her arms around his neck and drew him to her. Opening her mouth eagerly to his, she banished all doubts in favor of satisfying her own urgent desires.

"Tell me you want me," he instructed in a nearly desperate whisper. "I need to hear the words from you, Taylor."

"I want you."

"Finally," he breathed, as he moved to cover more of her body with his.

Now that he knew exactly what was driving him, Shane hurried to pull the shirt over her head. Much to his pleasure, Taylor was doing some exploring of her own. She had unbuttoned his shirt and splayed her fingers across his chest. She stroked upward, flattening her palms against his nipples.

"You have an amazing body," she breathed admiringly.

Shane thought he might explode with male pride. It was the first time she'd given him a compliment and it did incredible things to his ego.

"As do you," he murmured, propping himself up on his elbow as his fingers made easy work of the front clasp on her lacy wisp of a bra. As he covered one of her breasts with his palm, he noted her skin was pleasantly flushed, and he could feel her heart beating against his hand. When he teased her taut nipple between his thumb and forefinger, she sucked in a quivering breath and his hand stilled. "Did I hurt you?"

"Not exactly," she told him with a wry smile. "Unless it counts for me to admit that I want you so much it aches."

"That counts, honey. Big time," he said, grinning down at her.

"Why aren't you kissing me?" she asked, desperation in her voice.

"I'm watching. I like seeing the way your eyelashes flutter when I do this," he explained, tracing the outline of puckered, mauve skin surrounding the tight bud of her nipple. "Or maybe this." He delighted in hearing her sharp intake of breath when his mouth closed on her body. She went instantly rigid, then arched her back as her hands gripped his head.

Shane made quick work of dispensing with their

clothes, then took his time exploring every beautiful inch of her body. She was perfect, exquisite, and reacting to his touch with a primal, greedy honesty that convinced him she, too, felt more than just lust.

When he finally buried himself inside her in one heartfelt thrust, Shane was half out of his mind. It was so perfect, so right. She matched him move for move, as if the encounter had been choreographed. He tried to make it last, wanted this to go on forever. But when he felt her shudder, felt her teeth nip at his shoulder in the throes of climax, it sent him over the brink. He moaned softly, feeling his body shatter as his need spilled into her.

Much, much later, Taylor lay cradled in the crook of his arm, but it wasn't just the two of them there. Nope, she'd been joined by a large, heavy quantity of guilt and remorse and...*son of a gun, was that ever good!*

She had to remind herself that this was just sex. Great sex. Incredible *Shane* sex. But just sex. Not a lifetime commitment.

Good. Great. Perfect.

Exactly the way she wanted it.

I have to make my own way, build my own life. Then and only then, can I even consider sharing any part of myself with someone.

She could keep beating herself up, or she could get up and make sure it never happened again. Everyone was entitled to make a mistake.

Mistake, my foot! her conscience argued. That was some seriously toe-curling, mind-blowing sex.

"We'd better get back on task," she suggested,

clutching the sheet to her chest as she grabbed up some of her clothing.

Shane looked over at her, wearing nothing but a lazy, sexy smile that made her blush. "I like this task. Give me five minutes and—ouch!"

She elbowed him, then insisted he hand her the clothes that were out of her reach. "Focus, Landry."

"I'm focused," he assured her, nuzzling her neck.

Taylor's spine melted, but she managed to resist the temptation of spending more time in his bed.

Shane reluctantly got up, handed Taylor her bra and panties, then pulled on his jeans. He felt better than he had in, well, forever. Acknowledging to himself that he was completely in love with Taylor was the difference. Now, he just had to figure out a way to get her to see the light.

He turned, read the jumbled emotion in her eyes and knew he had his work cut out for him. He shrugged on his shirt, realizing she was uncomfortable at the prospect of dressing in front of him. He swallowed a smile, knowing she wouldn't appreciate the fact that he found that amusing. They'd just shared the most intimate encounter known to mankind and she was reluctant to let him see her naked.

"I'm going to get a drink. Want me to get you some water?"

She nodded.

"Be right back," he said, kissing the tip of her nose.

He went down the stairs whistling, feeling on top of the world. So happy it was everything he could do to keep from puffing out his chest and having a manly

Tarzan moment. Another thing he was pretty sure Taylor wouldn't appreciate in the least.

He had just come off the last step when there was a loud knock at the front door. Rolling his eyes, he wondered which of his nosy brothers he'd find on the other side. He also felt lucky that he hadn't bothered to unlock the door earlier, as was his practice. What if one of them had walked in on them? Taylor would have freaked. There was no way he was going to let any of his brothers mess this up. There was too much at stake.

He was going to make winning her heart his mission.

Starting now. By telling whoever was on the other side of the door to buzz off.

Twisting the lock with one hand while simultaneously turning the knob, Shane was surprised and annoyed to find Detective Rollins on his doorstep.

"Yes?"

"May I come in?"

"For what?"

"We need to talk. We can either do it here or at the station."

Shane eyed the man, curious, but also feeling alarm bells sound in his head. "What do we have to talk about that's so important?"

"The DNA results. You were a match to the evidence on the bloody towel found in the well."

"That makes sense, since my understanding is my parents' blood was on that towel."

"It was," Rollins agreed, shifting his weight from foot to foot. "Because we took DNA from you and your brothers, the lab was able to isolate the samples on the towel." Rollins pressed his lips together, then repeated, "I really think we should do this inside, Shane."

"Suit yourself. Come on in." He kept his tone even, but Shane had a bad feeling. That sense of foreboding caused the hairs at the nape of his neck to prickle as he ushered the detective into the living room.

Buttoning his shirt, Shane remained quiet as Rollins selected one of the chairs flanking the sofa, and sat down.

"So," Shane prompted, "what's the problem?"

Rollins pulled out his trusty little notepad. "What do you know about DNA, Shane?"

"Enough to know that people get half of theirs from each parent. Which totally explains why my blood would be a match to the samples. It was, right?"

Rollins nodded. "You and your brothers all matched two out of the three samples."

Shane relaxed, taking a deep breath and letting it out slowly. "So what's the problem?"

"The results showed an…*abnormality*."

"What does that mean?"

"Well, Shane, the lab people tell me you and your brothers should have matched the same samples, since you're siblings."

"We didn't?"

"No," Rollins answered, his voice solemn. "Can you explain that?"

Raking his hands through his hair, Shane considered the possibilities. "Sure. Your lab screwed up."

"Not likely," Rollins said.

"How can you be so sure?" he asked, catching a

glimpse of Taylor in his peripheral vision. He motioned her into the room. "You remember Taylor?"

"Yes," Rollins said, getting to his feet and extending his hand in her direction. "Not to be rude, Miss Reese, but I think Shane might prefer if you weren't in the room when—"

He draped his arm around her shoulder. *"Shane,"* he said, jaw tight, "has no problem with her being in the room."

The detective shrugged. "Suit yourself."

"Can I get you something? Coffee?" she asked.

Shane almost laughed. He knew her well—well enough to know there was a lot of hostility buried in that polite offer. "Don't bother. The detective won't be here that long. Detective? You were in the middle of telling me why your lab couldn't possibly have made a mistake?"

"If there was a mistake, then there'd be no way your DNA would match two of the samples."

"But I did match," Shane countered. "Right?"

"Yes. According to the lab, the sample provided by you is a blend matching the DNA identified as that of Priscilla Landry and the unidentified third sample."

"What does that mean?" Taylor practically yelped.

"It means," Rollins explained, "that based on the samples of the seven brothers, the lab was able to identify the bloodstains on the towel as belonging to Mr. and Mrs. Landry as well as blood from another, unrelated individual, probably their killer."

Shane's mind spun at a dizzying speed. "So you're telling me Caleb Landry wasn't my father?"

"That and worse," Taylor said, her large eyes lifted to his. "He's suggesting the DNA results indicate you're the killer. He's saying you killed your parents, Shane."

Chapter Nine

Chance Landry was seated in his customary seat at the family table, his eyes scanning the report for the second time.

"You're a doctor," Taylor practically yelled, "explain what this means."

"It makes no sense," Chance said, deep lines etched on either side of his eyes. "Where's Shane now?"

Taylor angrily blew at a stray hair caught in her lashes. "The detective had a warrant for another blood sample, so Shane had to go to the state police lab."

Chance shook his head, his expression a blend of anger and agony. "Shane *is* a Landry. I don't give a cra—crud what the DNA says. The samples were degraded. That evidence was down a well for fifteen years."

"That's what Rollins said. That's why he wanted another blood sample from Shane." Taylor felt like a caged animal, and a useless one to boot. "What can I do?" she asked, pacing restlessly.

"He left you here alone?" Seth chimed in after appearing suddenly in the doorway.

She glanced over at him. "He didn't have much of a choice. Besides, I got another call." She spent a few more wasted minutes bringing the brothers up to speed.

"You bought that one-week thing?" Seth scoffed, grabbing the phone, punching the keypad with a tad more force than necessary. "This is Sheriff Landry. I need a rush dump on incoming calls to this number." He ended that call and made another. "Sheriff Landry. Put me through to the bank manager, please."

"What are you doing?" Chance asked.

Seth covered the mouthpiece, then said, "I want copies of the bank records Rollins took. I'm not going to sit around and do nothing."

"Me, either," Chance agreed. "I'll see if I can't track down Shane's old medical records. Maybe there's something in there that can explain this DNA foul-up."

Taylor listened as the brothers mobilized, which was comforting, but did little to assuage her feelings of uselessness. Clayton was called, dispatched to the state police lab to obtain samples for independent testing.

The bank manager would have the copies within the hour, so Seth could deliver them to Sam for review. Chandler's job was to hunt through newspaper archives, pulling any stories written about the disappearance of the Landrys. Cody was all over old police records, using his FBI contacts to see if any similar crimes with the same MO might have been committed around the same time.

"I need something to do," Taylor insisted. "How can I help?"

"By staying put and staying safe," Seth answered. "I

asked Will to send one of the hands up here until Shane gets back."

She balled her hands into fists at her sides. "I would prefer something a little more proactive," she complained. "I can't do nothing!"

"Sorry, Taylor," Chance said. "The best thing you could do to help him is to stay here. We have to focus all our efforts on Shane right now."

A scant few minutes later, she was standing alone in the kitchen. That didn't last too long. Luke Adams knocked on the door and she almost didn't remember meeting him. Then she saw the tattoos on his knuckles and the flash of his cosmetically-corrected smile.

"Ma'am," he said in greeting, tipping the brim of his hat before removing it as he came inside. "Will sent me up here to sit with you."

"No need," she countered as politely as possible under the circumstances. "I mean, make yourself at home. I've got some things to take care of upstairs."

His eyes sparkled with interest. This time when he openly checked her out, she found it offensive. "On second thought, why don't you have a cold drink and enjoy the view from the porch." She hurriedly grabbed a can of soda from the fridge, slapped it into his hand and all but shoved him and his hat out the door.

Taylor raced up the stairs, ran to the attic ladder and climbed up into the musty darkness. Her hand ran along the wall until she found the switch and flipped it with the tip of her index finger.

It was a massive space, running almost the entire length of the large home. Taylor frowned when she noted that the boxes were no longer neatly stacked against the wall. Rollins and his warrant cretins had certainly made a mess. As she moved farther into the cavernous space, she cursed the detective, then coughed as her movements kicked up dust.

Taylor's search wasn't exactly a methodical undertaking, probably because it was her first ever. There had to be in excess of fifty boxes in the attic, in addition to several sealed plastic containers, old furniture and countless accessories and accent pieces.

"I can probably forget the cradles," she mused, distracted as she briefly admired the handcrafted items. The spindles and detail work were familiar; she recognized the same hand that had done much of the woodwork throughout the home. Shane was a direct descendant of the town founder.

"Or so we all thought," she muttered, still confused by the results of the DNA tests. They had to be wrong. A mistake, faulty, something. "A lot like my self-control."

Taylor felt a twinge of conscience, an annoying mix of regret and exhilaration as a memory of her morning tryst with Shane flashed vividly. "Tryst?" That didn't seem at all a fitting description for the explosive passion that still lingered in her system.

Banishing those thoughts for another time, she willed herself to focus on the task at hand. Problem was, she didn't really know what to look for. "Hopefully, it will jump out at me."

The only direction came from following Rollins's lead. She went to the spot on the floor where a ghost in the shape of a four-foot-by-three-foot, dust-free rectangle appeared. "The gun case," she whispered. She glanced around, hoping for inspiration, since the guns were in the custody of the police. She spied a box marked "Hunt Club" and figured there might be some sort of connection between guns and hunting.

"Or I'm just really, *really* desperate," she grumbled as she lifted the lid off the box and looked inside.

Unlike the childhood memory box of Shane's, most of the writing on these files was done in a sweeping, masculine hand. Caleb Landry's, she guessed.

In thirty minutes, she knew a lot more about hunting than she ever wanted to know. Caleb had served two terms as the club's president. She knew because she came across two pictures and a certificate that said as much. More photos were stuffed in an unlabeled file. Judging by the clothing and confirmed by the date stamped on the edge of the picture, they were from some party in June of 1967. Caleb and Priscilla were in all the photographs, some alone, some with other people.

"The year before Shane was born," she murmured as she flipped through the images. "Which means…" she looked away and counted backward "…nothing." Taylor frowned. June 1967 was more than ten months before his birthday, so there was nothing sinister about the pictures.

"Except bad fashion," she joked, taking in the trendy overuse of shimmering blue eye shadow, loud funky prints and frosted white lipstick.

She paused over one photograph, recognizing several of the people. Caleb and Priscilla, of course, but also a much younger Will Hampton, the ranch foreman, posed in the group of eight. She continued to stare at the woman with one arm around Caleb's shoulder. It was a familiar face. It was… "The woman from Webb's Market…Debbie, no, Doris! Doris Tindale," Taylor said aloud. She turned the picture over, hoping someone had noted the names of the other people in the shot.

No such luck, which was frustrating, because the other men were also familiar, she just couldn't place them. Rummaging through the box, she didn't find anything of real interest. Tucking the picture into the pocket of her top, she moved on.

It took another full hour working her way through boxes before she found something that might be significant.

"Date books," she whispered excitedly, dumping them onto the floor. For the first time she was thrilled that the Landrys were such pack rats. Until then, she'd loathed the fact that nothing ever seemed to get tossed out. Now, she was almost giddy to find Priscilla Landry's daily life chronicled year by year inside the pages of the school fund-raiser styled books.

Not just her life, Taylor noted, duly impressed. The lives of every member of Priscilla's family were tracked as well. Taylor discovered such mundane, normal things as Caleb's standing tee-off time, each Sunday at nine. And that Sam spent three years in art lessons in the early seventies.

Taylor opened each book, narrowing her search to the year Shane recalled having the special blood tests. If there was something to the fact that his DNA wasn't wholly Landry, that might explain those tests.

But why wait until he was ten years old? Why do it

at all? Unless Priscilla suspected Caleb wasn't Shane's father. Taylor got a chill thinking about it.

Unlike her situation, Shane had grown up with two parents. This might devastate him. Being a Landry was part and parcel of his identity.

Taylor thought of her own father in unflattering terms—as a sperm donor, nothing more. It wasn't as though she'd ever missed something she'd never had.

But Shane was different. Her heart lurched against her ribs. He'd only ever known a strong, warm, stable family. Until she'd come to the ranch, she hadn't given much thought to family. Certainly not on any type of personal level. In her mind, families were burdens, an unhappy blending of people forced together by a biological throw of the dice.

The Landrys were different. Or not, she acknowledged as she moistened her finger and started hunting through the pages until she found an entry for September of that year. "Shane, Dr. M," she read, drawing her lower lip between her teeth because there was no phone number, no address, not so much as a hint as to who this "Dr. M" was.

But, she realized, she had information. She had the name of the lab that had billed for the test. Maybe, just maybe, that would be enough for Chance to track down the mysterious Dr. M. She hoped so.

Tossing the date books back into the box, Taylor replaced the lid, saw movement out of the corner of her eyes and froze.

Luke Adams was standing near the entrance to the attic. "W-what are you doing?" she nearly yelped.

"Just checking on you," he stated. "Will told me to

keep an eye on you. When you were gone for so long, well, I got concerned."

When her heart rate returned to normal, Taylor managed a small smile. "No need, I'm fine." She strained, attempting to lift the heavy box.

"Let me help you," he insisted, his boots scraping loudly against the floor as he rushed to her aid.

"Thanks," she breathed. She could hardly wait to get back downstairs.

Luke lifted the box with seemingly little effort, following her down the ladder.

Shane was coming along the hall, his face twisted into a dark scowl. He glared at Taylor, then looked past her, saying, "What are you doing here?"

"Uh, I was just checking on Taylor."

"*Taylor,* huh?" Shane asked, making her name sound like a curse.

"I'll be on my way," Luke said, handing the box to Taylor before hurrying off.

"Good plan," Shane commented to the ranch hand. There was a threatening glint in his eyes as he turned his gaze on Taylor. "I'm out of the house a couple of hours and you—"

"Don't finish that sentence," she warned, each syllable careful and succinct. "I understand that you're having the granddaddy of all bad days, but that doesn't give you carte blanche to take it out on me."

"What am I supposed to think?" he demanded, his voice booming.

"That I'm not the town slut?" she suggested just as forcefully.

"Really, you seemed pretty hot this morning."

Fury burned inside her. "You can be a real ass, Shane, you know that?"

Stiffening her spine, she started past him, but he reached out and grabbed her arm.

"I'm sorry, Taylor."

"Yes," she agreed, yanking herself free, "you are."

Chapter Ten

"I'm really, *really* sorry, Taylor. I didn't mean that. It was a stupid thing to say."

"You've got that right." Taylor tossed the words angrily over her shoulder. She struggled under the weight of the box, but she damn sure wasn't going to ask him for help. She would have enjoyed telling him to go away. Or at the very least, giving him a little nudge to send him head over teakettle down the steps.

He was taller, faster and very determined as he stepped around her to block the head of the stairs.

"Give it to me," he insisted, putting his hands under the box. Seeing her sag from the weight, he asked, "What do you have in there, rocks?"

"No, those would be in your head."

"I am sorry, Taylor," he repeated, not the least bit strained as he took the box, carted it down the long flight of stairs, then headed toward the kitchen, Taylor behind him.

She hated that she was distracted by watching the

sway of his shoulders as he moved. Soft, worn denim hugged his trim waist, narrow hips and powerful thighs.

How was it possible to be so angry and so interested all at the same time? Luckily, her sense of urgency didn't allow for her to linger on that question.

Shane put the box on the edge of the table, sliding it toward the center and lifting the lid in one smooth, easy motion.

"Does carrying this get me out of the doghouse?" he asked, turning to face her as he absently rubbed a place near the crook of his arm.

"Not very far out," Taylor muttered, relenting. It was hard to be angry at a guy when he looked so...sad. Did men go to a special, secret class to practice that expression? That pathetic, impish, "I won't do it again, golly-gosh. Promise!" face was almost impossible to resist.

"I should never have lashed out." He took her hands in his. "I'm mad at a lot of things, but not you. Never you."

She peered up at him through the shield of her lashes. "'Never' usually only lasts until the next time."

"Come here," he said, his voice hoarse, making the request seem more like a plea.

Shane folded her against him, stroking her hair as he pressed her cheek against his chest.

She breathed in his familiar scent, listened to the strong, even rhythm of his heartbeat as her hand met his strong, solid body.

"Not with me, it doesn't," he said. "I'm not like the men your mother brought around, Taylor. Don't punish me for their sins. My remark was thoughtless—an idiotic, nasty lapse, and I promise you it won't happen again."

"Sure it will."

"I won't let it." She smelled his warm, minty breath as his lips brushed against her forehead. "Believe me?"

"It doesn't matter," she sighed, placing her arms around his waist.

"Yes, it does."

"Why?"

"Because I love you."

Taylor went still, unable to breathe, barely able to speak. "Don't" she managed to say over the lump constricting her throat.

"Too late."

Stepping out of his embrace, she stared at the tips of her shoes for a second as her eyes stung from the burn of tears she would not release. "I don't want you to love me."

"I know you've got some…issues, Taylor, and I'm the prime suspect in a murder investigation, so I'm not saying my timing is the best. But, honey," he began, bracketing her shoulders and setting her at arm's length. "Being in the middle of all this craziness has made me see that with amazing clarity. I am falling in love with you. Probably have been for years."

He looked down at her with eyes filled with sincerity.

That only made her feel worse. "I can't," she said, shaking off his touch. "I promised myself that I wouldn't even consider a serious relationship until I was well established as my own person." She saw her hand shake when she lifted it to nervously shove the hair off her face. "I'm almost twenty-eight years old and I've never even had a real job. There's—"

"What do you call the last five years?" he asked, his

light eyes sparkling with humor. "Sure felt like you had a real job when I was making the quarterly tax payments."

A frustrated rush of breath spilled from her gaping mouth. Didn't he get it? "I'm the housekeeper, Shane, and while it's good, honest, decent work, it's hardly the best use of my education."

"I'm starting to wonder about that education of yours."

"Meaning?"

He stepped forward and ran the pad of his finger along the hollow of her cheek. The action caused a shiver to slink the length of her spine, before her nerve endings started tingling. The result was total sensory overload. She was aware of everything: the sound of his deep, controlled breaths each time his expansive chest rose and fell; the subtle, comforting scent of soap that lingered on his skin.

Mostly, Taylor felt need flare to life in her belly, burning more brightly now that she knew what it was like to be in his arms. To feel his hands and mouth on her body.

The shiver evolved into a violent quake that hit her with considerable force.

"Obviously, there are some areas of the human psyche they didn't tell you about in class," he teased.

"R-really?"

"Yes."

When he was close, this close, Taylor's brain cells seemed to drain of everything but her awareness of him. It was a primal, purely female awareness that made every attempt to retain reason and rationality a real struggle. Shane was temptation. It was in the soft promise of his mouth and the easy smile in his eyes.

Most of all, it was knowing that it would take little more than a moment of weakness on her part and she'd be caught, hooked and reeled into the potential for a wonderful life.

But not the life she'd planned.

She stepped back, confused by the traitorous way her mind and body were derailing all the hard-and-fast rules that had gotten her this far.

The fact that Shane was giving her space actually made it worse. He simply leaned against the counter, his feet crossed at the ankles and his arms crossed lazily in front of him. It would have been easier if he'd thrown a childish fit. Anything would have been simpler than the patient, relaxed vibes emanating from him.

Shane had always been an instant-gratification guy, so this new side of him was…appealing. *Damn.*

His quiet eyes roamed over her face, then he asked, "What's in the box?"

Taylor gave herself a little mental slap and brought her thoughts back to the task. "Personal stuff," she said, tempered excitement building. Ignoring the rumble of awareness in her stomach as she moved past him, Taylor went to the box and started yanking out various date books and other items, laying them on the kitchen table as Shane came up behind her and peered over her shoulder.

Ignoring the rush of feeling caused by having his big body whisper-close to hers, Taylor thumbed through the books she'd scanned earlier, finding the entry for Dr. M. "We need the receipt from your file," she explained, flicking her thumb toward the pantry. "We'll compare the medical bills paid for the platelet test and hopefully come up with the name of the doctor."

"Good work, Nancy Drew," Shane joked as he rummaged for, then found, the paper. "Missoula Medical Center," he read.

Taylor's brow furrowed as she hunted for the phone book and skimmed through the relevant section. "Not listed."

"It was twenty-five years ago," Shane reminded her, stroking his chin. "Maybe Chance knows that lab."

While Shane made the call, Taylor moved around, trying to use up some of the annoying excess energy in her system. She felt like a cat ready to pounce, only she wasn't sure which way to leap.

It had been almost ten years since she'd mapped out her life plan. Every decision had been made with one eye on that plan. No exceptions. No deviations. Not even a mild temptation to do so. Until now. That was a sobering reality. A very scary one.

Shane's mind should have been focused only on the task at hand as he left a message for his brother. But that was hard to do when sneaking sideways glances at Taylor in her soft pink sweats. Even the loosely cut fabric couldn't hide the appealing outline of her body. A body he now knew was nothing shy of absolute perfection. He swallowed the groan in his throat, forcing his focus onto the corner of an old photograph sticking out of her pocket. Something neutral. Something that didn't remind him of the incredible sensation of holding her against him.

This wasn't the time. He rubbed his eyes as he came

back to the grim reality of his situation. "The DNA has to be wrong," he muttered as he turned a chair around and straddled it.

"Or altered," Taylor suggested. "What if…" Her voice grew more animated. "What if whatever the blood work stuff you had done as a child somehow did something to your blood to skew the DNA test?"

Shane felt a twinge of optimism. "Can that happen?"

She nodded. "I read an article about a guy who had something—leukemia, I think—and because of a bone marrow transplant, his DNA was different than the other people in his family."

Shane noted the enthusiasm in Taylor's big green eyes and wanted to find it infectious. "But I don't remember any treatments. A few shots, I think. Would that be enough to screw up DNA testing?"

"We should find out," she said. "Let's go see Chance."

"Let's wait for him to call back," Shane suggested. "Even though, according to Detective Rollins, I'm the prime suspect, I've still got a ranch to run."

"What if…" Taylor paused and placed her hand on his shoulder, giving a reassuring little squeeze.

The simple, innocent gesture inspired a litany of desires in him—none of them simple and certainly not innocent. But he couldn't push. Not yet.

"What if I talk to Chance? I need to go into town, anyway."

He felt that stab of fear in his gut and it brought him back to reality. He glanced over at her, locking his eyes on hers. "Are you forgetting the calls? The shot? The note and the knife? Not going to happen, Taylor. You're staying put here on the ranch until I can make arrangements to get you away from—"

"Are you nuts? I can't leave you."

"Why is that?"

She blinked rapidly. "B-because!" she declared. "You need help, Shane. The state police think you killed your parents. I don't want you to end up like Clayton, lingering for years in some cell for a crime you didn't commit. Besides, the caller said I had to stay, and because…"

"Because?" he pressed, seeing a possible hint of the truth in those pretty eyes of hers.

She looked away. A very telling move, in his opinion. "We're friends, Shane. I'm a smart woman who just might have a skill or something that can help you. You're hardly in a position to turn down help right now."

"I have my brothers."

"What?" she demanded, jerking her face back up and glaring at him with glistening eyes that were little more than narrowed slits. "You have to be a Landry to have something to offer?"

"They love me. What's your excuse?"

"I care about you, Shane."

It took every drop of his self-control to keep from reaching out for her, taking her into his arms and proving just how inane her remark was. He was ninety-nine percent positive that she wouldn't be offering to risk her personal safety if she didn't care more than she let on. And she sure as hell wouldn't have made love to him if she wasn't just a little bit *in* love with him.

Five years, he thought, shaking his head at the perverse irony. Five years to get them to this point, and now he was a murder suspect. The gods definitely weren't smiling down on him.

"Think about it, Shane. I can't be in any real danger. As you just pointed out, I'm not a Landry. The note, the shot, the phone calls, they were all really about you. I was just the messenger."

"I don't want to see the messenger killed," he said, standing and reaching up to capture a lock of her hair between his thumb and forefinger. He let the silken strands slip through his grasp. "I'm not willing to take any chances. I've already told Seth that I want you on a plane out of Montana tomorrow."

Taylor felt her mouth drop. "Excuse me?"

"It isn't safe here for you. You've always said you wanted to visit Hawaii, so I'm sending you to—"

"I hope you bought refundable tickets," Taylor interrupted. "Aside from the fact that there's no logical reason why I would be the target of anyone, there's school. I can't just blow off my last classes and my final exams. Not after all this time."

Annoyingly, Shane shook his dark head from side to side as she spoke. "Wrong," he said with absolute finality. "I've made the arrangements, so I suggest you pack."

"I suggest you rot." She turned on her heel and started for her room.

Shane left wearing his hat, a light jacket and a slightly bemused smile that had her blood on high boil.

She was not going to be shipped off to some tropical resort like an errant child inconveniencing the family. Taylor went to her room, changed into jeans and a coral sweater, slipped on some shoes and grabbed her purse. After stuffing the faded photograph and the spotty medical information into her bag, she headed to the front door.

She got one foot outside before she was stopped by the imposing figure standing guard.

"Should have known," she muttered as she offered Will a saccharine smile. "I'm going to the store."

"Shane says you aren't."

She sidestepped the old coot. "Well, Shane is wrong."

Will's craggy fingers closed on her upper arm. Taylor looked at his offending hand, then slowly and pointedly dragged her gaze up to meet the faded eyes of the foreman. "Are you planning on physically restraining me?"

Will looked perplexed. And annoyed. But Taylor didn't care. They stood locked in silent battle for about a minute until his hand finally dropped to his side.

"Thank you." She rooted in her purse for her keys as she started down the steps.

Will was right on her heels.

"What?" she snapped without looking at him.

"I'll come with you."

She was glad Will couldn't see the way her eyes rolled. "Suit yourself."

The trip into Jasper was long and painfully silent. She cracked the window, letting fresh air in to dilute the leathery, earthy smell of Will's lanky presence.

As it was everywhere in Montana, going to town wasn't a quick trip. Other than the dark blue truck that was little more than a blip in her rearview mirror, they were, as usual, alone on the road. She followed a forty mile ribbon of two-lane black highway that led east to the small, quaint town founded by the first Landry settlers.

Taylor liked Jasper. A beautifully manicured park lay at the center of town. At this time of year, the trees had just started to bud and bloom, adding a bright sea of chartreuse to replace the stark, barren landscape of a Montana winter.

The grass was waking from its dormant stage and the shrubs that lined Main Street were filling in nicely. Through the open window, the scent of ribs smoking behind the Cowboy Café wafted in, reminding Taylor that she hadn't eaten. Time for that after she'd spoken to Chance and dropped by Webb's Market for a little chat with Doris.

Chance Landry was the general practitioner in Jasper. His office was an old Victorian set slightly back from the road in order to accommodate a small parking lot.

It wasn't until Taylor slipped her car into a spot that Will spoke. "You sick?"

"No." She could be monosyllabic, too. She glanced at the clock on the dashboard, then added, "After I speak to Chance, I've got to get some things at the store."

"Okay."

Taylor expelled a breath. "I don't need a babysitter."

"Just watching out for you."

She thought about arguing, but knew it would prove futile. "Whatever," she said, cutting the engine, reaching for the door handle and grabbing up her purse.

Chance's nurse and receptionist, Mrs. Halloway, greeted her with a warm smile. Normally, she was perfectly coiffed, but today she looked quite harried. "Hi, Taylor, Will."

The foreman responded with a two-fingered tap to the brim of his hat. Taylor said hello, then asked, "Busy day?"

She nodded, sighing heavily. "Spring allergies. I think the whole county has been through here in the last week."

"Does Chance have a few minutes to see me?"

Mrs. Halloway nodded. "He just tried to return Shane's call. He's upstairs with Val and the baby. Want me to let him know you're coming up?"

"Please. Thanks."

"I'll wait," Will grunted, plopping into a chair and folding his arms over his chest.

Taylor shrugged, then went out the office door and walked along the gravel path leading to the staircase on the side of the building. She saw a flash of something blue out of the corner of her eye.

Heart pounding, she whipped around, feeling instantly foolish when she realized it was nothing more than a truck turning down the side street.

Mentally berating herself for being so jittery, and blaming Shane's paranoia for the effect, she took the steps two at a time, then gently rapped on the door.

Chance greeted her with the trademark Landry smile. Like all the brothers, he was tall, dark and handsome, and fairly oozed charm. In addition, he had a silly, new-father grin that probably made him more attractive.

Leaning forward, he kissed Taylor's cheek. "How are you?"

She followed him inside, astounded at the changes

in the place. Thanks, no doubt, to Val, the apartment looked great.

"I haven't been here since the purging of the doilies," Taylor joked, breathing in the baby powder smell.

"I definitely don't miss the doilies and crushed velvet furniture," Chance agreed, showing her into what had once been a formal sitting room dominated by the burgundy florals that had been a favorite of the original owners. Chance had purchased the practice lock, stock and barrel from Jasper's first medical doctor, prim decor and all. But now, as she followed him through the maze of primitive prints and casual, functional furnishings, the place seemed more suited to Chance and his wife. Val was part Native American, so interspersed with high-end baby gear and toys was some really interesting and colorful folk art.

"Val should be out in a minute," he said, reaching down to scoop up a small stuffed seal from a cushion. "She's trying to get Chloe down for a nap."

As she sat, Taylor pulled the papers out of her purse. "I'm sorry to bother you, but we're trying to figure out what this means."

She filled Chance in on the blood tests and Shane's recollections of the trips to the mysterious doctor.

"Shane was ten?" Chance asked, the skin between his dark eyes wrinkling as he mulled over the thought.

"Yeah," Taylor answered. "I'm thinking it has something to do with the hinky DNA tests."

"Like what?" Chance asked.

"That's why I'm here," she explained, shifting in her chair. "Why would someone need platelet tests?"

Chance stroked his cleanly shaved chin. "Specific disorders. Suspicion of some sort of virus or disease. Hell, Taylor, there are literally thousands of things in the blood. Any of them might be of medical or clinical interest."

"Specific disorders? Inherited things?" she asked.

The gravity of the implication behind her question hung in the air between them. Taylor could almost see Chance's mind racing through all the diagnostic possibilities. To some extent, she was doing the same thing, though she was limited to general information.

"What kinds of blood things are inherited?" she asked.

Chance shook his head. "Can't be," he mumbled. "I'd know if Shane had some sort of disease, Taylor. I'm his doctor, but more importantly, I'm his brother. Believe me, if Shane had some sort of hereditary disease, there would have been some symptoms. Besides, there are seven of us. If there was some sort of family disease or condition, statistically, more than just one brother would exhibit symptoms."

"Unless he's not..." Taylor didn't want to say it aloud. Not because biology could have made him any more or less a Landry, but because it was the one thing the authorities didn't really have. Motive.

Chance's mouth pulled into a tight, grim line. "That would explain it," he said, moving into the family room and flipping open a laptop.

Following him, Taylor was mildly distracted seeing his fingers fly across the keyboard. In the not-so-recent past, someone had tampered with Chance's patient records via the computer. Back then, Chance was barely able to boot a machine, and now, no doubt again thanks to his wife, he was as adept as an old pro. Val's computer savvy allowed her to help Chance when he really, really needed it.

Taylor felt a stab of guilt. Her attempts at assistance hadn't been quite so effective. So far, the only thing she'd discovered was a pretty decent reason why Shane might have murdered his own parents.

Chapter Eleven

Taylor's brain was pretty fried after Chance's crash course in blood disorders. When he'd promised to run tests as soon as Clayton had samples from the police lab, they switched to the issue of "Dr. M" and the Missoula Medical Center.

"I vaguely remember the place," Chance said. "It went out of business about five years ago. I'll call around and see if I can find anyone who knows where their old records are stored."

She stood and headed for the door. "Shane did not kill your parents."

Chance placed his hand on her shoulder, giving a little squeeze as she looked up into his eyes. "*Our* parents," he corrected. "No matter what, the blood tests don't matter, Taylor. Shane has to know that."

She let out a long breath. "I hope so."

"I'll walk you downstairs."

"You don't have—"

"Better safe than sorry," he insisted, placing his hand

at the small of her back. "I thought Shane was putting you on a plane out of town."

Taylor shifted so she could rummage around in her purse as she walked down the steps. Will was planted at the bottom, his eyes shrouded by the brim of his hat. "I'm not running away," she said, making sure she spoke loudly enough for Will to hear as well. "Shane isn't a killer."

"That's a given. But the calls?"

She shrugged. "Aren't about me," she insisted. "Whoever is making them is desperate and doesn't know the situation. If whoever it is really wanted to motivate Shane, they'd go after one of you. Someone truly close to him and not an…employee."

"You aren't just an employee, Taylor. You've got to know how Shane feels—"

"I almost forgot—do you know these people?" she asked, taking the old photograph out of her pocket and cutting off the conversation before he could continue.

At the base of the stairs, Chance took the faded picture and studied it for several minutes. He pointed to his parents, to Doris, then to Will. "I remember this guy," he said, tapping the image of the man seated next to Will. "Not his name, just him. How about it, Will?" Chance asked. "Do you remember his name?"

Taylor watched as he passed over the photograph. After a long pause, Will shook his head, shrugged and simply mumbled, "Was a long time ago."

Snatching the picture away from the unhelpful foreman, Taylor retrieved her keys, said another goodbye to Chance and impatiently waited for Will to shadow her to the car.

She was feeling pretty useless in the grand scheme of things, and having the silent foreman in her space wasn't helping. Steering into the gravel lot behind the small store, she parked, got out and walked briskly inside.

The store was deserted, save for Doris, who was seated on a stool behind the three-foot-long counter, thumbing through a tabloid. "'Lo," Doris murmured disinterestedly.

Glancing over her shoulder, Taylor watched Will lingering by the front door. Just as well.

Doris wasn't what you'd call a happy person. Taylor frequented the market at least twice a week, more often when Sam, Callie and the kids had been living at the ranch, and she'd never been able to engage the woman in conversation.

Now, however, she wanted information from Doris, but wasn't quite sure how to approach her. Stalling as she formulated a plan, Taylor grabbed a plastic basket and looped it over her arm as she strolled down the first aisle.

The market was little more than a glorified convenience store, carrying milk, bread, eggs and enough dry goods to save locals from having to drive the extra forty miles to the closest grocery. Originally, the building had been a quaint mercantile, the center of commerce in Jasper's infancy. The plank floors were smooth and worn after a century of foot traffic. The walls had at least a dozen coats of paint, and wires hung like garlands, connecting all the twenty-first century technology not foreseen by the original builder.

Taylor glanced up at the security camera, which buzzed as it methodically swayed in an arc around the room. Absently, she tossed into the basket some coffee she didn't need and some paper towels she did. Slowly, she was summoning the nerve to approach Doris.

The salesclerk was a harsh looking woman, with every year of her life etched into the lines on her face. Thanks to the local weekly paper, Taylor knew Doris had worked at Webb's since graduating from high school. Maybe that was why she was so unhappy.

"Hi," Taylor said breathily, slightly intimidated by the sour expression on the other woman's face.

Doris grabbed for the items in the basket, glaring as she waved a glowing red wand over the bar codes. "That be all?"

"No," Taylor hedged, easing the photograph out of her purse. She slid it across the counter, keeping her forefinger on the curled edge. "Do you know these people?"

Doris shrugged. "That's me. Where'd it come from?"

"I found it at the Lucky 7 and I'm trying to identify the people in the picture."

Finally, Doris lifted her sullen brown eyes. "Why?"

Because I have to do something to help Shane? Because I'm— Not going there! "I'm just trying to organize things in light of the...*discovery.*"

"Those Landry boys can't even sort their own pictures?" the woman snorted.

"I'm just trying to help."

Doris rolled her eyes as she tapped a chipped, overly long nail on the photograph. "They don't need help, sweetie. They have everything. And I mean everything. Not real good about sharing, either. Least not after Queen Priscilla took over."

It was the first time Taylor had ever heard anyone speak ill of Mrs. Landry. "She wasn't nice?"

Doris made a grunting sound. "She was a bitch." She paused and pulled a pack of cigarettes out from under the counter and lit one, drawing deeply before blowing a stream of blue smoke from her lips. The smoke curled up, partially obscuring the No Smoking sign taped to the wall just behind her head. "She swooped into town and sank her hooks into Caleb."

"Really?" Taylor heard nearly fifty years of bitterness in the woman's tone.

"Before she came along, Caleb and me had a thing. Can't believe he's dead. But I'll bet she had something to do with it."

"She's dead, too," Taylor reminded the woman, "so how could that be possible?"

Doris flicked ashes into a foam cup; there was a quick sizzle as hot ash fell into stale coffee. She reached up and patted her stiff, sprayed coif. "Don't you see it?" she demanded, poking at the photograph more fervently. "She was what we used to call a tease. Why, she'd flit around the Hunt Club parties like she was the belle of the ball. Looking for trouble if you ask me."

"Actually, I was asking you about the people in the picture. Do you know their names?"

Doris lifted her slightly hunched shoulders and sighed as she grabbed up the photo. "That's me and Will." She smiled briefly. "I spent an entire week's pay on that outfit. Drove all the way to Missoula to get me that store-bought dress." She took another drag of the cigarette. "In those days, we mostly made our own clothes.

All of us but Priscilla, of course," Doris added with a sneer. "Leona and I went all-out that weekend."

"Leona?" Taylor prompted.

"This one," Doris said, pointing to one of the other women in the picture. "Leona Drake. She was a lot of fun, that Leona."

"Do you know where she is now?"

"Dead," Doris replied flatly. "She passed away from the female cancer five or ten years after this picture was taken. Left her useless husband and that cute little baby all alone."

Taylor was happy to let the clerk ramble on. Maybe Doris's reflections would yield something more than the name of a dead woman.

Doris signed heavily, tossing the half-smoked cigarette into the cup. "Jack was a fine-looking man in those days," she mused.

"Jack?" Taylor prompted.

"This one." Doris pointed again. "He sure went downhill in a hurry. Started drinking after he got fired."

"Fired from where?"

"Where else? The Lucky 7."

"Why'd he get fired?" Taylor asked.

"Caleb claimed he was stealing. Will backed him up. After that, no one else would hire him, so Jack just started drinking. Leona stuck it out, though. She must'a really loved him 'cause she took a job in the school cafeteria and worked them long hours even after the doctor told her about the cancer. Died with her hairnet on."

"Do you think—"

Doris raised her hand, cutting off Taylor's question

in midsentence. "Take your things and go. If those Landry boys want any more information, they can pay me an hourly wage for it. You tell them I said so."

"But—"

"Go on now," Doris said, shooing her toward the door. "I've got things to do."

The woman grabbed up the tabloid and went back to reading it. Grudgingly, Taylor gathered the photograph and her grocery bag and headed for the door. At least she had something. Names. Jack and Leona Adams. If Jack was still sober, maybe he could identify the younger couple in the picture. Someone must know who they were.

Of course, it would be easier if the photograph wasn't so faded and the images were clearer. The man's face seemed familiar, but Taylor couldn't place it.

She stepped outside and found Will leaning against the edge of the building. Taylor's mind raced through possibilities. "Jack and Leona," she said. "Ring any bells?"

He just shrugged. "Yeah."

Gosh, that was helpful. She glanced across the street and had a thought. Pressing the grocery bag in Will's general direction, she mumbled something about being right back. After checking the two-lane street for traffic, Taylor jogged across to the Jasper Family Counseling Center.

A bell chimed as she opened the tinted-glass doors and went in. The small office was divided into three rooms. The reception area had a half-dozen mismatched chairs donated by various people. It smelled faintly of cherry deodorizer and was decorated with an array of framed posters and childish drawings.

Taylor smiled at the young woman behind the desk. "Hi, is Mrs. Grayson here?"

"In her office," the intern answered. "She's on the phone with someone. Can you wait a few minutes?"

Taylor nodded and thanked the fresh-faced student. Since she was working for college credit and no pay, Taylor went out of her way to be nice to her at all times. The counseling center was far from financially stable. It was dependent on volunteers and interns to be able to offer even the most basic of services.

Grabbing up a year-old magazine, Taylor sat and tried to focus on the articles, but she wasn't terribly successful. Hopefully, Mrs. Grayson, retired social worker and lifelong Jasper resident, might be able to put names to the faces. Taylor adored the older woman, had since their first meeting. Though close to eighty, Mrs. Grayson was as sharp as a tack and full of energy. She was also a great counselor. Many of their clients remembered her from her days as a county employee. For decades, Mrs. Grayson had been the only social worker in Jasper.

The few minutes turned into ten and Taylor's nerves were beginning to fray. She wanted to identify all the people in the picture. At least then she'd feel as if she was contributing to Shane's potential defense.

Tapping her toe against the edge of the rug, she tossed aside the dated magazine and glanced outside, waiting for a dark pickup to pass before checking to see if Will was still standing guard. She didn't see him through the tinted, one-way glass, but suspected he was lurking nearby. Will was amazingly loyal, so she knew he wouldn't shirk his responsibility to Shane.

Leaning back, Taylor heard Shane's voice echo in her head: "I love you."

A knot formed in her belly. It wasn't the right time for that. Maybe, just maybe, he'd wait. Probably not. He preferred instant gratification, and she had no idea how long it might take for her to establish herself in…what? Private practice? No bites on her résumé thus far. Teaching? Nothing there either. She drummed her nails on the arms of the chair. Forget career aspirations. What if Shane got arrested? Worse yet, what if he was convicted? Was that even possible? Could lightning strike the family twice?

Clayton had spent more than four years in prison for a crime he didn't commit. Was it possible that a second Landry brother could suffer the same fate?

She rubbed her face, then pressed her fingers into her temples. *I can't think like that. I have to stay positive and focused and…* Her heart squeezed inside her chest. How had everything gotten so complicated? *Because they found the bodies?*

No, it wasn't just that.

Because I slept with him?

No, it wasn't just that.

Because I'm in love with him?

Taylor shook her head, refusing to entertain thoughts that would completely derail her life plan. Like every other time she'd faced an obstacle, she had to fix this and move forward. That was the only way to make sure she didn't fall into the family pattern.

The door to the hallway leading to twin modest offices opened. Mrs. Grayson smiled. She leaned heavily on a cane. "This is a surprise."

"I need some help," Taylor said, standing and digging through her purse at the same time. "I found a photograph and I'm trying to identify the people."

"Nice to see you, too," her friend stated, placing her free hand at her ample waist. "Come on inside and we'll catch up. You haven't been here for two weeks."

"Sorry," Taylor muttered. "I guess I'm just flustered by everything that's been going on."

Mrs. Grayson looped her arm through Taylor's, ushering her down the narrow hall toward her practically barren office. "Are you sure that's all it is?"

Taylor sat down in a dated armchair they'd found at a local yard sale a year earlier. She held out the picture when the older woman had settled into her chair and balanced her cane against the arm. "Do you recognize this man or this woman?" She pointed.

Mrs. Grayson lifted the glasses dangling from a chain of brightly colored beads around her neck. "Well, well, this takes me back."

Taylor scooted forward and named the people she'd already identified. "The man looks familiar, but I can't place him."

"He does," Mrs. Grayson agreed. "Because it's a very young Brian Hollister."

"Senator Brian Hollister?' Taylor asked.

Mrs. Grayson nodded, the tight bun at the crown of her head bobbing. Lowering her glasses, she turned her inquisitive gaze on Taylor. "He couldn't have been twenty in this picture. Why does it matter?"

Taylor filled the woman in on what had been happening. As expected, the older woman's well-practiced expression didn't reveal anything she might be thinking. "I see. So, you're now on a mission to save the man you don't love?"

Taylor winced. "I didn't say that. I—I care about Shane."

"I think it's more than that," she countered.

"Not now," Taylor insisted, momentarily distracted by the sounds of approaching sirens outside. "Even if I did feel *something,* the timing couldn't be worse."

Mrs. Grayson offered a knowing smile. "Love has a way of cropping up at the most inopportune time."

"Not to me," Taylor said, perhaps more for herself than her companion. "I'm not going to perpetuate the family pattern."

"Ever think you've already broken the cycle of bad relationships?"

"No," Taylor admitted. "I have to be a whole person."

"Ever think you are a whole person already?"

Taylor reclaimed the photograph. "Has anyone ever told you you ask too many questions?"

"Occupational hazard," Mrs. Grayson said with a pronounced sigh. "You're a twenty-seven-year-old woman, Taylor, who, in my opinion, should be smart enough to see that you long ago stopped needing your unfortunate childhood as motivation."

"No, I haven't," Taylor insisted, gathering up her purse.

"Really? Then why are you so scared?"

"Because some lunatic has threatened us."

"Us?"

Taylor regarded her friend for a moment. "Don't analyze my every word."

"Can't help it. But I'll stop if you'll stop making Shane pay for the wrongs of the likes of Duane Treadwell."

"I'm not. I've got to—"

"Come quick!" the intern yelled as she rushed in.

"What happened?" Taylor asked.

"It's Doris."

Taylor's blood stilled in her veins. "Webb's Market Doris?"

The intern nodded. "There's police cars, and somebody said she's dead. Someone shot her."

Chapter Twelve

A gathering crowd formed a semicircle around the half-block radius cordoned off in front of the market. The acrid smell of burning rubber filled Shane's nostrils after he brought the SUV to a screeching halt in the center of Main Street and flung open his door.

Information relayed to the ranch was sketchy. He knew only that there had been a shooting in town.

Taylor.

Shielding his eyes with his hands, he stood on the truck's running board and scanned the crowd. His heart stopped when he didn't see her among the assembled faces. He knew he'd never be able to forgive himself if so much as a single hair on her head was out of place.

Jumping down, he strode purposefully through the crowd, lifting the yellow tape and ducking beneath it as he kept searching for a glimpse of her. Stepping sideways between the ambulance and a fire truck, he approached a small group of deputies and paramedics.

"Where's Seth?" he demanded.

"Inside," one of them answered.

A uniformed man he recognized as a rookie deputy looked as if he might block Shane's path. One pointed glare was all it took for the guy to step aside.

Just inside the doorway, a white sheet with the name of the local mortuary stenciled on the hem covered the still outline of a body. As he came closer, Shane found it impossible to take a breath. His heart literally squeezed so hard he was sure it would explode at any second. A tight, dry sensation strangled him as he took in the scene.

He was about a foot away when her name erupted from his lips in an anguished cry.

The activity in the room turned into a dull buzz in his ears. His gaze remained fixed on the blood, the body, and he had the very real feeling that someone had reached into his chest and ripped his heart out.

"Shane?"

It took a moment for the voice to penetrate his shock-numbed brain. Whipping his head around, he felt relief wash over him in crashing waves when he saw Taylor step out from one of the aisles.

He practically scooped her off the ground, holding her so tightly he could feel the breath rush from her small frame. He planted kiss after kiss on her hair, her forehead, pretty much any part of her he could reach before putting her down and sliding his palms up to cup her face.

He saw fear, torment and guilt in her eyes, but it didn't matter. She was safe. She was… "What the hell happened?"

Taylor blinked at the harshness of his tone. "There was a robbery. Doris was shot."

After placing one last kiss on her forehead, Shane cradled her against him and surveyed the scene over her head. Seth was huddled with a guy from the medical examiner's office. Chance was off in another corner, talking to a paramedic who was making notes on a clipboard. Will was back by the small dairy case, a quiet observer with his hat in his hand.

"Were you here? Are you hurt?" Shane set her at arm's length.

Taylor shook her head. "No, no. I was across the street with Mrs. Grayson. We ran over here when the emergency vehicles started to arrive."

"Thank God," he murmured, hugging her to him again. "When I heard the news I was so afraid it was you. I've never been so scared in my life. The whole way into town I was sure something terrible had happened to you."

"It didn't," she insisted, settling her cheek against his chest. "But it was a close call. I was in here talking to Doris not fifteen minutes before the shooting. Luckily, though, Will was outside the center waiting for me. So I think I heard him tell Seth he could give a description of the robber."

"So, it was really a robbery?" Shane asked.

"I know. I don't think it was either," Taylor said, apparently reading his thoughts. "If Will hadn't been here to witness the getaway, I'd be thinking the same thing. Jasper doesn't have much in the way of crime so the coincidence is kind of...*creepy*."

"That's one way of putting it," Shane agreed. He brushed his lips on her forehead. Leaning back, he gently squeezed her forearms and smiled down at her in relief. "Will you be okay if I go talk to Seth and Will for a minute?"

She pointed toward the door. "I'm going back across the street. I've already given my statement, and frankly, I don't like being in here with poor Doris's body. Do you mind?"

He shook his head. "Shouldn't be a problem. The street is crawling with cops and firemen and most of the town. Just to be on the safe side, I'll walk you over there, then I'll come back in a bit to take you home to the ranch."

Once he had Taylor safely secured behind the locked door of the Family Counseling Center, he jogged back to join his brothers, just as Doris's corpse was being wheeled out to the waiting ambulance. Several shocked gasps sounded in the crowd as the gurney was lifted and the doors slammed shut.

Will was waiting for him at the doorway to the market. "Glad you were with her," Shane said, extending his hand. "Taylor said you saw the shooter?"

The foreman nodded. "Tall, young, mid-twenties, thirty on the outside. Ran out of the market and hauled ass around the corner. Then a blue pickup truck squealed out of here heading north."

"Did you hear a shot?"

"Not so I could swear," Will said, almost apologetically. Shane watched as his longtime friend broke eye contact to stare off into space. "I wish I could have helped."

"I know you do," Shane said, patting the older man on the shoulder in hopes it might assuage some of the guilt he read in Will's expression. "Too bad about Doris, but I'm glad Taylor is safe. Thank you for that."

Will shifted from foot to foot awkwardly, which was very in keeping with the man's personality. Will kept everything close to the vest, so Shane was sure it was uncomfortable for a stoic guy like him to accept gratitude, compliments or any other remotely overt emotional response.

"Want me to drive her car back to the ranch?" Will offered.

"Good idea. Mind getting the keys yourself? I want to have a word with Seth."

"Consider it done. See you back at the spread."

Shane breathed his first genuine sigh of relief as he went in search of Seth. His heartbeat had finally calmed and the knotted muscles in his shoulders were slowly relaxing. Rolling his head to dispatch the last bit of tension, he again bypassed the deputies and stepped inside the somber building.

"...Dust every inch of this place," Seth was telling the crime scene tech. "And copy the tapes from the security cameras and send them to my office."

"Will do, Sheriff Landry."

Seth turned, his expression hard. "This stinks," he muttered as he grabbed Shane's arm and led him away from the others, waving for Chance to join them.

"It's a shame," Shane agreed. "Doris has been a fixture around town."

"That, too," Seth said, his voice quiet as he huddled together with his brothers. "I mean, it's bad she's dead, but this whole thing doesn't feel right."

"How so?" Chance asked.

Shane watched as Seth glanced down at his notepad. "The money from the lockbox under the counter is gone but the register wasn't touched."

"Meaning that most criminals are, as they say, all hat and no cattle. That's hardly newsworthy," Chance offered.

"Meaning," Shane suggested, "the perpetrator knew the place. Knew Doris kept the money from lottery sales in the box under the counter. Knew she kept little more than the float in the cash register."

Seth agreed. "Yeah, except they pulled the numbers night before last. If you were going to rob this place, wouldn't you do it the day after a ton of tickets had been sold? Increase your take?"

"Sure, right. So why wait the extra day when the lottery money would already be in the bank, and then leave the register untouched?" Chance asked.

"It could be a stupid criminal moment, or it could be something else," Shane agreed. "Was Taylor the last person in here before the robbery?"

Seth nodded. "According to Will, no one came in after she left except a tall white male in jeans and a beige Stetson who we have to assume is the perp."

"That describes roughly half the population of Montana." Glancing over his shoulder, Shane asked, "What about the cameras?"

"Look more closely," Seth answered.

When he did, Shane noticed that there was a film of something on the lens. Moving to within a few feet of where the camera was mounted in the corner of the room, he saw a puddle on the floor. "What's this?"

"Shaving cream," Seth muttered. "I haven't seen the tape, but I'm betting whoever it was covered it with foam."

"Smart," Shane acknowledged.

Seth blew out a frustrated breath. "I'm crossing my fingers that the camera got a look at him before he screwed with the lens."

"If the guy was smart enough to disable the camera, why not do a better job of the robbery?" Shane asked of no one in particular.

"That's another thing," Seth said. "Told you it feels wrong."

Shane met his brother's perplexed expression. "You're thinking the robbery was just to cover up killing Doris?"

"Too soon to tell, but I'm not buying the idea that my town is suddenly the crime capital of the county. I mean, what are the odds of someone taking a shot at Taylor, and then a few days later, a store clerk gets killed minutes after talking to her?"

Shane felt the blood in his veins turn icy. "You think there's a connection?"

"I do."

"I AGREE," Taylor said, shivering when she admitted as much to Shane a few minutes into their drive back to the ranch. She recounted her conversation with Doris, glossing over the very unflattering picture the bitter clerk had painted of Priscilla Landry. "I think Doris was killed to send a message."

"Which is?" Shane prompted.

Taylor drew her bottom lip between her teeth as she continued racking her brain for some connection that made sense. "She knew the history, Shane. I think she knew something else, too."

"Why?"

"Because she hinted that she'd be willing to sell it to you."

"What?"

"At the time, I thought she was just being…unpleasant. But she pretty much said that if the Landrys wanted information from her, they'd have to pay. It never occurred to me that she was serious."

Taylor turned, stealing a peek at his handsome profile. Shane's long hair was pulled back into a loose ponytail, secured with a soft leather cord. Tension was etched into deep lines at the edge of his mouth. Sighing heavily, she tugged at the shoulder belt and tucked one leg under her as she tried to think of some scenario that might logically explain the murder of a surly store clerk.

She was distracted when Shane reached over to rest his hand on her knee. Distracted didn't exactly cover it. His fingers felt like Tazers, sending pulses of electricity through her bloodstream.

Taylor hated herself for thinking vivid, carnal thoughts so soon after Doris's unfortunate demise. She justified it by reminding herself that it wasn't as if she and Doris had been friends. The woman didn't have any friends. Except for Leona, who was also dead.

Completely frustrated, Taylor shoved her hair off her forehead and tried to focus. Impossible. Shane was tracing maddening little circles against her thigh with his thumb. Even through her jeans, the brush of his touch ignited a small blaze in her belly.

She needed to get herself in check before they reached the ranch. If she didn't, she wouldn't trust herself not to do something foolish. Again.

"You're tensing," Shane remarked, punctuating his observation with a gentle squeeze. "What's wrong?"

Taylor turned and glanced at the passing scenery. She didn't want to have this conversation. She wasn't ready to have it. Besides, what could she say? *Shane, I want you so badly my whole body is coiled with need, but—* and it was a big but—*I'm scared I won't be able to walk away. And if I don't walk away, if I don't become my own person, I'll hate myself. And you.*

"It's been a tough morning," she remarked, hearing the overwhelming sadness in her own voice.

Shane must have heard it, too, because he said, "There's something else bothering you, Taylor. What is it?"

"Nothing," she insisted. Classic conflict-avoidance, she decided as they turned up the long driveway leading to the main house. "I'm just drained, I guess."

"You should lie down when we get home."

"Maybe," she agreed, in little more than a murmur.

It was a really beautiful late afternoon, which seemed almost disrespectful in light of recent events. Still, she couldn't help but appreciate the striking scenery. The Lucky 7 Ranch was a massive spread rimmed by the Rockies. Snowcapped mountains bracketed three sides of the ranch house built by Shane's grandfather. Along with the main house, there were several outbuildings— three barns, a bunkhouse, a smokehouse and some storage sheds.

Sam, the eldest of the Landry brothers, had just finished construction of a home for his rapidly growing
family on the eastern edge of the property. Taylor missed
them, especially the children. There was something
homey about the smell of baby powder and the shriek
of little children playing. Even though their new place
was technically on the ranch, it was at least a fifteen
minute drive from the main house.

Shane parked in the horseshoe-shaped driveway in
front of the massive home. They climbed the front steps
and were approaching the large mahogany doors when
she felt Shane's hand at the small of her back.

His splayed fingers inspired a little shiver to dance
along her spine. She closed her eyes briefly, taking in
the familiar, comforting scent of his cologne.

"I want you to go lie down," he said, latching the
door and guiding her toward her room. "I've got to
check in with Will."

"I should start dinner."

"Forget it," Shane grunted. "We'll wing it tonight."

"You don't pay me to wing it."

"Yeah, well, consider yourself on paid leave."

They reached her room. Shane. Bed. *Bad.* Taylor's
whole body was on alert. High alert. The walls felt as
if they would close in on her at any moment. Shane's
presence shrunk the space, aided by the strong, heady
desire pulling her insides into taut knots.

His hand fell away when he reached around her and
tugged down the comforter. "Take a break, Taylor." He
patted the soft mattress. "I'll be back in a while."

It took all of her personal strength to keep from

begging him to stay with her. But she managed, feeling alone and lonely when he pulled the blanket over her and kissed her on the forehead before leaving.

Taylor's heart actually hurt. This would all be over soon. A memory she'd surely revisit for the rest of her life. She'd worked too hard, come too far to change gears now. But what if Shane was arrested? It seemed as if the cosmos were conspiring to steal what little time they had left.

What to do?

Squeezing her eyes closed, she weighed the possibilities. Was she capable of having a casual affair with him? Was it really casual? No, he cared for her. And she…what? Admitting her true feelings, acknowledging them—even to herself—was not an option. That was about the only certainty in her life just then.

SHANE WAS ON HIS THIRD cup of coffee when he heard the water from Taylor's shower cut off. He took a long swallow of the muddy sludge, hoping his brain would focus on the hot liquid searing his throat. No such luck. What burned most was his fierce need to be with her. Pictures of Taylor naked and wet, standing under the stream of the shower, slipped in and out of his mind. He groaned aloud and suffered in silence as he heard her hair dryer, then the drawers, then finally the sound of her bare feet as she came down the hallway.

Normally, he would have been impressed by her display of inner strength. By the way she always managed to soldier on, regardless of the situation. He'd seen it every time a family crisis loomed. But this wasn't normal. Not by a long shot.

Normal didn't include his fascination with the smell of floral shampoo that arrived a split second before she came into the kitchen, wearing a plain white robe that seemed anything but plain when wrapped around her incredible body.

He allowed his eyes to roam freely and happily over her upturned face. He knew he should offer some sort of greeting, but he was afraid if he opened his mouth at that moment, it would be to insist that they go back to her bedroom.

As if reading his mind, Taylor stood still, her thickly lashed hazel eyes focused on him. Her lips parted slightly, allowing each breath to ease in and out of her pretty mouth.

A moan of strong, urgent need rumbled in Shane's throat. He felt a seizure in his gut and a tightness in his groin as his gaze dropped lower, to her long, delicate throat, and then lower still, to the hint of cleavage just above the V formed by the neckline of her robe.

Banishing rational thought from his brain, Shane took the two steps necessary to reach her, wrapped his arm around her waist and dragged her against him. The feel of her body against his was like finding his own personal little slice of heaven.

He wanted to take it slowly, intended to, in fact. But intentions were a memory the minute he dipped his head to brush his lips on hers. He felt the warmth of her mouth and tasted cool mint as his tongue teased her lips apart.

Taylor flattened her hands against his chest, enjoying the strong beat of his heart beneath her touch. Reluctantly, he loosened his grip and she stepped back ever so slightly.

Her eyes roamed boldly over the vast expanse of his shoulders, drinking in the contours of his impressive upper body where his shirt was tightly pulled. She openly admired the powerful thighs straining against the soft fabric of his jeans. The mere sight caused a fluttering in the pit of her stomach.

"So…" Her voice was soft and sultry, her eyes hot. "What are we going to do about this, since our respective self-control seems to have gone right out the window? I'm thinking it would be stupid for us not to sleep together."

"I agree." His voice was shallow, his breathing uneven. "I want you. But we aren't children," he felt compelled to point out. "We can't have everything we want."

"Does that mean you want me as badly as I want you?" Taylor held her breath, waiting for his reply.

He met her gaze. "Right now, your *safety* should by my primary concern. I should be putting you on a plane and getting you out of harm's way while I figure out who killed my parents."

Her arms wound about his neck. "I hear a but in there."

"Not a but." Shane smiled. "An 'on the other hand.' I want to stay close to you. Very, very close."

"I think we could get a lot closer in the bedroom, don't you?" she asked, unable to keep from smiling. She looked up at him, enjoying the anticipation fluttering in her stomach. The clock on the wall showed six-fifteen.

"You shouldn't make these kinds of offers, Taylor. Not unless you mean them."

She rose up on tiptoe to kiss his chin. "You know me. I rarely say anything I don't mean."

"We have that in common," he commented as he brushed his lips against her forehead.

Taylor took a deep breath and went for it. "Look, Shane. I'm asking you to go to bed with me. Nothing else. I need to be clear on that."

He moved and pulled her into the circle of his arms. "I wasn't expecting this."

"Me either," she admitted easily, adding, "I haven't been able to think of much of anything but you since we…since the last time."

Feeling safe and protected in the circle of his arms, Taylor closed her eyes. It would be wonderful to forget everything—all the baggage, all the danger. Just for a few hours. No memory of the calls, the knife, Doris, none of it. Nothing but the magic of being with Shane.

His fingers danced over her back, leaving a trail of electrifying sensations. Like a spring flower, passion blossomed deep within her, filling her quickly with a frenzied desire she had felt only once before. He ignited feelings that were powerful and intense.

Then he slipped the tip of his finger inside the neckline of her robe and she couldn't think anymore. Except maybe to consider begging when he stopped.

Shane moved his hand in slow, sensual circles until it rested against her rib cage, just under the swell of her breast. He wanted—no, needed—to see her face. He wanted to see the desire in her eyes. Catching her chin between his thumb and forefinger, he tilted her head up with the intention of searching her eyes. He never made it that far.

His gaze was riveted to her lips, which were slightly parted, a glistening pale rose. He could feel her pulse rate increase through the fabric of her robe.

Lowering his head, he took another tentative taste. Her mouth was warm and pliant. So was her body, which now pressed urgently against him. His hands roamed purposefully, memorizing every nuance and curve.

He felt his own body respond with an ache, then an almost overwhelming rush of desire surged through him. Her arms slid around his waist, pulling him closer. Shane marveled at the perfect way they fit together. It was as if she had been made for him. For this.

"Taylor," he whispered against her mouth. He toyed with a lock of her hair, then slowly wound his hand through the silken mass and gave a gentle tug, forcing her head back even more. Looking down at her face, Shane decided there was no other sight on earth as beautiful and inviting as her smoky hazel eyes.

In one effortless motion, he lifted her, carried her to her bedroom and carefully lowered her onto the bed. Her light hair fanned out against the pillow.

"I think you're supposed to get on the bed with me," Taylor said in a husky voice when he remained perched at the edge of the mattress.

With one finger, Shane reached out to trace the delicate outline of her mouth. Her skin was the color of ivory, tinged with a faint, warm flush.

Sliding into place next to her, he began showering

her face and neck with light kisses. While his mouth searched for that sensitive spot at the base of her throat, he felt her fingers working the buttons of his shirt.

He waited breathlessly for the feel of her hands on his body and he wasn't disappointed when anticipation gave way to reality. A moan of pleasure spilled from his mouth when she brushed away his clothing and began running her palms over the muscles of his stomach.

Capturing both of her hands in one of his, Shane gently held them above her head. The position arched her back, drawing his eyes down to the outline of her erect nipples.

"This isn't fair," she said as he slowly untied the belt of her robe.

"Believe me, Taylor, if I let you keep touching me, I'd probably last less than a minute," he assured her with a smile and a kiss.

Taylor responded by lifting her body to him. The rounded swell of one breast brushed his arm, and he began peeling away the terry cloth covering her. He was rewarded by an incredible view of her breasts spilling over the edges of a lacy bra that was sexy as sin. His eyes burned as he drank in the sight of taut peaks straining against the lace. His hand rested against her flat stomach, then began inching up the warm flesh. Finally, his fingers closed over the rounded fullness.

"Please let me touch you!" Taylor cried.

"Not yet," he whispered, releasing the front clasp on her bra. He ignored her futile struggle to free her hands, and dipped his head to kiss the raging pulse point at her throat. Her soft skin grew hot as he worked his mouth lower and lower. She gasped when his lips closed around her nipple, then called his name in a hoarse voice that caused a tremor to run the full length of his body.

Moments later, he lifted his head long enough to see her passion-filled expression and to tell her she was beautiful.

"So are you."

Whether it was the sound of her voice or the way she pressed against him, Shane neither knew nor cared. He found himself nearly undone by the level of passion communicated by the movements of her supple body.

He reached down until his fingers made contact with a wisp of silk and lace that almost constituted enough to be labeled panties. The feel of the sensuous garment against her skin very nearly pushed him over the edge. With her help, he was able to whisk the thong over her hips and legs, until she was finally next to him without a single barrier.

He sought her mouth again as he finally released his hold on her hands. He didn't know which was more potent, the feel of her naked against him or the frantic way she worked to remove his clothing. His body moved to cover hers, his tongue thrusting deeply into the warm recesses of her mouth. He ran his hand downward, skimming the side of her flesh all the way to her thigh. Then, giving in to the urgent need pulsating through him, Shane positioned himself between her legs. Every muscle in him tensed as he looked at her face, before directing his attention lower, to the point where they would join.

Taylor lifted her hips, welcoming, inviting, as her palms grasped his flanks and tugged him toward her.

"You're incredible," he groaned against her lips.

"Thank you," she whispered back. "I want you. Now, please?"

He wasted no time responding to her request. In a single motion, he thrust deeply inside of her, knowing without question that he had found his own personal paradise.

He wanted to treat her to a slow, building climax, but with the feelings sweeping through him, it wasn't an option. He caught his breath and held it. The sheer pleasure of being inside of her sweet softness was just too powerful. She wrapped her legs around his hips as the first explosive waves surged through him. One after the other, ripples of pleasure poured from him into her. Satisfaction had never been so sweet.

With his head buried next to hers, the sweet scent of her hair filled his nostrils. Shane reluctantly relinquished possession of her body. It took several minutes before his breathing slowed to a steady, satiated pace.

Rolling onto his side next to her, he rested his head against his arm and glanced down at her. She was sheer perfection. He could have happily stayed with her in the big, soft bed until the end of time.

Sadly, the telephone rang just then, disturbing the lazy tranquility of the moment. Taylor flinched at the strident sound. "I don't want to answer that."

Shane knew how she felt. "I'd better. Could be one of my brothers with news."

"I know."

He reached for the receiver. "Hello?" Instantly alert, Taylor read the absolute shock in Shane's eyes as he listened to the caller.

Chapter Thirteen

"What?" Taylor asked Shane as he hung up the phone.

"Something from the tape."

"The killer? That's fantastic!"

Shane's face was a mask of concentration as he shook his head. He shrugged into his shirt. "If that was the case, Seth would've told me. He just said it wasn't something he could explain over the phone. Said I had to see it."

"That's a little cryptic," Taylor offered as she hid behind the partially closed closet door in order to dress. Which, if she thought about it, was silly. Shane had already seen everything.

Curiosity piqued, she was grateful to have something to focus on aside from her sudden shyness and her complete and utter lack of self-control. She'd deal with her behavior later, as soon as she thought up a plausible way to rationalize her reasons for having sex with Shane a second time.

After running her fingers through her hair, she stepped into flat shoes and joined Shane in the foyer.

There really was no way to rationalize her body's immediate and primordial response to him. She absolutely tingled, and all he was doing was standing by the door, waiting for her.

Sex was supposed to have been the scratch for this itch. Surely satisfaction should last more than an hour. It wasn't emotionally healthy to want someone the way she wanted Shane. How many times had she offered such counsel to people? Explained that burning passion is usually temporary and rarely a good foundation on which to build a relationship?

What relationship? that annoying little voice in her mind shouted.

The one I'm not doing a very good job of avoiding.

"Sorry to drag you out so quickly," Shane said as he tugged her jacket off the brass coat tree by the door and handed it to her with a wink. "Believe me when I tell you I'd much rather have spent the whole night doing any number of wonderful things to your body and mind."

"Don't worry about doing things to my mind," she muttered as she walked with him toward the SUV. "I've pretty much got that area covered."

She heard Shane expel a loud breath, not that he'd done much of anything to hide the frustration fairly oozing from his pores.

"Damn it, Taylor. I can practically see that mind of yours working at full throttle. Still trying to convince yourself that there's nothing between us but excellent sex?"

"There *is* nothing more between us than excellent sex." Of course there was, but the second she put *those* thoughts out there, she'd be lost. "Which," she hastened to add, "is exactly as it should be. We're adults. Nothing wrong with us both wanting a satisfying sexual relationship. Neither of us needs to give up anyth—"

"Who's asking you to give anything up?" He was clearly annoyed. "I don't remember making any demands on you."

"You said you cared for me."

"I do. Consider the declaration, and the sentiment behind it, a gift. Not an obligation. At least it's supposed to be." When she didn't respond, Shane slanted his gaze in her direction. She was staring out of the window, her jaw set. *Stubborn woman.* He restrained himself from pulling over to the side of the road and kissing her senseless, or, he thought with an inner smile, loving the woman into submission. "Stop being obtuse and so damn single-minded about this," he told her, consciously taking the heat out of his words.

He didn't need Taylor's acceptance of his declaration to know that she just might be as crazy in love with him as he was with her. All he needed was the patience of a saint and the willpower of a monk.

It chafed to know that Taylor's position hadn't changed. Shane wondered what he'd have to do to get her to at least open up to the possibility that loving him wouldn't sound the death knell to her dreams and aspirations. Not an easy task given the reality of his situation. His timing couldn't be worse.

He turned the truck onto the highway, knowing he had to put things in the proper sequence. First, he needed to find a way out from under the dark cloud of suspicion. Hopefully, whatever Seth was onto would point him in that direction. Then he'd find some way to convince Taylor that loving him wouldn't ruin her life.

"Apparently our postcoital glow has disappeared," he said dryly. "How long are you going to give me the silent treatment?"

"I have nothing to contribute to the conversation."

He had volumes to contribute, but he bit his tongue. Time for that later. "Then feel free to open a new topic of conversation to while away the time it'll take us to get there."

Their eyes met. "Go, Grizzlies?"

Shane grinned as he brought his attention back to the road. God he loved her.

He parked in a spot adjacent to the municipal building in the heart of Jasper, and forced himself to change his focus.

Barely aware of the chill settling in the early evening air, he and Taylor climbed the steps and headed toward the door with Sheriff's Office stenciled in bold, black letters above a replica of the star his brother wore pinned to his uniform.

Taylor took his hand as they passed through the hinged, wooden half door that led past the secretary's desk. It was so distracting to feel her soft, warm fingers lace with his that Shane stammered when he greeted Lucy, the night dispatcher.

"Sheriff's expecting you," Lucy offered, continuing to file her fingernails as she spoke. "Hey, Taylor. Nice sweater."

Seth was seated on the edge of his desk. The chairs

were pushed together to make room for a small cart with a television set and videotape player. He had his thumb on the remote control, rewinding and playing the grainy image from Webb's Market.

"Recognize him?" Seth asked without greeting as he continued to replay the tape.

Taylor stared at the screen, scrutinizing the partially obscured figure of a man who kept his head bowed as he approached the camera, then without looking up, raised the hand holding the can of shaving cream to obliterate the image.

A large, light-colored Stetson hid his face. The security camera tape was black-and-white, so it was impossible to identify even the basics.

"Not me," Shane said.

Taylor moved closer. "Can you play it slower?"

"Yep." Seth rewound to the moment the man entered the market. "He brought the shaving cream with him."

The poor quality image flickered as about one quarter of the man's body remained visible in the left side of the frame. Then the shaving cream, then nothing.

"Again, please?"

"See something?" Shane asked, moving his hand to her shoulder as he leaned in close.

His warm breath caressed her cheek as she struggled to remain focused on the videotape. "What's that?" she asked, touching the tip of her finger to the screen.

Tilting her head, she waited for Seth to rewind and freeze one frame in particular. It was a close-up of the man's hand. Part of it, at least.

Squinting, Taylor stared at the hand, specifically the

knuckles. "See that?" she asked, feeling a rush of excitement as she pointed to the dark spots.

"A shadow, maybe?" Shane offered.

She shook her head, exuberantly declaring, "Tattoos."

"Yes, maybe," Shane said. "But they're too blurry to make out. Is there some computer tech that can—"

"We don't need one," Taylor practically sang. "I know only one person around town who has tattooed knuckles. Luke Adams."

"I know that name," Shane said. "He works for me. He's one of the new hires."

Shane grabbed Taylor and planted a quick kiss on her open mouth. "I don't care what they say, you are not just a pretty face, Taylor Reese."

She felt herself grinning like a child as she fought the urge to leap into his arms. Instead, she turned to Seth and asked, "Can you go out to the ranch and arrest him?"

"Already on it," Seth said, reaching for the phone and his hat in one smooth motion. "Have all cars roll to the Lucky 7," he told the dispatcher.

Feeling quite impressed with herself, Taylor took one last look at the screen as she started for the door. She stopped. "Wait. Look. See the door to the dairy case?" The Landry brothers did as she instructed, moving in close to where she pointed. "Doesn't that look like a man?"

"Hard to tell," Shane hedged. "The quality is so poor."

Taylor was almost certain she saw the faint image of a man's reflection in the glass. "It looks like a man to me."

"I don't think so, Taylor," Seth said. "Will only saw

one perp. Thanks to your keen observation, we have a pretty good idea who he is. You two hang back."

"Why?" Taylor asked.

"In case there's trouble. Luke Adams has an arrest record. No telling what he'll do when he's confronted."

"Seth's right, Taylor," Shane stated. "I'm going to drop you off at Chance's place. You can stay there while we go after Adams."

Her shoulders slumped. "That's not fair. I'm the one who identified him. I should be…well, included."

Shane shot her a glance softened by his very sexy, lopsided smile. "Really? What are you planning to do if he resists arrest? Beat him into submission with inkblots?"

"I'm saving that for you," she quipped. "I could be of help, Shane."

"Really? How?"

"Well…" She paused to take a deep breath while Seth was busy checking his gun before snapping it into the holster. "I could reason with Luke. The kind of thing a hostage negotiator might do."

"I'm not planning on taking any hostages, but thanks all the same," Shane said.

Seth rounded the desk, hat and keys in hand. "You two can stay here and fight it out. I'm going after the bad guy."

Ten minutes later, Taylor found herself seated in Chance and Val's above-the-office family room. Baby Chloe was teetering on the brink of sleep as she rested against her father's shoulder. Val was in the small kitchen, brewing some tea she insisted would relax Taylor's anxiety in no time flat.

Fat chance, she thought as she fidgeted in her seat.

Taylor managed a weak smile when Val handed her a steaming cup of tea that smelled faintly of cranberry. "Thanks." She took a sip to be polite and found the blend of herbal tea and fruit actually was soothing. "Should we call the ranch?" she asked.

Chance and Val smiled at each other, then looked at Taylor with a great deal of patience and compassion. Val spoke. "Honey, would you please put Chloe to bed? Just rock her for a while first."

"My pleasure." With the baby cradled in his arms, Chance disappeared down the narrow hallway, leaving the two women alone. Taylor felt her insides wind into a tight coil as the passage of time seemed to slow to an unnatural crawl.

Val patted her hand as she flopped next to her on the sofa, tucking one long leg under her body in an easy motion. "Hang in there. Seth and Shane will get to the bottom of this."

"I can't stand the waiting," Taylor sighed, raking her fingers through her hair after setting the cup on the coffee table. Sensing a change in Val's mood, Taylor asked, "What?"

"I found something," she answered, her voice low and her tone guarded.

"What kind of something?"

Jumping up, Val retrieved her laptop and brought it over to the sofa. "Chance and I have been researching DNA and the platelet test Shane had as a child. We've also been having the blood samples taken by the state police analyzed."

"And?" Taylor asked, feeling her heart rate increase from the anticipation.

"Von Willebrand disease."

Taylor said the words in her mind over and over. "Sound's bad."

Val shook her head vehemently, again patting Taylor's knee. "No, really. I mean, it can be, but it can also be a mild condition that goes undiagnosed until some catastrophic event."

"Shane has this…*illness?*" Her mouth was so dry it was difficult to get the question out. All sorts of questions ran through her mind. "How bad is it? Is he going to die? How did he get it?"

"Slow down." Val cautioned, her expression calm and patient. "I'll do my best to explain it to you. Whatever I can't answer, I'm sure Chance can. Know anything about blood disorders?"

"Close to nothing," Taylor admitted. "I think I read a story in a magazine about a woman who was struggling with a rare form of leukemia. Is that what this is? A form of cancer? Is that why the blood tests from the crime scene incriminated Shane?"

"No," Val insisted with some amount of force. "Von Willebrand's is a distant cousin to hemophilia. Simply speaking, a person with this condition might experience symptoms like bleeding from the gums, slow healing and frequent bruising."

"Bruising?" Taylor repeated, her mind's eye flashing the countless times she'd seen deep purplish bruises on some part of Shane's body. She'd never given them a second thought, which now made her feel intense guilt. "Val, I've—"

"We all have," Val insisted as she offered a weak smile. "Chance spent the better part of the morning beating himself to a pulp for missing the symptom all these years."

"Shouldn't Shane be taking medication or something?"

Val shook her head. "Maybe. Maybe not. You can bet Chance will have him tested every which way to make sure he gets whatever treatment is necessary. He's not in any immediate danger. There are different types of Von Willebrand's. Shane has the most mild form. It would only be a problem if he had surgery and the surgeon didn't know about the condition, or..."

"Or what?"

"He has children with someone who also carries the gene."

Taylor did her best to absorb the information. "So, if Shane has it, does that mean his brothers have it, too?"

Val gave her a straight look. "That's the million dollar question, isn't it?"

"WHAT THE HELL IS THIS?" Shane demanded as his brother brought the SUV to a screeching halt. The headlights of Seth's vehicle joined those of three other cars, cutting through the inky darkness to illuminate the front of the bunkhouse.

The marked police cars, lights strobing red and blue against the worn wooden building, sat idling, their doors open, officers hunkered down, weapons drawn.

Seth reached over, opened the glove compartment and gave Shane a hand gun. The weapon felt smooth and slightly cool in his grip as he checked the chamber and the magazine. He tasted bitter adrenaline just as one of the younger officers weaved his way over to the SUV.

"Adams is holed up in the bunkhouse."

"Why didn't I hear this on the radio?" Seth barked.

"Just happened," the deputy explained. "We went inside to arrest Adams and then, well, all hell broke lose. Everyone was filing outside all orderly and everything, then the foreman goes after Adams and the next thing we know, Adams has a gun and he's holding it to the foreman's head."

"Will? Will is inside with Luke Adams?" Shane demanded.

The deputy nodded. "Adams told us all to get out or he'd blow the guy's head off."

"Get on the radio and alert the state police," Seth instructed. "I want this area cleared of everyone who doesn't need to be here."

"I can do that," Shane said as he rushed from the truck. He crouched, zigzagging his way to the closest ranch hand half-hidden behind a nearby tree. "Get all the men out of here," he said.

"Will's in there with that lunatic," the man argued.

"We'll handle it. The last thing I need is a shoot-out. I want everyone out of here. Now. Make it happen."

The hand did as instructed. About two dozen men worked their way along the fence line, using the trees and fence posts as cover.

Shane's every nerve was on high alert. Through a small window, he could just see the top of Will's head. He felt a surge of anger tempered by uttered helplessness. There wasn't a lot he could do about the former, but the latter was assuaged by clicking off the safety and loading a round into the chamber of the gun in his left hand.

Shane was desperate to help his friend. Maybe he should have brought Taylor along. Not that he wanted her in harm's way, but perhaps she could offer suggestions, a way to talk Adams out of the bunkhouse without Will, or anyone else, getting hurt.

Seth joined him then, pressing his shoulder against the trunk of the pine tree. "There's a hostage negotiator on the way. He'll be here in an hour."

"An hour?" Shane repeated, infuriated. "What are we supposed to do until then? Ask everyone to take a sixty-one minute time-out for pie and coffee?"

"Wait him out," Seth replied as he used his thumb to dial his cell phone.

The sound of the bunkhouse telephone ringing incessantly cut through the night. Will moved out of his line of sight as the ringing went on for almost two minutes, before Shane heard some muffled arguments from inside, followed by a crash. Then there was silence.

"Must have yanked the phone off the wall," Shane guessed. "I say we rush the place. The son of a bitch has already killed a woman in cold blood. Do you think he'd hesitate to kill Will if it would do him any good?"

He felt Seth's fingers close on his upper arm. "I know how much Will means to you, but we're going to do this by the book."

"I'm not going to do anything stupid, but I need to

do *something*," Shane argued. "Let me go in, Seth. Maybe I can—"

He was silenced by the blast of a gunshot.

Shrugging off his brother's hold, Shane raced to the bunkhouse, right on the heels of three deputies in bulletproof vests. In tandem, the officers kicked in the door, splintering the wood near the lock as they trained their weapons on the interior.

As he'd been taught, Shane kept his elbows flexible as he stared down the barrel of his own gun. After a quick scan of the room, he focused on Will.

His friend was standing over the body of Luke Adams, a small-caliber revolver dangling loosely between his thumb and forefinger.

A handful of officers swarmed the long, narrow room. Shane breathed in the acrid scent of gunpowder as he strode toward Will. As expected, the older man showed no emotion as he said, "Didn't have a choice."

Shane nodded as he glanced briefly at the blood pooling from beneath the lifeless body of Luke Adams. "You okay?" he asked, knowing it was rhetorical, since Will would never admit to being hurt.

"I'm fine."

Seth joined them then, asking, "What happened?"

Will took in a deep breath and leaned back against the footboard of one of the unmade beds. Shane and his brother also moved out of the path of the incoming paramedics.

"The kid went off," Will answered, rubbing the day's worth of graying stubble on his chin. "Got the call that the law was coming for him, so I came to keep an eye on him."

Shane tucked his gun in the back of his waistband as he listened to Will. As always, the foreman's voice was devoid of emotion as he recounted the events.

"The cops burst in, and the next thing I knew he had a revolver stuck in my ear." Will paused, looking down at the weapon he was holding before handing it over to Seth. "I'm pretty sure that's one of my guns, too. Kid musta stole it from my desk."

"How come you didn't recognize him leaving Webb's Market?" Shane asked. "Seems to me you should have known it was Adams when you saw him running away after he killed Doris."

Will shrugged. "Happened really fast, and like I told Seth, here, I only caught a glimpse of the guy from the back."

"You didn't know your gun was missing?" Shane asked, perplexed since it wasn't at all like Will to be so cavalier with a weapon.

"It's calving season," he said. "We've been putting in twenty-hour days."

Shane listened, wondering why the explanation didn't ring totally true. It was crazy, since he'd known Will practically all of his life. If Will told Seth that's what happened, then that's what must've happened. Shane's brain knew that for a fact. Yet his gut was telling him differently.

Crazy was a good adjective to describe the way Detective Rollins looked when he burst into the bunkhouse. His eyes were narrowed and it was clear he was angry as hell.

"What part of 'stay out of the investigation' don't you understand, Sheriff Landry?"

Shane watched as his brother responded to the question with something akin to boredom. "How do you figure this was part of your investigation?"

Rollins glanced over at the body, then glared daggers at Shane. "Oh, Luke Adams was a big part of my investigation."

"How so?" Shane asked.

"He called me a few hours ago," Rollins answered. "Claimed he had information on the murder of your parents. He wanted to make a deal."

"He was playing you," Shane retorted. "Probably realized he was about to be arrested for the Webb's Market robbery-homicide."

"Adams claimed he was being set up on that," Rollins argued. "Said you Landrys were framing him just like you framed his father."

"His father?" Shane repeated, not following at all. He turned to Seth and asked, "Know anything about that?"

Seth shook his head, but Will cleared his throat and said, "It was a long time ago."

"What was a long time ago?" Shane asked, an odd feeling rumbling in the pit of his stomach.

Will shifted from foot to foot. "The thing with his old man. Adams is a pretty common name, so I didn't put it together when Luke signed on."

"What happened to his father?" Shane asked.

"Caleb had me fire him," Will stated. "Jack was the accountant here. He was siphoning money from the ranch. Stole nearly fifty grand before your dad and I discovered what he was doing. After that, the guy couldn't find work anywhere. Last I heard he was drowning himself in the bottle."

"When was this?" Shane demanded.

"Thirty-plus years ago," Will answered.

Chapter Fourteen

"Did you sleep?" Shane asked when he stuck his head in the doorway to the office.

Taylor was seated at the desk, totally focused on the computer screen until she glanced up. Her breath caught when she saw him. Even in the middle of a disaster, Shane had the uncanny ability to paralyze her just by showing up.

His still-damp hair was pulled neatly into a ponytail. His expressive blue eyes showed just a hint of the strain of the previous night's activity. But it was his broad, bared chest that sent her heart racing.

All instincts begged her to jump out of her chair, run into his arms and spend the next several hours in his bed. Luckily though, her brain was in charge and not her libido. Well, mainly in charge, she admitted privately when she felt a shiver of desire ripple through her.

"I slept a little," she said, waving him over. "Come look at this."

Shane finished buttoning his shirt as he came around

the large desk, then placed his hands on the back of the chair. It creaked under his weight as he leaned forward. His face was next to her ear, his warm breath tickling her neck. He smelled of heat and soap.

She had to give herself a little mental slap. This was not the time to be sidetracked by her physical fascination with this man. Then there was the added pressure of having knowledge of his blood tests before he did. She felt an odd mixture of emotions, a need to protect him from the truth struggling against her innate need to be honest with him. She wished now that she hadn't learned of the results first. Sometimes ignorance truly was bliss. Not that he'd be ignorant of the facts for long; Chance planned on telling Shane in the morning. Despite her argument that he be informed right away, Chance had wanted to do his research before he told his brother. He'd pointed out that twenty-four hours wasn't going to make any difference at this point. But they both knew Shane would demand to know everything there was to know about his illness. Chance wanted to have all those facts to give him. She would just have to keep the secret to herself for another eighteen or so hours.

Squeezing her eyes shut for the second it took to clear her thoughts, she said, "This is a fairly complete life history of the late Luke Adams. Well, as much as I've been able to cobble together so far."

"And you did this because…?" he asked.

She scooted to the side, thrown off her concentration by his closeness. Heat practically radiated from his large body and the scents of soap and shampoo filled her nostrils. Taylor was glad he couldn't read her thoughts. If he could, Shane would know that she really, *really* wanted to drag him down the hall to her bedroom and spend a lazy day in bed. She almost smiled. *Bed* and *lazy* were two words that didn't go together when thinking of Shane.

"Taylor?" he prompted, placing his hand on her shoulder and giving a gentle, prodding squeeze.

"Right. Sorry. Well, I got to thinking after last night. Why would Luke Adams go to all the trouble of getting a job here, then blow it by robbing the market and killing Doris?"

"Because he's a career criminal?" Shane suggested, moving around so that he faced her as he leaned against the edge of the desk. "You heard Seth and Detective Rollins. Luke started getting into trouble when he was in his late teens."

"But before that," Taylor pointed out, "he was an Eagle Scout."

"People aren't born bad," Shane remarked dryly.

"No," she insisted, "I mean that literally. He was an Eagle Scout. Look at these articles." She started handing him the pages she'd printed out. "Luke was only fourteen when he made Eagle Scout, which, by the way, is an accomplishment and a half. That was the year before your parents' murder and six months before his first arrest. Something bad must have happened to make such a great kid go down the drain so suddenly."

"You're analyzing a dead guy, you know that, right? A dead guy who killed Doris and would have killed Will had Will not wrestled the gun away from him."

Taylor nodded. "Yes, and I know that Rollins found

a prepaid cell phone on Luke and that the memory card in the phone proves that phone was used to make the threatening calls to me."

Shane rubbed his freshly shaved chin. "What's your point?"

"It's too strange," she argued. "I told you I met Luke."

"Yeah?"

"He didn't know who I was," she stated emphatically. "I had to tell him I was the housekeeper. So why would he call to threaten me if he didn't even know who I was?"

"Because he was a criminal?"

She glared up at him. "Think, Shane. Luke was here the day I went up into the attic. If he was some crazed killer, that was a perfect opportunity for him to rampage."

"But he had the cell phone, and preliminary ballistics on the gun prove that it was the one used to kill Doris. Pretty compelling if you ask me."

"Here." Taylor shoved a sheaf of papers into his hand. "Read what I printed," she insisted. "Luke was an above-average kid. Good grades, basically model behavior. Something happened to change him."

"That would have been about the time that his father was outed as a thief," Shane mused. "Will told me that even though no charges were filed, Jack Adams was a pariah after that. Started drinking, couldn't get a job, lost his house. Something like that would certainly change a kid's behavior."

"Speaking of that," Taylor said, her fingers flying over the keyboard as she spoke, "the father, Jack, made the papers a few times. Disturbing-the-public charges, mostly during court hearings regarding his son."

"Pretty fatherly behavior."

"Yes, but look at this quote," Taylor said, pointing toward the computer screen. "According to the reporter on scene, a very drunk Jack called the judge corrupt. Said the whole system was flawed and unfair."

"I think I said something similar when Clayton was convicted of killing Pam." It was clear Shane was only half listening as he riffled through the pages she'd printed. Clearly not impressed, he set them on the desk beside his hip. "Outbursts like that aren't all that uncommon in the heat of the moment."

"Okay. For the sake of argument, let's say it was nothing more than an emotional rant by an alcohol-impaired parent. It still doesn't change the facts. And another thing. Did you know Luke's mother and Doris were friends?"

That seemed to get his attention. His dark brows drew together. "And we know this how?"

Taylor shuffled some papers around until she found the old photograph. "This was taken at the Hunt Club the year before you were born. This…" she paused to tap one of the faces in the picture "…is Leona Drake. At least that's the name Doris gave me. I did a computer search and found that Drake was Leona's maiden name. She was married to Jack Adams and they had a son, Luke."

"Obviously, they knew my parents," Shane said, running his thumb over the aged image.

"Correct. When I spoke to Doris, it sounded as if she

and Leona were pretty close friends, which would mean Luke knew her as well. So why did he kill one of the only people in Jasper he had a history with?"

Shane frowned. "So what are you saying here? That there's some sort of connection between Luke killing Doris and the death of my parents? That seems like a helluva stretch. Do we know for a fact that Luke knew Doris?"

"One way to find out," Taylor suggested. "The father is still alive. I could go see him."

Shane started shaking his head. "No way, I'm not letting you go see some drunk alone. I'll—"

"Just make him crazy," Taylor interrupted. Closing her hand over his, she said, "If he started drinking because your father fired him, do you really think he'll be in a hurry to talk to *you?*"

"No."

"I'll go this afternoon, before my class."

"No way, Taylor. You are not running all over hell and gone by yourself."

"So come with me," she suggested. "But you have to wait in the car. No, make that completely out of sight. Killer or not, Luke was still his son and he's a grieving father."

"I hate the idea. A lot. But okay. You're better equipped to handle him."

She shot him a suspicious glance. "Are you making fun of me, Shane Landry?"

He reached out and cupped her cheek. His palm was warm and she reflexively leaned into his touch. "I'm

complimenting you, Taylor. That's what a person does
when they care about someone."

She stiffened. "Don't do that."

"Compliment you? Or care about you?"

Taylor scooted as far away from him as possible,
until the chair rolled to a stop against the bookcase.
"The latter."

The smile he offered was sad and caused a tightness
in her chest that made her feel as if she'd just kicked
his favorite dog. "Let's not do this now, Shane."

"Okay."

She hadn't expected such a quick and amicable surrender. Tilting her head slightly, she regarded him for
a few seconds. The man was sneaky.

She scowled. "Just 'okay'? No argument?"

He shrugged. "I'm willing to hold off on the full
court press."

She relaxed a little. "Good."

"For now."

Not good.

By MIDAFTERNOON, Shane still wasn't back and Taylor
was feeling pretty antsy. She was staring at the photograph, hoping for some sort of divine inspiration. All
the faces were familiar at this point, even if the picture
was more than three decades old.

Grabbing the telephone, she called directory assistance, then had the phone company automatically dial
the office of Senator Brian Hollister. It was a long shot
and she knew it.

Hollister was a very popular elected official whose

main claim to fame was carrying the torch of the common man into politics. Taylor navigated through a maze of administrative personnel before reaching the senator's personal secretary. Vaguely, she recalled meeting her—a petite woman with bright green eyes and a pretty smile—at the Landrys' funeral.

"May I tell Senator Hollister what this is in reference to?" she asked.

"I'm calling about Caleb and Priscilla Landry."

"Please hold."

A few minutes later the senator's assistant came back on the line. "Senator Hollister is in a meeting at the moment. Would you like to make an appointment to see him—"

Taylor almost groaned. Of course the senator was busy. What had she been thinking? That he'd drop everything because she called? Waste his time reminiscing over old pictures? Still, she had to try. Something about this picture niggled at her brain. "I appreciate that. But it's imperative that I speak to him as soon as possible."

Anticipating that the senator would see her in oh, about three months, Taylor impatiently listened as the woman's fingers clicked on her keyboard, apparently checking her boss's calendar.

"I have June 19 at ten o'clock or July 8 at three-thirty…."

"Neither," Taylor told her firmly. "It's vital that I see the senator, or at least talk to him, today."

"That's not—"

"Please. It could be a matter of life and death."

"The senator has a break between a luncheon and a

meeting at two-fifteen. Would two o'clock this afternoon suit you, Miss Reese?"

Taylor glanced up at the clock. If she left now, she could just make it. "Yes, thank you."

After she hung up, Taylor tried several times to track Shane down. He wasn't in the barn or up at the calving shed. None of the hands could tell her when anyone had last seen him, only that he was with Will. And, damn the man, he still wasn't answering his cell phone.

She left him a message on his voice mail. Just to be on the safe side, she also scribbled a note for him and left it on the table.

Contacting Shane was just a matter of courtesy, Taylor thought irritably as she quickly changed clothes for her meeting with the senator.

For reasons she did not want to analyze, she was ticked off that Shane seemed to have walked off the edge of the earth without telling her where he'd gone. Perhaps because they'd been on such high alert for days—first with his parents' bodies being found, then the threatening phone calls, and then Doris's murder. She'd quickly become used to having him there watching out for her. Silly to feel the loss now.

While there were still dozens of questions to be answered, there was no longer any threat of danger. Luke was dead. Shane wasn't obligated to tell her where he was every minute of the day, and she didn't need to feel strangely abandoned and vulnerable.

The drive to the office of Senator Hollister gave her time to think. Canyon Creek was north of Jasper, a small community at the edge of Helena National Forest.

Following the deserted black ribbon of macadam, she tried to organize the fractured bits and pieces into something that made a little more sense.

"Luke couldn't have killed the Landrys, he was only seven when they disappeared. Then there was the money," she murmured. "The hundred thousand dollars withdrawn from the account by Caleb Landry the day they disapp—*died*."

Fishing around in her purse, Taylor found her cell phone, placed it on the console as she attached the ear bud, then pressed Sam's speed dial number. His secretary put her through directly.

"Hi, Taylor, everything okay?"

"Fine," she insisted, filling him in on her plans for the day.

"Shouldn't you have waited for Shane?" Sam asked, his tone conveying genuine concern.

She was touched by how much Sam—heck, all the Landrys—cared for her well-being. "He was tied up and the senator only had a limited window of time. Listen, have you found anything relative to the money yet? Anything suspicious or strange?"

"One thing. Doesn't make a lot of sense, though."

"What is it?"

She heard the shuffling of papers before Sam said, "Beginning in 1978, there were large, semiannual withdrawals made from my parents' savings account."

"Shane would have been ten," Taylor remarked. "That was around the same time your mother took him for the blood test."

"I know. There's got to be a connection."

Shoving her hair off her face, Taylor asked, "Any thoughts? Theories?"

"Chance is trying to track down a nurse who worked at the medical center where Shane had the test. Maybe she can shed some light on why Mom waited until he was that old. I mean, if she knew her...*lover* had this disease, I don't understand why she'd wait all those years to have Shane tested."

"I know," Taylor agreed. She had an odd feeling as if she was missing something right in front of her. "I never knew your mother but I saw the records she kept on Shane. She didn't strike me as the kind of woman who would let a potential medical issue go ignored. Especially not for ten years."

"I did know her," Sam said. "And I'm having trouble accepting the fact that she cheated on my father."

Taylor heard the blend of pain and anger in Sam's tone. It would be ten times worse for Shane. "What about before then? What about the money stolen by Jack Adams? Did your father or Will keep the proof that he was embezzling from the ranch?"

"Yep," Sam answered, followed by the sound of more papers being shuffled. "For an accountant, Jack wasn't very swift at covering his tracks."

"What do you mean?"

"Let's just say that if I was going to steal from my employer, I would have done a better job of it."

"Give me an example." She turned north on Highway 279, adjusting the visor as blinding, bright sunshine streamed into the car.

"The ranch has a general operating account as well

as several investment accounts. Jack was a signatory on all those accounts. The unauthorized withdrawals were from the general operating account."

Taylor's brow furrowed as she tried to follow the gist of the conversation. She wasn't very successful. "Does it matter which account he stole from?"

"If you don't want to get caught, it does," Sam scoffed. "Back then, the bank sent monthly statements on the operating account to the ranch. Meaning Jack risked getting caught every thirty days."

"And the investment accounts?"

"Quarterly statements," Sam answered. "Easier to hide discrepancies that way."

"An accountant would know this?"

"Definitely. It's pretty basic stuff."

"So why did he do it?"

"I have no clue," Sam admitted. "I've been over this paperwork a dozen times and I can't find a pattern of any kind."

"Does that matter?"

She heard Sam expel a breath. "Normally, yes. If Jack was behind in his mortgage, you'd expect money to disappear at a set time every month. If he was gambling, the withdrawals might coincide with weekends. The theft in this case was pretty random."

"Why wasn't he arrested?" Taylor asked.

"I can only guess at this point. I can't find where the money went and I've got computer resources my dad didn't have at his disposal back then. I'm sure Dad ran into the same problem. It's hard to prove someone is a thief if you can't trace the money to them."

"But if he was the accountant…"

"*Knowing* someone is a thief and proving it are often two different things, Taylor. So far, I can only prove that the money was transferred to Western Union."

She felt hopeful for the first time in the conversation. "Wouldn't they have a record of some kind? A receipt, something?"

"No. Basically, Western Union gets the funds, then the recipient can go to any one of their authorized locations and claim the money."

"So it's a dead end?"

"I didn't say that," Sam said. "At the time of the embezzlement, there were only five authorized locations in Montana. I'm working that angle now."

"That's good, right?"

She heard him expel a long breath. "Only if the stolen money was picked up in Montana. If Jack had it sent out of state, I'm not sure we'll ever know what happened to it."

"Are you coming over in the morning?" Taylor asked, feeling her stomach knot just thinking about Shane's response to hearing the news.

"Of course. He's going to need you, Taylor."

"I…it's a family thing. I don't want to intru—"

"He needs *you,*" Sam stated simply. "You're going to be there for him, right?"

Her heart pinched in her chest and her next breath was something of an effort. "I think he needs his brothers more."

"No, Taylor. *You'll* be the one he'll want."

Chapter Fifteen

The offices of Senator Hollister occupied the first floor of a three-story building in the center of Canyon Creek. It was a small, well-manicured town dependent largely on tourism and a relatively famous drug rehabilitation center.

It was midafternoon when Taylor parked her car on the street about a block away from the office and strode toward the brick building.

She had to pass through a metal detector guarded by a young, uniformed officer, then a second set of glass doors before she was greeted by a pretty redhead wearing a headset.

The office smelled faintly of popcorn. The walls were lined with framed articles tracing Hollister's unlikely rise to relative fame.

"I'm Taylor Reese," she informed the smiling woman. "The senator is expecting me."

"Have a seat, Miss Reese. Can I get you come coffee, tea, a bottle of water?"

Taylor shook her head, thanked her, then watched the twenty-something woman disappear behind a door marked Private. When several minutes passed, Taylor began to grow restless. Lacing her fingers, she stood up and moved around the reception area, reading the articles that traced the history of the senator's career.

Hollister wasn't your typical career politician. In fact, he wasn't a politician at all, but a used-car dealer. Well, according to one article, that had been his focus until he'd gotten annoyed by a zoning issue and thrown his hat into the ring. The rest, as they say, was history.

Running as a regular guy willing to shake up the career politicians, Hollister had won his senate seat by the narrowest of margins. His constituents had latched on to Hollister's claims that he was one of them. According to one reporter, Hollister's rough-around-the-edges appeal negated the reality that he was a lousy businessman who had filed for bankruptcy twice before running for office.

His best asset was his wife, Elizabeth. One article even hinted that she was the brains behind the man's carefully orchestrated upset victory.

Taylor inched between two wing chairs in order to get a better look at the attractive woman waving from the front page of a news article. The color image was very flattering and very familiar.

Slipping the attic picture out of her purse, Taylor compared the unnamed woman to Hollister's wife, Elizabeth. They were one and the same. Pleased with her detecting skills, Taylor stuck the picture back in her purse.

The redhead returned then, wearing an apologetic smile. "I'm sorry, Miss Reese, the senator is on a conference call."

Checking her watch and doing a little math, Taylor said, "I can wait for a little bit."

"He may be awhile."

Taylor shrugged and sat on the edge of one of the chairs, grabbing a magazine and flipping—disinterestedly—through the pages. Five minutes passed, then ten, then twenty. He was pretty lackadaisical for a guy who only had a few minutes between appointments. Pressing her palm against her knee, she was attempting to stop the agitated tapping of her foot when her cell phone rang.

"Hello?"

"Please tell me you didn't go to Canyon Creek by yourself," Shane said with mild irritation.

"I didn't go to Canyon Creek by myself."

"Good. Where are you?"

"Canyon Creek."

He sighed for effect. "Do you really think it's safe for you to be running around alone?"

Taylor looked up to find the receptionist openly listening to every word. Placing one hand over the mouthpiece, she met the other woman's curious gaze and said, "I think I'll step outside so I don't disturb you."

Grabbing up her purse, she walked out to the street. "Luke is dead, remember?"

"Luke didn't kill my parents, remember? Seth is sending a deputy to follow you back to Jasper. I'll see you at home."

"I haven't seen the senator yet."

"I suggest you hurry it along because the deputy will be there in about a half hour."

"You sound annoyed."

"I was annoyed when I saw your note. I've moved past that to completely pissed, but we'll have that conversation when you get back here. I've got someone at the door, so we'll talk about this later. Bye." The line went dead.

She should have known there'd be hell to pay for going off on her own, but listening to his even, clipped syllables made her wince. For good reason, too.

Flipping the phone closed, she headed back inside, wondering when she'd gotten stupid. And it was stupid to drive all the way up here alone. Any number of bad things could have happened.

So why did I do it? she asked herself as she cleared the metal detectors for a second time.

Because if I can't be with him, at least I can help him.

And look what I did. she continued the mental lashing. *Like my mother and grandmother, I willingly put myself in physical danger for a man.* Her shoulders slumped. Obviously, her life plan wasn't working. She was making decisions—bad ones—based on a man.

It didn't matter that he was a terrific man, or that he was in trouble. All Taylor could think about was the chilling reality that being in love, acknowledged or not, had made her reckless.

Five minutes after her return to the waiting area, Senator Hollister opened the restricted access door and greeted her with a broad grin and a very enthusiastic handshake. So enthusiastic that her hand stung as she allowed him to guide her down the narrow hallway to his private office.

Thirty years ago, he'd been a thin, pencil-necked twenty-four-year-old. Now he was a silver-haired man with capped teeth and a sparkling pinky ring in the shape of a bear. When he sat behind a large, glass-topped desk, she noted that the bear's eyes were made of small garnet chips that glowed demonic red in the sunlight streaming through the window.

His cologne was a heavy, musky scent that Taylor actually tasted as she sat in one of two large, black leather chairs opposite the desk.

"If I'd have known you were such a pretty little thing, I wouldn't have kept you waiting," Hollister said, his brown eyes narrowed when he grinned.

Taylor didn't take offense. Instead, she ignored the inappropriate tone and content as just a generational difference. In her experience, men over fifty didn't always get that women her age loathed that kind of comment. "Thank you."

"My secretary said you have a picture you want me to look at?"

Nodding, Taylor pulled the photograph from her purse and slid it across his cluttered desk. The minute his brown eyes fixed on the image, his smile grew taut, almost forced. "Such a shame," he murmured.

"What?"

"Caleb, Priscilla, Doris, Leona," Hollister sighed. "Hard to believe they're all gone now."

"Did you know the Landrys well?"

Hollister lifted his shoulders. The action caused his double chin to press against the too-tight collar of his stark white dress shirt. "Not really. I mean, we all belonged to the Hunt Club. There were parties there almost every weekend." He shoved his cuff back to look at his watch, not bothering to be subtle. He was a busy man, granting a favor, and he clearly didn't want her to forget it. "Hell," he said with a small smile, "in the sixties, there were just parties, period. Know what I mean?"

Taylor smiled back. "What about Jack and Leona Adams? What do you remember about them?"

"Leona was a pleasant gal. Her husband was quiet. Pencil pusher type," Hollister said with a derogatory little sneer. "Sorry to cut this short, Miss Reese, but I have a meeting." He stood and came around the desk. "Thanks for stopping by," he said, holding the photograph in her direction. "If I can be of further help, you just give a call, okay?"

"I would like to know more about the—"

"I'm sorry, but I really don't have any more time today," he said, moving to the door and grabbing the knob.

Reluctantly, Taylor started past the senator, feeling very much as if she was being hurried along. He was in a serious rush to get her out of his office.

As she was leaving the building, Taylor practically fell into Mrs. Hollister as the older woman came charging up the stairs.

"Excuse me," Taylor said.

Elizabeth Hollister didn't exactly exude warmth. She was a thin, drawn woman who looked much older than her fifty years. A thick, chunky necklace clattered against the buttons of her suit as she brushed imaginary cooties from the front of her blazer.

"Are you okay?" Taylor inquired.

"I'm fine. You're the Landrys' maid, aren't you?" She

started nodding her head, her brown eyes narrowing slightly. "I vaguely remember you from the funeral."

"Yes, I work for the family."

"What are you doing here?" the senator's wife asked.

Actually, it sounded more like an accusation, which caught Taylor a little off guard. "I stopped by to see your husband."

"Well then, I'm sure he was helpful." Elizabeth started to walk away.

"Since you're here, is there anything you can remember about the people in this photograph?" Taylor called, whipping it out of her purse and holding it up.

"I remember it was a long time ago," Elizabeth replied, after glancing at it briefly. "Beyond that, you'll have to excuse me, Taylor."

Taylor? "But—"

A split second later, Taylor was alone, listening to the sound of her own voice echo off the building. She considered chasing the woman down, but then remembered that Elizabeth was the wife of a senator, and the deputy sent to follow her back to Jasper was pulling up to the curb behind a dark blue pickup truck.

Immersed in her own thoughts, Taylor barely mumbled the appropriate pleasantries as she was escorted to her car. The Hollisters were strange. And she'd bet her Ph.D. that they were hiding something. But what? And how had a woman who "vaguely" remembered her from the funeral several weeks ago know her first name?

The obvious guess would be that Hollister was

Shane's biological father. If her suspicions were true, why hadn't the senator come forward and said anything to Shane in all these years? If it was true, did Elizabeth know? And if so, why didn't she toss him out on his senatorial ear?

"And why," Taylor asked out loud, "are all the people in the photo dying violent deaths?"

Taylor was no closer to an answer when she stuck her hand out of the car window and waved off the deputy as soon as she reached the driveway to the Lucky 7. As she went up the lane she noticed that he waited until she'd come to a stop in front of the house before he drove on. She cut the engine and grabbed her purse.

It was already close to four, and she suddenly realized she wasn't even remotely prepared for her evening class. Calculating prep time, the visit to Jack Adams's place and the drive to campus, she wondered if she'd be able to do it all.

Almost at a run, she pushed open the front door, closed it behind her and started down the hallway to her room. She almost didn't see him there in the shadows. It wasn't like Shane to sit in the living room. Taylor knew instantly that something was very, very wrong.

"Welcome back," he said, his intonation completely flat.

"What's wrong?" she asked as she flipped on a light.

It seemed as if Shane had aged five years since breakfast. He was sitting on the sofa, elbows on his knees, his shoulders slouched and his chin resting in one hand. His gaze was distant, his mouth bracketed by deep lines, his brow furrowed and that little muscle at the side of his jaw tensed.

A fist tightened around Taylor's chest as she walked into the living room. "Shane?"

He patted the cushion next to him and waited until she sat. When she did, she noticed him pressing the heels of his palms against his eyes. "Detective Rollins came to see me this afternoon."

Her heart skipped a full beat. "And?"

"It's all there, in black and white." He indicated a neat stack of papers in the center of the coffee table. "I had to haul Chance out here to explain it all to me."

"What?"

"Let's see." He began ticking things off on his fingers. "There's no way I'm Caleb Landry's son. The up side to that is I may not be the killer. According to Detective Rollins, they can't make a one-hundred-percent match of my blood to the blood on the towel that was recovered with the bodies because of the age and poor quality of the evidence. But I do have the right blood type, so I can't be excluded, either."

Dread filled her. "And?"

"And I have a hereditary genetic disorder."

She wanted to take him in her arms and comfort him. Instead Taylor reached out to give his shoulder a gentle, reassuring squeeze. "I'm sorry, Shane."

"Nothing I can do about it," he said numbly. "This Von whatever-it-is disease isn't deadly, so I guess that's something."

"Of course it is," she insisted. "I looked it up, and so

long as you take precautions before surgery, or if you have a bleeding episode, it won't impact your life one iota."

His brows arched as he fixed his gaze on her. "Looked it up?"

Taylor sucked in a breath. Bad. Very, very bad.

"What were you doing? Thumbing through a medical dictionary? Why would you be looking up a disease no one has ever heard of?"

Damn it. She'd told Chance not to wait to tell Shane. Now look at the position he'd put her in. Shane was never going to understand this. And who could blame him? "I went to see Chance yesterday. He gave me a crash course on platelet disorders."

"You knew about this?"

Shane felt completely out of control, as if his life was one big wave about to crash onto shore. Knowing Taylor had kept such an important secret from him didn't exactly help.

She grabbed his hands, holding them tightly in hers. "I didn't say anything because it wasn't my place."

He cast her a sidelong look. "A hint would have been nice. Better than hearing it from a detective."

"I know," she agreed. "I'm sorry."

"That helps," he remarked sarcastically as he expelled a breath. "I don't understand why you would keep this secret, Taylor. Wait, that's a theme for the day, isn't it? I don't know why my mother had an affair."

He stood and started to pace, needing some way to release the explosive nervous energy knotting his insides. "Know what I did when the detective was explaining to me that my father wasn't really my father, and 'oh, yeah, you have a disease'?"

"That's an awful way to find out something like this. What did you do when he told you?"

"I got mad," Shane admitted. "Then I felt guilty about being mad."

"Normal reaction. Often when a person—"

He paused and glared till she fell silent. "I don't want to be analyzed, Taylor. I want to understand all this. How could my mother have cheated? Did my father know? Maybe that's why the two of us clashed. Maybe I was a walking, talking reminder of his wife's infidelity. And the big one. Who *is* my father?"

"Caleb Landry was your father in all the ways that matter, Shane. I have a feeling when you're not overrun by conflicted emotions, you'll see that clearly."

Taylor twisted a lock of hair between her thumb and forefinger as she continued, "People have affairs for all sorts of reasons."

Shane massaged his tense shoulders. "Well, I'm not like you, Taylor. You're fine with not knowing who your father is. Hell, you're comfortable with anything so long as it doesn't have any strings attached."

His words hurt more than she thought possible. "That's not fair, Shane."

Lifting his head, he met her eyes. "Really? You're so good at ascribing motives to other people. Ever turn that mirror on yourself?"

"I'm comfortable with who I am."

"No, Taylor, you hide from who you are. From what

you feel." He blew a breath toward his forehead. "We've lived together for too long. Know how I know?"

Mutely, she shook her head.

"'Cause I actually get you. You don't choose not to love me, you don't know how. If you did, you would know that when someone you love has been given some pretty devastating news, you offer comfort, not analysis."

"I'm trying to be comforting," Taylor argued. "I spent the afternoon running all over creation just to gather information that could help you."

"It would have been nice to have you here," he told her honestly. "I needed you, Taylor. Not Will or Chance or anyone else. You."

His brother had been right. Shane *had* needed her. "I had no way of knowing that Detective Rollins would come here. I don't know what else I can say or do."

"And that's the heart of the problem, isn't it?"

"It doesn't have to be a problem, Shane. You're making it one."

"Then we shouldn't have made love."

Her eyes narrowed angrily. "Convenient of you to decide that after the fact. What a…a *man* thing to do."

"No, Taylor, that's the problem. I'm the only one here interested in a relationship. You're just jerking my chain until you have your diploma in your hands and you can be on your merry way without a backward glance."

"Well, you got the jerk part right. You promised me that you wouldn't do this again."

He balled his fists at his sides. "Do what?"

"Lash out at me because you've had some unpleasant news."

"Unpleasant?" he mocked, astounded by her understatement. "Swallowing a bug is unpleasant. Discovering you don't know who your father is falls under a completely different heading. Tack on knowing that your biological father murdered your parents and dumped their bodies down a well to rot takes it to a different level, wouldn't you say?"

She folded her hands neatly in her lap. "I'd say you have every reason to be confused and emotionally fractured."

"You going to charge me for this office visit?"

"What do you want me to say?" she snapped. "I'm really, really sorry this happened. I'm sorry you found out this way and, well…hell, I…probably do…love you."

"Well, I'm sure basking in the warm glow of that proclamation of love."

"It's the best I can do," she insisted stiffly.

"You know something, Taylor? The sad truth is, I agree with you." He willed himself not to walk over to punch a gaping hole in the wall. But he sure wanted to hit something. He wanted some way to alleviate the crushing emptiness in his chest. Anything that wasn't an analysis of his motivations.

Oddly enough, as devastating as it was to hear the news of his parentage, it paled in comparison to knowing that he had no future with Taylor. Nothing that would leave his sanity or his heart intact. That much was brutally clear.

Walking to the coat rack, he snapped up his jacket, turned to her and asked, "Coming?"

"Where?"

"I'm going to see Jack Adams. While I'm there, maybe I should ask if he's my father."

"Then of course I'm coming," Taylor replied, scurrying off the sofa, grabbing her own jacket and fairly chasing after him down the front stairs.

Chapter Sixteen

It wasn't until Taylor had her second arm in its sleeve that it dawned on her she had said the words to him. *I love you.* And nothing. No response, no whoop of joy, no…anything. Nada, zero, zippo. Granted, her timing sucked, but never in her wildest dreams had she ever considered that if and when she said those weighty words, they'd be tossed off like an unwelcomed insult.

The late afternoon air couldn't hold a candle to the chill in the air inside the SUV. Taylor guessed she should do something to smooth things over. After all, the man, obtuse moron that he was, *was* in crisis.

She winced, glad he couldn't see her face in the dull glow of the dashboard lights. *He's right. I do make everything sound clinical. Lord, life was a lot easier when we were limited to playful, pointless banter and I didn't have to weigh the importance of every word.*

"Off the subject," she said facetiously, "I understand your anger, Shane. You're hurt, and you feel betra—"

"Do *not* reduce what I'm experiencing to one of your textbook cases. Yes, I'm hurt by this, and damn it to hell, *yes.* I do feel betrayed that you—*all* of you—knew this and kept it a secret." He put a hand up when she tried to talk. "I understand that Chance wanted to present me with all the facts. Intellectually I get it, okay? I get it.

"Just give me a second here to assimilate everything I've learned. In the meantime, why don't you tell me about your visit with Senator Hollister?"

He wasn't going to talk about the elephant they'd left back in the living room. Fine with her. She had a little adjusting and assimilating of her own to deal with. She recounted her visit to the senator's office. "He couldn't get me out of there fast enough. Any ideas why?"

"Not really. I barely know the guy. I remember him coming by from time to time, but that was way back, around when he opened his second used car lot. Mostly I just remember that Hollister ran these really cheesy TV commercials in the middle of the night."

"He likes playing the good old boy. What else do you know about him?"

"What I read in the papers. Married to Elizabeth, who used to be known as Lizzy until she clawed her way up the social ladder."

"I met her as well," Taylor said. "She wasn't what you'd call warm, either."

"Rumor has it Lizzy's from one of those old Southern families. The grandfather made a few millions—textiles, I think. The money only lasted one generation, leaving Lizzy and her cousins in the position of having to make it or marry it."

Taylor nodded. "That fits. Is that how she ended up with Hollister?"

"Sure. I think she was probably still in her late teens when she married him. My guess is that she was facing college or the secretarial pool, so Hollister and his used car empire must have looked pretty damn good to her."

"So, they knew your parents? Socialized with them?"

"*Knew* might be a little strong," Shane murmured. "The Hunt Club was Jasper's version of a country club. If you paid the annual dues, you were a member."

As he continued to speak, the tension in his voice lessened. There was still an edge, but not as pronounced. "I remember my parents talking about the parties they used to attend, but that ended when I was still in elementary school."

"Why? Did it close down?"

"It's still open," Shane said. "I haven't been there since my ninth birthday. My…dad took me there to do some skeet shooting."

She felt a stab of pain, hearing him stumble over the reference to Caleb. She was respectfully quiet for a moment, then asked, "And not after that?" In the dark, without seeing his face, she could tell that Shane was thinking the same thought.

"My mother took me for the platelet test not long after that."

"Okay," Taylor mused. "So, we know that something happened when you were ten years old that made your mother get you tested. Were you sick? Anything?"

"No."

"Why then? Why wait so long?" Taylor still had that nagging feeling she was missing something, an integral piece just there, out of reach. It was frustrating as sin.

But it was easier to hone her thoughts on who'd killed the Landrys than to delve into her feelings. Lord knew they were a jumbled mess. Mostly of her own doing.

Where was her all-powerful life plan when she needed it most? "Maybe Jack Adams can tell us."

That seemed very unlikely a half hour later when Shane turned down a rutted, overgrown road. Road was a generous description. It was more like a trail, complete with deep gulleys and small boulders that had to be negotiated like a giant slalom.

Dust sprayed in through the air vents, causing her to taste dirt as the car rocked and lurched up the steep incline. It was dark as pitch and Taylor still didn't see any signs of a house.

"Are you sure this is the right road?" she asked.

"Yes. According to Seth, there's an old cabin about a mile back from the main road. He failed to mention that the road was this rough."

"I'm getting a bad vibe about this," Taylor said, feeling the hairs on the back of her neck prickle. "Maybe it isn't a good idea. His son just died. He probably won't welcome the intrusion."

"I don't think Jack Adams even remembers he had a son named Luke. The way I hear it, the guy's been living inside a bottle of cheap Scotch for years."

"Look! Look!" Taylor cried, pointing at the shadowy outline about fifty feet ahead.

As impossible as it seemed, the house was in worse shape than the road. The wood exterior was cracked and several of the logs hung askew. The roof was patched with a rusted slab of corrugated aluminum and the windows were so dirty that they absorbed the beams from the headlights.

There was an odd smell, offensive and sweet all at once, and very strong as soon as they exited the car. "What's that?" she asked, bringing her jacket sleeve up to mask her mouth and nose.

"Poor housekeeping?" Shane suggested wryly. Leaving the car lights on, he slammed his door and strode toward the shack, Taylor hot on his heels. "Hello? Anybody home?"

There were no lights inside. No movement, no nothing, not even after Shane pounded on the door for several seconds.

Fear shot through Taylor as she crept over to a window and tried to peer inside. She had to step over a heap of assorted debris, bricks, twigs and other things she was sure she'd hate seeing in the light of day. Grimacing, she used her sleeve to clean a circle of glass. The interior grime was too thick for her to make out much beyond the vague images of a table and chairs.

"I don't think he's here," Taylor said.

Shane whipped out his cell phone and a few seconds later was speaking to Seth. The conversation lasted a minute or two. When he finished, he turned to Taylor, his face pinched in a frown. "Seth checked with Detective Rollins and apparently no one has been able to find Jack Adams. A fact Rollins failed to share. The state police have been by here a few times."

She spotted something by the front door. Something that appeared fresh, new and very out of place. "That explains this," Taylor said, reaching down and gingerly picking up a crisp, white business card with the state police emblem embossed on it. On the back side, someone had written, "Please contact us immediately." Showing it to Shane, she added, "Tough way to find out your child was killed in a hostage standoff."

Shane reached for the door handle, feeling the cold knob turn easily in his grasp. "Mr. Adams?" he called.

"We can't just go in," Taylor grumbled as he shoved the door past a high point on the floor that caused it to scrape and stick.

"Mr. Adams? Jack?" Not getting any answer, and fully aware that lots of folks in Montana shot first and asked questions later, he felt for Taylor and tucked her protectively behind him. He listened for sounds of life, but there was nothing but the gentle rustling of the trees and distant cry of a wolf.

"We shouldn't do this," Taylor repeated, though he didn't hear the same sense of conviction in her tone.

Groping along the inside wall, he found the switch plate and flicked on the light. A single, naked bulb dangled from the ceiling. The harsh glare blinded him for a second as the smell of stale cigarette smoke filled his lungs.

Once his eyes adjusted, Shane surveyed the sparse, single room cabin. There was a small, round kitchenette table with three chairs. All the seat cushions were split, most having been repaired with rope or duct tape. One chair sat at an angle to the table, as if someone had pushed it back to stand up.

Shane's conclusion was further supported when he

walked over and smelled the remnants of the nearly empty glass. "Scotch," he confirmed.

Taylor was still plastered to his side. Not that he blamed her; the cabin was creepy and dank and generally nasty. It was also deserted. Glancing around, Shane cataloged the contents as Taylor's hold slipped from his waist. A camp stove, crusted with baked-on gunk, sat on the chipped counter. Shane placed his palm on top of a small, dorm-size refrigerator and felt no vibration from the motor. Maybe the bad smell was coming from inside the unconnected appliance. He decided not to check.

He looked up to find Taylor crouching beside the unmade, metal twin bed. She picked up a small, framed photograph. "This must have been his wife, Leona."

Shane murmured some sort of acknowledgment as his eyes darted around the room, looking for something, anything. A clue of any kind would be welcome at this point. He had no idea what he was searching for, or if it was large or small. Jack Adams lived a spartan life. In addition to the kitchen and bedroom areas, the only other furnishings were a lumpy old recliner and a small, tin tray table holding a twelve-inch black-and-white television with a wire coat hanger and tinfoil rigged as an antenna. There wasn't a drawer in sight. Nothing to rifle through.

Dingy, graying paint and plaster were chipping off the wall. A large, moldy water spot on the ceiling drew his attention to the far corner. To a narrow door.

"A closet," he said, as if he'd discovered the New World.

"What are we looking for?" Taylor asked as, with a grimace, she got down on her hands and knees to peek under the bed.

"It'll jump out at us when we find it."

"If *anything* jumps out from under this bed, I'm back in the car."

He was still grinning as he opened the closet door. The narrow enclosure had a single clothes rod and a single shelf holding two boxes. Four plaid shirts hung on hangers and a large pile of dirty laundry was shoved into the corner. Okay, he wasn't touching that, either. A pair of worn hiking boots sat on the floor.

Shane reached to the shelf, grabbing first one box, then the other, and placing them on the bed for inspection.

Taylor stood, flipping her hair back and dusting her palms on the edge of the sheet. She grimaced and shivered. "This is a vile place."

"You can take a long bath when we get home." He was lifting the flaps of the box when he stopped abruptly and looked at Taylor's flushed face. "You missed class."

She shrugged and reached across to slide the second box closer to her side of the bed. "It isn't like I'll get detention or anything."

Tilting his head, he watched her briefly, trying to remember the last time Taylor had skipped a class. Never. Not once in five years. He'd seen her drag herself out of a sickbed to drive several hours in a blinding snowstorm. That Ph.D. was the most important thing in her life. But tonight, now, when he needed her, she'd bailed without so much as saying boo.

For a few seconds, he allowed himself to believe that

she'd done it because she actually did love him. In that small amount of time, his heart sang. The heavy pain of the day's disclosures vanished at the mere thought that Taylor was capable of loving him the way he wanted her to. The way he needed her to. The way he loved her. Then he gave himself a little mental reality check.

The temptation to take whatever crumbs she tossed his way was strong. But in the end, he needed more. A lot more. He needed her to feel what he felt. The blinding, white-hot, intense kind of love like…well, like he'd seen his parents share.

Shaking his head, Shane brought himself back to his now strange world. Caleb wasn't his father and the marital relationship he'd so admired his whole life was, apparently, a sham. That didn't change the fact that he was responsible for his parents' death, albeit indirectly. That was the only logical conclusion in light of the DNA results. So, following logic, his biological father was the killer. Why? If he could answer that, he could come to grips with himself, his brothers and his future.

His maudlin thoughts were interrupted by a triumphant little sound from Taylor. "What is it?" he inquired.

Slowly, she ran her fingernail along the edge of an old wedding album she took from the box. "There's something behind the cardboard."

Moving quickly, Shane went to her side, helping support the album as she coaxed two envelopes out from behind a photograph of Jack and his new bride. "What made you look behind the picture?" he asked, trying to fill the time as she took great care not to tear the photo.

"See the outline?" she replied.

In fact, there was a ghostly image, roughly the size and shape of a standard envelope, creased into the picture. "I probably would have missed that," he admitted.

"My grandmother did the same thing," Taylor said. "She used to hide money in frames behind my annual class pictures."

"Good a place as any, I suppose."

"A relatively safe place. The kinds of men she brought home weren't really the family type—oh, wow!"

"Wow is an understatement."

The papers were bank statements. Based on the post-marks, she knew they had been mailed to the Lucky 7 when Shane was roughly fifteen, three years before the Landrys were killed. One was addressed to Caleb and Priscilla Landry and the other was for the general operating account. "Why did Jack have these and why did he save them?" she wondered as she opened the envelopes, removing the statement and the canceled checks.

"This is from my parents' personal checking account," Shane said, examining the checks in turn. "Feed and Seed, Webb's Market, Guy's Pharmacy, Feed and Seed, Amanda Grayson, Cash—"

"What?" Taylor interrupted, trying to snatch the checks out of his hand.

"Cash," Shane repeated. "My mother wrote this check. It's for five thousand dollars."

"No, not that one. The Amanda Grayson one."

Shane sorted backward until he found the check. "Here it is—Amanda Grayson, twenty dollars."

Taylor checked the memo section. "Hunt Club?"

"Probably some sort of fund-raiser," Shane suggested, going back to the checks. "Yes. That's gotta be it. Here's another one two weeks later. Amanda Grayson, twenty bucks."

"Amanda Grayson would not belong to the Hunt Club. She wouldn't help with a fund-raiser."

"I told you, it was a social thing, too."

Fervently, Taylor shook her head. "I don't care if they were raffling off a night in Buckingham Palace. I'm telling you, Mrs. Grayson would not support a hunt club. She's staunchly antigun. Trust me, Shane, I've worked with Mrs. Grayson for two years and I know with every fiber of my soul that the woman would not be involved with anything even remotely related to ammunition, targets, guns or weaponry of any kind."

"Okay," he agreed. "But that's a forty dollar thing, Taylor. Look at this. In one month my mother paid out five grand from her personal account and another five grand from the operating account. Both payments are to cash." He handed her the checks. "See?"

The checks were identical. *Too* identical. "I need light."

"For what?"

"Bring that stuff."

Without waiting for him, Taylor went outside and sucked in a deep breath of much-needed fresh air. Going to the front of the SUV, she placed the check Priscilla Landry had written from her personal account against the warm, bright light of the headlamp. The light made the check almost transparent. Then she overlaid the second check, the one from the general operating account.

"I think I know how Jack Adams embezzled money from your family."

Shane leaned beside her, his breath warming her neck in short bursts as he looked more closely. "He traced my mother's signature? Not very high tech."

"He traced the amounts, too," Taylor said, seeing how perfectly the script matched. "Basically, Jack used your parents' personal checking account as a guide for what to steal and when to steal it. These two checks are a month apart, so I'd bet that if we compared all the checks, you'd have irrefutable proof of Jack's theft almost down to the dollar."

"So, Jack was a thief. And his son is a killer? But Jack couldn't have killed my parents because Detective Rollins already verified that he was in prison doing six months on a drunk and disorderly charge. Luke is on videotape killing Doris, but Luke couldn't have killed my parents because he was in juvenile hall at the time. So we can prove that they are both criminals, just not the *right* criminals?"

Taylor nodded grudgingly, rubbing her chilled arms. Bugs flew in and out of the beams from the headlights. "Pretty much." She turned and leaned against the car, utterly frustrated. When Shane reached for the checks, his fingertips brushed her palm, sending a small shiver up her back.

Slowly, she looked up into his hooded gaze. She swallowed once, twice, waiting anxiously as a kaleidoscope of raw emotion swirled in his eyes. Tucking the checks into his shirt pocket, he slipped his hand inside her jacket, resting it on her waist. He lifted the other to her face, gently caressing her cheek with the pad of his thumb.

Shane wasn't the only one whose thoughts and needs were jumbled and confused. Taylor wasn't handling her own inner turmoil too well. His mouth was inches from hers as his gaze flickered between her eyes and her mouth, finally settling on her lips. Fear, longing, anticipation—all of it pooled together into a consuming puddle in her tummy.

Pressing her palms against his chest, Taylor fully intended to stop anything before it started. Not that she didn't want his mouth on hers; she did. Desperately. But this was neither the time nor the place. Except that her rational mind kicked in a fraction of a second too late. Far too late.

All she needed was the feel of his rapidly beating heart beneath her hand and all her good intentions evaporated. The sensation of his thighs pressing against her became the focal point for her desire-addled brain. He smelled warm, inviting and familiar. His touch made her feel safe and…loved.

Getting up on tiptoe, Taylor tried to press her mouth to his. Shane deftly shifted his position, leaving her standing against the cool metal grill of the car.

"No more."

"No more what?" she managed to gasp, wondering when her voice had turned so whiney and pathetic.

He dug in his pocket for the car keys. "No more sex, Taylor. We're done."

Chapter Seventeen

The dashboard clock read quarter to eight when Shane called Sam and gave him the updated financial information they'd found at the cabin. It was pretty amazing to listen via the speakerphone as the Landry brothers agreed on which bank official to summon back to work. Power definitely had its advantages.

As did compassion, loyalty, kindness and many, many other attributes Taylor could assign to Shane. It was very dark, but as she sat in the passenger's seat, she finally saw the light. A scary, thrilling, wonderful light. Crispy, clearly, unequivocally.

She'd spent her whole life planning how *not* to include a man. So she'd never actually thought about her life *with* one. She'd never considered what it would be like not needing to be with him but *wanting* the experience. Choosing it.

And not her mother's choices, either. Not bad ones. Not necessarily safe ones, but the kinds of chances you have to take when your heart is as involved as your head.

Glancing over at Shane, Taylor was practically bursting with the need to share her epiphany. She took a deep breath. She even opened her mouth, but nothing came out. The words, the feelings, jammed in her throat, too powerful, too all encompassing to verbalize.

This was the scary part and it would pass. Then she could tell him that she really did love him. Really, truly.

And he'll believe me this time...why?

Euphoric, her heart pounding as adrenaline raced through her, she fell back against the seat. How was she going to regain his trust? How was she going to convince him that she was utterly sincere? And how could she even begin to describe this feeling of lightness? This feeling of...*rightness?* Taylor felt giddy with her self-realization.

"You're quiet," Shane said.

Not inside I'm not, she thought dryly, as her mind raced. "I'm thinking." Thinking about their future possibilities like a butterfly flitting over a flower garden. She glanced out at the bright, even slashes of white as they drove beneath the lampposts through town.

"About the murders? Me, too."

Okay, I can change gears. For now. "Let's stop by the Hunt Club. Will it be open?"

"Should be."

"That place is the only common denominator in all this."

"Maybe. Or it could just get us another piece that doesn't fit. I thought you'd want a bath after Jack's place."

"Two baths. But right now I want information more."

He reached out and rested his hand on her thigh. It was just enough to keep a flicker of hope alive. She

entwined her fingers with his, her heart waiting for a re-
ciprocal gesture. Without looking at her, Shane turned
his hand over and held hers.

The breath Taylor had been holding eased a little.

Baby steps.

The Hunt Club was a large, two-story building with
a smattering of cars parked in the lot. Trucks, more accurately. Taylor recognized some of them and mentally
went about matching people to vehicles while Shane
selected a spot to park.

He didn't take her hand again once they exited the
car. Taylor felt a chill run through her as they walked
on the gravel path toward the club. The twang of a
country song blared a greeting when Shane opened the
door and escorted her inside.

She was as acutely aware of his hand at her back as
she was of the dozen or so pairs of eyes tracking her.
No wonder they called it a "hunt club."

A large, utilitarian bar, dotted with bar stools,
spanned the length of the room. Only three were
occupied. She recognized one man from town but
couldn't recall his name, so just smiled.

"Hey, Shane, ma'am," the bartender began with an
uncomfortable smile. "Sorry, but it's still a private club.
Members only."

"We just dropped by for a little history lesson. That
okay?" Shane asked easily.

The thin man shrugged and slapped two napkins
down on the thickly varnished bar. "Whatta'll you have?"

"A beer and…?"

"Red wine," Taylor stated, slipping up onto a stool. "How long have you been serving here?"

The bartender placed a glass of wine in front of her, then opened a long-neck bottle of beer for Shane. "Monday, Wednesday and Friday for the last twenty years."

Taylor swallowed her disappointment along with a sip of her wine. "Is Amanda Grayson a member?"

His brow furrowed as his graying brows drew together. "No, ma'am."

"Ever been a member?" Taylor pressed.

"Not as long as I've been around. I think she tried to get a permit to picket us once. Something about the annual turkey shoot contest being cruel to birds." He snorted. "She's probably one of those who thinks the turkeys in the grocery store died of natural causes."

"I believe her objection was that the contest is on a family holiday and there's often more drinking than hunting." Taylor's back stiffened as she defended her friend. "Alcohol and family stress can be a bad combination."

"Thanks for the tip," he said, wandering off to wait on another customer.

"When did you become the Jasper Temperance League?"

She sighed. "I'm not, really. I just happen to agree with Mrs. Grayson on that issue. People do stupid things when they're drunk."

"More wine?" Shane teased.

"When they drink to *excess*."

"So?" He rested one foot against the boot rail and

said, "This field trip is turning into a total bust, don't you agree?"

"No I don't. Look. There. Behind the bar."

"Trophies? So what? Lots of local clubs sponsor sports leagues."

"How many are co-sponsors with Hollister Motors?" She reached out and grabbed a fistful of his shirt. "Follow the years, Shane. Hollister Motors and the Hunt Club co-sponsored teams until 1978."

"The year my mother took me in for the blood test. The last season before my father stopped bringing us here to shoot."

"There has to be a connection."

"Hollister is a freaking senator, Taylor." Shane struggled to keep his voice at a whisper. "If the connection is Hollister—and that's a big *if*—why would he kill my parents? By default, that makes him my biological father, and I can't believe he'd have risked his political future on a child he obviously didn't want. Play it out to the end. If Hollister was my mother's...*married lover,*" he spat the words, which left a bitter taste in his mouth, "he'd have every reason to want to keep it a secret. Killing them doesn't accomplish that goal. Fast forward fifteen years, and now explain to me how he can be involved in any of the weird stuff that's been going on.

"First it was the calls and the note stabbed into your car seat. Hollister is too public a figure to be running around town with knives, taking potshots at you."

"Probably."

"Definitely," he insisted. "He lives and works in Canyon Creek. You tell me how he got Luke to fake a robbery in order to kill Doris. How did he turn Jack into a thief? I'm starting to wonder if all these events are even connected. And what does any of that have to do with a blood disorder my own mother didn't know I had until I was ten years old?"

"*Because* she didn't know you had it."

Shane gaped at her. "Huh?"

Taylor slipped off her stool. "Hurry up and pay. We've got to go see Amanda Grayson."

A few minutes later, they were on the road again. It was getting late by ranching community standards. Most people were up with the sun, so anything after 10:00 p.m. was considered an all-nighter. High headlights, from a truck following a reasonable distance behind, were bright enough that he automatically adjusted the rearview mirror to cut the glare.

Taylor gave him directions, then Shane called the ranch to check in. The latest update was a half-dozen new calves. He was sure Will was pulling his hair out, but Shane knew the man never balked at hard work. "The birthing barn must be crazy with activity," he said. "I guess at some point I'll have to talk to my brothers about, well, about my taking care of the ranch and…"

"Don't be a jerk. Do you honestly think one blood test can change the way they feel about you?"

"I don't know."

"Sure you do," Taylor retorted. "What if the shoe was on the other foot? Would you turn your back on one of your brothers?"

"No."

"Then have some faith. And turn at the next corner."

AMANDA GRAYSON TUGGED at the edges of her robe. Her long gray hair was braided, dangling to well past her waist as she led them into the kitchen of her modest home.

"I'm glad you're here," she said, filling a teakettle and placing it on a burner. "This has been weighing on me for some years."

"You've been expecting us?" Taylor asked.

Her smile was warm but tempered with sadness. "Not you," she said, then turned her eyes on Shane. "You."

He was slightly taken aback as he took the seat she offered. "Why me?"

"I've been holding something for you. Something from your mother."

Shane felt his stomach drop into his toes. "And you never got around to giving it to me?" He reached out for Taylor's hand, comforted by the feel of her fingers lacing with his.

"It wasn't my place, Shane. I made a promise to your mother that I felt ethically bound to keep."

"She was murdered."

"Which made my position more difficult," Amanda said as she hobbled over to a drawer next to the stove. Removing a sealed envelope from the drawer, she presented it, saying, "Take this into the other room. Taylor and I will have some tea."

He hesitated for a second, then squeezed Taylor's hand before taking the thin envelope. He had it opened by the time he settled into a chair.

The letter was several pages in length, all written in neat precise script, dated February, 1986:

Dear Shane:

I wanted you to hear the truth from me sooner but I never summoned up the courage. Now, if you've found your way to Amanda's doorstep, she can help me tell you all the things I was never brave enough to say aloud.

You'll be eighteen in two weeks. The last of my sons to hit that milestone. I'm very proud of you, Shane. We both are. Your father and I love you very much. No matter what, never question that.

I want only good things for you and your brothers. Most of all, I want you to be as happy as I am at this moment. I need you to know that you boys and Caleb are how I define myself. Not what happened eighteen years ago. Don't let it define you, either. Even if I could change the past, I wouldn't do it, not if it meant not having you in our lives. Neither would your father.

Before I say anything else, think back, Shane. Remember all the good things. Separate your conception from your life. That's what your father and I chose to do, and we're so glad.

Okay, so now for the hard part... We were attending a party at the Hunt Club. I went outside for a breath of air when it happened.

In those days, we didn't have words like 'acquaintance rape.' All I knew was someone grabbed me, threw a tablecloth over my head. I was attacked and it was over. I stayed outside for a while, trying to figure out how to tell your father.

You know his temper. I understand now my feelings of shame were normal. But that night I was shocked, embarrassed, scared, angry, and all I could think about was going home to my children. I didn't want anyone to know what had happened. Especially not your father. I know it wasn't my fault, but it was a different time, Shane. Not like now.

I didn't see my attacker's face that night, but his voice was familiar. He was a friend of your father's. I didn't know how to handle it. So I hid. From everyone, including your father. I didn't say anything to him, not even after I found out I was pregnant. I've never been ashamed or sorry about you, Shane. Not for one second.

I'm not sure how, but I kept my secret. It wasn't like I intended to deceive your father or you. At first I was ashamed, then afraid, and then one day it didn't matter anymore. You were our beautiful baby boy.

I can tell you it wasn't something I consciously thought about. Not for years.

Then when you were about ten, I got a phone call. I recognized the voice. It wasn't the man who attacked me, but he knew all about it. I didn't believe him at first, but then he told me about this strange blood disease and told me to have you tested.

I should have gone to your father immediately,

but I didn't know how. I did take you out of town to a doctor, who explained the disease and swore to me you had a very mild form that shouldn't affect your life.

The man who called me was having some financial difficulties, so I gave him some money, hoping that would be the end of it. That went on for about a year. I finally broke down late one night and told Caleb what happened, but not that I'd been paying money to keep my secret.

I was braced for his temper. Instead, your father kissed my forehead, then went into your room and kissed you as well.

It never mattered, Shane. You were—you are—our son. I know that doesn't change what I did, all the lies that have come home to roost, but I never intended for anyone to get hurt. Least of all you.

Last night I told your father about the money. He's really mad at me—you know him. He pretty much dared anyone within earshot to call you anything but his son.

We're going to fix this money thing, Shane, and then your dad and I will sit down and talk with you. I hope when all the dust settles, you'll understand why I made the choices I made.
Love, Mom

A lump the size of China clogged Shane's throat as he wiped tears off his cheeks with the back of one hand. His emotions ran the full gauntlet from anger to sorrow and back again.

His body felt drained as he rose and walked toward the kitchen.

"Can I get you something?" Amanda asked.

"A name," Shane said, astounded he was capable of making the request sound reasonable. He wasn't feeling very reasonable.

"I don't know his name." Mrs. Grayson pursed her lips and shook her head. "All I know is that Priscilla said the man she was paying worked on the ranch."

Chapter Eighteen

"Hollister worked on the ranch," Taylor said later when Shane careened into a parking space near the sheriff's office. "He told me so when I met with him. It has to be Hollister."

"I've got my own plan for getting a blood sample," Shane said, smashing the heel of his palm against the steering wheel.

"I don't think this is a *good* plan," she cautioned. "Talk it over with Seth. Then do it legally. If we're right, and it is Hollister who's been behind all this, you want the man punished, don't you?"

"There is no 'if,'" Shane said, his tone grim. "Trust me, he will be punished."

"I don't think it's a good idea for you to go off half-cocked," she stated as they reached the entrance.

The dispatcher, seated with her feet on the desk, straightened when they burst inside. "Seth's on his way. Said for you to wait if you got here first."

"Just great," Shane groused.

Watching him was like watching a wounded animal

looking for a target. "There's a vein threatening to explode in your temple," Taylor said softly. "Take a deep breath. This will all be resolved soon."

"I'll be calm a few minutes after I put my fist through Hollister's teeth."

"Very manly," Taylor said dryly. Grabbing his arm, she shot a men-will-be-men smile at the dispatcher, who was watching them. "But there are much better ways…." She tugged him into Seth's office and closed the door, then pushed him into one of the visitor's chairs. She nodded at the closed door. "She'd make a wonderful witness for the prosecution. Take that deep breath. Seth will be here soon."

Shane jumped up and started pacing his brother's office like a caged lion. "I just want to do this. I owe it to my mother's memory."

Taylor turned her chair a little so she could watch him. She sympathized with his impotent rage and frustration, but he *couldn't* go off half-cocked. They'd prove that he hadn't killed his parents, but if he assaulted Hollister, there'd be no going back. "She'd probably like it more if you didn't go to jail in her name. Do this inside the legal system."

"I'll take the sheriff with me. Seth can legally watch me pummel the guy into hamburger. Satisfied?"

She opened her mouth just as the door burst open. "Saved by the cavalry."

"Let's go," Seth said shortly.

"Hello? What about…me?" Taylor said into the echoing silence after the door slammed behind the two brothers. They had taken off, oblivious to everything and everyone.

Taylor was panicked. Raking her fingers through her hair, she thought for a minute, then grabbed the phone and dialed Sam. She told him what she knew and asked for his help. "It's not that I necessarily care what happens to Hollister, but I don't want Shane ruining his life."

"I'm on it, Taylor. You stay put."

That should have been reassuring, but she still had a nagging doubt swirling in her head. And nothing but time on her hands. Time that was moving so slowly she actually flicked the clock twice just to make sure the hands weren't stuck in place.

The television and VCR were still in Seth's office. Taylor cued the tape and started playing and rewinding the footage of the robbery. With each pass, she struggled to find even one more detail. The robbery was the one element that didn't quite fit. Assuming Hollister was guilty, how was he connected to Luke?

"He isn't," she murmured. At least there wasn't any connection she could find. She tried expanding her search of the videotape. Other than taking up thirty minutes of her time, she didn't learn anything new, so she went back to the few frames that she thought depicted the shadow of a second person reflected on the dairy case.

"Jack, maybe?" she wondered. He was unaccounted for; he was a drunk and a thief. It fit. Except that Jack couldn't have killed the Landrys, and that was the key.

"Or the Hunt Club is the key," Taylor argued, feeling a little silly that she was debating with herself in a closed, empty room. "Or Shane's paternity is the key. Or—" The phone rang, making her jump. "Yes?"

"Will's here," the dispatcher said. "He says Shane told him to take you back to the ranch."

How typical of Shane to think of her in the middle of all this. "Thanks, I'll be right there." Feeling completely thwarted by her lack of progress, Taylor shut off the television and the VCR and left the office.

She was out on the street, uttering a third, effusive apology to the craggy cowboy, when she saw something that made her stop dead in her tracks. There, idling at the curb, was a dark blue pickup truck. Strobelike, a series of images flashed in her brain.

"I know this truck," she murmured. "It's—"

"Courtesy of Hollister Motors," Will said, jabbing a gun against her rib cage. "Get in."

The door swung open and Taylor found herself staring into the cold, narrowed eyes of the occupant who'd been shielded behind the vehicle's tinted windows. "You've been a real pain in my rear end, Miss Reese. But we're going to rectify that now."

Right outside the sheriff's office, Taylor was lifted off the sidewalk and dumped onto the pickup's bench seat. Senator Hollister sat on one side of her, while the ranch foreman quickly slipped in the driver's side and closed the door.

"You?" she demanded of Will. The bitter taste of fear-inspired adrenaline coated her tongue. "Both of you? Together?"

"We're a team, aren't we, Will?" Hollister asked, chuckling softly.

"What are you? Jasper's version of Leopold and Loeb?" She winced when Hollister's elbow caught her in the cheek.

They were headed back toward the ranch. Which made no sense. The place was crawling with people—many of whom were Landrys. She chewed her lip as Will drove the speed limit out of town.

"Curious, aren't you?" Hollister mocked. "Why the ranch? Well, I happen to know that at least two of the Landry brothers are on their way to Canyon Creek. I know this because Will tells me everything, don't you, buddy?"

Again, the cowboy said nothing, though Taylor felt his body tense where their shoulders touched.

"He doesn't have a choice," Hollister continued. "Will did a bad thing years ago, so now Will has to do whatever I ask him to do, right, Will? If he doesn't, he goes to jail for a long, long time."

"Really?" Taylor asked, buying time to think. "What bad thing did Will do?"

"He got very drunk one night at a party. So drunk that he didn't remember what he did until I reminded him."

"Shut up, Hollister!" Will growled. "We've got enough trouble. She doesn't need to know all this."

A scenario was falling into place in her mind. "A party at the Hunt Club?" she asked.

"Yes." Hollister's tone wasn't quite as confident. "Very good, Miss Reese."

Yes, she thought. Almost as good as committing a sexual assault and then convincing some poor drunken sap that he was responsible. "Why go back to the ranch?" Taylor asked.

"You tell her, Will. Tell her how you've been holding out on me all this time."

"Money's there."

"What money?" she asked.

Hollister leaned over, placing his vile mouth very near her ear as he said, "The money Priscilla Landry was supposed to cough up the night I killed her. With everything that's happened, I'm going to need all the traveling cash I can find."

Taylor wiggled closer to the driver. "If she was paying you off, why kill her?"

"That wasn't the original plan," Hollister explained. "See, thanks to Will's...*indiscretion* and the resulting birth of the youngest child, I should have been able to feed from the Landry *trough* well into my golden years. Like I told Will, he put that tablecloth over her head so she'd never be able to identify him. And hell, she'd pawned off the youngest as a true Landry, so she wasn't going to put up a fuss. The Landrys were like our own personal ATM until Priscilla had an attack of conscience and spilled everything to Caleb."

"Still doesn't explain why you killed her," Taylor said, seeing the lights of the ranch up ahead. As their destination grew closer, the bubble of panic in her stomach got larger and larger.

"Why, once Priscilla told Caleb, we didn't have a choice. Will would have been arrested, and that Caleb— he was a vindictive son of a bitch—he would have tracked me down, too, because of my financial interest in the matter."

Taylor was torn between her fear and a burning

desire to take her shoe off and beat Hollister bloody. As tempting as that was, it didn't solve her immediate need. Staying alive did.

"There's no money at the house," Taylor pointed out. If there was a large amount of cash, she'd know.

"Tell her, Will."

"There is," he admitted.

"Yes," Hollister agreed, scratching the lower of his two chins with a small-caliber handgun. "I've forgiven Will for holding out on me all these years but he's promised to turn the money over to me in exchange for Shane's life. I'll take this money and what little I could get from my personal accounts and be on my way out of the country."

Will parked the pickup in front of the house. Taylor realized she had to get Will on her side, and to do that she had to break Hollister's hold on him. Unfortunately, she was pretty sure the senator would shoot her before he let her finish a sentence. "Let's go get my money, Miss Reese. Then I can watch you die."

Not if I watch you first, she thought as she slowly climbed the steps to the door, the two gun-wielding men flanking her. There had to be something she could use to her advantage. *Think. Think. Think.*

"Where to?" Hollister asked.

"Money's in the attic," Will answered.

No it wasn't. She'd been through every box in that attic. Nothing was making sense except the certain knowledge that she'd be dead in a matter of minutes if she didn't do something. Fast.

Her eyes darted around the foyer. The only thing

between her and the staircase was the hall table. It held nothing more sinister than a house key and lamp. So, she reasoned as she pretended to stumble, something was better than nothing.

She palmed the key and kept moving. The edges weren't at all sharp, but she kept it hidden just in case an opportunity presented itself.

Hollister was breathing heavily by the time they reached the bottom rung of the attic ladder. "Him first," he said, yanking Taylor back so that she was sandwiched between the two of them. He rammed the gun into the small of her back as Will started to climb.

"WAS THE DISPATCHER positive?" Shane asked his brother again.

"Very."

"Will told her all this? Word for word? In, like, sixty seconds?"

Seth heaved a deep breath. "He told her to watch until the car pulled away. She did that."

"It was Hollister? She's sure? Because it's really dark out."

"For the hundredth time, yes. She saw his ruby pinky ring, the one with the bear head that he wore in all those dumb-ass commercials. Will said that as soon as they drove away, she was supposed to call and tell us the killer was going back to the ranch."

"How does Will know about Hollister?" Shane asked.

"We can ask him in about five minutes if you'll shut up and let me drive. I know you're worried about Taylor. We'll get there. Nothing will happen to her."

"She's with a killer, Seth. She isn't safe."

The car was still rolling to a stop when Shane leaped out, rounded the pickup and bounded up the stairs. Carefully, he eased open the front door and tried to detect any sounds over the pounding of his own pulses. Nothing. Nothing. Yes.

Stealthily, he climbed to the second floor, reaching the hallway just in time to see Hollister's foot disappearing up the ladder into the attic.

"Wait." Seth was just behind him, chambering a bullet into his gun.

Waiting was not an option. Not when Taylor was in danger. Shrugging off his brother's cautionary hand, Shane started up the ladder.

Hollister had Taylor by the hair, roughly shoving her toward a pile of boxes. Shane had barely processed that bit of information when he realized Will also held a gun. His first instinct—beyond the one telling him to rip Hollister's spleen out through his nostrils—was to call out. Until it sank in that Will had his gun trained on Taylor, not on the senator.

Taylor was on her knees, rubbing the back of her head with one hand and cringing as she waited for Hollister to put a bullet in her brain. Then she saw it—a brief, beautiful flash of movement. Shane.

Her heart practically leaped out of her chest. "Since you're going to kill me anyway," she began, slowly working the pointed end of the key between her third and fourth fingers, "maybe now is a good time for me to tell Will he isn't a rapist."

The second she had the last syllable out of her mouth,

she ducked and rolled, using her momentum to plant the key deep into Hollister's thigh.

"What?" Will yelled.

Then the room exploded, literally.

Hollister was falling backward, his leg wound bleeding like a geyser, but his finger squeezing the trigger of his gun. Wood splintered; bullets ricocheted. All Taylor knew was there was no way on earth she was going to let an evil Hollister or a misdirected Will have a second chance at destroying the Landry family.

Stretching to her very limit, she made a fist and punched the key deeper into Hollister's leg. He yelped and cursed, and then Shane's large body was sailing through the air, falling on top of the larger, older man.

She counted one more gunshot before being blanketed in an eerie silence.

Taylor half crawled, half lunged to Shane. There was so much blood. "Are you hurt?" she screamed, rolling him over and touching him everywhere.

"No. You?"

He started at her scalp and worked his way down, scanning anxiously. Other than a slight bruise on her cheek and some wood fibers in her hair, there didn't seem to be anything wrong with her. He was finally able to breathe.

Shane devoured her mouth, lacing his fingers into her hair as he tasted her lips, her cheeks, her eyelids. "You're crying," he murmured, tasting the salty remnants of a tear.

"Delayed stress reaction."

He groaned. "I don't want the clinical explanation,

Taylor. I was thinking along the lines of something more personal."

"Um, Shane?" Seth said, his voice somberly echoing off the attic walls.

Hugging Taylor to him, Shane glanced over and saw Will slumped against the wall. A bullet, either Hollister's or Seth's, had found its way to him.

Dipping his head, Shane said a silent prayer for his friend's redemption. He had no such charitable feelings for Hollister. The senator was still bleeding from his leg. His face had gone stark white and his breathing was shallow and labored.

"Go call an ambulance, okay?" Shane told Taylor, kissing her forehead.

Then he removed his shirt and crouched over Hollister, pressing the fabric to the semiconscious man's leg.

Her throat suddenly felt thick with unshed tears. "You're a good man, Shane Landry."

He rose, helping her to her feet. "If he lives, he'll do so knowing that I gave him life and not vice versa."

She got up on tiptoe and kissed his chin. "You're an *exceptional* man."

"I am," he said, patting her behind.

"You'll make some woman a fabulous husband," she called over her shoulder.

"Are you asking me to marry you?"

"Maybe."

Epilogue

"Dr. Taylor Reese." She beamed as she read the name-plate Shane was affixing to the side of the freshly stained wooden building.

Thanks to him, it had taken less than six months to get the place refurbished and opened. It was a perfect, perfect day. The sun was shining, the trees glowing with rich golds, greens and yellows. The furniture was in. The wallpaper was up. Everything was done. She was official.

Shane draped his arm over her shoulders. "So, is it the way you imagined?"

"Better," she exclaimed, squeezing him tightly. "There's privacy and yet it's still, technically, in town, so people will come. We have a playroom for children and a real computer system for me. Nothing could make this any better."

Well, that wasn't completely true, but close enough. As in the six months they'd been working on the building, Shane hadn't once said he loved her. Not even now that she said it freely—heck, *hourly*—to him. He'd been a regular saint, too. Dodging almost every one of her attempts at seduction. Of course, Shane had two secret weapons—Sam and Callie's twins. Since Sarah and Kasey had arrived, Shane used the babies like shields to keep her at bay.

Nuzzling his chest, she breathed in his scent and smiled. He'd cave. She knew it. He'd already stared to crumble. She tested her theory, dancing her fingertips along his spine just to change the rhythm of his breathing. Worked every time. She could be patient. She didn't want to, but she could.

"We should probably go get the ribbon you're going to cut for the grand opening," he said.

"I have a new couch. We could take it for a test drive—ouch!"

He swatted her fanny and looked down to see the sparkle in her hazel eyes. She was happy. That mattered, a lot. She was happy with him. That mattered more. "You're a Ph.D. now, Taylor. You can't proposition me on the street anymore. It isn't professional." He went inside and returned with a bag. "Per your request, a large red ribbon across the entrance for the grand opening."

It was like watching an old woman on Christmas morning. Taylor carefully removed the ribbon from the bag as if she was going to save it for posterity. Did women reuse opening-ceremony ribbons? he wondered, amused. He managed to maintain his cool for a little while, then lost patience. "Sometime before we grow old is fine."

"This is really big for me, Shane. I'm savoring every

moment. I'm going to look back on this day when I'm ninety, and I want to remember every…"

He'd never heard such a deafening silence. Shane had attached the ring to the very end of the ten-foot-long red ribbon. "I love you, Taylor. Will you marry me?"

Her eyes misted. "I was wondering if you'd ever get around to asking."

He brushed away her tears with his thumb. "I needed to know you could be happy here. With me, doing this."

"I am. I love you, Shane. I'd be happy even without this," she insisted, waving her arm in a wide arc. "This place is like a fantasy for me. One I would never have dreamed if it wasn't for you."

"Are you sure?"

"I am."

"Then put the ring on and give me a second," he said, rushing back inside for a second bag. "Now try this on for size."

Taylor opened the bag and found an identical name-plate to the one he'd just installed.

"You don't have to do it," he insisted when she didn't say anything. "I just thought, that, well…"

"Dr. Taylor Landry," she said, "has a very nice ring to it."

He held her to him. "Goes nicely with the clinic, too. Don't you think?"

Taylor felt her smile all the way down to her toes. Wrapping her arms about his waist, she grinned up at him. "I think another Landry is exactly what the Caleb and Priscilla Landry Clinic needs. We all know there aren't enough Landrys in Jasper."

He smiled. "That's something else we should talk about."

Taylor gave him a mock outraged look. "Are you telling me you won't be the last Landry, after all?"

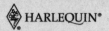

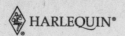

#909 INVESTIGATING 101 by Debra Webb
Colby Agency: New Recruits
New recruit Todd Thompson skips basic training and jumps right into danger when he helps researcher Serena Blake investigate a horrifying case involving stolen identities and missing children.

#910 MURDER ON THE MOUNTAIN by Cassie Miles
Rocky Mountain Safe House
While hosting Homeland Security exercises at her lodge-turned-safe house, FBI agent Julia Last discovers the body of a five-star general in a locked room. And when a sudden blizzard traps her and the local deputy sheriff in with the murderer, will they become the next victims?

#911 AT CLOSE RANGE by Jessica Andersen
Bear Claw Creek Crime Lab
Can rival CSIs Seth Varitek and Cassie Dumont set aside their differences to take down a serial killer who has returned west and trapped them within close proximity?

#912 THE SECRET NIGHT by Rebecca York
43 Light Street
Every lover Nicholas Vickers takes, he eventually loses forever. But when a young woman pleads for his help on his doorstep, he can't refuse. But can he resist her before his horrible secret dooms them both?

#913 UNEXPECTED FATHER by Delores Fossen
Lilly Nelson awakens from a coma to find she's given birth to a daughter she didn't even know she conceived. But when she finds her baby in the protective care of a tough-as-nails Texas cop, Lilly will do anything to make up for lost time, including tracking down the people who put her in the coma in the first place.

#914 WHEN A STRANGER CALLS by Kathleen Long
Camille Tarlington tried to bury the senseless tragedy of her past, but when a young lawyer with a shared secret presents her with new evidence, she's forced to reconsider everything she ever held true.